Supernova
Rivers of Time
by
Raymond Walter
Seibert

Copyright © 2007 by Raymond Walter Seibert
Published by arrangement with
Advanced Concept Design
Library of Congress Control Number
to be assigned
International Standard Book Number
ISBN 13: 978-0-9799723-0-0
ISBN 10: 0-9799723-0-2

First paperback printing October 2007
Printed in the United States of America

Dedicated in Loving Memory
to
Martha Gilmore

Acknowledgments

The first and foremost help in my life and with this book is the continuous and constant encouragement and help by my wife Jean, who has put up with me through the thirty years which it has taken to bring this book to print. Her editing and support are the pillars of my life, and she is my beautiful friend.

There are many others, and I am bound to leave someone unmentioned, but you know who you are, and I will somehow make it up to you. You might be a character in here, but you will never recognize yourself.

Introduction

This book was begun in 1972. The neutron star in the center of the Cancer nebula had just been discovered in the constellation Taurus, in the tip of the horn of the bull. Also, the human genome project was just being talked about, and the space shuttle was on the drawing board.

Inspired by these remarkable goals and astounding achievements of man's quest of the unknown, I began to think about and extrapolate some of the far reaching consequences of these discoveries and goals. Now much of what was once conjecture, is reality. The world moves forward with frightening speed. To match the change that our fathers saw from horse and buggy to jet airplanes, we will soon reach for the moon and near planets, and our children will reach for the stars. That is unless warfare drains our energy, and our myopia of the environment dooms us, before we can get started, as it has through much of my own lifetime.

New and incredible breakthroughs are just around the corner. Rise up, rise up, on tongues of fire, you children of the earth. Rise up and strive with all your might, and do not miss your berth.

Raymond Walter Seibert
June 2007

Contents

Chapter One The Oracle

Uris was sitting silently in the snow, imperceptible, certainly to human eyes, but more. Covered over completely with the soft white flakes, no part of her showed, just a bump in the rounded side of the mountain, sitting quietly in a hollow and waiting.

Thoughts washed to and fro in her mind. Thoughts of the hunt, thoughts of her father. Thoughts from long ago, the clash of arms, the face of her weapons master. Faces of all the various masters of all the disciplines in her life swirled about her, admonishing her, cajoling her to greater effort, all of them flowing by in her trance-like state.

A slight wind stirred the still morning air, swirling the snow in and around the crags of the mountain side, dancing like a devil wind, whipping and twisting down into the chasm below her. Soon, the first of the twin suns of this binary system would break the horizon, spreading first orange and then a fuchsia deepening into the magenta of the sunrise.

She did not stir as the bright yellow orb crested the hills far across the valley. She was still sitting deep in trance when the twin brother arrived, much smaller and much dimmer than its brother, who was much smaller on this winter solstice day. In summer it far out shone its brother, who being more massive and thus the center of the system, kept almost equidistant from the planet, giving as a result, a delightful three spring times per rotation, but a propensity for very severe earthquakes at the end of each summer. The planet was considered extremely unsafe, and especially in the mountains, during these four-to-five-day periods three times each year.

It was her father's favorite winter hunting retreat, or so it seemed to her. As far back as she could remember, her father had brought her the dream of the winter solstice. His finest passion was to hunt the gru that roamed the high passes in the mountains. She never really fathomed why. The meat wasn't especially tasty, certainly not prized like the Chen fowl of Lapin Tor or the Mur fish of their own family world of Ur. She could only remember two that he had taken in his entire life. One of the kills, she only knew from hearing that he had been on Calaban hunting when she was born. He had returned to find himself, widowed, with a suckling baby daughter. As Mez had recounted the story to her, her father had cremated the carcass of the gru on the carved alter stone that was the only remains of the ancients or their odd ceremonies from the family wars at the dawn of the House of Ur.

How curious she had found this stone. She played on and around it in the great slab stone courtyard that was their walled garden, serving to protect her from kidnappers and enemies of the House. Once it had formed the main floor of the ancient temple, but long since, even before her grandfather's birth, it had been cut away, and many of the stones had been used in the garden wall. Here her father had burned the gru's carcass. Here, he had buried his young wife.

"Even then," Mez had confided in an introspective mood to Uris, when she had asked of her mother, "he shed not one tear as if he knew All the Names of Life. Although, the rest of us cried enough for him. Why he burned the gru?" Mez had shaken his head. "Well, perhaps, he had flown it halfway across a galaxy to show her. It was a triumph of discipline to him, and then to find her gone and you, little one," Mez had tussled her curly hair, "arrived before your time. Aih, it was a strange day. Uriah was never the same after your mother's death. And then, the ceremony with the gru and the way he forced all to stand while he burned it, came very close to crime against the state enforcement of the laws against religious practice. But who would have reported him? The day was so strange." Mez came back to it, his eyes distant. "It seemed like the failure of all scientific disciplines, and then the burning of the gru, was so like an act of...."

"Go on, Mez," she had entreated.

"Religion," he knit his brow and strode solemnly away leaving her to rub her fingers over the cool and strange embossing of the stone.

The only other time that Uriah had succeeded at the Solstice hunt was the year of his departure on the Draco exploration journey. They had hunted the same ridge that she now crouched on. He had left her at the timberline, leaving her to tend the camp and keep a continuous fire. The hunt had taken three days, a tremendous will of discipline for the young girl. She had been nodding in a semi-trance state, practicing the same discipline that her father used above her to a more extreme degree, when Uriah returned. His mellow, smooth voice stirred her from her slumber.

"The meat is here. Have you kept the fire alive?"

"Yes, yes, father," she had started awaking and not knowing where she was or being fully awake had reached out to feed the fire, but she tripped over something in the snow, and her father was laughing. What was it that had tripped her? It was so long ago. Uris tried to remember. Why was her father laughing? She seemed to be the girl in the snow again. She had tripped over the body of the slain creature. No, that was long ago. She had been dreaming. She was awake now, in the rigid posture called, 'wait for the kill'. So, why was her father still standing there and what was he laughing about?

"Meat's here. Have you kept the fire alive," he seemed to whisper, but his mouth only smiled.

Suddenly, she was fully conscious. She sensed the creature's warmth in front of her. She must strike quickly, before it sensed her presence from her growing body warmth. She flexed her hand, which rested on the knife sheathed on her leg. When she felt the handle, she drew it and sprang. The light covering of snow flew away, and she was on the gru instantly, slicing its throat, with one upward movement. The creature lay bleeding it's life into the snow, it's heat seeking, eye-like tentacles lying limp.

She began to take deep breaths of the crisp air. The exhilaration the experience, the thrill of the kill, the cold, it all hit her at once. But it was the haunting feeling that she had heard her father laughing, had really seen him standing there, that made her shake.

She made her way back to the timberline. She camped and set about to break her three days fast. The two binary suns would be eclipsing within a few hours, marking the center of the winter solstice. She skinned the carcass, and prepared the meat in a quiet joy, savoring all the smells. She seemed more alive than she had ever been before. Her senses were sharp, as never before. A wonderful experience. It was the way she best remembered her father. The hunt was her homage to his memory and now she felt good, like he was with her even now. She had felt his absence more keenly, having never known her mother. She lost herself in hours of remembering the things they had done, the wanderings, much of it on the surface of this planet.

The solstice passed. The gru was excellent, much more from the three days of hunting. She would have lingered another day, that had been the plans, but suddenly, she wanted to break camp, to sleep in her own bed on her own world so far away. A vague impression that something needed tending, that something had gone awry.

4

The ship was several miles down into the flatland, but she carried the two hind quarters with her. The animal was too hard to kill to be left behind, and it was her first.

The sleek craft was nestled in the tall grass near the stream that drained the slope she had hunted. Looking like a giant egg, there were no seams showing, until at a command word from her, a door appeared, sliding back noiselessly. She entered inside. Shortly, the egg hummed very slightly, rose slowly upward, and with an ever-increasing velocity, disappeared, curving up and out of sight within a twinkling, leaving silence, and then, a few seconds later, the resounding clap of a sonic boom reverberating through the valleys.

He eased the throttles back to twenty-two fifty on the tachometers and readjusted the trim. The sleek little twin went into an easy gliding descent. Below, the uniform housing of the outer suburbs had given way to the patchwork of the squared blocks of tract homes built in the last century. The commuter trains fairly screamed along the track below. They were passing him now that he was descending. Everywhere, locust-like cars were beginning to crawl up on the freeways. He reached the transponder and gave the dial a spin. It came up one-twenty-one seven from years of experience. A voice cracked out at him.

"Approaching aircraft contact Love Tower one-eighteen three, when approximately five miles out. Winds are stable aloft, two- seventy degrees at fifteen knots per hour. Gusting winds from the West to twenty-five knots. You have information Foxtrot."

He let it play through twice more while he repacked some papers with the letter head Cryogenic Solarus, into a briefcase beside him, then gave the transponder a second spin.

"King, Victor, Victor calling Love Tower, come in, over."

"We have you King, Victor, Victor. What's your position, over."

"Inbound, over wee- Waxahachie, Daniel, is that you? Over."

"Morning to you, Stark. You're a little early this morning. Early bird that gets the worm, Eh?"

"I can't say about old sayings, but I get the worm this morning. Political breakfast," he closed the mike and laughed to himself.

"Say Daniel, it's been nice modulating with you but we better cut this chit-chat before the FCC slaps our hands. Over."

"Right O, you're third on a left base for runway number eighteen. Over."

"Thank you, Love Tower, KVV over and out."

He sat back and aimed the Nightingale's nose at the left corner, bottom of the approaching field. He sat back for a moment, automatically adjusting the trim control a tad. He mused for a moment, counting on his fingers as if he were clicking off the things he had listed for himself and making sure of his memory. He turned on a second radio giving it a minute to warm up. He enunciated distinctly into the microphone, giving the office number. The voice activated dialing connected him. The phone rang twice, and then a female voice came on the line.

"S. G. Raven Enterprises. I'm sorry Mr. Raven is out. If you will leave your name and phone number, Mr. Raven will be happy to reply. You may leave as long a message as you wish. Thank you."

"Thank you, Ms. Chore," Raven laughed into the microphone. "Voice Lock," he said. He waited for the relays to react. "Stark Galileo Raven," he said plainly.

"Verified," came the monotone response.

"Computer section," again he paused until he heard the faint click of the connection to the computer. "Internet search," a pause, "what do we have on a Congressman Albert Flutter and Senator Samuel Prickle, personal dossier and known corresponding interest."

He laid the microphone down. It would take some time to get the information gathered and placed in a form he could peruse. Now, he had a plane to land.

****

"I see here that he made much of his early money in communications systems for businessmen," Representative Flutter peered over a manila folder at his overshadowing companion. The big man shifted uneasily in his chair, ground his cigar, which was already out, in the center of his breakfast remains.

"Who does this guy think he is? I've got a plane to catch," Senator Samuel Prickle was being true to his name.

"We're booked on several flights," his aid interjected, in an attempt to be helpful. The burly man gave the younger aid a sour look and then turned to gaze absently out a window, sucking pointedly on his teeth, failing to notice the object of his frustration was arriving.

"Gentlemen, pardon my tardiness, I've come a long way this morning," Stark gripped the congressman's hand. "Congressman Flutter, I'm pleased to meet you," he pumped the man's hand in the good ol' boy way. "This is one of my top aids, Enrico Ramirez."

"Congressman," Enrico exchanged pleasantries with the Congressman while Stark turned his attention to the Senator. They sat down to order breakfast.

"Senator," he reached his hand across the table. The big man paused and scowled a moment before reluctantly taking the offered hand.

"Mr. Raven," the Senator responded flatly.

"We've met before, Senator, but you probably don't remember, twice in fact."

"Is that a fact?" The Senator touched and parried like a fencer warming up. He opened the folder in front of him. "I saw that the Federal Space Administration has granted you permission to operate communications satellites, but I don't remember the particulars. I may not have even been present at your hearing."

8

"Yes, Senator, you were," Stark stirred his coffee, watching the other man, enjoying his momentary advantage. "But then, my hearing was right after a boy scout group and right before a church group. I'm very aware the sky is crowded, Senator, and always felt you did a good job regulating that problem. We met once before, two years before, also a regulatory hearing, when I got my company's microwave transmission license. It was the old Microwave Transmission Commission, before it became the Directed Energy Beam Transmission Commission."

The Senator was still at the head of DEBT Com, and he began to feel Raven's cuts.

"I'm afraid I don't recall either incident, Mr. Raven. You have the advantage on me."

"Well, no matter, time goes on, and I am a member of the fraternity, also, so to speak."

"Yes," the Senator agreed, "you seem to have made good use of your opportunities."

"But I don't usually play in your ballpark, Senator, which leaves me with a puzzle. Why did you invite me here this morning?" Stark let an edge creep into his voice. He remembered the Senator on the previous two occasions. The Senator had voted against his licenses on both occasions, on the grounds that the services were already being adequately delivered by existing companies. He also remembered the stream of secretaries and lobbyist that took the Senator's mind elsewhere, in those days.

"I beg to differ with you Mr. Raven, but you have far outstripped your competitors. Cryogenic Solarus is a by word in its field."

"I didn't realize that I was kicking up that much of a fuss, "he looked at Enrico. Enrico returned the look. Both found it interesting that this attention had been drawn.

"We have felt that it was past time that we met you, and we have a problem that we hope you may be able to help us with."

"Many, I am sure, Senator, but I do what I can. The world is large and full of misery, who exactly is we?"

"Well, myself and Congressman Flutter."

Congressman Flutter nodded in eager agreement. "There are many areas where your business laps over into government-controlled areas, and we would like to know more about you."

"I take it that you mean various boards and commissions that I have appeared before would like to know more about me. Well, you will find me fiercely independent for your taste, Senator."

"Is that a fact," Senator Prickle began to see Stark's drift, and his hackles started to get up. "It's too bad that such a talented man is anti-social."

"You miss the point Senator, I'm not anti-social, I carry on any number of relationships with the government. I'm afraid I'm a bit old fashioned, faith in the people and all that."

"The problems of our society require more government all the time."

"You have to teach people to govern themselves."

"You sound like an anarchist, the Senator was stunned with the thought. "I thought I was coming to see a rational businessman."

This made Stark laugh. "Rational is related to point of view, Senator. In fact, let me expand on that. We are both being cagey. Let me just come right up front. I know why you called me here. You are a leading figure on the Atomic Energy Commission. You are in fact one of the most powerful men in this nation. Now, you have come down here to eat breakfast with me because you need something. Security for your power. You know that I built a series of the best security systems in the world.

That is a credit to the group of people that work with me, just like Cryogenic Solarus or any number of other ventures into the business world. You need some company here in the United States, in your power block, to build you a security system for your nuclear waste. Is that not the fact?"

"I hoped this could be discussed in private," the Senator looked sincerely disappointed as if something he had counted on was not going to work out.

"There is nothing secret about the nuclear world since the John Phillips' Atomic Bomb design of the 1970's"

"That is exactly the point," the Senator got down to brass tacks. Someone had sold him on the idea that this was the man that was his best hope. "With the information so widely disseminated, we must keep the waste under control."

"No one is more disturbed than me about this, Senator. But the sun is in the sky for all to see."

"But you could help us. Your company is the most advanced in its field. Your security systems offer the most promise for a fool proof system of control."

"You don't understand, Senator. I know I have a good series of security system designs, but you have an impossible problem. Atomics spill over into our lives out of the material world, carrying us into a spiritual world. It is replete with such history. Like the scientist who pulled up the emergency brake of his car, when the first blast went off at Ground Zero in White Sands, and a verse of the Bhagavad-Gita passed through his mind, "I am Shiva, I have become Death." I don't expect that you will understand what I am trying to say, but the more you try to put a lid on something like that, the more it unravels in front of your eyes. I'm sorry gentlemen, but I can't help you. I wouldn't want the responsibility, even if it were a 'rational' thing to do. Atomics never belonged in the hands of the government, and the government will never successfully stop the entering into the picture of private individuals. Just look at the problems. You couldn't talk about security in Washington, not in your office, not in my office. Perhaps at a casual breakfast table, you think no one is listening, but I knew you were coming, and why. Enrico is taping our conversation," he pointed to Enrico, who smiled and tapped his coat. Others could be aware, in ways you can't understand or believe. If the company that designs the system is known, the system could be considered compromised, and your idea of a private meeting is a joke. A restaurant, come on Senator, don't even you see the ludicrous, impossibility of what you were attempting here this morning, a casual first meeting about a top-level security system?"

"You'll be sorry that you have taken this attitude," the Senator snarled at him.

"No, Senator, but you will."

"We will see when your license comes up for renewal at DEBT-com."

"I've never needed your vote before, Senator."

The Senator was hopping mad now.

"Well gentlemen, sorry I couldn't help you," Stark and Enrico stood up. "I will say this. If I were in your position, I would take all the nuclear waste under guard to Cape Kennedy and rocket it into solar orbit and burn it up in the sun. You can't hope to dispose of it by successfully storing it. That is an impossibility." He turned to go. "Congressman, it's been real, interesting," he paused. "Give my best to the President."

He gave a perfunctory nod to the Senator, who was still blanching and reddening at the same time with rage and despair, and they were gone, leaving the waitress holding a tray full of their breakfast and a twenty-dollar bill. The Senator's mouth was flapping, aimlessly, for the absent cigar. But a light had dawned in the congressman's eyes.

"Powering down."

"Roger, CAP Com," Colonel Derek Ramirez eased a look at his copilot Jason Richards. The two men exchanged a nervous glance. No one went into space without thinking of Challenger.

"Passing point of maximum aerodynamic pressure. All green. Over."

"We've got minimal pogo," Richards returned information on vibration of the ships passage through the maximum stresses, keeping an eye on his gages. "She's a smooth bird." The second-generation shuttle rose majestically through the dark blue sky. She was a sleek machine. A Porsche, compared to a nineteen-fifty-seven Chevrolet.

"Telemetry good. Coming up on Madrid. How is your LOX temperature? Over."

"LOX green. Over."

"Passing point of maximum pressure. Coming up on booster separation. Over."

"Go for separation. AOR. Over."

"Booster separation." The two solid fuel booster rockets were blown away by explosive bolts. Spent, they fell away toward recovery platforms where they would land vertically to be caught in giant forks and refurbished for reuse.

"Mississippi, this is Madrid control. Separation good. Telemetry, good. Mississippi, you are PRESDEMECO."

"Thank you, Madrid," Ramirez eased his clenched fist. "Powering up. Mississippi confirms. We are "go" for orbit."

The shuttle rose quickly into orbit velocity. Climbing quickly to over eighteen thousand miles per hour, the Mississippi climbed upward and outward from the pull of the earth's gravity. Traveling over seven times the speed of a high-powered rifle bullet, she streaked into low earth orbit and turned her belly toward the sun spilling the excess heat from launch into the cold of space.

Under the cargo bay doors, the cargo was contained in a metal box like a giant sea lane cargo box with a small rocket engine on one end. Blunt nosed and cumbersome, it was meant to fly only into the void of space.

After a couple of cool down orbits, the Mississippi moved into a higher orbit. Richards and Ramirez had little to do but monitor gages being monitored down below, as the mission specialist suited up in a pressure suit and checked the cargo bay for any obstructions that might have shaken loose during launch. The launch specialist went through the payload launch list.

When the payload crew was satisfied, the pilot maneuvered the Mississippi into a payload launch attitude. The craft had to be taken to high earth orbit where the payload was sprung into space. The Mississippi backed smoothly away.

"CAP com," Lt. Colonel Ramirez called earth. "Ace Garbage Trucking Co., the load is dumped, and we're ready to come get another. Bring us home, ground control. Over."

"Good job. Come on home."

The craft was maneuvered into the upside-down reentry positioning. The retro rockets fired and the Mississippi began the short fiery trip back to earth.

Shortly after the transport was back on earth, the cargo container was put into its launch trajectory and the small rocket fired taking the cargo and the container into a

15

slow looping trajectory that would eventually take the cargo and container into the sun.

Seven months later, the container, traveling at tremendous velocity, began entering the corona of the outer solar atmosphere. The steel container vaporized as it peeled away, exposing its cargo of ceramic coated plutonium.

Plutonium was the byproduct of a steadily increasing number of fast breeder reactors that were used to supply earth's voracious need for electricity. Making its own fuel, the reactors also produced excess fuel that presented a storage problem for the nation states that depended on them. Storage was expensive. Security had proved unreliable. The plutonium was literally too hot to handle. But it was proving to be a needed shot in the arm for NASA. The increasing threat of nuclear terrorism had led the United States to dispose of its excess plutonium in the sun. Sealed in a ceramic coating in case of an accident during launch, the six kilograms of plutonium in each ball would withstand the impact of explosion or reentry and impact on earth.

Now exposed to the Sun's Solar atmosphere of one million degrees Fahrenheit, the ceramic glowed white hot and grew even stronger as ceramics do under heat. The force of the stream of photons pouring out from the surface caused the ceramic balls to skim the surface like a rock on the surface of a pond.

As they spread out over the surface, prominences swallowed them in superheated gases, and they added their small force to the hot exploding hydrogen. Others skipped into areas of sunspots, where the nuclear reactions went beyond any physics yet understood on earth. Falling into spots of special distortion, caused by the forces of gravity in these localized areas, where the gravitational force was so great that even photons were pulled back into the solar core.

Many of the plutonium pellets exploded at this point, but occasionally, like a bullet to a bullseye, the trajectory was such that the ceramic coated plutonium entered a localized Schwarzschild radius, where time itself was distorted along with space. Here, depending on their entry angle, they could obtain velocities many times the speed of light. Entering this distorted region of time and space, they fell right through the core of the star and entered hyperspace, coming out the other side, spewing up and down the timelines, and spreading out willy nilly over the past, present, and future of a galaxy halfway across the Universe. They were scattered throughout, according to the unfathomable star growth singularity function, and traveling at fantastic speeds. One is deflected by a sinister figure, with a technology unknown to any other, for a fratricide most hideous.

Nuclear blackmail was a frighteningly familiar term, complete with its media symbol on the five o'clock news.

The first unauthorized, in the sense of government non-sanctioned explosion, occurred in Tokyo, and had nothing to do with blackmail or money. One eighth of Tokyo was destroyed in a single instant, by what authorities termed a 'crude homemade device of low yield'. Its origins remained a secret, however, its motives were totally political, and credit was generally given to and claimed by an organization known as SOUL-Servants Of Universal Love.

That was just Tokyo though. It hardly made a ripple in New York but made them take a nervous glance. Nor did the explosion two years later that followed an abortive attempt to have partisans released from a Columbian jail. America, whose industry and power companies produced plutonium waste, slumbered at these rumblings. Tittered, as various fools tried robbing banks with 'atomic bombs' in paper sacks, held its breath while a man almost blackmailed New York out of a billion dollars, but couldn't back his bluff and lost his life. They would have paid it, too, if they could.

It wasn't until one Christmas, several years later, that the country came awake like a derelict from a nightmare. This time it was real, unexpected, and totally devastating. Someone, a girl in a light-colored dress and sunglasses, it was believed, had driven a van with an atomic device concealed in its rear area. The van or some type of vehicle had been parked in front of the Los

Angeles police station, and at three-twenty-three in the afternoon, a three-block area was vaporized.

"The death toll has how reached forty-three thousands, "the grim-faced T. V. commentator in pallid makeup droned out at him. Scenes passed through the camera flashing the appalling reality to the nation. The phone rang, and he picked it up halfway through the ring.

"S. G. Raven," he said in his business voice.

"Stark," Carlo's voice seemed drained.

"Carlo," he cut the other man off. "Thank God, you got through. All the communications are out, and the frequencies are jammed out. I've tried to raise the ranch all day."

"Stark, it's terrible. I was inside a building. Some outside can't see, and their ears are bleeding."

"Is everyone all right," he asked lamely? He heard Carlo choke.

"We've lost some people, "he said with hard-won control. "All the people on all the boats. The explosion was near the waterfront, every boat sank," his voice broke. "Angelina," he sobbed, "I think Angelina is dead. She was in the city and," he completely broke up.

"Hang in there Carlo," he offered ineffectually. "There are planes and people bringing supplies up to the ranch. I'll be with them. I'll see you later tonight."

He hung up the phone and crossed to the window looking out on the city, but the luxury of height was not pleasing. Instead, he had that feeling of wanting to rush somewhere, and there was nowhere to rush. An urgency was on him, and he needed to be doing something to escape some as yet unforeseen danger. Now the danger was no longer unseen. The suffering was all around him, echoing in his ears, the T. V. commentator gave the latest gruesome statistics. He strode quickly over and shut off the remote control. The picture's flat screen blinked out. He sat in the darkened room staring abstractly out the window, letting his mind drift over the possible future events. Now and again he unconsciously shook his head and let out a slow heavy sigh.

****

Infinite space, forever spread in all directions, dotted to the eye like the sequins on a dancer's black gown. If the eye could see farther, what brilliance it would find as the black faded away. Even had someone been looking, it would have been virtually undetectable. With suns being born and suns exploding all around, such a minor disturbance would certainly have passed unobserved. Even prominences capable of creating a world went unrecorded. Who would have looked twice at a simple series of solar spots? What difference could it make? The sun they occurred on was hardly even named. It only had a number and name because it lay within the scoping of an established dimensional space lane. Its configuration was well charted. It always had stable mass, in the past. True, the spots would affect the gravitational coefficients to a small degree, but nothing requires attention. The navigational computer would take it into account, along with hundreds of other minor solar disturbances along the way and automatically make the course correction when the error reached one millionth of an arc of degree. Some of the high-speed vessels had constant corrections, but Commander Rune was well satisfied with his ship, and his assignment. True, there were more lucrative assignments than the ambassadorial shuttle. He could be plundering and subduing any number of worlds throughout the galaxies. It would bring more immediate wealth, but then it also carried a certain risk. This was the unpleasant aspect of conquering new territories for the glory of the Imperium. Better to let younger, more foolhardy men, lead such expeditions. He had done his share of it. It had let him gradually work through the myriad ranks of captains to this position. There were fringe benefits that were not immediately apparent, attached to a diplomatic shuttle. What good was wealth, if you didn't have the influence to hold on to it? No. He had chosen wisely when he left the corps. He had made many friends, who would serve him well, when the time came. He possessed a home on the ruling world, and more influential friends, all the time. But now, his mind was not occupied with power politics. He was more concerned with what species of slave girl he would use for his amusement when they reached Regis Xinor.

A smile came to his lips at this thought but inwardly, it was more of a sneer. He let himself back in his chair and envisioned his homecoming with several different species, pondering the question of which one he would choose. They were all good at their craft, or they would not be on Regis Xinor. It was one of the fringe benefits that he liked so well. His revelries were untimely interrupted by the swish of the automatic door sliding back.

"Pardon me, Captain Rune," came a whinnying nasal voice. "I hope I'm not intruding."

"Not at all," Captain Rune lied. "What can I do for you ambassador Mephor?"

"The trip has become so tedious, that I thought I would come up to navigation."

"I'm afraid that the trip is just as long here."

"To be absolutely frank, my dear captain," the creature slid into the computer console chair, behind the captain, blinking huge, but beguiling orbs, at the man. "I wish to have a talk with you, before we reach planet fall."

"Well, we should have time for a real heart to heart then."

"Actually, my dear Captain, I have been waiting to speak with you alone. May we speak freely?" Mephor accented the question by fixing Rune with a narrow stare.

Rune thought of recording devices in his cabin, in the galley, in fact, in every part of the ship except navigation, which was where the monitoring was done. The two regarded each other for a long moment.

"You may speak without worry, Ambassador," the captain reassured the ancient creature.

"Captain, you are a man of growing importance. You will soon be the senior officer in the fleet and, as such, will become Captain of the Emperor's Flagship."

"It's possible," the Capitan offered. "There are several others that might be offered the post."

"With a word in the right ear," the Ambassador countered.

"Calpin is too old, he certainly will retire. Tolmac intends to put out to one of the outer rims, carve out a piece as far from the center of things as he can, but there are still five or six others."

"But it might be you," the Ambassador smiled a toothy grin.

"Yeah, might be. What's in it for you?" The captain leveled his voice. He had no patience with politicians.

"My dear Captain, we have been watching you with interest, for some time."

"Who is we?"

"My dear Captain, let's not be coy. You are familiar with my master, Metastophiles?"

The captain's blood turned icy at the name.

"Your Master? I thought you are Viceroy of Pandamon."

"Captain, we really must be direct, if we are to get anywhere."

"Alright, Mephor," Rune lost his composure. "What's it going to cost me?"

"Nothing you won't be able to easily afford," the creature raised the patches of fur above the yellow orbs. Rune nodded his understanding.

"A man has to make use of his opportunities."

"We simply will wish to know the location and intended travel plans of the Emperor and his family."

"I want no part of assassination plans."

"Captain Rune, I'm shocked. My Master is a simple businessman. The Emperor's movements, those of his family stimulate trade, portend all sorts of things of interest to a businessman. Who would be able to provide a better source of information than yourself?"

"Your master was never a simple businessman," Captain Rune snapped back. "Don't play me for the fool."

"We know what type of man you are, my dear Captain, which is precisely why I have taken this tedious journey on trumped up reasons. Now do we have an understanding? Captain, it is your decision."

"Each piece of information will be valued separately," Rune aimed a finger at the Ambassador.

"Captain, you know that my master can provide any advantages."

Rune laughed heartily as his imagination fired over this last break of fortune. 'All the advantages,' he let the words carry him along a tide of fantasy.

The Ambassador reveled in the bargain, smirking a smile. Mephor's Master, however, had a different idea for him, as these two, and those with them, became the first casualties of a new epic.   The ships' sensors didn't have time to ring a bell or flash a light. The deflector screens barely slowed it, but they started it going critical. One ten thousandth of a nanosecond latter, the ceramic coated plutonium ball, weighing slightly less than six kilograms, tore through the outer skin of the ship, struck Ambassador Mephor in his mouth, and went supercritical, about where the Ambassador's head used to be, vaporizing

the ship and throwing pieces of it all over that part of the
galaxy.

His hands were sweating so badly the micro access desk was slipping through his fingers. If he were caught with it, he could be executed.

He worked in the central computer section and that gave him use of any of the processing equipment. The disk cost him plenty. Every favor that he had out. All the Kronegs he could beg, borrow, or steal. But he had to have it, it meant everything.

With his twenty-first birthday, he would be marked. The counsel be obliterated, he'd be damned to death if he was going to be made one of those sadistic, privileged dandies, who glutted themselves all day.

Closely chaperoned, the 'free ones' turned to sadistic games of perversity in a social order that valued power and prestige at the court. He had always tried to keep his distance from it, but now, he would be pulled into the center of the court. Pandamon was indeed a strange society.

His hands moved swiftly across the keys. He was enamored of many of the extravagances of court life, but he had not been lazy. He had made good use of his time. And with a natural proclivity for computers, he had landed a job in the central processing section, even though as a member of the Royal Household, he would have an interesting job to do, and the money helped.

He lifted fingers now. He typed faster than he had ever typed before, rapping his fingers on the desk. "Come on, come on," he coaxed the machine impatiently, as he waited for the control program to boot. He looked nervously over his shoulder. He did not want anyone to find him here. He had the right to be in this section, but he didn't want to explain what he was doing. If the disk wasn't back before the morning shift, there would be no ending of the trouble.

"Come on," he pounded on the machine. It clicked and a light came on, the program came up on the screen. "Shit," he cursed. There was an access lock on the program usage as well. He knew how to run them all. He tried over and over to break it. He pounded the desk in frustration and bit his lip. The consternation made him type that much more furiously.

Sometime, about dawn, he was whipped. He slumped in his chair. He would never be able to get access to this program again.

Suddenly, an idea flashed in his head clear as a bell. He rejected it. It came back with certainty.

METASTOPLILES, he typed. He returned control. The program whirred and ran. A creeping feeling came over him. He was in. He knew how to do this now. He looked through the reams of information on himself, looking for the files he was after.

"History," he typed in. It responded with a menu on the file. He typed in 'Origin', the machine blanked out and the flashed back a list of vital statistics.

"Terra," he read, "Solarian System." It meant nothing to him. He scrolled the screen upward.

"Birthplace: Lawrence Kansas
   Hospital: Wythe Memorial Hospital
   Address: 1225 Beltline
   Mother: Amy Hodge
   Father: M
   Genetic Typing: ACTG sub-chromo BETAZOID

That was what he was looking for. His heart stood still and he felt sick.

"No, no," he groaned.

He knew exactly what the future held for him. He was destined for what the Noble Princes called the Royal

26

Stud Pen. He would be one of the future rulers of Pandamon, which he reflected sardonically, was not all that it was cracked up to be. He had hoped not to rise so high, to get lost in the bureaucratic shuffle, to be of such little significance so as to lead a life of quiet mediocrity.

But it seemed, his genes would thrust a different, and dubiously desirable future of distinction on him.

He worked feverishly to put his plan into motion. He made copies of his history. He didn't know why. He had a pirated copy of the operating system, but without the equipment he could never run it, and he hoped to be far away from both.

He tapped in an order for himself to assume a guard position at the spaceport, on a night that he knew how to penetrate their security. A cadet was having an affair with a reservations clerk. He made himself a nice little diplomatic package with his lip, finger, and eye print, a nice piece of work. He smiled at himself, at this deed and congratulated himself on his cleverness. Now, where would he be going? Anywhere, it just had to fit with his time schedule. He pulled up a list of departures.

"Saphos, it is," he said satisfied at last. He knew what he must do. He quickly collected his gear.

Not a second too soon. The director of the complex arrived.

"Good morning, Thane Marx," he secreted the access disk into his books on his desk.

The older man came over to him turning on lights, his eyes darting suspiciously around.

"What are you doing here, Kurege," he demanded?

"I'm running a statistical analysis of fuel consumption and air transport on the planet."

"Is that so?" Thane Marx stepped to a console and brought it up.

"It may come up with some savings of Helium III isotope. The super cryo-fluid is expensive to Pandamon.

The balance of our imports from Xinor itself is accounted for largely by this one item. This program is a modification of the eco-stochastic alpha, that was in the files. It has a correlation factor on aberrant data that is a possible refinement," he was glad that he had thought to cover his tracks by running a statistical program he was working on developing.

"Yes, I see," the director perused the screen. "Someone has accessed the main file."

"I tried to have the program run for inter galactic consumption also, but the mains would not engage that information to my terminal," he had covered the program that was run, but he couldn't get rid of the run time record, and then the backup would exist for twenty more hours, if Thane Marx was curious enough to go downstairs. "Very good, Kurege. You're to be commended. We will miss you if you are transferred."

"I would miss the center sir," he thought that it sounded like it was an afterthought. Did the director know? They looked at each other for an awkward moment.

"Well, I think I'll go to the commissary, sir, and grab some breakfast before my regular shift starts," he excused himself. He picked the book up that contained the disk.

"Kurege," the directors voice froze him as he turned to go. "What have you there?"

"Where?"

"In your hand."

"A book, sir."

"I can see that. What is it?" The director approached him. He took the book from him, Kurege thought he was going to vomit. His stomach churned. He tasted bile in his throat.

"A book on statistics."

The director held the book in his hand and studied its title for a long moment. He examined its binding and looked at the author. "Stochastic Binary Representation," the director read. "Harrumph," he grunted. "You study too much."

"I like it," Kurege reassured him of his good nature with his sweetest, innocent smile.

"Yes," the Director licked his lips. He handed him back the book.

Kurege's legs would barely support him all the way to the big central dinning area. The man that worked in the central processing file room was waiting for him.

"You're late," he accused.

"I'm lucky to be here."

"Give me that disk. I'll be lucky not to get caught. We'll both be killed." He prised off down the hallway, in the little fury that he generated, all around him. "Don't forget your part of the bargain," he threw over his shoulder as he disappeared around the doorway.

Kurege ate quickly. There would be many loose ends to take care of, and now he would have to pull his entire standard shift, unless Thane Marx left at some point during the day. He would never get off sick, now that he had been seen. He would have to go back to work and watch for an opportunity. Unfortunately, he had to work his entire shift. It didn't leave him much time.

He arrived at his apartment within less than an hour to get dressed for his false role as spaceport security. He frantically pulled the papers from the space in the air handling system in the ceiling, where he had secreted them. He checked them quickly. They must be in the proper order. Satisfied with his work, he shoved them in his pocket. His expertise with the computer and access to the central system, had served him well, again. A talent he had traded on very successfully, and a mainstay of his abilities to maneuver his way into the central file room.

Now, with all his questions answered, it was time to burn his bridges, and head for somewhere far away, as the last dance had been done. His options were being shut down, but he had been preparing. He had known. A hundred things around him had shown him exactly what was happening. He had noticed changes in the way his superiors treated him. There were certain interviews and tests. The visits to the medical doctors and then the psychiatric evaluation. But most of all, there were the dreams. He was being smothered or trapped, imprisoned, and starved. Worst of all, he was milked of his seed. These wet dreams were the most horrifying out of control entrapments of all except in some of them, a faceless woman controlled him, and he liked that, in spite of himself, although, he was left with an extremely uncomfortable, empty feeling at the end of these dreams, and a sticky mess.

His adolescent mind was primed for escape, and he readied himself with the special diplomatic jacket, sown inside out, of the spaceport security guards uniform. Sewing was another talent which he had developed for himself in his idle time. It was all part of the exploration of the insatiable market on Pandamon for false identities, passports, clothing, and software to penetrate security.

Kurege had a lively little black-market business going on the side, not for the Kronegs, but for the favors. This approach had not only saved him considerable taxes but had garnered him enough favors to make good his escape, he hoped. He nervously dressed. Taking six deep breaths, and trying to compose himself, he left for the spaceport.

He handed his security clearance to the Charge of Quarters, at the central security station at the spaceport entrance.

"Trevon Capsan," the guard looked disinterestedly at him. "Where is Jalap tonight?"

"He came down with a sudden illness, they didn't say what," he hoped the vague reference to someone upstairs would end the conversation."

"I've never seen you before."

"I usually work at the Macron gate," he jerked his thumb toward the far side of the port. "They pulled me in on my rec night," he groused. He hoped his ill humor would mask the need for further conversation. He threw in a shrug, as if 'what's a peon to do', and a conspiratorial smirk.

"Yeah, they got no mercy around this place," the guard commiserated with him. "Trevon Capson, on the Cestus gate. Here is your security lock and tesloc disruptor, now get going, you're late. The guard you're replacing will have a sore ass. He's got a hot engagement. So, you had better move it."

"Aye, aye," Kurege rushed on up the terminal.

The guard gave him a hard time for being late, but not too hard, as he was in a hurry to get gone.

He waited until the Cestus Warp shuttle was boarding and then stepped into an alcove and changed identities by reversing his jacket.

He handed his identity card to the stewardess, who was in charge of boarding.

"Ambassador Kurege of Sol," she spoke the identity that he had created for himself with conviction, and a shading that hinted she was both impressed by him and his title. "We are pleased to have you with us on the Cestus. Where will you be disembarking?"

"My positioning is on Saphos," he took back his identification.

"Oh," her face dropped. "We don't get much traffic going that way."

"I understand that it's not a large post."

"No, but I've heard that it is a beautiful little place. We have three compartments that might be suitable for your excellency.

"Thank you."

"Let me guide you to them," she led the way along the companionways. He followed her to the first one and chose it.

"This will do nicely," he insisted.

"If there is anything else you need," she said hospitably.

"Thank you. I'll let you know."

"Please do."

She closed the door and left.

He centered himself on his escape and felt much better thirty minutes later when the ship left Pandamon on time. When they fell through the Warp Star Cestus, and were safely on the other side, he began to feel safe. Any chase now would have to be carried through the warp. The tachyon message of his escape would have a hard time overtaking him now.

He began to relax at last. He needed to sleep badly. He lay down and closed his eyes. He was sound asleep in a few moments.

Kurege was dreaming. The specter awaits, stalking the night like a cat, seeking to take: no giving in its heart. A ghost, a shadow, a half-seen figure lurks just beyond this reality. In sleep, he was seeing these beings, both real and imagined. Wild fantasy-dreams of gardens surrounded by high walls filled his mind. A garden peopled by beings known and unknown, his associates, his blood-kin, his secret lovers, his wishful thoughts, his dreaded fears, his noble aspirations, were all there, awaiting his sinking into the great depths of mind.

Hear me Oh God! I am a mortal man and yet, a god, also. I am asleep and desire to awaken from these dreams and See.

A feminine Voice speaks.

"Then you must toil and sweat and from your cries will come the awakening into life. Yours must be the long and difficult path, full of illusion and traps, prepare well, for what is to come will be of Hell. This you know but prepare your mind as well as your body. There is great work to be done. Perceive truly and weigh each deed, carefully, and tarry not, least you be swept away like pebbles in the flood."

I open my eyes
I open my ears
I open my Heart
I open my Mind

He awakened with a start. Uris was standing in the doorway looking at him. He knew her but did not know her.

"I was having a very strange dream."

"Not as strange as reality. Come with me," she motioned for him to follow.

He awakened a second time. The first awakening had been into a second dream, but a dream so real it seemed like reality. He didn't know who the woman had been.

"Not as strange as reality," she had said. "Come with me," and motioned for him to follow. He was intrigued. As a dreaming species, he knew that not all species dreamed. He knew that sometimes his species dreamed of the future, this was the déjà vu that the writings spoke of in the library. He was vaguely familiar that his classification as a betazoid sub-cromo carrier had something to do with all this. He puzzled over it and the woman in the dream. He seemed to know her, trust her.

"I'd follow you anywhere," he said to no one in particular.

He called for something to eat and a progress report. He was pleased to see that he was two warp stars and thousands of parsecs from Pandamon. He hoped grimly that it would be far enough. He would be glad to get to Saphos and lose himself in the city. From there he could go anywhere.

Space, limitless space reaches forever. The Void is the form from which space is carved by what can be called God, or any word that might be chosen, light; at the speed of light, growing bigger, beyond any comprehension of size, growing always, at the speed of light.

It flows in all directions, and it carries the energy of its emptiness with it. It flows to be full and is full, therefore; it flows. Rivers meet and join. Particles of light meet and join. Great deltas of rivers are fabric formed. Great pools of light gather in the emptiness of space. What is lost travels on until meeting. One particle joins another, as rivulets are formed from drops, flowing into rivers, and on into the sea. Also, light joins light.

Deltas give rise to great mountain chains. The weight pushes down and the fabric pushes back. When the gathering is great enough, the surge comes.

So it is in Nebulae, or in Star Birth. The light gathers from the infinity and begins its dance.

At predictable spots in space, a nebula will gather. The future world. The Devi dance of totality. The billion-year squeeze that brings Star Birth and solar systems, eventual decay and climax in Nova.

Light is bent as it travels by the mass fabric of space. The river of light carves; not inward as a river might be seen to carve, but outward. Imagine two great rivers that have carved canyons through the globe and have met in the center of the earth, with their waters rushing suddenly together. Light carves outward into space and, as it carves, it sometimes carves through the flat surface, for the world is indeed flat. Two great rivers of light which are very far removed from each other come together and flow together through a hole in the fabric of space. It can be understood that in drilling holes in a three-dimensional space only a limited number of holes of any certain size can fit into the object without crossing each other at some point or doing away with the object. In the material world, the drill bit is the size of the photon. This is also the rate at which holes are being made. Fear not, however, for the fabric of space is big indeed, bigger than three dimensions when taken in a straight line. Space has grown in some direction, from a single point, the Universal Singularity. Therefore, it is, at most, in thickness, the distance light has traveled from the beginning. But there is no reason to assume that it is round, or that light has grown uniformly from the Singular Beginning. In fact, there are good reasons to assume that it would have grown in random, preferred directions. Therefore, space is very much thinner in some places, or times. The Universe can be seen in this way as a flat, but curved or twisted surface, growing in preferred directions. Space, the limitless void, is a straight line, but light, if it bends any, and it is bent by its totality, must curve back on itself. Where it curves back and touches itself, special conditions arise: The Supernova.

Many of these rivers of light are so filled with the velocity of the exchange between the two rivers that nothing else can go out, only things go in, like whole galaxies. These rivers will erode the fabric of space, and, some think, destroy it totally.

Some of these rivers of light are navigable to ships sufficiently shielded, and like a bridge over a river of water, can make the other side a lot closer.

Uriah was awaiting the building of such a bridge. He had carefully, and at great cost of time in his life, traveled into down time to chart the formation of the Neutron Star Draco, which was about to go supernova.

In Xinor time, the doorway would be open, creating the seventh navigational star of the Regis system and opening unmeasurable areas of time and space. It would be the single most important event of the last eight hundred standard Xinor years.

"It will blow soon," Uriah spoke calmly to Dav, keeping one eye on the instruments in front of him.

"A Pandamon warship has emerged from up time. They are taking a position directly across the path we must take away from the explosion."

"We expected Metastophiles. He's right on time. He can pick us off when we come out from the explosion of the surface of the collapsing star. We will be blind from the electromagnetic flux. The shields may not form either."

The two men looked at each other a long moment.

"I want better data than they are going to get," Uriah turned back to his gages at the console.

"I'm with you all the way captain. We will sleep side by side tonight."

"I must do this for the House and for Uris. Metastophiles will come through the Cestus Warp to get to Draco, and he will attack Saphos when he does. The House of Ur will have to move deeper into a new and uncharted area. I must give them the edge that the data from this supernova will reveal about the new warp star. For Uris it will be a matter of survival."

"The data must be complete, if we are to have first pass at the new hole," Dav smirked a ribald spacers joke.

Uriah smiled at his friend. They both knew that they would not see another day. "So, Dav," Uriah fixed him with a hand on his shoulder, "escape if you can."

"I have always wanted to die with you in battle. This is as good a day to die as I have ever seen."

"Look, the star implodes."

They hurriedly took the measurements they had come through fourteen years of real time to gain. Dav transferred the data to an escape pod. He armed and programed a decoy of a more detectable engineering and set them free. In the electromagnetic confusion of the supernova, the pods could easily get lost from the pursuers.

"Arming weapons system."

They both hollered an old battle cry of Ur as they charged on the Pandamon battle cruiser.

The cruiser blew through the weak shielding that was beginning to form and utterly destroyed the proud craft.

On the other side of the river, as things now flowed, many light years of distance, the light from that explosion would eventually reach a blue-green planet around a M class star in a galaxy called the Milky Way, in the year ten-fifty-four AD. In that year, Chinese astronomers observed a supernova in the tip of the horn of the bull in the constellation Taurus. It was so bright that it was visible for several weeks during the daytime, as well as lighting up the night like a second moon. They called it 'The Guest Sun'.

Kung Sung turned to his general and gave the order to attack. A great battle began on the Yangtze River. Tremendous warships with twenty-three paddles, eleven on a side and one in the rear, attacked each other and the fate of China was given over to the Sung Dynasty, unrivaled.

In England, Edward the Confessor proclaimed his heir, William of Normandy. The Pope of Rome excommunicated the patriarch of Constantinople. William, who would be called 'The Conqueror', had just returned from a visit to England, and made up his mind to attack it.

The Turks overturned the Empire of the Caliphs. In each instance, these decisions were accompanied by a sign from the heavens that they were absolutely correct. A great astronomical event like none that had ever happened before; A second sun arose in the heavens.

William of Normandy thought God had decided to let him have a spot next to him in heaven and ordered immediate preparations for the attack on England.

Light from this explosion had been traveling for eons, when it first began reaching Earth in 1054 AD. The explosion left great clouds of matter, which we came to call the Crab Nebula. In the center of the Nebula, a great star was discovered in 1972. A rapidly spinning neutron star of dense material and unbelievable gravitational forces was found to be existing in its center.

Kuo Hsi, the founding master of Sung dynasty landscape painting, must have found that the landscape was more interesting than usual with two suns.

None of the men who thought about this phenomenon or presumed it to give blessings to their personal fortunes and ambitions, could have in their wildest dreams understood the real implications of this incident. None could have imagined what it would mean to their children's children. Indeed, it would be unbelievable fantasy in any previous time. The doorway that had opened would be clear of turbulence and star surface material, and would be navigable, letting two worlds of time and space join sometime in the early years of the 21st century-earth time.

The towers of Ur gleam like polished bronze, and indeed they are surfaced with an alloy of silicon, high in copper content. It is not vast as capital cities usually are, nor are there multiple complexes of megalithic monoliths developed to do business, as always, on a galactic or multi-galactic scale.

In contrast to other capital worlds Saphos is tiny but like its name "gleaming light", considered a jewel in the dust. Surrounded by high mountains and inaccessible except by vehicles capable of a sixteen-thousand-foot vertical climb, it seemed to grow from the cliffs, gleaming bronze against rock, white as snow, and green entrapped gold in the spring.

The peaks and valleys all around were arranged with many types of communications equipment, that would have been both familiar and strange to the human eye. The common radio and television, radar, microwave, and radio telescope arrays similar to Arecibo, would have made an earth man feel at home, but the round column like cryogenic receivers of the tachyon galactic communications system, five hundred meters tall, and twenty meters thick of molded, faceted, polished crystal, would have seemed alien, and stood out to be noticed among the more overshadowed planet and solar system communications and radio telescopic devices.

No one could fail to miss these strange machined, annealed, quartz columns. The transmitter counterparts, which suddenly command attention by emitting an almost inaudible resonance, or perhaps it is the rocks around it that are making a sympathetic noise to the thing that is taking place inside the transmitter. Over a thousand meters high, poured and annealed quartz towers, these transmitters, along with the receivers, form the backbone of a galactic communications system. These towers are part of the tachyon communications system that is the link with the neighbors, of which there are few. Such a galactic understatement needs clarification.

The tachyon towers, other than adding a fairy kingdom type of effect to Saphos, by completely dwarfing the gleaming buildings with glistening quartz towers, also form the backbone of Ur as a world and member of the Guild of Houses, and Ur as a ruling house. The message is sent to a relay station, where it is couriered through a navigational doorway leading into an adjacent galaxy. Only the Guild members know the navigational secrets. This is how safety and security is maintained.

Space folds on itself. The stars are created like organic growth at mathematically predictable junctions between almost infinite rays from other suns. The energy accumulates and localizes, birthing stars. Eventually, growing out, it becomes strands of star filled galaxies. In special places, these strands bend back, and double stars exist that are only the thickness of the fold separated. Space folds on itself, not at every solar body, but as if someone had dropped string, and where these strings cross, a special star exists, that at its death, will become a supernova. This double star, at its death, collapses into its gravitational center, literally warping the fabric of time and space, wadding it, and wrinkling it like a ball. The couriers warp through where the message is tachyon transmitted to a second courier, who navigates a second warp, and so on, to where the message is sent by tachyon to Regis Xinor, where a reply is made up, if only to confirm the system integrity. A little less than a one day process in Terran time, from warp star to warp star. A good three days ahead of the fastest shuttle, in the case of Ur, and the Hyperbolia Warp Star.

The towers hummed and hummed today.

"They are burning up the quartz today," Eljer spoke through the door. Mez was standing in the frosty air gazing across the valley. The younger man joined him outside, leaving the massive door ajar. It swung with the wind pressure with amazing ease for its weight and size.

"Here is the first message, I knew you would want to see."

Mez took the message from Eljer and read it.

"All members of the Navigational Guild are requested to depart for an emergency council meeting of utmost importance to galactic security. Ordered this time Pandamon 10638-2-23. High Commissioner Beel."

"Look where this one is from," Mez exclaimed uncharacteristically.

"Pandamon," Eljer cut his eyes upward, craning his neck back and squinting against the morning sun. It was light for hours when the sun finally crested the peaks, the rays were warm. This door was the front door of the castle like structure, called the Morning Gate because it was the first place the sun's rays struck the valley floor each morning. That was why the ancient fortress stood in exactly the same spot and why the palace was built here with the rest of the city around it and in the heart of the mountains.

"At least they've toned it down from yesterday," Mez pulled another note from his pocket and reread to himself.

"It is by Imperial Decree that all Ruling Houses send all ranking Navigational Guild members to Regis Xinor immediately, 10638-2-21, Emperor Leo XIV."

"Just the same, I wish Uris would return early." Eljer searched the patch of blue green above them letting his eyes come to rest on the stonework engraving above the Morning Gate's massive door frame.

'Worlds Collide, The Family Endure,' written in the ancient script of a long dead language.

Eljer was one of the few that could read this writing, and the words gave him a sense of security, the same as the massive structures all around him had always given him that same feeling of being safe. "I'm going to try to raise Uris again. She should be on her way back by now." He turned and left his white-haired companion, where he had first found him, soaking up the bright morning sun.

He raised the Pearl on the fourth try, but even with all possible speed, it was almost dark when she made planet fall. The sun had long disappeared behind the mountains and the air was frosty when the little egg-like Pearl came noiselessly sliding down between the crags and then hummed into the shelter that had opened with a great popping of ice some minutes before. Appearing almost magically out of the stone mountain side, a door had opened inward on cryogenic, magnetic, frictionless, bearings.

A room, which moments before had held twenty forms clustered in groups around the walls, was now alive with activity. Almost before the ship touched the floor of the enormous chamber, the doors had swung noiselessly and quickly shut. Carpets were rolled out, and men in five or six different kinds of uniforms came to a snappy attention. In fact, all who moments before had been lounging peacefully, were now doing their best to be busy whether writing forms, or toting crates. They did find time to stop their busy tasks as the door of the little Pearl opened. Even the character slouching by the main entrance hallway, straightened.

For a brief moment, the room seemed entranced. Uris had emerged from the tiny craft to confront them carrying the hindquarters on one shoulder and the rolled skin in her other hand. Mez had caught his breath; she looked so much like Uriah on that day long ago.

"Madam," was all he managed to say. She stood looking at them all over one by one, eventually stopping on the figure slouching by the causeway, which now came almost to attention with the pressure of her piercing gaze. She did project an extraordinarily savage picture. Knife in sheath at her hip, with the meat on her shoulder, piercing ice blue eyes, golden hair and legs wide, she confronted them all. Something she didn't like, and it made her nostrils flare. "Madam," Mez broke the spell of the moment.

Suddenly, the workmen went about their work. The men in uniforms all pressed forth asking for her attention, some calling her Princess, some Regent, or by her name. She waved them all away with her left hand, which still contained the gru skin.

"Gentlemen, I will see all my Generals, and all members of the Guild of Navigation in the general counsel chamber in one hour." As she spoke, she pushed her way through them. She handed the skin to Eljer and hooked her left arm through Mez's. "Let's go," she whispered to them, and they started moving toward the main hallway. "I'm very tired," she said first, cutting them both off, but I will want to see you both in my chambers in twenty minutes," and then to Eljer, "Eljer, I would like a pair of boots made from that skin. Can you see to it?"

A disgruntled look crossed the old man's face. "I suppose, I can."

"As Master of Crafts, I would think you could," she taunted, they had reached the causeway and had come up to where the young man, whom her eyes had come to rest on last, was still standing, surveying the scene with a look that betrayed silent amusement at all he saw. Uris stopped in front of him and confronted him directly.

"Who are you," she demanded?

"This is Kurege, Princess Uris," Eljer conferred for him.

"Has he no tongue, Eljer," she turned to the old man?

"I am Kurege, lately arrived from Pandamon," he said clearly.

"Little enough to recommend you in that," she stated flatly. "Why is he here?"

"He is the rotational Ambassador, from the Guild Office."

"Another bright young native," she cut him off. "I'm sure you have found our kitchen," she proffered the hind quarter to him. He accepted it gripping the leg just above her hand, letting his finger just touch her.

"Certainly, Milady," he smiled with his borderline sarcastic smirk. So self-assured, she thought. Just an ego maniac like all the Pandamons, she conjectured to herself.

"Well see that it gets to the butcher," she threw back over her shoulder, as she strode firmly away with Mez still in tow. Leaving Kurege still unceremoniously holding the leg, and Eljer muttering to himself.

"I'm Master of Crafts, not a tanner," he muttered. Kurege shouldered the leg. "I build space ships, not cobble."

"What's wrong Master Eljer," Kurege turned away from following Uris down the tunnel with his eyes, and turned back to the old man?

"A galactic war breaking out, the whole world coming apart, and she wants some goat skin boots."

"Well, you know how women are about shoes," Kurege smirked. "Let me see," he took the skin from the older man.

"I haven't time for this. She always gives me every mundane thing, as if my responsibilities aren't demanding enough."

"Don't fret," Kurege offered, "I'll do it."

"You mean, yourself," the old man quizzed? "No Ambassador, I couldn't ask you."

"It will be my pleasure."

"Well, if you want to take care of it, as a diplomatic gesture," Eljer scratched his white hair. "Are you sure you can?"

"But of course, I'm a bright young Native," he said wryly, looking after Uris, who was disappearing into the distance of the hall.

"Gentlemen," she said entering the room. "We will be getting immediately underway. The counsel rose to its feet as she entered. "Everyone, please be seated," she said

quickly sliding into her console seat at the head of the large oval conference table.

The men and women around the table followed her lead quietly. "What is this about, Princess," an older and firm disciplined man two chairs to her right ventured. "We all have rumors: Galactic war, a traitors plot. What do you

think? Why all the Guild members summoned?" He summed up the questions on the faces around her. All the other people at the table nodded in ascent.

"Well put Zethuras, as always, straight to the matter," she paused. "I don't really know for certain, but I do have theory, but for now, let us assume that Galactic War is breaking out. That traitors are among us. Now," she punched a button in the array of buttons in front of her, "this is what is known. Officially, an Ambassadorial shuttle was attacked and destroyed by an attacker of unknown origin. It is being considered an attack from outside the ship, as no natural phenomena can account for the craft's destruction. The record box, which survived the explosion intact, as it is protected by a magnetic containment field designed to survive an atomic explosion, and is plasma proof, as you know the diplomatic ones to be, shows the screens penetrated by a projectile in hyperspace. Also, evidence tends to indicate that it was a projectile of some sort of fissionable material. The word has leaked from a freighter that was the first to arrive in the area, that traces of isotopic forms of lower unnatural elements were in the area. Isotopic forms of elements ninety-eight through about one hundred and ten, with traces of element 306, which can only be formed in an atomic explosion occurring in hyperspace. So, we can see, if an explosion occurred that would make matter found in only the middle of some of the most intense supernova gravitational holes in the universe," she paused and punched the figures up. "You see," she continued as the figures came on the screen, the projectile was traveling way too fast to be natural. Therefore, we must infer an attacker."

"But Madame," one astonished commander blurted, "there is no such weapon."

"Correction," the woman to his left," pointedly interjected, "hasn't been until now."

"Exactly, Surula," Uris responded to the woman and regained the focal point. "We cannot assume anything about this situation. The old Family Wars may begin again. It may simply be an attack on the Ruling House."

"But there is no good reason for the total Guild being summoned. It has never been done," Zethuras pointed his finger at the table. Eljer, who sat between Uris and Zethuras bobbed his head up and down in approval that someone had finally stated his point. "It's unheard of. It smells like a plot. It's like Beel."

"And that is exactly why I think it isn't," Uris cut him off, quickly setting her eyes on the young Pandamon Ambassador sitting in a chair provided away from the table. "Besides, I have other information. Several of these explosions have occurred. The first was last spring in the Moria system. There have been three others that are presently known about. She flashed three different sets of star charts on the viewer. "No, the Guild office and Beel himself are obviously worried. I have too many reports of their inquiries."

"But, Milady, these inquires could be a deception on the part of the Guild to capture and slaughter the members, thereby, dividing the whole Empire, to be restructured as the Guild Chairman sees fit."

"Yes, Beel and Pandamon stand to gain in his mad quest for the Empire," she looked straight at Kurege, who returned her gaze steadily and unflinchingly. "But he is genuinely seeking information. I want it to go no farther than this room," she said, as if to Kurege alone, then broke the gaze. "Beel is worried. It is too early in an assassination plot or a war for certain things to be happening."

"May I presume to ask, what specifically leads you to this conclusion, Princess?" The fair haired man who had been corrected by the woman earlier, voiced the skeptical side again.

"Yes, Simezon, you may. I need help with this thing," she smiled at them all. It was like warmth that she wanted to share with them before she broke the icy news. "Metastophiles, it is reported, through a reliable source, has come out of Down Time, and is present on Pandamon. The Baron is reportedly residing in the official executive building." She paused and fixed the response of each one to this piece of news. Each was visibly disturbed. She failed to notice the Pandamon Ambassador's quick upward dart of the eyebrows in surprise and perplexity. By the time she looked to his corner, he had his best diplomatic face in place. She noticed his mask, and it drew a line between them. He was an unknown.

"Now," she began over slowly, "this can only mean that the Guild is as much in the dark as we."

Some were skeptical, but none disagreed. Heads went side to side or nodded in assent. No one spoke.

Uris continued, "the Guild is frightened. Leo is frightened. I am sure they feel we are being invaded by someone from outside the Houses, whoever that might be," she waived the idea off. "I am not saying that something ominous is not happening. However, we should not panic over it, as the other Houses seem to be doing. "We will not withdraw diplomats, ask stupid questions, or risk the entire Guild of this House. However," and here she sighed, "I will personally be going to Regis Xinor." She held up her hand to the uproar. "Enough," she commanded. "I have made my decisions. This is a top-level meeting, and if the whole Guild does not go, then I must go to lead. It will be considered as a breach of the request, no matter which course we go. These communications are filled with the panic and the desperation of not knowing what is happening. No panic, we will return to them a top diplomatic gesture."

"Not alone, Milady. Not in just the Pearl," Zethuras forcefully but respectfully demanded.

"No, of course not," she looked at him crossly, and then her face mellowed realizing his concern for her. "Full Military Regalia will be appropriate. I will fly in the Dragon's Tongue. Zethuras," she motioned toward him, "will command it for me. As I will travel as Princess Regent of the House of Ur, Surula, you will command the Pearl. Simezon, you will fly the Scorpion. Each of you pick one ranking Guild member as your Second in Command. All others will stay on Saphos. Military alert is moved to the highest level, until further notice, by my order. Eljer will preside in my absence. All ships' personnel will be unconscious and under scan when Warp occurs, except of course the two Guild members," she looked at Kurege again. This time he noticed a worried look across her face. He tried not to look puzzled but didn't entirely succeed. She saw something he was trying to hide, and the seed was planted. She suspected him. There was an unknown. Unknown was suddenly everywhere. She was tired and dismissed the meeting.

As the meeting broke up, she conferred with the woman on her left.

"Has the Pandamon Ambassador been personally summoned," she questioned the woman?

"Not to my knowledge, Milady. He is not a full Guild member until he has finished rotational service at all the House's," she informed Uris. "I know that this is his last House, and he is gorgeous."

Uris looked at her perturbed. "If he asks to leave Saphos, he stays," she cut the other woman off. "If he does not ask, then see that he is on board the Dragon's Tongue, when we depart for Regis Xinor." She rose and left the table. "I will rest in my chambers until departure time," she told an attendant. "Send Eljer to me two hours before the ships are ready.

Swirling clouds of galactic dust obscure the stars on the port side, starboard, the awesome majesty of a thousand million suns, each of enormous proportions, pour out from the galactic center like bubbles from champagne.

"Matter," she observed, "grows faster than we can comprehend." The words echoed hollowly down the access shaft that led up to the observation bubble. "Yet, we creatures go on cheating, killing, and lying for a cool piece of it." Her musings were interrupted by the intercom.

"Pardon me Princess," Zethuras's mellow voice poured into the room.

"Yes," she responded?

"We will be attaining hyperspace shortly."

"I will be right there," she shook off the dazzling enchantment.

Taking one more look around the ship from the vantage point revealed through the transparent material of the floor of the chamber. The ship spread out below her like a flying pitchfork, or Neptune's trident. A design, not on purpose, but purposeful, to the efficiency of the gravitational flux concentrators. The ability to stretch them out linearly had improved performance over oblique structures or spheres, like the tiny Pearl, that hove into sight, swinging back from an abreast pattern to follow the leader.

The Scorpion, looking like a spear with an egg tied to its butt, swung in directly behind the little Pearl. They were all lined up in a row, now. Getting in single file, setting an azimuth as tight as possible. From hyperspace jump to the Warp Star, all three ships would hold a singular course, aimed at the center of the Warp Star. That would fix them into present time on the other side of the warp. Any variation off center, would send a craft whirling off through timelines, past and future, or down time and up time, as Uris knew it. Seeing the crafts in line for the course through to Hyperbolia, brought back one other flutter of memories. It was the Hyperbolia System that her father, Uriah, had passed through, on his way to Draco, those many years before. A day never passed that she did not remember Uriah.

The ships were lined up and the jump into hyperspace was obviously close. She walked briskly out of the access chamber, and along the ornate corridors. The Dragon's Tongue, the Flagship of the House was a crown jewel. Ornamented and embellished with all the craftsmanship of the best craftsmen. Built to impress intergalactic dignitaries, luxuriant, would be a gross understatement. Three-Hundred-year-old masterpieces of the most beautiful scenery in the galaxy vied for space along with more contemporary works of pure pattern. Works arranged, so as not to look to crowded, hung on walls. Mosaic pictures done in jewels, reeled by as she walked along.

She dropped down the gravity tube, stopping neatly at the next level. She passed through the equally elegant state rooms, along another corridor, and emerged into a room similar to the observation bubble, at the tip of the center point. Zethuras was strapped into the navigation console. He indicated her chair.

"You better sit down, or I'm going to have to take us on a big swing," he said with impatience showing in his voice. The jump consisted of a real energy barrier at the speed of light and like any change of state situation, backed up static resistance to the changing body, like water trying to become steam. Uris sat down quickly.

"How long, if we jump now?"

"Forty-five seconds, approximately," he answered her.

She began to work feverishly with a notebook on her console. "Give me a readout on Periyus," she queried.

"It's on your readout, now."

She worked at the figures efficiently, her hand flying over the pages.

"Alright," she said making a decisive last jot on the paper. "We are ready. I confirm."

"You don't miss one iota do you," Zethuras smiled.

"By the book, and the rule is, two navigators must confirm any warp course."

As if to punctuate her statement, the ship lurched in a jerky forward movement, pressing them into their chairs, just as the ships dove into the center of the Neutron Star. The electronic gear, the metal, and plastic, everything around them, seemed to ring with the transition.

"Let's see your figures," she challenged him.

"I let the transverses axiter take it on auto," he kidded, handing her his notes.

"Uh huh," she smiled at him sideways. Zethuras always acted and talked irresponsibly to her, having known her since she was a child. She knew it was a satire on his own meticulous nature. She nodded in agreement with it until she came to the roster, then her eyes flashed.

"Someone has the Pandamon Ambassador on your roster and not on mine," she was already moving out the door.

"I don't know anything about it, Milady," he offered lamely, to no one, as she was gone out the control access. He picked up his notebook and looked at it. "First I've heard of any passengers-minimum crew," he stopped explaining his innocence, as she had already disappeared out of the door.

Kurege was lying in his bed in one of the Ambassador's staterooms. She had noted that in the quick look at the roster. She pushed through the door without waiting to be announced. Not expecting him to be there but expecting him to be loose somewhere on the ship, she threw a quick look around the room and was about to leave.

"Hello," he called, "whatever you are, I'm in here," he said in a bilingual joke. She pushed through the bedroom door. He straightened and sat up.

"Princess, I apologize," he said flabbergasted.

"What are you doing," she demanded, looking quickly about the room.

"Resting," he replied. "They didn't tell me anything."

"Why are you conscious," she asked sharply.

"I felt the jump, but I assumed that I was on my way back to Pandamon."

She sneered at him unbelievingly and turned to the intercom on the wall. "Medical, to the Ambassador's quarters on B deck," she cracked the command into the intercom.

"But no one told me anything," he continued in his own defense. "Just get my belongings and report to the space port."

She said nothing. He rose to his feet under the pressure of her stare and then reached for a shirt to put on, as he was naked from the waist up. The medical personnel came in with an emergency kit. She took one look at the situation and lowered her eyes. Uris motioned for her to give Uris the black case that the woman carried.

"You won't be needed," she dismissed her. The girl fled from the scene, stumbling hurriedly backward.

"Roll up your sleeve," she said flatly, pulling a syringe and a bottle from the case.

"Princess, you wouldn't use that thing on me would you?" He protested but started to obey. "I know we made

the jump. If I had been recording, it would be too late."
He stopped that line of protest when he saw her reaction.

"You know that I could keep you on Ur the rest of
your life," she warned?

"Great," he brightened.

She disconcertingly stuck him hard, with a solid
jab.

"It wasn't my fault. No one came to put me under,"
he protested again, but she knew that was the fact.

"Don't let it glitch your star," he smirked, as he lost
consciousness. It was a bawdy comment. A pun in their
language that connected star quakes to sex. It was a
harmless saying among spacers, but hardly appropriate for
a Princess Regent. She fingered the knife at her side and
then drew it, feeling the edge. She saw nothing funny in
what he had just said.

She pulled up on the handle and turned it slightly.
The knife was now an electronic sweep. If any recording
devices were running, it would detect them. None
registered. She snapped the knife back to its knife shape
and replaced it in the sheath at her side. She thought that
there might still be something to find, and she began a
search of the room, tearing it apart. Spilling and pulling
everything from the closets and the drawers, like a
whirlwind.

She only stopped when she came to a boot in the
bottom of the closet. She drew it out, along with the
companion piece of fur, for the other boot. Recognizing
her gru's skin, her expression went through a series of
changes, and then she looked back at Kurege. She looked
at him as one seriously misjudged, and she was sorry for it.
She replaced the boot to its exact position, and began to
reorganize the room, trying to make it seem the same as it
had been before she tore it apart.

Hyperbolia is the first Warp on the way to Regis Xinor, when a ship is coming from Ur to the ruling world. Hyperbolia was also the path through Up Time that Uriah had used to gain access to the Draco System. The Family had originally resided in the Hyperbolian System until the Family Wars had caused them to retreat deeper into unknown space and time. The nearest habitable planet to Hyperbolia is Ka, which orbits the star Cester. It is on Ka that the Family of Ur maintains its diplomatic relationships with the Imperium. The tachyon communications system is maintained and staffed by only the most trusted and accredited members of the House. It is a lively and worldly place, enjoying an excess of life, which trade centers always do. They disembarked for Ka together in the Pearl just after nightfall on the planet, and after sixteen hours of hyperspace.

"That's the first hop," Zethuras looked up from the copilot's controls. Surula had been left in charge of the Dragon's Tongue, and Simezon had turned the command of the Scorpion over to his second. They departed from the landing bay of the Trident Class War Ship.

Uris sat without saying anything, surveying the planet below them. Her mind was naturally suspicious, fueled by a life filled with unexpected tragedy.

The port would be much like the landing hanger on Saphos, only larger with many ships and many creatures around them. It was always a shock to realize humanoid shapes were not the predominant form for creatures in the galaxies. Only occasionally, did the disturbing fact come to Ur. An occasional ambassador brought through the Hyperbolia Warp. On Ka this fact was everywhere, and the sentient species mixed freely, if not totally unprejudiced of each other. Each had found something in the other that it wanted, and trade strengthened this tie.

"What is wrong, Uris," Zethuras questioned?

"Nothing, really," she returned dreamily. "I was just thinking of father," she mused. "I suppose that I will finally have to admit that he is dead and will not return. The last possible time slot passed almost a year ago."

"I'm sorry for you, Uris," Zethuras started out slowly, and cautiously. "You feel perhaps that he abandoned you."

"He did," she said flatly.

"No," Zethuras shook his head. "Uriah was changed after Ursula's death."

"He blamed me," Uris said, in the same flat voice of acceptance.

"No, how does one blame life for death, or death for life. But, he was confused in his emotions."

"I was never even told he was leaving, until he was gone."

"He wouldn't have gone, but when he talked to me, he was deeply disturbed about leaving but felt compelled. He talked incessantly of the need that the House of Ur would have for data on the new Warp Star. He felt it was his mission that he must chart the Draco Supernova.

"But it was unkind of him to leave me behind. I was only eight years old when he left. He came to me just before he left. He said he would be gone for a while, and when I asked how long, he started crying and left the room. I think he knew then that he would never return."

"He thought that perhaps it would take twelve years."

"Why would he waste his life in a pointless search into Up Time for one more Warp? Space is full of places to go."

"But, Princess, most of them are known and mapped. When the family Wars came, The House of Ur used its last card with the move into Hyperbolia. The Imperium navigators knew as much as we knew about any other time and space. All other choices were just too easily violated. The Hyperbolia Warp is the last barrier against the Imperium and against Pandamon. It is thought, that from now, it would take a thousand years to unlock its secret."

"Exactly," she said, "what was my father's point in wasting his life? Choosing to die in the cold blackness of space, or lost in hyperspace, and lost in time, for the rest of his life?"

"I don't know the answer to that Princess, but I do know that with your father, also went one of the most outstanding men ever to come from Ur. You do not remember Dav. He was not part of court life. However, he and your father were like one when it came to the Draco expedition. I don't know if Dav put it in his mind or the opposite, but they reinforced each other with absolute fanaticism when we tried to dissuade them. If they ever talked of their motives, it was in guarded and mysterious terms, of their destiny," Simezon used one of the old words that had fallen into disuse since the ban on the spreading of religious concepts.

"You know," he continued, "twenty years ago the atmosphere was different. The Inquisition was still a power in Leo's Court," Zethuras looked at Uris to see how she took this. He saw the curiosity on her face. "Of course, this generation hardly seems to be restricted and reserved in religious matters. They don't seem inclined to the concept of any religion. Then, association with the full scope of creatures always seems to bring a hassle of religious views followed by an embracing of materialistic concepts of life. A predictable result of too many things and too much diversity. But Uriah never saw life in this way, and he was much more adamant in his ways of thought then anyone I have known, except for Dav."

"Well, whatever his reasons," she interrupted, he is not coming back. She began to unbuckle herself from the console. A scout ship from the Scorpion had landed ahead of them, coming down to bring Simezon and Zethuras back to their commands. They had joined Uris in the landing bay of the Dragon's Tongue while still in orbit and had come down in the Pearl for the arrival ceremony. The Pearl was just coming into the port. "I calculated the trip myself. It could not have stretched beyond fourteen years. The last possible time slot for a return happened over a year ago." She opened the hatch and stepped into the hanger. The occupants came to attention. Obviously, she was going to have to go through a ceremonial greeting. Outside, the Pearl could be seen starting to disembark people from its side. Zethuras and Simezon fell in step on either side of her as they made a way through the standard bearers to the presiding official.

"Crotus is presiding," Simezon offered.

"I know the smell of him," she returned.

"Welcome Princess," Crotus purred at her with up lifted palm. "To what do we owe this visit to this corner of your realm."

"We pass this way to Xinor the Free where everyone comes," she responded with the Imperium's saying on the fact that all Guild Members knew the way to Xinor, through the Warp Star Regis, but no one knows where his neighbor's House is or even when, for that matter. But Xinor the Free was a standard salutation from the out world on approaching Imperium governors.

"On business or pleasure?" Crotus continued.

"On Guild business. You may send a message of arrival to Xinor and state our intentions to proceed there from here tomorrow."

"Thank you, highness," Crotus bowed low. "Your quarters are ready."

They passed by the proscenium and were joined by an honorary guard. They had made the anti-chamber leading from the hanger when two men stepped up at attention in full dress colors of the House of Ur.

"We await the return of the King," they saluted her and chanted in unison.

She stopped and looked at the two men a long and sad moment. "The King is dead," she said directly, as if stating a simple fact, long understood by everyone.

The two men looked at each other startled by her response. "Long live Princess Uris and the House of Ur," the one Simezon knew as Urvin spoke.

She pushed past them. Their words stung her. With Uriah's death the last male heir passed from the House. If she married someday, the House would pass from her care- taking to one of her male cousins.

"Milady is this wise," Simezon cautioned, realizing that this action would bring immediate speculation in the family as to who would ascend the throne. Uris could hold it as long as she never married.

Dismiss the honor guard, Simezon, fifteen years is too long. He cannot return. The last possible time slot slipped by over a year ago. My enemies will use irrational actions against me. They know he can't be returning, and it is time that we made it official."

Yes, Milady," he stood aside and let them pass. He made his way back to the color guard.

"The Princess wishes to dismiss the color guard and proclaim her father dead," he instructed them. "You are dismissed. You will be reassigned." Simezon turned to follow after the disappearing diplomatic troupe.

"Fine kettle of fish," one guard said to the other. "I just get things going good on Ka, and now, it's probably back to Saphos for us." He turned up his nose at the thought. "Let's go over and get cracked," he gripped the other man's shoulder.

"Leave me alone," the other shrugged his hand off, beginning to fight back tears.

"What is wrong with you?"

"I'm not going to abandon this post. I'm sure that maintaining this station is important to everyone on Ur." He wiped his face with the back of his sleeve with a determined look on his face. "You go on if you want, Curos, I'm staying on post."

"Urvin, it's not a matter of want. Princess Uris, herself has ordered this post abandoned, the act has diplomatic overtones. This will elevate her from Regent to Ruler." Curos tried to reason with his friend. "You can't defy orders, especially when they have come directly from the person who will shortly become Queen," he forcefully tapped Urvin's chest.

"I know this post is important."

"How? What makes you believe that? You know that the timelines make it an impossibility for a ship to return from the Draco explosion time. The probabilities have been becoming less and less for several years."

"I just know."

"You've gone a half bubble off level, my friend, and I am not going to risk my career, or waste time on this futile effort. This posting has been a bore and useless for the years that we have been here."

"Go on, perhaps you are right. I've gone to far down the line. Glitched in the head, whatever. This is something that I have to try. I just know it."

Curos looked long and hard at his companion, shook his head in disgust, and finally gave up on persuading him, turned and stalked off, headed for the nearest bar.

Urvin settled in to a lonely post, and a determined look, with a clinched jaw line, stood his post with determined posture.

That posture had slumped after several hours, but he was still with it, when some time after midnight a signal began to blink on the console in front of him. He didn't see it at first, as he should have been relieved some hours earlier, and was almost dozing in a half-asleep state. When the blinking light was not acknowledged, a beeping noise began to come on and off, set to draw attention. Urvin came awake with a start, and quickly reviewing the board, saw that a signal with Uriah's ship's signature code was coming out of hyperspace from the direction of the Hyperbolia Warp Star. He was stunned, and for a few moments he didn't know what he needed to do. Then he remembered that the Pearl was in the landing hanger, only a few yards away. But he would not be able to gain access to Uris. What would he do, go over to the guard detail and ask them to wake her?

When his brain cleared a little, he realized that the Dragon's Tongue, Ur's heavy warship was in orbit, and the Scorpion was there too. He had the ability to hail either or both from his station. He hailed the Scorpion, because he knew Captain Simezon, and had received his commission from him when he had been assigned to the Ka posting.

When the knock came to the captain's cabin door, Simezon was deep asleep, and had been very busy and tired from the activities of the evening, and he and Zethuras had returned to orbit only a short time before midnight. He was not in a good mood when he looked at the time, but knew that something must be happening, if he was being disturbed.

"Captain Simezon," the duty officer tapped again at the captain's door. Simezon pulled on a cloak and opened the door. "Sir," the officer began, "there is a hail from the surface, from an officer Urvin. He is reporting a signal from Uriah."

Simezon came awake as if from an electric shock. "I'll be on the bridge directly," he snapped and shut his door and dressed in haste. In less than a minute he was in the command center. He took Urvin's hail.

"Captain Simezon, Urvin, what are you doing?"

"Captain, I have stayed on station, and about ten minutes ago, a sensor detected a signal from Uriah. It is a tachyon signal from a ship coming out of hyperspace from the Hyperbolia Warp."

"You were dismissed from that post this morning," Simezon stated the obvious.

"Yes sir, but I felt that I could not abandon the station. I just could not give up...," Urvin could not explain.

The navigation officer signaled Simezon that he had the probe signal and placed it on the Captain's console. "I am looking at the signal now, Urvin, we will talk about this later." There was a pause, neither man spoke. "Good work," Simezon commended him. "I'll take it from here." He shut down the hail with a gesture to the navigation officer. "Hail the Dragon's Tongue, and tell them to follow us, now," he ordered. "Make an intercept course for that pod signal, and give me hyperspace, as fast as possible, without burning these engines out."

"Aye, Captain." Navigation began to break orbit. When Ka control was slow to answer, protocol was forgotten. The Scorpion broke orbit and streaked away from Ka. The Trident Class warship, with Zethuras in command, was soon right behind. Zethuras tried to hail the Scorpion, but it had already attained hyperspace, and he had to slow down to communicate with Ka, or follow blindly. He chose to follow blind. He knew Simezon would not be leaving Ka except for some extremely important reason, and with Uris protected by Surula who had resumed command of the Pearl on the surface, he knew that the Princess would be protected. It was a good decision.

On the Scorpion, things were getting clearer. It was near morning on Ka, when the ship reached the intercept point, and broke out of hyperspace, they were able to get a clear reading that the ship was an escape pod.

A message was immediately tachyoned back to Ka. It was adrift, apparently, its field had collapsed from a lack of coolants. Hope sprang up that Uriah and Dav were on board. But as they drew near, the navigation officer reported the alarm.

"Captain, a Pandamon Azreal fighter has broken from hyperspace. They are hailing us."

"Open communications," Simezon returned. "Charge weapons systems. Battle stations," he spoke to the ships company.

"This is Captain Simezon of the Scorpion," he hailed the Pandamon ship. "You are in Ur Space, state your intentions."

"We are in hot pursuit of a thief that has crossed through Pandamon Space from Cestus through Hyperbolia. Stand Down," the Azreal fighter captain, failing to identify himself, smugly commanded. The Scorpion was outmatched and the Pandamon ship knew it had the advantage.

"If you continue to charge your disruptor weapons, you will be fired upon," Simezon stated clear and cool. "This escape pod is no thief, and you will not take it."

"He has cut the communication link, Captain," the navigation officer reported. "He is continuing to charge his weapons system."

At that moment, the Pandamon ship fired a disruptor blast at the ship's engine section. The shields held. "Captain," navigation warned, "We can only take a couple of his hits like that one."

"Do not retreat. Do not fire. Divert all power to shields," Simezon ordered. The Pandamon ship fired again, and this time it rocked them to their teeth.

"He is recharging, and this time he will destroy us," the navigation officer warned. Then, "the Dragon's Tongue has emerged from hyperspace."

Zethuras was an experienced and battle-hardened captain. He sized up the situation in a heartbeat, and brought all batteries to bear on the Pandamon ship, at the same time the Scorpion fired its weapon, and the confrontation was over. The Pandamon ship was dust.

They tractored the escape pod into the landing bay in the belly of the Trident, Dragon's Tongue, and Simezon joined Zethuras in the landing bay. When it did not open of its on accord, they sent a command to the pod to open, and hoping to find Uriah, were sad to see only a data box strapped into one of the seats.

Uris had paced all day, with no word coming from the two ships. She could not understand what was happening or why the ships refused to answer, although they both sent a carrier wave, so it was known that they were intact.   Almost a day and a night later, back on Ka, Zethuras delivered the report of the incident to Uris. He had made the decision not to inform anyone of the confrontation and its result, until he could bring the message to Uris in person. It was with mixed emotions, and holding back tears, that she received the data recorder which her father had sent up time to her. As she held it in her hand, she knew that it was a miracle of chance.

The three ships slid smoothly into a parking orbit.
Uris punched in a scrambler signal and called the escort
ships.

"Captain Simezon, Captain Surula, this is a
scrambled and encoded transmission," she paused a
moment to allow the men to make the adjustments to their
equipment.

"Locked in," Simezon quipped in precise military
fashion.

"Communications lock secure," Zethuras assured
them. Being in the Trident Class Warship, he took
responsibility for electronic surveillance, as the massive
warship had the most sophisticated gear.

"Crowded around here, isn't it," Simezon spoke
impulsively. The cat-like fighter pilot was nervous, and it
showed in his voice.

Uris tapped three buttons on the console in front of
her, and the images of the man and woman appeared on a
split screen in front of her. She felt the tension too,
something she had noticed, but couldn't ferret from the
back of her mind.

"Princess," Zethuras was staring at his display.
"There are over sixty-thousand ships in orbit. He glanced
incredulously at the monitor then turned and said
something to a console operator beside him. "Eighty-three
percent are in defensive posture."

Simezon whistled softly through his teeth. "This
could be one hell of a bar-room brawl, if trouble were to
break out."

Uris swore under her breath. "Orbital defense,
stage two," she ordered. Now she understood her

uneasiness and was angered that she had not understood earlier. The ships were spread out in concentric rings instead of close proximity in the same plane of orbit. Obviously, an anxious situation even to the eye without electronic information. In this way, each spaceship had the ability to leave orbit without consulting one another. This freedom of lateral movement allowed for quick and independent departures, in case of trouble.

The fighter escort craft took the lower orbit. The Trident warship took the outer position, settling over the Pearl like a mother hen over an egg. In this way, the Pearl was protected from above or below, in a diversion.

"Xinor control is calling for identification," Surula informed them. "They are calling on one hundred eight-point six Megahertz."

"I will respond," Uris adjusted a receiver to the frequency and prepared the transmitter to a tight laser beam standard response pattern. The Xinor control was calling asking for identity and giving their triple co-ordinate configuration.

"Xinor control," she signaled them. "This is Uris of Ur, Princess Regent of the House of Ur. I am responding to the emergency meeting called of the Navigational Guild."

"Welcome, House of Ur. Please continue your carrier wave and hold for an encrypted message from the High Commissioner."

The High Commissioner and Uris were cousins of a sort. Although the blood relationship was distant. Their fathers studied at the central academy. The main branch was a university that produced brilliant woman of unusual grace. Uris had even met this cousin once in childhood on one of a few trips made to the ruling planet. The relationship and love felt for Uriah by High Commissioner Surilen's father was reflected in the fact that he used the

House 'Ur' incorporated in Surilen's name as was the family custom.

Uris flicked the telecommunications screen on and noticed the encrypting signals that were available between the two computers. A private family channel code was being used that varied the frequency and type of signal as well as a specifier mode.

"Surilen," Uris spoke in greeting. "You wear your office well." It was a conversational greeting for a bureaucrat, but not disrespectful.

"My office wears me well," Surilen returned, in a twist of words, but the concern lines in her face had already conveyed her mood.

"Well, we all bear these burdens," Uris attempted to mollify her, but it fell lame. Apparently, the woman's concerns were extremely serious. She should have known. Surilen was a renowned sociopsychologist. She was never known to say the wrong thing or be at a loss for words. Reputedly, the woman was smooth as silk. But she would not be reassured, and Uris doubted a simple strain of nerves would leave her at a loss for words. The two women viewed each other for a long, long moment.

"Uris," Surilen spoke at last. I trust you, and I need to speak with you. I was worried that you could not be found. Then the monopole message came that you had been found and were on your way here. You were expected two days ago. But when you were delayed on Ka, I was afraid that you would be late for the meeting. A central question will be debated in the morning, and I wish to brief you on something beforehand. You need to fall in here as soon as you can. What is your status?"

"I'm at your disposal Commissioner," she used Surilen's title not wanting to appear chummy, if this was an official request. "I must clear immigration and file our arrival report to tachyon home but I am autonomous here and can break away and fall to at once."

"Good my sister," Surilen used a family endearment term to let Uris know that the request was of a personal nature. "I will expedite immigration for you."

After signing off, she called Surula on the Pearl and instructed that an arrival report be filed, and that she would be falling down to the surface and would be with the High Commissioner.

When she arrived at the Spaceport Central, she was pleasantly surprised to see Surilen there to meet her. She waved eagerly to Uris as if they were close friends. When they clasp hands together, a warmth exuded that was infecting. It was no wonder that the woman had risen to a top administrative post.

"Uris, it is wonderful to see you," she smiled.

"I am likewise delighted, cousin," Uris embraced her back. "But I must admit, this meeting of the Guild and circumstances about my trip here are disturbing."

"Yes, we heard about your trouble on Ka." She looked vexed. "Follow me," she beckoned and didn't speak again until they were off the tarmac and into the transport car. They whisked silently upward, except for the hum of the cryomagnets inside the anti-gravity units. They were soon whizzing along the tops of the mile high buildings, headed for an open area some thirty kilometers away, with the most magnificent building at its center, that Uris knew was the Museum of the Universe, with the most marvelous of all the things from all the worlds of the known galaxies. A building so vast that a lifetime could be spent without seeing it all.

"I wish you to see something at the museum. It is a piece of the puzzle, and I hope you will be able to fit it into place. So far none of our people can. In many ways, it relates to the root cause for the special Guild meeting that has been called." She had been in office but three years, but the excitement of the capital city made her seem so very grand that Uris seemed suddenly provincial to herself.

Surilen caught the sign of it somewhere. "You see, it is your mathematical and navigational skills that I need to depend on," she reassured.

"The urgent element," Surilen continued, "began to unfold about one solar ago. Uris mentally computed the Xinor time period to her own on Ur, and decided that the time had been just before she had gone hunting.

"Negotiations are going on over a sphere of influence rivalry that is taking place between Pandamon and the home world of the Pran. You know the Pran world," Surilen questioned?

Usually, aliens did not affect Uris. She was not bigoted, but the cold blooded exopiles left a metal taste in her mouth. "Yes."

"Well, last period and going back to a short time after my election, I began an initiative to avert more bloodshed in the area. I was involved in communicating with the Commission and succeeded in bringing about discussions and a cessation of hostilities.

The trade pact that we had made, struck a common good deal for both parties and a framework for a solution had been designed. Mephor, the Grand Ambassador of Pandamon, was proceeding to the Pran home world, when something struck his ship. It was an Imperial ship, impervious to disrupter, let alone anything else. Yet, it was vaporized."

Uris took this astounding news in. Mephor was her father's enemy, and she delighted in the news of his death, but what could break graviton shielding. Something that could protect a ship going right through a Neutron Star? What could penetrate or disrupt that? Nothing she knew of. It made her mouth fall open.

"The explosion happened in deep space, and an investigation was possible," Surilen continued, "I shudder to think what would happen if the evidence was destroyed by falling into a star or planet. Of course, each side accused the other of sabotage. It was only fast footwork that had avoided major hostilities. With the aggression pacts the way they are, the Imperial Union could break up. Some of the social scientist say probabilities of dissolution are over sixty percent."

They were approaching the museum. Coming down in altitude, the details of the massive structure were becoming clear. Uris had spent many days wandering through its endless corridors. Under construction for over ten thousand years, an individual could spend ten lifetimes wandering its halls and galleries and not see it all.

"What I wish to show you is inside the museum," she put the little ship on a glide path into a landing strip on top of the main building. Surilen continued to explain what she knew to be at the core of the reason for the hurriedly called Guild meeting. "The whole explosion scene was tractored. We have every atom of that ambassadorial shuttle, and some interesting incongruities have arisen from our laboratories' analysis."

They had landed, and Surilen maneuvered the air car into a parking spot. She stopped the engine and sat for a moment. She seemed nervous. "Let me explain some things before I show you what I brought you here for. There have been electronic surveillance devices found in my executive offices, and we have not been able to maintain our security. It has us all seeing ghosts. The air car is clear as far as we can tell." Surilen paused and looked straight at Uris. "The Ambassadorial shuttle was vaporized in a nuclear explosion."

Uris had reports of this already. The implications were obvious. No nuclear explosion could have passed through the ships shielding. It was made to withstand the explosive force of close passage to a Neutron star. No known reaction could generate the kind of force that it would take to break that shielding. The logical conclusion was sabotage. The device had to have been inside the ship.

"But if it were sabotage," Uris leapfrogged ahead, "why would they choose such a detectable and obvious ploy."

"And how could a radioactive isotope be smuggled on board a secured star ship, as these shuttles are," Surilen added the obvious question? "These are the contradictions that the incident raises. But there is more. The lab says unquestionably the explosion was an isotope of plutonium."

"Primitive is my first reaction to that," Uris curled her lip.

"And so dirty," Surilen continued. "Easily detectable, as if they wanted to let us determine that the explosion was sabotage."

"If the security of the ship were violated, why use such a dirty device. They could have easily hidden the means for destruction in any number of ways," Uris finished the thought.

"Exactly."

"What motives could they have had?"

"Perhaps to engender the speculation that is leading to accusations flying in every direction. The Guild meeting may break apart in accusations about every sore spot among the members. The procedure starting in the morning promises to be long, but not tedious."

"Yes, we noticed the tension when we first fell into orbit."

"Yes, almost all the sentient groups of any power have defied my order to maintain a non-military status. I rescinded it before your arrival. Better no order, than something we can't enforce. Just the way things are happening, is leading to total dissolution. If I don't find a solution, the way some are chafing," she left the thought unfinished. "That is a very brief synopsis of events, but I think you have enough background now to see what I want to show you here."

Suilen lifted up the door of the transport and stepped out. Uris followed her lead. As they walked to the entrance way, she had a moment to take in the grand structure. No expenses had been spared. The facade of the building was a continuous relief of creatures from every time and place. The building was situated on a long, low plane. In the distance, modern structures towered a kilometer above it. She knew most of the building was underground. The above ground portion was a few stories high, fifty or so she guessed. Just enough to give grandeur without being so remote from the ground that it became inconsequential. The building sprawled over a several kilometer base, but open area was expansive all about its base. It was a breathtaking view.

Surilen lead her through giant copper doors, green with age. She knew this to be the original complex, thousands of years old, and unique in all of the known galaxies of time and space.

Uris followed. They took a fast elevator down and down. They disembarked down a seemingly endless corridor. Anterooms and galleries of collected specimens of historical interest were carved from the solid basalt. The museum was carved mostly underground from a solid and stable rock. The strata were chosen for its geological stability.

Surilen led her to a small and insignificant chamber in the geohistorical section. Some artifacts of dead sentients civilizations were also displayed. She came to stop in front of a glass case and pointed. "What do you make of this," she asked pointedly? Uris looked at the round almost rock looking fragment in the case and switched on the holomem, choosing a familiar language.

It began to quote, "This ceramic projectile was found on the dust planet Darimon, in the Skela system by

Anus Timon the famous early time explorer and map maker," the accompanying holographic image appeared in front of them showing the planet and the location of the find. "Because of impact evidence (more information available) and the plutonium core just short of critical mass, the object was located by scan. It is thought to be a projectile gone astray from some ancient war among species that are totally unknown. No other specimen like it has ever come to light, and the markings in relief on its surface are totally unknown, both in Timon's day and now."

"How old is the artifact," Uris asked the holomem.

"Unknown. The object was on the surface of Darimon seven thousand -six-hundred and forty Xinor standard periods, before Timon located it. This is accurately known from several dating techniques. Would you like more information." The programs loved to hear themselves talk, so they would try to lead.

Uris stepped to the edge of the glass and squatted for a better look at the markings in relief. They were charred and worn from friction but still distinct. Some sort of beaked animal, with wings, and an insignia or shield in front of it. The creature looked imperial and powerful. The markings above the creature's head read in a script she had never seen before.

"U. S. A.," and under the creature's talons another embossed script, "D. O. E."

"I do not believe this to be a projectile at all," Surilen spoke.

"What could it be, if not an implement of war?"

"Primitive Garbage,"

"Garbage?"

"Yes, and I need your mathematical skills to prove it before the Guild meets."

Uris stepped back from the ceramic coated plutonium ball and looked Surilen full in the face to fathom her intent.

"I believe," Surilen restated, "this is primitive garbage. The material is the by-product of the most elemental fission reactions. The Guild is divided. Some smell a plot by the Pandamon Empire to force the mapping issue. The mapping wars continue to be the major source of conflict up and down time. If a mapping dispute breaks out in Regis, as is threatened with the supernova in Draco twenty years ago, the Federation of Worlds will be torn apart.

"What do you know of the Guild summons, Surilen?"

"Xinor is rife with rumor, but I believe that it will breakdown at the meeting to three sides. You understand better than most, that since the species met in Regis ten thousand years ago, no map, no total map of space time has ever been made. Guesses exist. But the world is full of disinformation about where and when. Navigational information is the highest prized of secrets. Mostly, we stick to the known space lanes and try to keep our probes out of other species' worlds. That way, we all stay safe and out of conflict. But there are many currents that run counter to this flow of information. Power isn't one of them."

"That is very true," Uris agreed.

"The status quo is to colonize uninhabited space with one's own species, keeping the location in time and space secret by whatever means deemed necessary."

"Our family," Uris added, "has always chosen backwashes of time and space that few travel. No trading opportunities and dangerous primitive conditions."

"But we've learned to cope," Surilen smiled approvingly. "It's what keeps our species viable. We don't get soft and too much in our minds like the Krell do."

"I will take this information on the strange bird-crested object back to my ship to analyze."

"You must work quickly," Surilen cautioned, "the Exos are lined up firmly behind each other. In their paranoia of Metastophiles, they are certain that Pandamon is preparing for war and wish to join in co-ligation to the humanoids in a war on Pandamon. If no deal can be struck, then they are determined to go alone. These actions fly in the face of what is known of the destruction of the Ambassadorial shuttle. An Exo shuttle was bringing Mephor, the Pandamon Grand Viceroy home to Pandamon, from the Pran world, when it was destroyed. The Pandamons are raising hell about it and so are the Exos. Exos say it was an act of war by the Pandamon Empire. The Pandamons say it was nothing. Just a random piece of nuclear star material that had warped somewhere. Purely accidental, but something that couldn't happen if mapping were more complete. So, they're back to asking for a vote on the total mapping of known time and space."

"Oh, you know how that is going to fly with the independents. The Houses have always found safety in burrowing back or forward into time and space, far, far, from the centers of government."

"That is why a compromise solution must be found," Surilen's eyes pleaded.

"The mapping must be stopped. We need information. My senses are telling me that for Pandamon, there is more to this than meets the eye." Uris thought of the Pandamon Ambassador that she had on ice back at her ship. He might prove to be useful after all.

"We are probably dealing with a new species, or perhaps a group of humanoids, hitherto unknown to us. I will see what I can determine with this information," she gestured to the holomem, and the ceramic coated plutonium ball. Uris did not tell her that she had four other possible occurrences that had been observed in Hyperbolia. With six possible sources of place and time, she might be able to calculate the original origin point of the plutonium.

"I will visit you tomorrow on board the Pearl," her cousin placed an arm around Uris. Uris noted the code number of the exhibit and then arm in arm they spent the rest of the afternoon in just that small area of the great museum.

That night, as Uris poured over calculations feeding numbers into her machine, she discovered several interesting things. Following the trajectory of the ceramic object back using its potential energy estimate from the dust planet analysis, she calculated vector of flight path and probable velocity component, which would have been tricky had the dust planet had an atmosphere but with the dust surface being barren and without atmosphere, she could be fairly certain of her estimates. That gave a direction, but no time, or a time with no direction. She chose a direction and that direction traced into unmapped and unreachable space in the Draco system. Draco would be its nearest Neutron star!

Now, she was really getting interested. Each section of space was named after its nearest Warp Star. This projectile was from a far distant star series that when Draco became navigable would be near time to Saphos and in Now Time to Xinor, itself. This was the great breakthrough in time and space travel that her father had spent his life researching. It was the single most important thing to happen in Uris's lifetime. It was the discovery of millions of new worlds, perhaps many millions of new worlds.

She was fascinated now. She worked on the figures faster. She looked at far-fetched calculations. She looked at the momentum and center of gravity of the particles of the Ambassadorial shuttle, waiting several hours for the scan information of the wreck site to come from the surface files. It was at this point that her security systems made her aware that someone noticed her using this information. That was interesting.

The total kinetic energy of the wreck as calculated by her computer, compared very closely, almost a correlation of one, against the potential energy of a twelve-pound ceramic coated plutonium ball going critical while traveling at high warp.

By recombining centers and letting the time variable float, she was able to substitute the earlier solution from the dust planet vector analysis, and the other four known occurrences in Hyperbolia, and integrate one real solution that fit all the parameters. If she assumed a real time for the Ambassadorial shuttle, she got a real time solution of a star called Sol, in the Cragor system, soon to be Draco. Until twenty years ago there was an immense distance across the galaxies. Now through the space time doors of the warp stars, it would become next door. Soon, the Draco Star would be navigable, and her father had given his life to make sure that they had the first chance to be the first of the Houses able to use this door. Thanks to that guard that wouldn't give up, she had this information from the escape pod of her father's ship. She reached out and touched the data box. Sleep would be slow coming. Surilen and she must plan. Surilen would know what they might do. She must sleep now and think on this. How was the Pandamon Ambassador involved in this? She must speak with Kurege in the morning. Perhaps he could shed some light on these events. She fell asleep at her desk.

When she rose, she refreshed herself and went to the Ambassador's quarters. He was asleep. She had had him drugged and fed intravenously for the three-day trip. He looked puffy. She knew he would be sick for a day or more when he awoke. She turned the dial to shut off the chemical that made him sleep and began to pump a stimulant into him.

Kurege began to come around. "Wha, what happened," he licked dry lips, and looked through puffy eyes. "You," he licked his dried lips again. He thought he was going to be sick. He fought the wave of nausea. "You drugged me," he accused weakly.

"Get dressed," she jerked him to his feet and shoved him through the bulkhead toward the head. "Get a shower. You'll feel better in a minute."

She ordered some black coffee-like stimulant and flat bread. He didn't look much better when he came back.

"I feel terrible," he groaned. "What did you give me anyway? How long have I been out?"

"Three days."

"You could have killed me. I feel like excrement."

"Shut up and try to listen."

"Lady, I'm tired of being shoved around, and right now, I'm in no mood," he raised his voice.

She caught him with the flat of her hand on his forehead, hard, quick, betraying hours of training.

"Ouch!" He protested rubbing his forehead.

"Shut up."

"Well, all right, if you feel that strongly about it," he rubbed his forehead.

"I could have killed you," she told him flatly.

"I believe it."

"Give me straight answers, or I will kill you," she said looking levelly at him. "Do you believe that?" She continued fingering the knife at her belt.

"Hey, now slow down. What is going on?"

"We are on Xinor."

"Xinor?" He reached for it foggily. "Regis Xinor?"

"Guild Imperial Summons."

"I remember. The meeting on Saphos."

"Unexplained. Can you shed some light?"

"No. No. Things were quiet when I left Pandamon."

"No Pandamon plot to map the continuum?"

"Pandamon's classic position is free and open sharing of navigational information for the safety of all."

"A good party line."

"It makes sense."

"Not for the smaller fish."

They looked each other over. He didn't want to fight with her. He had to stay calm. She tried to fathom what she might do or say that might reach him. What would bring him to her side of the issue?

"Do you follow the cult, in the worship of Lord Metastophiles?"

"Metastophiles? Now there is a name. Lord of Pandamon, it has been two generations since we've seen him. He is deep in down time, if he ever means to come back. If he was on Pandamon, when I left, it was not generally known".

"Oh, he will come back," she clenched her fist until the knuckles turned white. "I have proof of his whereabouts less than twenty years ago. I can assure you, he is forward slightly. He is soon to be with us again, if he is not already in Standard Time."

"It has never portended any good for the people of Pandamon," Kurege shrugged. "We are primitives, in his power."

"As we all are."

"But I can tell you this. As strongly as the cult was in our grandfather's time, a thirst to be free runs through this current generation. Few of them will cheer the Baron's return. Most are secretly in contention with Chancellor Beel and his conservative, tyrannical, crew."

"Rest and recover," she counseled him. We will talk again later."

She left him under security lock and called a guard to be posted outside the Ambassador's door. She wanted to rework her calculations before Surilen arrived and she had one new idea she could check.

She worked the morning away, until Surilen arrived. She summoned Kurege and after introductions the three of them left for the Guild meeting, which was already under way, on the surface of Xinor.

"You must have decided to let me live," Kurege whispered to her as they left for the conference.

"Only as long as you prove useful," she shot back.

The meeting room was immense. The Guild was actually limited to three thousand. There were ten species that had met, basically falling into two categories. Exo skeletal and endomorphs. The endomorphs were considered loosely humanoid. Mostly bipedal.

Surilen, Uris, and Kurege were humanoid, bi-pedal, and also, sleepers, and therefore dreamers. A great many of the species were totally literal minded. All of the Exomorphic species were totally centrally controlled, and very mechanical, predictable, and literal of mind. They tended to be somewhat paranoid politically always accusing the humanoid races, and especially the Pandamon Empire, of attempted genocide against the Exos.

The pure facts were that in map disputes the Exos were quick to swarm in down time and up time to strengthen their hold on the politics of the Xinor time realm. They were also quick to use whatever ruthless measures that they could get away with, Uris reflected to herself, as she looked the great chamber over.

The gallery was composed of the later expansionist, Royalist, or colonial empires based on worlds of corporate, private, and royal influence, and investment. The floor drew her attention. Beel of Pandamon was sitting serenely in the Chancellery Chair.

"Beel," asked Kurege questioningly? "Where is Mephor?"

"Where indeed," Uris reflected the question back to him? She studied his face. He was obviously unaware that Beel had replaced Mephor. She was satisfied that he knew nothing at all. His face was genuinely perplexed. "Mephor was the Ambassador killed on board the Exo shuttle."

"You mean assassinated by the Exo's?"

"No one knows. The ship vaporized in the explosion. The last transmission from the ship was the automatic beacon flashed when the shield was struck. So, whatever it was, it came from outside the ship."

"And thus, the Guild Meeting?"

"Yes, the Exos are screaming paranoid fantasies about the Pandamons, and Lord Metastophiles, as usual. They say it was an attack from a new weapon."

"Is it," asked Kurege? He thought about the awesome shift in power that comes to warfare with new technologies.

"Possible, but I have another theory." Uris had a look in her eye like she knew a secret. She let that hang for the moment. A speaker was in progress, droning on at the podium about humanoid behavior, his antenna whipping frenziedly about his head, his arms waving, manically. Kurege was listening intently. 'He has his antenna out too', thought Uris, as she watched him.

Speaker after speaker came and went. Witnesses prove that no Exo could have been involved or could have made a mistake or missed a bomb. Several pounds of plutonium, missed, "How absurd?" Beel listened, gaveled for the next and continued to call members from the other side of the isle, who stated that it was some accident by chance. The plutonium was a piece of Neutron Star formation from some ancient nova explosion. Cragor has produced much of this type material in recent time. This was the plausible explanation. These witnesses always ended with the same line of reasoning; "If only more and better maps and charting of the continuum could exist, these accidental tragedies could be prevented."

This brought grumbles all around from Exos, and humanoids alike. The members from the Pandamon Empire being the only cheerers for this idea. Kurege kept his peace and listened.

Then there was the paranoid fringe in the other direction. This was mostly coming from the inner worlds. The Federation was under attack, but from an outside force. Under attack from an unknown species or alien life form. Uris could see this played right into Beel's hands.

A probe vote was coming. A major navigational decision which would give access to much new territory for the Federation to control, and, therefore, Pandamon control. Beel fed the hysteria artfully. The inner worlds were going to overpower the colonial coalitions. This would be very bad for Saphos. Its survival had long depended on the cloak of secrecy that it maintained by legal force of arms. She pushed the button to be recognized.

Beel noticed it, and in no more than a moment, gaveled the current speaker into submission. "We shall hear now from the Princess Regent of the House of Ur."

"No longer Regent, Chancellor Beel," she boomed forward. "My father's time has passed, and it is no longer possible that he will return to our time." She didn't reveal that the data box had returned from the supernova explosion.

"Proceed, your Excellency."

Uris took a moment to gather herself and look around the chamber at all the members. "Each illustrious member here has added much to our understanding. Now hear me, as I have labored long to analyze the math of the explosion of the Exo's starship carrying High Chancellor Mephor." She paused another moment for the translations to be made and understood. "I find that we should search for another life form, although I think that they are doing this to our space lanes by accident. She paused again, finding it somewhat uncomfortable to be in the same mind set as Beel. "We therefore propose that the probes be set to send back, only when they detect plutonium. This is the specific material that marks the primitives that we search for. No advanced civilization within our numbers would allow the artificial production of this element. Therefore, navigational secrets, and Anonymity, could be maintained. Yet, this type of tragic circumstance be averted by finding this unknown civilization and stopping the production of this element."

This brought murmurs of approval. Beel frowned at this. It wasn't what he was aiming for, but half a loaf was better than none, and he would find a way to get the other half under the table.

The proposal was made formal and put through. It didn't carry enough votes, the first time through. The wrangling went on, the haggling increased until everyone's emotions were spent. They came back to it as a compromise, and this time it passed. No mapping to be done. But probe ships to be manufactured to fire probe droids up and down time to confirm the advanced civilizations, but to leave them unmapped. But the fact that the probes were going out would mean that the information was gathered, and that would lead to mapping of the continuum for the first time. The information would be supposed to be a state secret, but it would lead to war. That had always been foreseen by every socio futurist throughout the Houses. Yet Uris knew that it would be a long time before the offending new species, just on the other side of the Draco Supernova, would ever be found by probes sent through Cragor. It was on the literal other side of the Universe. Uris noted this as the vote carried. A strange set of ironies. It was funny how some places and times could be practically right next door, but impossible to get to. But this spot would not be impossible to get to very much longer.

She and Surilen were engrossed in conversation when they left the conference. They didn't notice the tail they picked up, but Kurege did.

The Puma medicine man gazed serenely into the faces of his three young initiates. His was the job to initiate these young boys into spiritual manhood. They were to understand the secrets of the inner self. He had them eating figs and drinking sulfur water for three days. Their stomachs were completely empty from the purgative effects. The young braves were on the point of hallucination from lack of sleep and fasting. Now he had them ingest a button of the peyote cactus. They would be soon drawn into their own inner world.

"Before you depart on your inner journey," he spoke softly to them, his voice echoing and resonating through the cavern that they sat in, "you must know of the valley of lights." He built up the fire and drew them around.

"Toward the rising sun, one day's ride from the trail that the Comanche has that runs to the Southern lands, three days before the crossing of the great white canyon, is an area that you must not let your people or your young chief's venture. It is taboo, forbidden, to all of our people. The gods that come and go there, shine with great light, and ride faster than the hawk. They are not our gods. They have nothing to do with our people, and no one who enter their valley ever returns."

Sam Keogh was seated at the bank of gauges and dials that read the boiler pressure for the Pantex complex. Maintenance duty wasn't too bad a way to go, as it was inside, and not too hot or cold. Any field work was likely to be on some of the hydrogen producing wells, which were also tended by the plant. He congratulated himself. True, sitting on top of several hundred nuclear bombs, at any particular time, made him nervous, but Pantex was the only game in town, if you liked West Texas. He had grown up here, and the wide-open spaces were what he needed to feel like himself.

The boiler room seemed cramped, and he got up and moved around, examining gauges and pipes as he walked. Sam liked the quiet time of the graveyard shift. He ambled slowly down the corridor, patting his leather holster absentmindedly. His uniform was flawless. Sam had learned years ago that there was much of the world out of his control. This only made him much more determined to control the little pieces of it in his charge.

He was perplexed by a mystery. Sam didn't like mystery. He didn't like surprises either. He knew that many times, one was contained in the other, and they usually meant some sort of unpleasant experience for him.

Sam prided himself on being the best at his security job. Hell, he was the best. Didn't he have the highest security job in the nation? If the security of the graveyard shift at America's only nuclear weapons assembly plant wasn't the top of the security world, he would like to know what was. If only the salary was commiserated with the position. It was good for West Texas. He thought of Pantex as his place. He felt like a mother hen to all those nuclear eggs that he would personally like to see hatched over Moscow, Peking, Bombay, Berlin, and even London. He didn't like foreigners. And, he didn't like not knowing everything about his hen house, as he doubled as a combination maintenance and security man. Right now, he had a mystery, and it was giving him a gut ache. He hated mystery. It made his stomach turn knots, and, right now, he had knots on knots.

He had been noticing for years that a lot more crap came into this place than ever went out. At first, he consigned it to shipping crate size. But lately, he had been having a thing with one of the girls in accounting. She was privy to the Blue File stuff. The Atomic Energy boys wrapped everything in blue. But the fact remained that more plutonium came into this place than ever went out the front door. Not officially, put on paper, but it did it.

And another thing that had been bothering him for months, where did that damn air pipe go? He had walked the perimeter of the building many times. This inside wall did not jive with the rest of the building. Keogh removed the filter grill of the air conditioning return air duct that was at floor level. He peered inside. Just as he suspected, the duct continued into darkness, whereas on the outside, according to the plans, the wall apparently terminated the interior of the building. He got his tiny flashlight out and turned the screw switch. He placed his gun and holster inside the duct to the right and crawled in. It was large enough to crawl into and was put together with S and drive metal where the sections came together, so fortunately, there were no screws poked into the interior of the duct where he might come down on them with a knee or hand.

Keogh crawled a long way. The air was hitting him in the face. He knew there was an opening somewhere ahead of him. He came to a branch opening. He couldn't fit into it. Here, he could hear noises like machinery running. There wasn't supposed to be any forklift work on any of the graveyard shifts that he knew about. This made him even more curious, and he started on farther down the main trunk pipe. He came to another branch. He could hear machinery noise, and a barely audible conversation. He stopped breathing, and strained hard to hear what was being said. He couldn't catch a word. It did seem to have a totally alien sound to his ear. He thought it must be Chinese or Vietnamese. It was totally unfamiliar. He crawled on.

He hadn't gone very much farther down the pipe when he came to another branch pipe. Light was coming in from somewhere just around a ninety-degree elbow. This pipe was round and small, leading to some conference room, probably. Screws were sticking into its interior at each seam. Drive screws, with super sharpened points. He could just make them out in the dim light. He could hear voices, quite distinctly coming from just beyond the elbow.

"The glitch in the Draco Neutron Star will be clear soon. All must be in readiness."

"All will be in readiness, Lord Sargon," another voice said.

"The processing of the protofetal material is proceeding ahead of schedule," a third voice stated.

"There is a new schedule," the first voice resumed.

Sam recognized this voice through its thick accent. It was the voice of Reginald Tellur. He recognized it from the Firing Line program that he had seen just the previous Sunday. His Indian hair on the back of his neck stood on end. A strange feeling ran up his spine. The man who was responsible for the production of all that plutonium was just a few feet from Sam's head.

"There are," the voice continued," six Azreal type drive fighters coming through the deep-down time vector. Tachyon reports, running ahead of the craft, indicate that one will emerge and make planet fall by sometime tonight. Its cryogenic condition will be critical, and it will have converted all its Helium three. It will be coming in hot and fast to the Amarillo Hydrogen well at Nader tonight. One sixth of the protofetal material will be placed aboard and the craft is to attempt a return to Regis to await The Lord Metastophiles," Tellur said.

"Yes, my Lord Sargon."

"How is the betazoid sub-chromo content of the protofetal material?

89

"Excellent, my Lord, the percentage is the highest in my experience. It is the highest anyone that I know has ever seen." The clone graft into these humanoids has produced an incredible ten to minus third grams per cubic milliliter of general populous fetal material.

"And the clone graft here is barely over seven thousand years," the third voice added.

"There must be plenty of cryohelic fluid available," Tellur continued, glossing over the glowing reports. "Five more craft may be expected, and if these fail, more will be right behind."

"What about the plutonium my Lord?"

"It will have to wait. The protofetal material is to take precedence over everything else until I receive word that an uptime supply has been secured."

Keogh didn't know what the hell these guys were talking about, but he knew he didn't like it. He was afraid now, and sweating.

"The Draco system will clear and an up-time supply of the protofetal fluid must be ready. Beel has informed me that a probe droid is unavoidably on its way. We have a year or two. The plutonium may be sent down time for storage."

"All of it?"

"No," the voice of Tellur, was reluctant. "It seems that some of our garbage has gotten in someone's way. Mephor is dead."

There was laughter all around. Keogh had heard enough. He started backing out. But what he heard next, made him stop.

"We may not have time to get the plutonium out. Draco may not clear in time and now with all the attention it may be impossible. We will not know until Lord Metastophiles comes into the Regis system from down time. That makes the protofetal material, and whatever we can salvage out of the Helium three operation, that much more important. It may be that this operation may be terminated."

Sam Keogh knew what terminated meant, and he had a real bad feeling about the meaning of 'this operation'. He clawed his way backwards, out of the duct work.

Sheriff Jim Knowles had just pulled out from the pizza house where he had been putting the make on the waitress. He hadn't gone but a block, when he saw Sam Keogh, driving without his lights. He figured that Sam had drunk one too many. He was going to hate writing him up and running him in. A DUI would ruin him with his security job at Pantex. He was surprised to see him making a mistake like this, and he thought that it was Sam's night at work. He put on his lights, and hit the siren with a short burst, to get Sam's attention, as he went barreling by. He could see Sam shaking as he approached the car.

"Sam, you OK," he asked, approaching the car with some caution. Opening the door, Sam came out babbling.

"Jim, Jim, the abortion clinics are in league with the Devil. Plutonium, all that plutonium," he moaned. He was frothing at the mouth, slobbering with fear and stinking with sweat. Sam totally surprised Jim by pulling his revolver and placing it under his chin.

"No," Sam yelled, holding the gun tightly in his hand and firmly under his chin. "You must believe me, you must believe me," he repeated over and over.

"Calm down Sam, I believe you. It's OK. Give me the gun."

At that moment, the air was split by the supersonic passage of a great ball of light. Always written off as a meteorite, it streaked across the sky illuminating the environs bright as day.

"They're here!" Sam screamed, as he dropped his gun and fell to his knees. He was crying like a baby.

Jim hadn't seen anything like that in a long time. He hadn't seen lights like that since his childhood, and the lights that streaked overhead in the nineteen-fifties. But he had seen it before. It made his hair stand on end. He looked at Sam shaking and crying.

"What in the hell is going on here?"

He loaded Sam in his squad car and took him into the Pizza parlor for some coffee.

Sam tried to keep the cup of coffee steady in his hand. Jim watched his friend uneasily. His hat was still on his head even though they were sitting in the back booth at the Pizza Mom drive in.

"God, Jim, don't you know I know you think I'm crazy."

"I've known you a lot of years," his voice reflected his concern. "We've been on the firing line a couple of times, together."

"That's it. Sam snapped. The Firing Line," he was getting excited again. They were drawing attention. Sidney Porter, the freelance news hound for the local paper, had come in not long after they got there. He had noticed the two of them, and now he picked his cup up, and came over to join them. Jim was beginning to wish he had just run Sam on in to Wayfarer, the middle-class mental hospital.

"Howdy boys," Sidney greeted them.

"That was some meteor pass. Just like way back in nineteen-fifty-seven, huh?"

"That's it, that's where I knew him from, Reginald Tellur," Sam babbled on.

"Take it easy, Sam."

"Tellur," the news hounds ears picked up. His eyebrows went up, and he looked at Sam with renewed interest.

"I'm telling you, I'm absolutely sure that it was the voice of Reginald Tellur, the nuclear scientist, you know, the weird, hairy Gnome of a man, with the big bushy eyebrows, that is in charge of the President's commission on Nuclear Technologies. He's a real big wig. He's always pushing fast breeder reactor technology."

"That's right," Sid slid in beside Jim.

"Sid, we're not feeling real sociable right this minute."

"Huh, OK, sorry boys, I'll catch you later."

"You Sidney Porter, the newspaper guy," Sam put a hand on him?

"That's right."

"Don't go. I need to talk to you," Sam pleaded, obviously overwrought.

Sidney stopped and looked at both men, wondering what he had gotten in the middle of. "Well, if I can help."

"You can't," Jim said flatly.

"Yes, you can," Sam insisted.

It was starting to get a little sticky for Sid. "What's this about Reginald Tellur?"

"I heard him talking tonight."

"Where, on TV?"

"No, out at the plant."

"Plant? You mean Pantex?"

"Yes, I'm a guard out there. Oh, my god, they'll miss me. They'll know I was there."

Sam was thinking, in panic, of the traces of his presence that he had left at the plant. To Sid, he seemed to babble. Jim did a little circle around his left ear, and pointed at Sam. Sid could see he was confused, but a guard going crazy at Pantex, the nation's nuclear bomb assembly plant, was news, even if the guy was crazy. But imagine, he thought, if Reginald Tellur were inside the Pantex plant at night sometimes? What a story. That could probably be checked out.

"Sid, now really," Jim cautioned, "I'm a friend of his, and I'm trying to save his job and keep him from getting a record on this. Keep this off the record."

"I can't promise anything Jim, but that I can keep you out of it, if it all works out all right."

Jim knew he had him there. Jim was a policeman, protecting a Pantex security guard. That could get him hung. It shut him up anyway.

"Now Sam, Sam, look at me. What's this about Tellur?"

"He was at the plant."

"At Pantex?"

"Yes."

"Where did you see him?"

"I didn't see him, I overheard him. I was in an air duct and I overheard him talking about weird stuff. They said they were shipping out some fetal fluid, and that there might not be time to get all the plutonium moved out. I got scared. I ran. I've been up all night."

"Why didn't you turn it in to security?"

"Christ, you are stupid," Sam looked at him with loathing. "If Tellur were in the building, he would have security wired. I'm going to go to the head office and say, 'little green men are exporting plutonium and fetus material to Mars?"

"That's your job."

"That's the government. Do you know who Reginald Tellur is?" Sam shook his head in frustration.

'Incredible,' thought Sid. It's beyond imagination, yet how could one man's fantasy fit another. Uncanny coincidence, no doubt. Yet, he had been around the Amarillo and Lubbock area for years. He knew the old Indian legends. The old cowboy stories, about the Chicago boys and the XIT ranch, were plentiful, in the mythology of the area. The politics and power plays didn't come any bigger. This crazy story about flying saucers in Northwest Texas kept coming up every few years since way back in the twenties. Then he had traced a story found in a family account of Potter County, Texas, of the eighteen hundreds. The stories of lights in the sky of West Texas went back as far as any history of the area.

"I know you both think I'm out of my head," Sam said, "but I know what I heard, and how bad it scared me. Now, I haven't had any sleep, and I'm acting funny, but I'm still going to remember this tomorrow."

"Would you go back up to the Pantex office?"

"No way," Sam shook his head. His eyeballs were showing. He was obviously scared.

"I'm going to make a call," Sid excused himself.

"Ah, Sid, don't do that."

"Don't worry Jim. I'm not going to call the paper. I'm going to call a wealthy industrialist friend of mine."

Sid punched the call in on his cell phone address book, marked 'Stark'. He took a chance and dialed the private number that he had for Stark Raven's ranch. The phone picked up halfway through the ring.

"Hello," a mellow voice came on.

"Stark, I took a chance that I would find you there. This is important."

"It better be Sid. I'm up to my asshole in tax forms. You know how it is in January, so I'm in no mood for bullshit."

"Well S. G. old buddy, you're probably going to think I've gone 'round the bend, but I've got a gut feeling on this one."

"What is it, Sid? Lubbock under terrorist attack?"

"I wish," he paused before launching in. "You know my weird fantasy that I'm always laughing about, saying it's the only solution that fits the circumstance."

"Clue me?"

"You know, about flying saucers exporting plutonium from the Pantex facility."

"Yes. The only way to account for all the plutonium being manufactured, I believe you said," Stark wasn't feeling amused, "so, go on," he hurried him.

96

"I think I've got proof."

"You say, 'you've been drinking'," Stark laughed. "What proof was it? You're ever so clear."

"No, stop it Stark. I'm serious."

Something in Sid's voice brought him up short. Stark stopped his guffaw and snapped upright in his chair. "No shit? What kind of proof?"

"Well other than poundage, that I've told you of before, I've got a guard that overheard a conversation."

"That could be anything."

"He overheard Reginald Tellur inside Pantex."

Now Raven was fully alert. He had other axes to grind with Tellur. The man had shot holes in every sensible energy program Stark had proposed. They fought on a daily basis at the Department of Energy headquarters in Denver. During the 1980's, he had shot down every sensible solar funding, while letting con artist, and the pork barrel lobbyists line their pockets. He had pre-programed great sections of the DOE to fail from waste and extravagant grant studies of misapplied and over technological usages of alternative energy solutions. The results became so statistically skewed that the programs all went down in scandals.

Sid, on the other hand, was the one man who could call him in the middle of the night and say, "The Martians have landed, and bring the minute men," and Stark would have to respond. The bond was deep. They went all the way back.

"Think I better come up to Amarillo."

"I think so."

"Can you pick me up at the little airport West of the city, out by Helium Road?"

"Sure."

"I won't get in until afternoon. It depends on if I can pick up a tail wind, which this time of year is unlikely at lower altitudes. I'm going to fly a Cherokee single engine, so I don't attract any attention."

"That sounds like a good idea," Sid confirmed.

"See you, tomorrow."

"For sure," Sid rang off.

Chapter Thirteen Metastophiles

A consciousness there is that never rests. It roams the realms of time and space, and ravages where it will. So long has it lived, so deep into down time, that none can penetrate its purpose. A being with the most perverse of mind, a thorn among the flowers, from the Foundation, when the Houses first were met, Isis pierced the Regis Star from its side and entered Xinor. Lord Metastophiles was there, waiting. This is what the legend claims. No species had ever met another. The Wars began.

Azbael had excellent news for his lord this morning. He walked swiftly by the cryo-tomb. That wouldn't be necessary, now. With the news that had come in this morning, they would be going home. He had thought only yesterday how he would never see home, never see Pandamon again. The supply of life-giving fluid that Metastophiles had to have for his blood disease, had grown low. The Master, it was thought, would have to be put in cryo-suspension. That had been enraging him. The slightest provocation sent him into an acerbic display. Azbael grimaced as he remembered the screams of the technician who had failed to hit the vein the first time with his needle.

He was making his way along the corridor of the medical rejuvenation section. This was luxuriously decorated. It was where the lord spent most of his time these days. Azbael opened the central door and walked softly in. The pretty little humanoid medical technician was holding Metastophiles hand.

"Thank you dear," Metastophiles dismissed her in his high little voice. It was usually most beguiling, but in his weakened form, it was thin and hollow. The nurse left them alone.

"What have you today Azbael?"

"Great news, my lord."

"It had better be," he spoke from under puffed eyelids and red eyes. "My kidneys are going. I must go into cryo-suspension. I haven't got the energy to be mad about it anymore." He looked forlorn and hopeless. Azbael would have felt sorry for him, if he had known how. He simply knew to obey his master.

"Cryo-suspension may not be necessary. The first ship carrying a supply of life fluid, has emerged from Cestus, and will be waiting, just a few hours up time from us."

"What system," Metastopliles asked weakly?

"The Solarian system. The humanoid planet Terra, Earth."

New life seemed to come into the ancient creature's eyes. "Earth?"

"Yes, and the tachyon reports running ahead of the ship are saying that the analysis is the best ever on the fluid."

"The protogene nesting of the third core DNA? This crap is worse than useless he screamed," pulling the syringe from his arm. The puncture began to bleed. For a feeble man, Metastophiles startled Azbael, and he stepped back and began to talk very fast.

"Yes, my Lord, the proto-gene nesting has been achieved, and even more."

"This is a weak and dying race. We must move from here. The Draco system will open soon. We will be able to move against the Regis system. How are the reports of other news."

"Just the news of the life fluid. More ships are coming behind it. The best part I've saved for last."

"What is it?"

"The betazoid content is the highest ever seen The clone grafting of the Terran humanoids has proven highly beta active."

"This is marvelous, Azbael," the sick old face took on hope.

"We will go up time to meet the ship. Chart us a course to the nearest touch point."

"Yes, my Lord."

Azbael backed away and followed his orders quickly. Things would happen now. The times had come so sullen lately. He had given up hoping to see the historical moment. He thought his destiny had passed him by. But now with a single stroke, he was going to see it all. The re-emergence into Regis and the final conquest of Xinor. Xinor would soon be humbled with the plutonium bombs made up time by the clone mutant humanoids of earth, who would be stripped of their lives and processed into oblivion, as so many other cloned races before. Infused and genetically controlled to give the life fluid that Meastophiles and his close cohorts required to maintain their incredibly ancient bodies.

They could come out of down time now and face the Xinor realm in a show down. Azbael busied himself with gaining a few extra seconds to the approach of the special craft, made to make the run to the other end of the universe, to the end of the timeline and back. Earth had been chosen for the clone graft because it was remote and inaccessible from Xinor. That would all change with the opening of the Draco Star. At last the final conquest of Xinor could begin. They had not been in the Regis system for one hundred Regis years. All other time was judged by Reg years. The time and space of the capital world set the standard. He knew rewards would come with just finding an extra second shaved off the time that Metastophiles was separated from the life fluid he desperately needed. He spent most of the day in navigation.

When all had been accomplished and the Master had been rejuvenated by the proto-fetal fluid brought from the Solaris system, Azbael sought the medical section head.

"How is the Master?"

"He is almost rejuvenated."

"Would it be good to go in?"

"He is in an exceptional mood."

He passed on, and into the rejuvenation room.

"Azbael," he was met with a high forceful greeting.

"How are you feeling, Master," he inquired with polite concern?

"This is the best ever," Metastophiles flexed his hand and fingers, and made a fist. The change was remarkable. Where a withering old man with sunken and redden eyes had lay, now a man in the prime of his life, dark hair, bright eyes, bubbled forth with conversation.

"This means a step up in the timetable. I must have more of this immediately. The chromo-typing is perfect. The gene splicing is taking root in the graft. The rejuvenation is more complete than ever. I must return to standard Xinor time. A way must be found to penetrate the Draco star, the Cragor route is too time-consuming. With Draco coming clear, these humanoids will be discovered. These humanoids must be drained before they are detected. The fluid must be moved up time. The plutonium must be brought from Terra to Pandamon."

"My Lord, we move into the Cestus system within the hour."

"Cestus, you say? That will make a good base in this time. Pandamon is too far from Cragor."

"My thinking exactly. We can use Ka as a base. We have found a traitor among the Guild. We have turned a member from Ur, named Curos, to our way, and he has given up the location of Saphos."

Metastophiles looked at him with contempt. If Azbael were 'thinking' for himself, that would have to be stopped. He made a mental note of this, to be taken care of in the near future. It would not do to have close aides thinking for themselves. "Only The House of Ur and Saphos will remain in my way. We will sweep it aside." He swept the table in front of him crashing bottles across the floor.

"Make for Regis present time immediately and lay into the Hyperbolia system, from there. What excuse can we find for taking Saphos?"

Azbael consulted his record computer. The most recent point of contention is an extradition request that has gone without response from Saphos. It is concerning the escape of a young man named Kurege, of a primitive house of no consequence. Also, there is a report of a confrontation and destruction of a Pandamon Azreal fighter that was in pursuit of one of the escape pods that was sent out from Uriah's ship during the Draco Supernova."

"All the better. It will do perfectly," he gloated. "I want every inch of Saphos searched. I must have Uriah's data on the Draco Supernova. He sent it into up time in a way that I could not follow it, but no doubt by now it has found its way back to Cestus, and on to some secret destination through Hyperbolia."

Metastophiles continued to grow stronger and more virile looking as the minutes went by. "You know, Azbael, the betazoid content of the cloning is incredible. I can feel it working, putting wrinkles in my brain. You know, I think I can read your mind."

A look of panic crossed Azbael's face.

"My, my thoughts be always on you, my lord," he blushed and recovered.

"Hmmm, yes. Indeed. Now see how quickly you can get us into Xinor Standard Time," the voice beguilingly crooned.

Ch. Fourteen Hmax=Velocity*Cos45*Time of Rise

The New Mexico countryside slid smoothly past. Nobody on the highway, he put his foot in it. Jacob Martin was in a great frame of mind. The day was high and blue, the road was dry and straight, and the little Japanese number that he was driving was a smooth machine. He congratulated himself on the decision to plunge for the forty-five grand, to hell with the balance of trade.

He was on to the story of his life. He graduated summa cum laude from Texas Agricultural and Military College, but growing tired of corporate life, he had fallen into writing technical articles for a growing number of science fact and technology journals. Now, he was free-lancing full time.

He had gotten lazy lately. His income was down, and with the new car purchase, he was going to have to crank up the old P.C. and hit it again. He needed to churn a few out, or try to resell some of the old ones, after an update.

Martin didn't like to think about this, and he grimaced and checked his speed slightly. If what he was on to here was as good as he thought, he might be able to chunk all that.

He thought back over the events that had put his feet on this particular road. Bryan Mallory and he had been roommates back at A & M. Mallory was straight arrow. Square jawed, perfect physical specimen, military skin head all the way, but a nicer guy with a bigger heart didn't exist.

"How can you rot your brain," he would complain when Jay came in and kicked back. That stuff is gonna kill you," he would chide, as he gathered up his books and made for the library to avoid being contaminated. But Bryan never turned him in, although they were testy a few times during exam times. They would laugh, and say it was male equivalent of PM, a high aggression period, once a month.

Mallory had joined the military after graduation and had become a career man. Martin had gone on the construction circuit for a large Houston construction firm. He was all around the country, but often back in good old hot, smelly, humid, crowded, Houston, the ass hole of Texas. All the sewage of every Texas major city ended in the bay at Galveston, and along the coast. Bryan ended up there on assignment.

And so, their friendship resumed, and continued on long fishing trips down the piers and coast line south of Galveston and Corpus Christi. They loved the early morning surf fishing for shark, drum, red fish, sea trout, and in winter, flounder, which they would gig in the shallows. They took long trips out to the reefs for Red Snapper fishing. On these trips, they became closer than brothers. The interaction developed into long-term dependency. They needed each other to brag to, to argue with, to reflect bad ideas on. They functioned better together, neither finding wives. Although, they shared plenty of sisters, they never dated the same woman.

Now, Mallory had been stationed outside of Cheyenne Mountain in Colorado Springs. Their fishing trips were down to two a year, and they both felt deprived.

For three years now, Mallory had been busting with something that was going on. Martin couldn't put his finger on it. When he questioned him directly, he clammed up tight. It was big all right. Martin had figured from the drift of their talks that it was something to do with superconductivity. Whenever they hit that exciting new field, Mallory's eyes lit up.

"You're on the fast tract there," he hinted to Jay.

Then last July, during a long bay fishing trip, after a couple of six packs, Bryan had made a slip. Just a name; "Chingigcook." He had come down to "The Tomb," the name they call The Mountain, from Chingigcook. Jay had jumped on it like a pit bull, but Bryan had sealed up like Cheyenne Mountain.

Next, about a four months later, in December, they were after Sea Trout, fishing the jetties around the circle at Northern Padre from Red Fish to Aransas Pass, and back to the Corpus side of the Bay trying their luck first one place and then another. They were not doing any good but having fun.

The talk turned to high tech, as always. Bryan was hedging again, when it came to talking about his work. They fell into a long silence, just listening to the lap of the water, and feeling the sun and salt air.

"Jay, I'm going to tell you something," Bryan looked up, fixing his eyes squarely on Jay. "But you've got to promise to hold it under your hat. They're beginning to assemble the press people, and I want you to have a little lead. But you have to sit on this until I tell you."

"Sure, Bryan," Jay returned his stare level. "You call the shots."

Bryan took a deep breath and let it out slow, as if a great weight were being lifted from his shoulders. "Something big is coming," he started, "a completely new technology, it's going to change everything. Everything!" Bryan gestured an all-encompassing circle with his arms raised to the sky.

"Biotech," Jay questioned apprehensively?

"No, hardware," Bryan shook his head. "Let's just take my job. You know I've been working for NASA on the military side of the fence. You've heard of the new Pathfinder technology, that is supposed to be ways of using lighter rockets, better fuels to go to Mars. That's mostly smoke. Star Wars defense spending, more smoke. The old Supercollider experiment, now there is a story, but a lot of smoke also. Experience with the magnets, that's what they were after. Experience with superconductivity, of a grand scale. That part is called Tecumseh, in inside talk. It's the cryo boys and the magnet heads, we call them. The other part is at Alamogordo. The plasma physics boys. That part is called Adonis. A discrete solar image. It's all led incredibly fast. I've been in charge of the civil engineering stuff, that is undoubtedly the most outrageous piece of engineering ever to be done. I've bored a fifty-two-foot diameter hole over one hundred miles through the base of a mountain."

Jay whistled in comprehension and amazement, "What in the world," he exclaimed.

"It's a new launch system and the deployment of Space Based Defense System all at once. We've built a magnetically levitated train that is going to get going so fast that it's going to fly right off the surface of the earth. We can throw things into space with magnetic linear accelerators. We can place things in orbit through a thirty-foot hole in the top of a mountain, and that's not all. They've learned to contain plasma in an electromagnetic bottle and accelerate it to tremendous speeds with magnetic fields. We have a plasma cannon capable of shooting down missiles in orbit. The whole apparatus is being mated and made operational."

Jay made him tell everything in even greater detail. The afternoon wore into twilight, and they were still talking. Jay was just beginning to understand the magnitude of the change.

Now he was barreling along to Colorado Springs. Bryan's note had just said, "Tecumseh mated to Adonis. Mohamed, come to the Mountain. Now!" He had been on his way within the hour.

He made the long run down from Ratan Pass in good time. He found himself in the outskirts of the city before he knew it. He beat a path west on the loop halfway around the city to get near the Mountain before he called. Pike's Peak was the backdrop.

"Bryan," he said when Bryan picked up the phone. "Mohamed is here."

"Great, Jay, come on up to the mountain. We've got to get you checked in and processed. And, I do have a surprise for you," Bryan chuckled.

"Oh, yeah?"

"Yeah, so hurry up. Just come to the main gate. They're expecting you."

As he hung up, he wondered what he was getting himself into.

Cheyenne Mountain defies description. Massive blast doors greet the eye on first sight. Unbelievable construction is the common place, on a grand scale at this complex. Bryan came down to meet him and guide him through the processing. It was early afternoon when they finished, and he was famished. They made their way to one of the underground mess halls. The chow smelled great to Jay. He was voracious. They walked the line and picked from an abundant buffet. Jay piled his plate until he was embarrassed.

"I guess my eyes got too big," he remarked as they sat down.

"They're going to get a lot bigger when you hear what I have to say. I've been able to do something for you that I can't even do for myself," he croaked it out, with obvious envy in his voice.

"Ah, oh," Jay stopped shoveling chow. "What makes me think I'm not going to like this?"

Bryan looked gleeful. "That is if you've got the balls for it. I've got you on the Big Ride. This thing goes operational, one hundred percent, next week and the

109

NASA manager has decided to take some civilian reporters on the third run. One of the men tagged for the nonaffiliated spot came down, sicker than a wormy dog. He's runin' at both ends, so he's been scratched. I talked them into sending a freelance, and then held my breath. Sure enough, your name came up because of your technical writing on the Supercollider. I said that I knew you, and that you were the perfect man for the job, and of course, I would have to abstain from the vote. Well, of course, that did it. There's no clout like abstention." Bryan chuckled to the inside joke. Jay was frozen with a bite of mashed potato in his mouth.

"So, if you can pass the physical, and, of course, you will, you'll be headed to space. I forged you an application about a year ago to NASA Civilian in Space Program. So, now you, my little CIS, if everything goes smoothly with launch one and two, you'll be in space three weeks from today."

Bryan beamed. Jay sucked air and mashed potato down his throat and had a coughing fit.

The following morning, they were up bright and early, although, night and day makes no difference inside the Mountain.

The conference room was absolutely packed with scientists and reporters from the major universities and newspapers, the four major networks and the cable and satellite feeds. Jay recognized many of them. Dr. Hans Remy, professor of physics at Stanford, Dr. Frank Frady, America's foremost authority in the cryo-sciences. The list of PhD's went on like a reading list of who's, who of American science and journalism.

A uniformed man in blue approached the podium. He pounded a gavel three times.

"Gentlemen and Ladies, I'm Admiral Standford Hughs. Please take your seats." He paused for a moment and then continued officiously. "The Navy is here courtesy of the Air Force today, "he nodded toward a group of high-ranking air force brass. "We have this great honor and focal role, for three main reasons. We were interested in it from its inception, and frankly few people felt in nineteen-twenty-one, that this idea had much merit. That is how long Dr. Ellerson, and a few others, have been working on this."

Bryan punched Jay and indicated an ancient man to their left.

"This project fell to the Navy, because it is basically a device for the conquest of deep space, the moon and beyond, and that has been left largely, as it should, to the Navy. Also, the defense of the home shore is also the proud duty of the Navy and that is what leads us to today," he paused, and poured a drink of water and took a sip.

"During the funding of the 'Star Wars' era, this project began and is a combined venture of the Space Agency and the Department of the Navy. But this project should be seen as a national effort, and indeed the Secretary of State will talk to you shortly, after I've given you this preliminary briefing. The long and short of it is, we will go operational today with a new launch system, that has been a super-secret operation. It involves throwing objects off the surface of the earth with super magnetic force. From this spot to a mountain peak one hundred and thirty-one miles from here, a tunnel has been constructed, over the last twenty-one years, with the extracted material being disguised as coal moving to eastern power stations and dispersed as fill for erosion in coastal areas needing repair. The tunnel is lined for its entire length with super conducting magnets, which will accelerate a projectile capable of carrying people and freight to an enormous velocity. Upon entry into the atmosphere, scram jets will propel the craft to altitudes near space, where small rocket engines will lift the craft into orbit high enough to utilize the curvature of the earth to gain escape velocity, in the most economically efficient system yet to be designed and built. These craft will carry military, scientific, and, eventually, even tourists into space. Returning to earth as a glider, and powered by the scram jet motor, the craft will land at one of several Space Ports, which have been under preparation in New Mexico, Oklahoma, and Texas.

The CAP as we have come to call it, will carry several tons at a time and launch costs will be less than three million per ton of payload." This news brought an excited murmur from the crowd of reporters. They hadn't caught much so far, but dollars per ton, they understood, fully, what that portended. Admiral Hughs continued, "Today, this system will become fully operational. Today, we reach for the stars. But in addition to the NASA deep space effort, the thrust of this first mission will be military defense. The payload today will be a first-generation ICBM killer. This weapon fires a plasma ball contained in a cryogenic maintained magnetic field and is accelerated to near the speed of light. The energy ball is capable of hitting an ICBM coming over the horizon. Capable of firing many minutes at thirty loads per minute, this defensive weapon is the perfect choice, as the plasma ball is dispersed by the earth's atmosphere, making this weapon useless against Earth-based targets, unlike laser weapons."

The crowd murmured its approval. "Now before you inundate me with questions, let's take a tour of the facilities, and perhaps many of your questions will be answered."

They were led into a large open area and divided into groups of ten for the tour. To Jay's disgust, he was put in the same group as Reginald Tellur, a hideous and ancient little gnome of a man, with a strange look and devilishly strange eyebrows, which he combed out in an exaggerated and flamboyant way. He had a sour look on his face, Jay thought amusedly that he must not be having fun today. This was not his bailiwick. He was into nuclear power and more ICBMs. He was on the President's Brain Trust in the eighties, and his opinion was always consistent- more and bigger bombs and weapons. On the civilian side, he was known as the 'Father of the Fast Breeder', which brought to Jay's mind a dirty joke. He thought sardonically, that if there were anything really dirty, the man was into it. If it meant more dirty plutonium was brought into the world, he was for it. Jay studied him. He thought the man looked insane.

The tour lasted three hours, and then they broke for lunch. Bryan was beaming.

"If you knew how long we've kept this secret. Man it is so great to get to expose this project. Christ, the civil engineering on the tunnel alone is the eighth wonder of the world. And, to think, we got the nuclear digging technology from the Russian's," he chuckled, and rubbed his hands together.

Jay had to admit, it was something, the tunnel, the magnets, it all reminded him of the fantastic Empire of the Krell that Dr. Morbius showed the two Navy men in the old first color movie, "Forbidden Planet". It seemed too fantastic to be believed, yet it was real. They gave them a tour up the tunnel, by magnetically levitated train, explaining that the projectile or CABIN would travel in this same magnetically levitated and frictionless fashion. They were shown how certain parts of the tunnel was evacuated of air as the CAB increased in velocity. They were told how many g's a rider would sustain at any portion. Generally, a launch was such that even a softy could stand it. While military payloads, without people, could be launched at much higher velocities.

They had thirty minutes for a break, and then the Secretary of State was to give a press conference, before the launch. Men were already gathering around the

113

podium looking nervous, like security men always do while trying their best to be cool, calm, and collected.

"Gentlemen," Stanford Hughes did the gavel work again. "The Secretary of State of the United States," he quit the podium. Jay recognized Secretary Ingersoll, who replaced Hughes on the speaker's platform.

"Today, we realize a long and cherished dream. We realize freedom for the entire world. My great regret is the man who had the vision and determination to place this all in motion, President Ronald Reagan, is not here to see it, but we feel his spirit is with us. We are thankful for his family members, who have joined us here today to dedicate this facility. The long and cherished dream of freedom for the world from Nuclear Tyranny. Ever since the buzz bombs of World War two, machines flying above the earth's atmosphere have rained death and destruction all over the world. The fear of death from the skies is the most ominous fear of our modern time. Today, for the people of the United States, and all peoples who will join us in harmony and equitable relations, and for any who ask our protection, on humanitarian grounds, this fear is ended. After today, this nation will not tolerate a rocket above the earth's atmosphere, if it is on a mission of destruction."

The room exploded in cheers. The men were on their feet wildly exultant. Jay thought Reginald Tellur of Chicago, looked chagrined, as he remained in his seat.

"The United Nations, and nation states of the world are being notified by the President of this deployment as we speak. Now, gentle people, if you will follow me into the observation room, let's make history."

The launch and deployment was accomplished before the supersonic shock wave rolled the hundred and thirty miles back down the valley grumbling like thunder from the force of the projectile leaving the end of the tunnel and meeting with the thin air at the fourteen-thousand-foot level. It was heard all the way to Salt Lake

City. Within minutes the military payload was in orbit, unfolding itself, it was ready to defend itself within less time than a missile could shoot it down. The excitement waned. The crowd thinned. The news men made a bee line for the bank of phones and computer links, now open to them, as their cell phones would not work inside the Mountain.

"Exhausted," Bryan quizzed?

"It's a long day," Jay grinned.

"Well, it ain't over yet. You're due at the Medical Section. You've got to start getting ready for the ride of your life."

"Man, that is some roller coaster."

"What's the matter, nervous?"

"Sure, a little."

"I'd give anything to be in your shoes, brother."

"Yeah, well maybe you can just have them."

They laughed and pounded each other on the back as they started for the medical section.

The giant galactic probe droid fell by in close warp star orbit. Even with the thick shielding, at this orbital distance, the radiation was unbearable to the men. If the heat from the torrent of radiation pouring on them from the outside wasn't enough, the inside of the droid was an inferno of furnaces and industrial processes. It couldn't be called a ship because it had no engines. It wasn't a station because only a skeleton crew, which remained a very short time, observed the production.

Thousands of deep space probing and transmitting devices were being manufactured. At mathematical predetermined intervals, these devices were launched into the Schwarzschild Time Warp of the neutron star.

"When you stop to think," observed one of the radiation suited crewmen to another, "that there are hundreds of these droid ships at all seven of the 'Doors of Reality' searching all the time space continuum, it is awesome."

"Somebody wants the answer to where and when and right now. I think war is brewing again."

"And what would we fight with," the crewman asked coldly?

"Groten, it's hot," the first complained changing the subject. They had been chosen for duty with differing political views on purpose. They weren't supposed to get along, just do their jobs or else. That was part of the strange shake-up, and everyone knew of the meeting of the Navigational Guilds of the Ruling Houses.

There was obviously something big going on. There was enormous expense involved in the universal time space search. It had never been attempted in the thousands of years of the Empire. The funding had never been available, and besides, many people had many places they didn't wish for the Imperial troops to come snooping around. Even this massive search effort would reveal but an infinitesimal part of the whole.

"But you know the really strange thing," the first one mused again?

"Huh?"

"These probes aren't mapping probes."

"That's crazy, what else could they be?"

"I've got a friend in programing. She works on function programming. They bring the brains in and put them in, last thing before the probes are dropped. SI stuff, very hush-hush."

He pointed at the heterodyne tachyon unit they were installing.

"These probes don't give back any signal unless they spot what they are looking for. They transmit when they find what they are programed to spot."

"What are they looking for?"

"Radiation of an artificial type, only one particular type."

"That would indicate an outside adversary, wouldn't it?"

"Or an inside one."

When the probe fell into earth orbit, it wasn't noticed at first. The computers just regarded it as an unknown piece of space junk. It was later discovered that some unknown operator of the ECHO SDI system, the new system capable of protecting the satellites, upon which the country now depended, had penciled in a question mark and a 'where did this come from'. That was a week before it moved. When it moved, to say it was noticed would hardly be enough. But to say that the world almost came to an end, that all military powers went on alert, each accusing the others of attacking in a surprise attack, would have characterized the crises correctly. No one knows if the others had given their control over to a computer with no human in the chain. That one caused some pause for thought. There was a tense moment in the cabinet when it was reported falling on the United States. But it was falling on White Sands, New Mexico, and it was landing without the characteristics of a plane or rocket ship. When a tank approached it, the tank was crushed.

Uris knew there was trouble when they came out of warp in Hyperbolia. She had avoided the Cestus system by going another route through rocky terrain as it were, a gas nebula and a different warp star. One that only the family knew about. It was well off any trade lanes.

The air waves were dead. The Tachyon carrier wave, that stayed in operation all the time, was not functioning. She feared the worst, but nothing prepared her for the horrible destruction that she saw as she descended into the mountainous city of Saphos.

The tachyon towers had received a direct energy blast. The shields had broken down under bombardment. Rubble from the surrounding mountains partially buried the city at the edges, where the buildings ran up against the shear walls of the cliffs. Melted rock showed the amount of bombardment that the shields had withstood before the generator blew up, taking the power station and surrounding area with it.

She was choked with tears as she made her way over the rubble, and through the once proud ancient doorway. The Portal was cracked and hanging from its corbeled arch. The word Endure in the family motto was cracked through.

She searched for the dim recesses of what was left of the palace, and could find none of her family. She called their names, hopefully at first, and then in screams of desperation. She heard someone moaning in one of the basement wine cellars. She got a bar and broke the old lock.

Mez was sprawled inside, holding the head of his dear friend Eljer, whose lifeless eyes stared back at Uris with cold reproach.

"Mez, Mez, what has happened here," she held the old man up. He tried to speak. He could make one trembling word.

"Metastophiles."

He began to cry, but no tears would come. He hadn't the moisture left.

She left him for a moment and found some water in a courtyard fountain that had escaped being fouled, and rushed it back. He drank greedily. In a few minutes, he was able to talk with great effort. His voice was hoarse.

"They came on us suddenly, without warning, their ships above the city in a mass bombardment."

"Don't try to talk."

"I must," he whispered, "You must know. My heart, it could give out at any time," he spoke haltingly.

"Rest."

"They were pretending to be looking for that Ambassador you took with you to Xinor. The young one, Kurege."

"Kurege," her eyes grew fierce. "So, he was part of this after all."

"That was a pretext. They were really looking for information on the Draco Supernova," he clutched her shoulder. "They killed Uriah," he sobbed. I heard Metastophiles say it, himself. They caught him coming out from the measurement of the exploding Supernova. They said that they were searching for the Pandamon Ambassador, but they were looking for the data they said Uriah sent back from the Draco Warp Star."

"Yes, I received the probe at Ka by luck. There was a small incident over it."

"Well, that is the incident that they used as provocation to open fire on us. They were searching desperately for that data. They tortured Eljer to death. He would tell them nothing. He would not speak to Metastophiles, or any of his men. He kept his silence all

120

the way to the end, and they did horrible things to him, but he was immune to their drugs and torture. They kept me to run the computer system. I let them have everything we have, they had it anyway, and I knew that we didn't have the data that they were looking for."

"I have it."

"My liege, you must be careful. Metastophiles won't stop until he has that data. I heard them talking. They plan to subjugate the entire Regis system. They have been stockpiling munitions, enough to attack Xinor, just up time at a juncture where Draco will be clear for navigation. Metastopliles has been preparing for this ever since the star was identified as a future navigable star eight hundred years ago. Uris there is more. Do you know how Metastophiles and his cohort of buddies, Azbael, Beel, Mephor, Sargon and the rest of them live so long?"

"They stay moving in down time. Anyone can do it, if they wish to leave everything and everyone behind, and travel at warp all the time."

"That's not all there is to it." Mez drew her face close to his. "I heard some of the technicians talking. They have devised a way to make cells immortal. They have found a proto-fetal sub chromosome clumping that exists in humanoid fetus, that has regenerative powers. They are clone grafting their own genetic structure into humanoid races and then extracting the life essence out of an entire world. Using them up, before going forward and backward in time doing this hideous thing throughout the galaxies of time and space, to maintain their own twisted lives," he stopped in a coughing fit.

"I'm going to go get you some help. There must be some survivors. I can't find any of my family."

"He disintegrated them. He lined all the House of Ur up on the front steps and destroyed them." He wept, and she wept with him. Now her tears turned to blinding anger.

"I must get some help for you," she said. She
really meant to go back to the ship and kill the Pandamon
Ambassador, but as she walked, the more that this seemed
a futile and childish way of destroying an innocent life.
As she looked around her, she saw too many innocent lives
in ruins. She began to help with the injured, once she had
found some men to go for Eljer's body, and Mez had been
given comfort.

When the people saw who it was, they began to
take heart. They called to one another, and the city began
to show small signs of life left yet. She worked tirelessly,
and by dark there was beginning to be some organization
and hope. Food, light, warmth were the things she focused
on. That was what they needed now.

At one point in the afternoon, she had gone back to
the Pearl to confront Kurege, since this had been done in
his name. She entered his room with her hand on her
knife. "Who are you, Kurege, Ambassador of Pandamon,"
she spit it at him?

He was startled by her sudden entry. He had seen
no one but his guard for days nor anything other than this
room, that was his cell. He looked at her levelly. He
could see something was terribly wrong.

"I don't know. You know me as an ambassador. I
was brought to the central world when I was very young. I
have no memory of any other place."

"How do you know you were brought there?"

"There are rumors as to things."

"What things? I warn you be specific. I'm not in
the mood for a game of words."

"You cannot imagine life on Pandamon as a
member of the aristocracy. The young men are privileged
in all ways. We lead a life of unimagined luxury. We are
privileged in all ways except one."

"What way is that?"

"I would rather not go into that right now, if you don't mind, but suffice it to say, that it made me rebellious, and I escaped."

"Escaped?"

"Yes. I'm not really an ambassador at all. I'm really due to be locked up in isolation on Pandamon."

"Are you some kind of criminal?"

"I'm not exactly a criminal," he blushed under his olive complexion.

"Be specific, I warn you," she pulled her knife and pointed it at him. "Do you know what this is?"

"I do," he sat up nervously.

"And what it can do?"

"Yes."

"I can torture you with this device."

"I know that well, my lady."

"Now, answer me straight."

"I will try. The rumor is that all the humanoids of the privileged class, and I use the term loosely, are genetically related to the six clones of Metastophiles, or in other words to the old man himself, since the clones are genetic replicants of Metastophiles."

"I know this."

"Well, what you don't know, is that Pandamon is one huge genetic engineering experiment."

"What?"

"It's the central gathering place for genetic material up and down time."

"How do you know this?"

"I got into the central computer records. That's why I escaped. I found out that I was going to be incarcerated."

"Why?"

"I found out that I'm a high betazoid, and they were going to lock me up," he shrugged, hoping that she wouldn't ask him anymore.

"What does that mean?"

"It seems, and this is just speculation among the men involved, that a sub chromo genetic unit exists, that has incredible regenerative powers."

"Go on," she commanded. This jived with what Mez had reported.

"It seems that the Betazoid, high dreamers, are selected for even more of the desired genetic quality, so I was to be put in prison."

"For what," she was genuinely puzzled?

"Do I have to spell it out for you?"

She shook her head. She still didn't get it.

"To be milked."

"Oh!" Now it was her turn to blush and be embarrassed.

"So, life on Pandamon is not all it's cracked up to be. I figured to get out on some Ambassadorial shuttle, and just get lost in the crowd, but you put a hold on me, and I couldn't get loose."

"I wish to heaven that I had let you go," tears welled up in her eyes.

"What is wrong, Uris?" Suddenly, he just knew, beyond a shadow of a doubt, what had happened, as if he had seen it through her eyes. "OH, no! Oh, no!"

He went to her and grabbed her and hugged her to him. She shuddered and let the knife fall with a clatter to the floor. She sobbed and sobbed against him.

"Shh," he comforted as he held her. "Shh. It will be all right."

Chapter Seventeen Starquake
(How She Glitched the Imperium's Men)

Desperation is the enemy of logical choice. It places the mind at the mercy of its own imagination, when circumstances least afford. But survival instinct, can still run true. Both Kurege and Uris were in desperate frames of mind. One, with nothing to lose, and the other having lost everything.

In their newfound intimacy, they both found solace. He attempted to take care of her, sensing that she was in shock. He coaxed her to the galley. He placed her in a padded booth, that formed the crew table. He spread a throw over her, which he retrieved from his room. Then he busied himself fixing her a soothing drink, but before he was finished fixing her a sandwich, she had slumped down. It was too much for her to take, and she had got extremely tired. Once warm and secure she had let down and gone to sleep, but she jerked fitfully betraying her sleep to be as troubled as her awake life.

He fixed himself some drink and watched her as she slumbered. She had dismissed the guard on him, so they were alone inside the Pearl. He blew on his cup of soothing drink and tried to organize his thoughts. He was restless and couldn't be still. He hoped she wouldn't wake and went outside.

The carnage that met his eyes was unbelievable. Rubble was all that was left of the bright and beautiful, bronze colored city. The proud towers lay in dust, shattered to pieces. She said that all this was done in his name.

This filled him with anger and a foreboding. To think, that the almost mythical Metastopiles, sovereign of Pandamon, was aware of him, filled him with fear. To think that he, Kurege, was being pursued, numbed him with a paralysis that he could not shake. He could not understand what value that he would have to the master of time and space. Besides, Metastophiles had not personally appeared on Pandamon in three lifetimes. That he would appear now, looking for Kurege was unfathomable to him.

He shook his head and went back inside. He would wait for her to wake. She was still sleeping when he came back to the galley. He made himself something to eat and then busied himself with the sewing that he had been doing. He was putting the finishing touches on the pair of boots he was making for her from the skin of the gru she had taken on Calaban, what seemed like ages ago, but was actually less than a moon cycle, on Saphos.

She awoke and saw what he was doing. "Making that may have saved your life at one point."

"Is that so?"

"When I wasn't sure of who or what you were."

"And now you know?"

"Yes, I think so. But you are no ambassador."

"No, just one of Metastophile's clone breeding stock."

"But an important one, evidently."

"Or, it has nothing to do with me."

"I think we should assume that you have some value to him."

"I don't understand what it could be."

"There have been rumors about Pandamon, and its purpose, and the reason for its mode of organization."

He waited for her to clarify. He could not understand what interest he could be to anyone.

"Evidently, Metastopiles is doing humanoid genetic engineering on a galactic scale, for some purpose of his own."

"What could it be?"

"Well, there is really only one thing that obsesses him, so the rumors go. He is obsessed with growing old. That is the reason that he stays in down time almost always. He has been in and out of the affairs of the Xinor Empire since the humanoid race of Isis pierced the Regis Star. Metastophiles was already on Pandamon. The other species came in the next one thousand years, but his clones, Beel and the rest of those bunch have only come and gone as Viceroys in Metastophiles name, for the last three hundred years."

"Mepor had newly replaced the old minister Sargon, who has gone back down time," Kurege informed her.

"Yes, that happened several years before Mephor was killed in the shuttle explosion that led to the Guild meeting on Xinor. Beel assumed the Chancellery when Mephor went as Ambassador to Pran."

"But why would they seek me?"

"Perhaps it was a convenient excuse to take Saphos out of the picture. He killed my father over a territorial dispute, involving the Draco supernova. Saphos lies between the doors leading from Pandamon to Draco."

"Whatever he is up to," Kurege perceived intuitively, "the answer is on the other side of Draco."

"It would seem that is a fair assumption. But, the distance to the other side is very far downstream. Much real time is involved in getting there. That is what intrigued my father," Uris mused. "The Draco system will clear soon, and then what was many years around, will be right next door."

"My earliest memories are of growing up on a ship on a long hyperspace voyage. We were in cryosuspension after I was about four. It took ten more years to reach Pandamon," Kurege added idly.

"Perhaps you came from the other side of Draco," Uris added. "It's about the right distance. It is about

fourteen years one way. My father made it once, and he
sent back data on the Draco Supernova."

"The answer to what Metastophiles is up to may be
on the other side of Draco," he repeated with conviction.

"If it is clearing, it explains why he is here." She
wrinkled her brow. "We need help, and there is no help
left here on Saphos," a tear came in her eye. She fought
hard not to bring those memories back. "We must go to
Regis Xinor and get help from my cousin Surilen. She
knows some of this already. She must be warned that
Metastophiles has returned into Xinor time, and means to
attack the capital.

"Can she help us?"

"She is powerful," Uris looked determined. "She
can help us. I must see what I can do to restore order here,
and then we will leave."

They left the next afternoon. The counsel
protested, but she took no one with her except Kurege,
ordering her aids into positions of government
responsibilities and charging them to do what they could to
relieve the suffering of the people.

They had barely warped the Cestus Neutron Star,
when they knew they had made a mistake.

An alarm came on. The voice activated battle
computer reported.

"Heavy military scan of us," Uris told Kurege.

"I feel helpless," he said. I don't know anything
about your ship. I'm useless."

"Just hang on tight," she flopped one-hundred-
eighty degrees upside down, and dove straight back into
the Cestus Warp door. She headed slightly up time,
hoping to lose the pursuing Pandamon Battle Cruiser. She
had gotten a glimpse of its weapon studded profile, as she
kicked the little craft back into hyperspace. "I just lost us
a month of real time," she observed to Kurege, as they
came out the other side. "It will take them a standard

period or less to sort through the time eddies for our track, but they can find it," she bit her lip.

"Sit here. Just hold this course," she showed him the instrumentation of the flight console. He grasped it quickly. It was not difficult.

"Just hold that course," she pointed at the navigational instruments. "I have an idea that I have to work on to see if it may be an option to us. They're standing between us and Xinor. We're obviously not going there. We must have a way to hide from that cruiser. They will figure out where we've gone and come after us. They'll overtake me like I was crawling."

She sat down at the pilot console and began working feverishly at the computer screen. She went to a storage file and came back with the data box that had come through down time in Uriah's drone ship and had found its way to her by a miracle tenacity and of good luck.

She plugged the information into her navigational computer and began a statistical analysis of the Draco Supernova, in its electromagnetic and time distortion sense. The program would run for a long time even with the enormous capacity of her computers. They were the best cryo type of $+ -$ magnetic bubble. They could walk and talk and several of the android extensions of the Pearl did.

Andro, her principal robot, was on board and in storage, until now. She brought him out to keep a constant scan for the Pandamon Battle Cruiser. Kurege was startled.

"What is that?"

"Oh, don't mind Andro, he's a pussy cat."

"Yeah, he looks it," he shrank back. The machine was a massively intimidating military robot type of the latest cryo design. It floated to a communication console and plugged in and began to do its thing.

"Andro, keep a sharp watch out for a Pandamon Battle Cruiser."

"Got any more like him?"

"Not any more exactly like him," she grinned, he is a prototype.

"Maximum scan milady."

"Oh, no," he groaned, a talking tin head." He hated talking machines. To him it was an inconsistency.

"You prejudiced against the droids?"

"It's just the social situation I come from, you understand," he apologized. "We are subjected to a good deal of machine violence on Pandamon."

"I thought you were a member of the privileged class?"

"I had eyes. I could see what was going on. In my own small way, I was striking back."

"What way, and why would you strike out?"

"I've already told you, life at the Royal Court was no picnic. For people like me, well I was no more than breeding stock. For the lower classes life was an enforced routine, that of the genetic scientist. They draw the best from all over the galaxies, because the money of Pandamon is strong and they pay opulently, but Pandamon is also an expensive place to live, and they mostly end up working all the time. The rest, their lives are unspeakable. The damned, we call them, except it has a double meaning in our language that is a slang word for Prince, so that if you say 'our children are the damned' you also say a phrase that means 'the blessed children of the Prince'. It is a morbid pun. As you can see, Pandamon leaves much to be desired."

"Who are these damned ones?"

"I thought you knew. They are the products of the genetic experiments. Most are unsuccessful mutants, that are headed in some direction of mutation. They are kept alive for their genetic material. That is why they are in a sense, the children of the Royal Family, although, really, they are a symbol to us because they are a product of the laboratory gene splicing. The real purpose of the genes of the Royal Princes, we do not know, but it can only be something even more monstrous than Pandamon itself."

"Yes, Pandamon has never gone along with any of the treaties outlining the controls that must be placed on genetic engineering, nor will they sign non-interference agreements to allow natural selection in the worlds that they control, where there are primitives, with no intelligent species present. It has long been rumored that they are using these worlds as laboratories."

"It is a nightmarish place of sadistic kingdoms."

At that moment the nightmare found them. "War Cruiser coming into real time, milady," Andro interjected, matter of fact.

"Andro, give me a reading on that data you've been crunching in the mains, on the Draco Supernova."

"Data is incompletely analyzed at this time. There is apparently a path of sorts. The fabric is still tearing at the edges, the time door would be highly unstable and unpredictable."

"Andro, continue to analyze the data and make ready for a hard warp through the Draco Warp Star, and possibly a crash. Make ready the escape pod."

"What are you going to do?"

"Run for it."

"Run where?"

"In there," she set a course into the heart of the Draco Supernova.

"Milady," Andro spoke, "It is not advisable to warp the Draco Star at this point in time. I am receiving information from current readings on the neutron body of the star, and a further contraction would be certain."

"We've got no choice."

She set the course and hit the thrust. "Strap down," she warned getting into a harness. "Andro, do the best you can, it's all yours," she never let computers handle warp commands, but this time no humanoid could react fast enough to go through.

"The Pandamon ship has followed us in," Andro warned. It was starting to get rough. The force field was singing from the stress, making the whole craft vibrate, and shake. "They have fired inside the door," and this time Andro's usually mechanical voice took on a distinct note of surprise.

"The fools," Uris screamed. The explosion tore and rocked them before the words left her mouth.

"Glitch!" Andro yelled a warning.

Alarms went off and red lights flashed across the console and around the control panels. The force field was overloading. The craft experienced a tremendous shock wave and Kurege and Uris were knocked unconscious from the sudden molecular shift.

Uris didn't know how long she had been out when she came to. A totally unfamiliar star field filled the viewer.

"We did it," she said groggily. Kurege was still unconscious. She went to him and felt him. He was alive and breathing. He would recover it a few minutes, she guessed. She turned her attention to Andro. She was still working on him when Kurege came around.

"Oh," he groaned. "My head feels like it's gonna come off."

"I've made a soothing drink," she pointed with the glass ergo probe that she was sticking around inside Andro, taking measurements.

"Tin head has a headache too," he observed, but the joke wasn't worth what it cost him. He grabbed his head.

"He got pretty messed up, but I think I can get him going," she kept working. "We are going to need him. We need his sensing capabilities."

"For the War Cruiser?"

"No. We've seen the last of them. When they fired at us inside the doorway they glitched the neutron star, causing a further contraction of its super dense matter. The cruiser was undoubtedly caught in the star quake and destroyed or caught in an eddy of time and sent into oblivion. No one has ever come through a glitch, no matter how much shielding they went in with."

"I guess that will fix them as far as chasing us any further," he stirred some sweetener in his drink.

"No, we need Andro to look for something else. The field was over strained by the star contraction. The Helium III is seriously depleted. Without a high-tech civilization, we aren't going more than a few hundred parsecs. We can cross this galaxy maybe twice, but that's it, and once we come out of hyperspace, no warping, that is for sure."

"What if we don't find one?"

"Then we are going to run out of power. With no way to keep the field coils super cold, we can't maintain. We will have to set down on some M class, oxygen rich world. Hopefully, with a little Xenon, which won't hurt you, but will keep me from getting sick."

"The prospects of being marooned don't seem good."

"Some men would welcome the opportunity," she threw him a nervous glance.

"It can get pretty primitive," he noted the flirtatious comment, but didn't react to it.

"Well, we know Metastophiles has a base here somewhere. He has been going the long way around to get here, and now that will change, with Draco becoming navigable."

"Finding his nest may not be such a good thing to find."

"Considering how scarce Helium III is, it is the only chance we have," she determinedly worked on Andro. "Glitch," he came alive!

"It's all right, Andro."

"Oh, me, Milady, I seemed to have smoked my cryo circuits."

"This will get you fixed up. Kurege, help me lift the cowling and hold it up, while I reroute some of his damaged circuitry."

They worked on the robot until they had done what they could.

"He's not new, but I think his scan functions are intact." They began a sweep of the Milky Way Galaxy in a spiraling course to get them near as much of its area as possible.

"We better find something soon," she looked at Kurege, with concern. How is your head?"

"I'm going to be all right," he answered her, and continued to scan with a radio wave detection setting. "I'm picking up some weak electromagnetic waves way down in the kilohertz band."

"That's it. Fix a direction and track up that signal, paralleled to its path out from its origin." The ship changed course. The stars flashed by as almost straight lines, as they maintained hyperspace from the acceleration they had obtained in passing through Draco. "It better be young, and not far away, because if these waves have traveled very far," she didn't finish.

"Young and near, Milady," Andro responded. I'm picking up more sophisticated transmissions. We are moving up their timeline very rapidly. The signature is young and near. Approximately eighty parsecs."

"Great news," she checked the console. We just might make it. There is enough He III to sustain the hyper drive, but may not be enough for a planet fall, if the planet is of much size."

"I'm picking up low frequency visual now Milady. Its strength of origin is very low. The planet is near."

"Approach with maximum fuel efficiency. We are in a hurry, but we want to get there."

"Certainly," Andro seemed offhanded.

"Can you get a lock on separately grouped signals?" Kurege questioned Andro. "We might be able to get a look at them, if the signals are video."

"I think that I can separate some of the signals, successfully." Images of nineteen-fifties black and white television came on the screen. Followed by color images from later dates.

"Well, at least they are humanoid," Kurege observed. Uris was too busy to look up. The field was starting to collapse from the depletion of the Helium III that maintained the superconducting field around the magnetically contained plasma, that powered the gravity concentrators. Without the field, they were a rock, falling through the sky. She diverted power from all other sources to keep the Pearl flying.

"I have the planet, Milady," Andro hummed with success.

"Make for it."

"Landing coordinates?"

"Anything. Skip through the atmosphere and let the hull take as much as it can stand. We're going to lose the field and this thing doesn't glide very well." She climbed into the shock straps that were suspended from floor to ceiling. "It's going to get pretty hot in here," she warned, pulling her straps tight.

Joe Le Blanc, he thought the moon, she be joule bon, tonight, as he tended his nets. The shrimp, they run good, and he was wet with sweat with the heavy work of harvesting the drag net. He cursed and stabbed at a Sting Ray whipping its tail menacingly in the net. He threw it over the side with a respectful Cajun saying.

"To the moon Monsieur Tato," a reference to a local mythical demon of which the voodoo swamps of Lafayette Bayou were full.

He gasped as the white-hot ball streaked across the sky and exploded the water fifty yards away, with boiling, hissing steam. He could see the water boiling as the white-hot Pearl settled to the bottom of Lafayette Bayou, in about thirty feet of water.

He pulled his nets aboard as quickly as he could when he had recovered his senses. He started his boat's engine, and drew slowly, very slowly, closer to the boiling cauldron. The craft had lost its white heat and was no longer glowing.

"Oh, Joe Le Blanc, what you say? Flying Saucers in Tibaldo, you know no one gonna believe dis," he sing song chanted to himself, in the bayou dialect peculiar to the South of New Orleans, along the coastal area.

"They never gonna believe dis up in Oakdale," he continued. "Maybe Daniele, maybe she believes, she crazy in the head, like Joe Le Blanc." He stopped right over the turbulence. He dropped his anchor and cranked up his old ship to shore radio.

"Oh," he yelled into the receiver, when he got the dials adjusted. He whistled loudly. "Henri! Yo! Yo there, Henri."

"What you want, Joe Le Blanc," Henri came back, with a sleepy voice. "Yo know what time she be?"

"Henri. Yo get yo dive lungs and lights and get out here rit now, maybe she be good idea."

"Joe Le Blanc, what you say?"

"I say yo come rit now."

"Where you be?"

"I be up Lafayette Bayou. Yo come out. I see yo come out the creek. I flash yo, three times."

"She be right there."

Henri Usay was a good man, Joe Le Blanc think he be the best. He would come right away, no questions.

Joe had just gone to the bow, and looked intently into the water, when two military jets made a low pass just to the South about a mile. He watched them circle and run a pattern, going farther to the South. He killed his lights and turned one of his many radios to the coast guard band. He wasn't the only one who had seen the meteor, or whatever it was, come plummeting into the sea. Fortunately, no one seemed to be sure of the exact position of the splash down.

He didn't have long to wait until Henri Usay's salvage boat came around the bend and out from under the Chatham Bridge and out into Barataria Bay. He took a powerful spotlight and blinked it in Henri's direction. Henri raised him on the radio, but Joe gave him some smuggler jargon to get off the air waves.

"Joe Le Blanc," Henri called as he pulled alongside, "you one crazy Cajun, yes. What you get me out in the middle of the night for." He cut his motor.

"Turn those lights out," Joe called.

"What you up to Joe Le Blanc?" Henri did as he was told.

"Something, she fall from the sky. She fall rit here," he pointed down his anchor rope.

"Meteor?"

137

"I no think so."

"Airplane?"

"Some kind, foisure. She not from dis world."

"Joe Le Blanc, you drunk maybe jus' a'little?"

"Yo shut up, and hand me one of those tanks, rit now, and that's fo sure."

The two men suited against the cold and strapped on the lungs, then slipped into the murky waters of the inter coastal canal, just out from Barataria Bay. They clicked on the powerful spotlights, but they did little good. The visibility was almost zero from the turbulence of the crash. Le Blanc had managed to get the boat positioned right over the top of the fallen Pearl. They hadn't gone but about twelve feet below the surface until they came to its top.

Usay was stunned. He pulled the other man near him. Joe motioned downward. Henri took a deep breath and tried to control his breathing. He was an experienced diver in murky water, but this was scaring him. He was hyperventilating.

They started around the smooth side of the Pearl, feeling their way, inching downward. Suddenly, a seam opened under Henri's fingers, and he fanned back as a great rush of water gushed into the interior of the Pearl. A door was swinging open from the smooth side. Le Blanc pushed away, but Henri could faintly make out his light.

An unearthly, ethereal, and elfin, face and floating hair, was transfixed, luminous in Henri's powerful light. Blinded, Uris grabbed out, and grabbed Usay's mask, and pulled it off. He grabbed her arm and whirled her around in self-defense and started for the surface. She struggled momentarily and then went limp.

"Henri, Henri, Henri," he heard Joe calling his name over and over as he broke the surface.

"Joe, over here."

"Henri, what you catch," Joe swam out from the boat. He had pulled a life ring from where it was tied on the edge of his boat.

"She be a girl, I think," Henri's voice was edged with doubt.

"Take this life ring. I'll go back and see if anyone else be in the wreck. What kind of plane you think she be?"

"No plane like we ever see before, I can tell you." He took the life ring and put it over the limp form of Uris. "Help me get this one in the boat."

They put Uris in the bow of Le Blanc's boat, and after checking to make sure she was breathing, went back to the Pearl, feeling their way back along the seam to the door. Fortunately, Kurege had not made it out of the ship, as they might never have found him. He collapsed in an air pocket in the top of the ship that had formed when the door burst open. They could find no one else. They abandoned the Pearl, and carried Kurege back to Joe Le Blanc's boat. After they had the two wrapped in blankets, they backed Henri's big salvage boat over the top of the Pearl and scooped it into the net. The cable strained as Henri reeled it in, on the old salt encrusted hoist, but the rigging held, as both men gave a sigh of held breath.

Having accomplished their task, they rolled smokes and sat a moment studying the Pearl snuggled in the net behind Henri's boat draining water and the two survivors tucked onto the bow of Joe's shrimp boat.

"What you thin they are, Joe," Henri was wide eyed?

Just then the two military jets made a low pass directly over them. "We go upriver. We better move soon, I bet you, for sure."

"What you think?"

"I think these two do no good, if the government get them."

"Let's put some distance from here."

Making sure that the two stayed warm, the two boats headed away from the scene, beating a crooked path, back up the river in the bayou backwash swamp land. Finally, coming out near the bridge and passing into the open and then back into the tangle of bayou on the other side, slowly making way upriver in a pirate's path centuries old. Once they figured they were a safe distance, Joe pulled up.

"Where we go, Joe," Henri yelled?"

"Follow me. We need a doctor, and a secure place. We go to Danielle's"

"Rit behind you."

They beat on up the river in the darkness, keeping a sharp eye out for others, running without lights.

Danielle Usay blew softly on the steaming cup of half coffee and half chicory, which was the preferred blend in the bayou country. She watched the two forms sleeping, curled in the front of the shrimping boat, which was pulled up in the back dock, near the loading door of her shrimp processing plant. Her brother, Henri's salvage boat was backed beside where she stood.

She looked with curiosity at the paper she held in her hand. It had appeared tacked up all over town by good daylight this morning, and Cutoff Louisiana was being crisscrossed by men in plain brown cars, with whip antenna. She read the notice once more in disbelief.

"Title 14, Section 1211 of the Code of Federal Regulations, implemented on July 16, 1969, makes it illegal for U.S. citizens to have any contact with extraterrestrials or their vehicles."

She took another thoughtful sip of the liquid still steaming in the cool morning air. Her brother Henri and Joe Le Blanc had pulled into her shrimp processing plant at around four in the morning. She had heard them when they had come into the dock and had been getting dressed when they had come into the house with an excited chatter going on between the two.

"Sis," Henri had called to her, "yo never gonna believe what we catch tonight."

"What you crazy Cajuns doin'," she called from the bedroom. "Is that pirate Joe Le Blanc with you?"

She had made some chicory coffee and sat them down to hear the story, and then they had gone down to check the two in the front of Joe's boat. Kurege and Uris seemed to be all right, and they did not disturb them, as it was useless to try to get a doctor at this time of the night or take them to an emergency room, where they would have sat for hours waiting for attention. They were not bleeding, and were breathing, and it was decided to wait for morning light and see what the two said for themselves when they awakened. There was some concern about concussions, but the thought of an emergency room visit or calling an ambulance seemed a bad idea for these two. This was an area of the country which mistrusted authority and depended on self-reliance. They simply watched the two and kept them wrapped and warm.

The warehouse was Danielle's, inherited from her father, while Henri had inherited the boat. Danielle was a reading teacher in the fifth grade of the local elementary school, and at six o'clock had gotten on the Internet, and arranged for a substitute for the day. Henri and Joe had used the big hoist, which rolled on an I-beam out over the dock area to transfer the Pearl from the back of the boat to the inside of the warehouse. They had placed a sump pump inside the Pearl and emptied it of most of the water before they had brought it higher than the hatch, which had fortunately ended up on top when they had scooped it into the net. They had carried the craft trailing mostly submerged letting its buoyancy partially support its weight. With the water pumped out, they were able to transfer the netting to the hoist and under the lights of the shrimping dock, bring the load into the processing shed. All normal activity, seemingly, for this time of the morning, for men who had been out all night drag netting for shrimp.

They had not taken the Pearl into the shed for more than a few minutes when Danielle observed the first of the brown cars with the whip antenna come slowly past on the street in front of the house. It was coming slowly and stopping often to look at each facility. About first light, it or one just like it, had returned and she had seen a man get out and tack up the notice that she was now holding onto.

She had gone out and removed it from in front of her telephone pole in front of the house, when the car had moved on down the road. Joe and Henri were busy pumping out the rest of the water, when she brought the notice into the shed and showed them.

"Federal regulations from 1969," Joe had exclaimed. "The government has been aware of this type of thing for that long," he scratched his long white hair. "Military jets came right over us not long after the crash."

"What you think we should do, Danielle," Henri questioned his sister?

"I'll have to think on that one a while," she responded. "Anyway you cut it, this is going to be trouble," she told the men, thinking about the various smuggling activities, and the tax evasion, and all the various agencies that would descend on them. These were agencies that bayou people just naturally avoided. Danielle's tendency had been to try and stay legal, and she did the best that she could, having paper for her school teacher's job, and inspections from the health agencies involving the shrimping business, but like all independent and small operations, they were slowly being buried in paperwork, and no one could stay in compliance with all the regulations anymore, unless they had a full time compliance officer whose only job was to do the paperwork to keep all the required policy enforced.

She pondered all of this, and sipped the chicory coffee, as the men moved around and talked inside the plant. The first stirring of life was moving under the blankets, and in a moment, Uris sat up with a start and looked around. Her eyes locked on those of Danielle's, and the two stared at each other for many moments. Uris felt for her knife. It was missing from the scabbard. She felt totally vulnerable, but when Danielle moved toward her, and held out the cup of chicory coffee to her, she recognized it as a friendly move, and accepted it. Danielle

143

had sipped it just before she handed it to Uris, and Uris understood, and took a sip of the insipid liquid. She made a grimace that made Danielle laugh and handed it back to her. Uris recognized the laughter as a friendly sound, and felt the hot strong liquid stimulate her system. Danielle spoke to her, but the language was strange to her ear, and completely unknown, but she realized that it was language, and tried to separate the words, but could not really hear them. Danielle took the cup and pulled back.

Uris realized that Kurege was beside her and pulled the cover back and shook him. He moved but was slow to revive. After three efforts, he opened his eyes and looked at her. He was slightly concussed and his eyes would not focus, but he could see two of Uris bending over him, and in a moment, he reached for her. They embraced for a long moment, and as his head cleared, he began to be able to see his surroundings.

"What has happened," he asked her.

"We have survived, by some incredible chance. The creature looking at us, has given me an awful tasting liquid, but it is warm and some type of stimulant. Drink some." She reached up to Danielle and Danielle handed her back the cup, which she helped Kurege hold while he sipped the coffee. He made a face with a downturned mouth, and Danielle laughed at them again. "At least, this planet is humanoid, and this one seems friendly enough." She held the cup for him again and then took another sip herself. It strongly stimulated her system, and she could feel the jolt as the caffeine raised her blood pressure. Kurege began to shake, and Uris pulled the covers around him, setting the cup beside her on the deck. Danielle turned and walked into the warehouse to tell the two men that their visitors had awakened.

Danielle called from the doorway, "Henri, Joe Le Blanc, our visitors have gotten up, and I am going to fix some food." She turned out the doorway to the processing shed and walked to the two story house that sat up the embankment. It was small, and frame, but neatly painted white, with flowers along the side, and Danielle picked a handful as she walked along the way and disappeared through the back door that led into the kitchen.

Joe Le Blanc and Henri Usay appeared at the bay door of the processing shed, at about the same time as Danielle disappeared into the kitchen, and Uris could see them from over the rail on the slightly raised fore deck that formed the bow of Joe's boat. She recognized Henri, vaguely, from the underwater meeting of the night before, and she had a unclear impression of Joe Le Blanc's long white hair and beard. She reached up and felt her own hair and felt that it was matted and stringy.

"How yo ah," Joe said to her, as he raised his hand in greeting. She gave him a blank stare. Kurege dropped the blanket away from his shoulders and Joe reached down and gave his hand a shake.

"She look a little blue to me," said Henri Usay.

"I had limp handshake before, but this one got no clue," Joe observed, scratching his chin beneath his long white beard. They were assuming that one was a man and the other a woman from the obvious breast that Uris had beneath her clothes, but their faces seemed to favor each other from the men's perspective, and they all stared at each other for some time.

"They have to be cold from this damp," Henri finally observed to Joe, and they both stepped back and began to motion for the two to follow them. Danielle appeared at the doorway and yelled that breakfast was ready.

"They want us to follow them," Kurege told Uris. She rose in agreement, and the two followed Joe and Henri into the house, as they walked ahead, and motioned the two repeatedly to follow them in encouragement. A pirogue with a man at the oars hailed the two with a friendly 'hallo', and Henri 'hallowed' him back. The man gave the four a curious stare, and stopped in his rowing, until the foursome had disappeared into the back door. Then scratching his head, he rowed on down the bayou.

"That Etienne, he be curious, and nosy, you batcha'", Joe observed.

Danielle met the two with towels and led them into the middle part of the house, where she put Uris in a bedroom and gave her dry pants and shirt to put on from some of her own stock. "A little big, she observed, but it will have to do, hon." She led Kurege into the downstairs bathroom, and gave him some of Henri's clothes, which he kept in the spare bedroom upstairs. She had thrown away all of her late husband's clothes, when he had died the year before from lung cancer, after smoking himself into an early grave. She was still mad about that and had kept none of his clothing to remind her of the smoke.

"That's going to swallow you," she observed to Kurege as she left him to figure it out.

The three of them were sitting and talking, buttering croissants, and slapping mayhaw jelly on the top, when Kurege and then Uris came out of the respective rooms and stood at the doors leading to the kitchen.

"Come on and sit down," Danielle spoke softly to them and motioned them to the table. She rose and lifted the lid off the cast iron skillet, and the smell of a scrambled egg omelet with an inside stuffed with chopped Bourdain sausages and shrimp creole, with melted cheese on top, wafted out into the room. Kurege looked at Uris, and had to laugh, and she laughed back at the way he looked, and then they moved to the table and sat, with the three watching them for every move. The eating implements were strange to them, but they watched the other three and imitated their moves.

The food was unfamiliar in taste, but they were ravenous and made the three smile as they soon stopped their tentative pokes, and scooped it into their mouths like they had never done before. It was good to be alive, after what they had been through. They topped it off with the chicory coffee, and about halfway through the meal, Danielle made the introductions.

"Danielle," she said, pointing at herself, and then pointing at her brother, said, "Henri," and then "Joe." Each man reinforced the speech with pronouncing their own names and pointing at themselves.

"Kurege," he responded, pointing at himself. Uris took umbrage at Kurege introducing himself first. She was not used to being upstaged by anyone, at any time. She gave her official title, "Queen Uris of the House of Ur," and looked hard at Kurege, with narrowed eyes. He just inclined his head at her and repeated only her name and pointed at her. The three knew that some minor quarrel had just happened, and Danielle repeated their two names with a nervous laugh.

"Well now, Uris and Kurege," she divined the proper protocol. "Now we have a starting point."

They let the two guests finish eating and sip another cup of coffee, until their visitors had their fill. Danielle motioned them to follow her, and she showed them through the bottom floor and then upstairs. She was delighted with Uris response to the view out the upstairs porch but tried to redirect her from the outside. She was still aware that the brown cars with the whip antenna were crisscrossing the small town repeatedly.

She led Uris into the upstairs bath, and showed her the water closet, which Uris found somewhat curious, as they had disintegration devices for this function, but quickly divined the purpose, and when Danielle turned on the water in the tub and adjusted the water, she knew exactly what she wanted, a long hot bath, to wash the salt and sweat from her. When she finished, she took a long time looking over every item in the bathroom, smelling and exploring each thing. The hairbrush was one item that she knew how to use, and she was very glad to get her hair unmated. When she emerged, the bedroom door was closed, and her clothes had been washed and dried and even the belt with the empty scabbard was lying on top. She felt longingly for her knife of many uses and thought that she would never see this gift from her father again.

When she came down the stairs, Kurege was nowhere to be found in the house, and Danielle pointed her toward the processing plant, and led her out the back, taking a nervous look around.

When they reached the shed door, she was amazed to see Kurege standing on a bench with his head inside the Pearl's hatchway. She gave a delighted whoop and climbed up beside him. He was holding a container and opened it to show her the boots made of the gru's skin that he was working on.

"They are undamaged in the sewing box that you gave me. I'll get them finished now."

"That's good," she said, but she was more interested in looking for something else she had lost.

Joe Le Blanc was adjusting a pump at the lowest point to suck out the last of the water, and she saw immediately the knife on the floor, and practically dived head first onto it.

"Woah," Joe cautioned, as she dove past him and scooped up the precious weapon.

She turned it over and over and examined it from every angle, and then climbed out of the Pearl, with Joe curiously watching her. She walked to the door of the shed, and Joe climbed out and they all followed her to the dock area. She made a quick adjustment to the handle, and stepped forward on the dock, pointing the tip at a rounded post top near the middle of the edge of the dock. A thin blue light blazed out from the tip, and the upper part of the post sizzled and neatly plopped off into the water, leaving a stump of creosote blazing for a few seconds, and water boiling out beyond the post, toward the middle of the river, where the thin blue line had entered the stream.

"Mon Dieu!" Joe exclaimed. Henri just gawked with his mouth wide open. A look of fear crossed Danielle's face, and she screamed and turned her face away from the sight, fearing it would explode. The post fire died away, and Uris readjusted the knife handle, and with a satisfied look on her face, reinserted the knife into its sheath.

"Now look what you've done," Kurege admonished her.

"What," Uris questioned?

"You've frightened them."

Uris looked about her at the startled faces, looking from one to the other. She did not feel regret, as she never considered herself as needing approval for her actions. She turned with a shrug and started back for the Pearl. Kurege followed her. "Uris," he began again, but let it drop, and he realized that she was not going to listen or be lectured to. They left the three flabbergasted people on the dock. They were talking very excitedly among themselves, and the two men began to examine the post, being careful not to burn themselves, as it was still smoking.

Uris climbed back into the Pearl and began to survey the damage. The inside of the ship smelled of ocean water, and the smell of salt was heavy.

"This is all going to have to be washed down with fresh water, and everything cleaned," she said to Kurege, who was looking in on her from the entrance. She began to right everything that had tumbled from where it should have been.

"I have seen them using fresh water in this building from a fixture like the ones in their water closets," Kurege told her. "Do you think that it can be put in working order?"

"It can all be cleaned up, and I know how to take it apart and put it together again, but it is a very large job, and every panel and control will have to come out and be cleaned. Andro may be able to help, if I can get him up and running. He has some damaged circuitry from the passage through Draco, and the overload that was created when the Pandamon ship fired on us inside the Neutron Star doorway. She gave a heavy sigh. "And, it will never fly again without a source of Helium III. That's not something that you can get just anywhere."

The faces of Joe Le Blanc and Henri Usay appeared along with Kurege at the portal entrance, and seeing what Uris was up to, Joe joined her. He began to pass loose objects out the door to Henri, and Henri sat them in a part of the floor with a drain and began hosing them down with fresh water. This began a workday among the four of them, and in this way, they made some headway cleaning up the ship.

They began to naturally learn to communicate, and the word 'water' was soon known. Kurege learned quickly to say their names, and was better at it than Uris, who had trouble with the s and soft c sounds. She could say 'Henri' pretty well, and it sounded very French when she pronounced it, but the best she could do with 'Joe' was a sound like Oh. Danielle had gone back into the house to clean up the breakfast dishes and do some house work that was needed, but she came and went, and Uris used her name several times, and this also sounded very French, so Henri and Danielle were pleased to hear a sound that was familiar to their ears. She fixed boudain sausage sandwiches, chips, and orange soda drinks for them at lunch time and brought them out to the processing plant. Fortunately, it was off season for the commercial shrimp industry, and Joe had only been out the night before filling the home freezer for their personal use. Danielle met the few people that wandered by to talk about the activity. She side tracked them from the processing shed.

"No," she told them, they had seen nothing unusual and had not seen the bright meteor that had streaked overhead. "I can't imagine what they are doing," she said to the curious locals concerning the government agents that continued to crisscross the town and waterfront asking questions of the local people. She realized that it was just a matter of time before someone would show up to question her.

In the evenings, they sat around the small kitchen after dinner and Danielle passed children's reading books around the table and after she had taught them their ABC's, began to teach them to read and pronounce words of common nouns, starting with animals like cat, and bird, and fish. Kurege showed more interest in this than Uris, who would drift back to the processing shed and sometimes work until late at night on the inside of the Pearl. She worked on Andro more than anything, and after a few days, had his self-repair program beginning to work.

Henri and Joe went to their homes late in the evenings, but were back every morning to help, if called upon, and Kurege often helped them to tend their ships, and mend the fishing equipment, which was always in need of repair. Kurege was especially interested in the mechanical devices, like the wenches and the hoist, and most especially in the diesel and gasoline engines on the boat and generators, and in various stages of repair and disrepair around the inside of the processing shed. It was not many days until he had the hang of the way they worked. Uris and he had never seen this type of engine, and they were fascinated with the automobile. It was not many days before they wanted to try to drive one, and Danielle let them get behind the wheel and drive them around the lot but cautioned them not to get outside the compound. She made it clear with the paper notice that they were being sought.

This made Kurege apprehensive, as he could easily understand that the government of this world might not be friendly to them. He still thought of himself as a fugitive from Pandamon. Uris, however, reasoned that making contact with the authorities might be of benefit. They talked it over until late into the night on several occasions, Uris taking the position that they would have to seek the precious Helium III from a major source of political power. Kurege had a different feeling about this, and persuaded her to wait, especially when they came to understand the meaning of the notice, and that there was a federal prohibition on the association of citizens with beings from other planets. This was puzzling to them, but so were many things that they were seeing. Caution, until they knew more about the society, they found themselves in, seemed the prudent action.

It could all wait, and they were learning every day. Uris slept and had a room in the upstairs bedroom, and she loved the view and the experience of this life, free of the responsibilities of her place in the government of her planet. When she thought of it, it grieved her not to be with her people in this time of need, but she accepted the reality of the crash, and she was freer than she had ever been, and she liked being with Kurege. He kept a respectful distance, but the intimacy that developed between them was obvious to the Usays, and to Joe Le Blanc. They watched the interaction with amusement and could see that these two were falling in love. Kurege was so solicitous of Uris, that it was obvious from the beginning to the three of them. But occasionally, an argument would break out over something that Kurege said and Uris would stomp off to her room to be alone, and Kurege would look baffled at whoever was there to witness these outbreaks. He kept his distance and camped out on the sofa in the living room, the last to bed and the first one up every morning before daylight. He had developed a taste for the bitter coffee, and had it waiting each morning, and would be sitting on the back porch when Joe and Henri arrived.

Danielle took extended leave from the school, and since she had never missed a day before in twelve years, she had months of time coming. She was teaching every day to Kurege, who drank up the language lessons with an almost unquenchable thirst. And when Danielle showed him the Internet, he was on it most of the day, so that Uris complained to him that she could use a little help cleaning up the ship. He would reluctantly leave the computer, and come out to the processing shed, and then sneak away to be found at the computer again.

One day he came out to the Pearl to find her and was very excited.

"I have found my mother," he exclaimed.

"What is this," Uris asked?

"I have found her name and address in the state of Kansas, and I have found articles written about my abduction," he told her. "I can't understand it all, but I can read a little of it, and I know that it is her, and there are articles about me, and a picture of me, as an infant."

He motioned for Uris to follow him into the house and noticed that she stumbled in climbing out of the hatch of the Pearl, and there was a slight tremor in her hands as she reached to catch herself. He took a good close look at her and noticed that she was beginning to take on a bluish tinge to her color.

"Uris, what is wrong with you," he asked?

"I am feeling tired. It may be that this atmosphere is slightly lacking in the Xenon that is in the air of the home world. It has become a necessary component of the air that our House must breathe, and although I can go without it for some time, eventually, I am going to need to find a source for this element. This planet must have some, or I would have been sick very quickly. But it is evidently not quite high enough in content to satisfy my metabolism.

"Perhaps, now that I have learned to use the Internet, there will be a way to solve this problem," he tried to assure her, as he reached out and steadied her. She let him help her, as she was suddenly feeling weak.

After he had shown her the articles about himself, which were only a couple, he tried to search for the gas that she needed. With only a limited knowledge of the language, and no knowledge of technical words, he was frustrated at every turn and was soon at a loss to know what to try next.

"Kurege," Uris asked? I am needing to get away from just sitting at this house. "Could we just take the car and drive around a little? Do you think that we could manage that?"

"I don't know why not. It seems pretty easy to do with the automatic transmission," he said using the English words for it, as their language had no such words in it.

"Can we just slip away for a little while," she pleaded with her eyes, and she touched his arm.

"They won't like us just leaving," he said thoughtfully.

"We won't go far," she stroked his arm, "we'll be back before they know it."

He got the keys to the car from the rack where they stayed, and like the teenagers that they were, they slipped out the door, and closing the door to the car very quietly, started up, and with butterflies in their stomachs, backed out the driveway.

Kurege drove slowly down residential streets, but kept the waterfront in sight, and made his way some miles South. Turning off on a small road, they wound along the river until the road narrowed down to a dirt path and then got out and walked hand in hand to the water's edge, and stood for a long, long time, just letting Uris get her breath. He was not going to break this magic spell, and finally when she turned and looked into his eyes, he bent and kissed her, and she did not stop him. But, when he tried to kiss her again, she stopped him.

"We need to go back," she said, and pleased with the breakthrough in their relationship, he nodded, and they headed back to the car, arm in arm, and drove back to the house.

When they pulled into the drive, there were two brown cars with whip antennas. One was in front of the house and the other was pulled all the way back toward the processing shed. They got out and walked cautiously to the small door on the end and looked in.

There were several men inside, and Henri, Danielle, and Joe were in handcuffs on the floor. A man in a suit had Uriah's data box in his hand at the workbench on the side, where Uris had been cleaning on it earlier in the day, and he was examining the connections and turning the box over to examine the bottom. Three other men were standing over the Usays, two with guns on their hips, and one holding a gun at the ready, pointed at Joe Le Blanc. Another man, who Uris and Kurege knew as Etienne, was standing near the man at the bench. The man at the bench pulled out a walkie talkie and punched the send button.

"We've got it, close in," he said.

Joe Le Blanc was very red in the face, and he yelled at Etienne, "You damn Judas, you pay for this, you be sure." The man nearest him gave him a savage kick in the side. Uris had seen enough, and she quickly and deftly drew her knife and set the handle.

She opened the door wide, and stepping into the opening, cut the man holding Uriah's data box in half, just above the waist. A look of utter surprise crossed his face, and he had time to smell the sizzling flesh, and see himself fall into two pieces, before the blood pressure dropped and he was instantly dead. The man who had kicked Joe Le Blanc had his gun at the ready, and he turned and fired, striking the door frame beside Uris, who stood her ground. It was his last move, as she cut him in half, and Etienne, who was standing beside him, lost part of an arm, with a hand attached. Uris had been careful not to hit the Pearl behind them. Danielle screamed and shut her eyes. Joe and Henri looked up from the floor with eyes as big as saucers. The other two men ducked behind the Pearl, and she could not get at them.

Kurege sized up the situation in a moment, seized Uris and began dragging her toward the car. He realized that re-enforcements would be arriving at any moment, and that they would be caught in a crossfire that they could not escape from. Uris gave him a fierce look, but came with him, and by the time he put her in the car, she was going limp. He backed out and tore off down the street, and as he made the first turn, he saw another brown car drive up to the house.

Kurege kept winding slowly through the streets, changing directions, but driving with the other traffic, and not attracting attention. When he looked over at Uris, she was very blue.

"I'm not feeling very well," she told him.

Jacob Martin was on top of the world, not literally, but that is where he had come from. His ride into space was the biggest news story in twenty years, and he was sitting in the catbird seat.

He opened his apartment door. The mail had stacked up high. It had been more than a month. He dragged his suitcase in. He needed a bath, a shave, and some sleep, to get over the jet lag. The debriefing had gone on for days, meantime, he was being scooped from his own story. He walked over the mail, threw his suitcase on the bed and began to unpack. He turned the hot water on to let it warm up the bathroom and turned on the heat lamp and adjusted the thermostat. He took off his wristwatch and threw his billfold and change on the dresser, while the phone recorder played on and on. Looked like there were going to be magazines pursuing him for once. His luck had definitely taken a turn for the better.

He turned the recorder's sound up as loud as it would go and let it run. It was mostly magazine contacts and advertisers, sprinkled liberally with insurance companies. He heard one from an Amy Hodge. It didn't ring a bell, but there was something familiar about the voice. He rewound the recorder to that message and listened to it a second time.

"Mr. Martin," the middle-aged voice began, "you probably don't remember me, but some year ago, you were very kind in helping me get some media exposure for my kidnapped baby, Michael Hodge. Please call me," she left a return phone number.

There were three such messages, each a little more insistent until the end of the tape. He puzzled over it a moment and made a note to call her back. Frankly, with this new cryogenic stuff, and the story he was going to do on the Pathfinder Project, he felt he probably wouldn't, in reality, get back to making the call. He had just got dressed when the phone rang. He started to just let the machine catch it, and then, with a heavy sigh, he picked it up.

"Hello."

"Jacob Martin," the middle-aged female voice on the other end, inquired?

"Yes."

"Oh, thank God, I have gotten you at last, Mr. Martin. I've tried over and over."

"How can I help you?" He thought he recognized the voice.

"This is Amy Hodge, mother of Michael Hodge."

"Yes, Mrs. Hodge," he remembered her more and more, with the recording to jog his memory. "How are you doing?"

"I'm fine Mr. Martin. It's just that I don't know very many people, and I need some help again."

"Well, I'm glad to help you, if I can. Did you ever have any luck in your search for your son?" He was afraid to ask, but it was a logical question, plus the way she answered it, would tell him a lot about her state of mind.

"That's what I called you about Mr. Martin."

"Call me Jay," he said. "I'm less formal these days."

"All right, Mr. Martin. It's just that my son has come home."

"Wonderful, Mrs. Hodge."

"No. You don't understand. He claims he was kidnapped by men from outer space."

"Oh, I'm sorry," he paused and thought. "Mrs. Hodge, there are some unscrupulous, and conniving people who take advantage of an unfortunate situation and try to bilk people of their resources. Be careful."

"No. No," she cut him off. "Oh, dear me, this is coming out all wrong. You misunderstand. It is my son. I am totally sure of it. We have plenty of visible proof."

"Oh, I'm terribly sorry. Perhaps counseling. How has he become disturbed?"

"No, you still don't understand. He is not mentally disturbed, and well, there is this woman with him, and, well, she is different. I need to see you to explain it. I can't explain it over the phone. You were the only one I could count on."

He was such a sucker for a sob story. This was crazy through and through. He didn't have time for this nonsense. He was tempted to be scornful and get rid of her by being rude.

"I can't break loose here. You will have to come and see me," he heard himself saying.

"The woman is ill, but somehow, Jay, we will get there."

"When will I expect you, Amy?"

"We will have to come by car from Kansas, and it will take a day and a half on the road."

They said goodbye and rang off. He shook his head and scratched an imaginary itch on the back of his neck. Life was getting hectic. If things went any faster, he was going to get dizzy.

Jay buried himself with incidentals. The recorder drowned on. "Jay, your printing bill is overdue on your last vanity printing. How about some money, honey. Morty, in case you don't know." A kissing sound. Disgusting. He would have to make a payment to keep from experiencing that call again. "Mr. Martin, this is the condo committee. You must keep your grass mowed and you must repaint your house to match the new color scheme."

"Shit on that," he had a story to write. Now, if he could get it done before the electricity got turned off.

Martin was too busy with his story on the Pathfinder system operations. Amy Hodge was the last thing on his mind. His doorbell rang two days later. He looked through the peep hole and recognized Amy's face. It had grown matronly somewhat over the years. Although not a bad looking woman, he thought.

"Amy," he greeted her warmly. "It's good to see....," he stopped. What he saw now made him stop mid-sentence. "What the Sam Hill!" He exclaimed.

Uris face stared at him out from under the cowling of the hooded coat she was wearing, pale blue from the lack of atmospheric Xenon. She was waning, ethereal, and weak.

"May we come in Mr. Martin, Jay," Amy stammered.

"Yes, certainly. Come in," he let them go by him and then checked the entrance porch to see if anyone had seen them come. He closed the door and led them into the living room. They laid Uris on the couch.

"What's wrong with her," he asked?

"We don't know for sure. Something is lacking in the atmosphere."

"Atmosphere? Wait a minute, on the phone, you weren't kidding. You think this girl is from outer space?"

"Look at her."

"She looks a little blue."

"She doesn't look strange to you?"

"All the kids look strange these days. No. She doesn't look any stranger than the kids from anywhere in the USA. Look, I'm sorry, but this does seem like a fantastic story." He sized them up. The girl was unconscious; she could be on drugs.

"Jay," Amy stepped forward, "this is my son Michael Hodge."

Kurege stepped forward to Jay and took his hand. His mother had him practice the introduction. "Pleased to meet you sir." His accent sounded like a German native, who was just beginning to be taught English by a Cajun school Marm.

"You might as well know right now that I am suspicious of you."

"Jay, it is my son's fingerprints from the birth certificate. It is Michael."

"Yes, but kidnapped by people from outer space?"

"I can't make out the whole story, yet" Amy filled him in as best she could, "but evidently, my son Michael was kidnapped and taken from earth. He can't speak English good enough that I can make this all out, but evidently, he found his records on computer. That is how he knew about me and came to find me. The beings who kidnapped him kept a record on me."

"Please, sit down and take your time."

"Yes," they sat down in the kitchen, and Jay put some water on to boil for tea.

Kurege was concerned about Uris and stayed near her, standing between the conversation that was developing in the kitchen and Uris stricken form on the couch.

"The child is sick. She is known as Uris. She saved my son and brought him back to me," she looked lovingly at the unconscious girl. She must have a special component in the air she breathes, or she begins to smother."

"Why don't you get her to a doctor?"

"From what my son Michael, who calls himself Kurege, tells me, they crashed in Louisiana some twenty days ago. The army saw their ship crash but said nothing to the public. But they are being hunted. The people who helped them when they crashed, didn't think the government finding them was going to do them any good."

"Probably right about that," Jay smiled.

"That's when Michael decided to seek me out. I was skeptical at first, like you, only I recognized him. He bears a striking resemblance to one of my daddy's brothers. It was like Uncle Jim was standing there. Anyway, I didn't turn them away, and when I checked his prints from his birth certificate, it was obvious."

"Is the government still after them?"

"We haven't had any trouble, but they must be. Michael told me that a ship recovered the spaceship that they came to earth in," she obviously believed him. "They recovered the craft before the military got to the crash site, and have it stored. But they were seen, and the military has been all over the area, searching. They told the local people that it was a meteor crash, as many people saw the light in the sky. But Uris and Michael had to leave. The authorities were getting zeroed in on their location. That's when they came to me. I checked out the story in the New Orleans Herald, for May sixth. It was written up as a meteor, but it doesn't prove anything. They are terrified of the authorities and won't let me take them to a doctor." Kurege had not told her about the fight at Danielle's warehouse.

"I don't know what I can do."

The girl had regained consciousness and was looking at him with sunken eyes. She was so unearthly looking. It was totally crazy, but he believed the story.

"Look, I just don't know how I can help."

"You were my last hope. I didn't know who else to turn to. I finally convinced Michael because I showed him the articles you wrote on his disappearance."

"Help us," Kurege grasped Jay's shoulder. They looked at each other.

"Well, there is one thing that I can think of, that is a possibility. I know this newsman out in Amarillo. He is really chummy with this far out industrialist. A sort of space cowboy. If anyone can help your sick friend, this man can, without the government getting wind of it."

"Call him," Amy pleaded.

Jay put through a call to his friend of slight acquaintance, Sid Porter, on the Lubbock Sun. He wasn't on the desk. They suggested that he try Sid at home, as Sid was on leave of absence. Fortunately, there was an S. M. Porter, with a listed phone. Jay dialed the number.

"Sid," he could feel his face flushing as he heard Porter's voice.

"Yes."

"It's Jacob Martin, Jay Martin."

"Who?"

"Jay Martin, you remember, in Dallas, at the Anatole, we talked philosophy and politics at the piano bar. I'm the science article writer."

"Oh yeah," Sid rejoined, "the guy with the bee hives."

"That's me."

"What can I help you with Jay?"

"Well, this is going to sound off the wall, but simply put, I've got a space woman here in need of medical attention, and I can't take her to a local hospital."

"Space woman? What can I do for you Jay?" Sid thought he had a personal problem, but the word 'spacewoman' had startled him.

"You know that wealthy space industrialist, Stark Raven?"

"Yes, I do," Sid sat up.

"Well, I think he might help. The girl lacks something that she has in her atmosphere. Raven might be her best chance. Turning her over to the government would only get her vivisected."

"You're serious."

"I'm on the level. No prank, Sid, and time is very valuable. She is dying, and I think she might prove very important to us. We may need her."

With the events of the past few days, with the guard, Sam, and Sid was very receptive to this line of thinking. "I have a little space story I want to share with you too," Sid confided back."

"That so?"

"Yeah, about Pantex."

"Pantex?"

"Yeah. You know what Pantex is and does don't you?

I know you do. Well, the aliens are into there."

"No shit?"

"No shit!" Porter stood up. "I think we better not talk on the phone."

"Can you come here? They brought the girl, and she is very sick."

"Do you have more than one?"

"A young woman, and a young man crashed in a spaceship. The young man was kidnapped from earth nineteen years ago. He found his mother, and she turned to me because I had helped her with exposure to the case years earlier. Do you think Mr. Raven will help?"

"I know that he will. Give me your address and number. I will see what I can do."

"Hurry, the woman's life is ebbing away."

Porter hung up and tried to reach Stark.

"S. G. Raven Enterprise," the crisp voice came on.

"Mr. Raven please, Sid Porter calling."

"Mr. Raven is out of the office right now Mr. Porter. I can give him a message."

"It is extremely urgent that I reach him at once."

"He is in transit, but I'll try to relay a message and have him call you. He is in transit in the far East, and there has been only spotty cell phone coverage in the area."

"Thank you," Sid said, leaving it in her hands, which he knew he could do. The far East, bad news, he was half a world away building another telecommunications empire no doubt. There was nothing he could do but wait.

Sid waited through half the day for the return call. Waiting for the phone to ring drove him crazy. He talked with S. G. Raven Enterprises several times during the day. The girl at the other end was very apologetic, but Mr. Raven was in Sumatra, and the telecom link was breaking up for some reason.

He left instructions with them to keep trying but gave them Jacob Martin's phone number in Houston with instructions that he should be found at that number.

A haze hung over the city as he flew into Hobby. The Johnson space center was out his window as they circled for the approach. When he arrived in Houston he took a cab from the airport, and directed the cab down Interstate 6, and exited Westheimer. Long faces met him when he finally reached Jay's condominium, on the West side.

"Sid, thanks for helping," Jay met him at the door. They shook hands, and he led him into the troubled little group. "This is Amy Hodge," Jay introduced, "and her son Michael."

"Hello, Mr. Porter," Amy said.

Kurege took the hand that Sid offered him and shook it in the firm style he had learned from Joe Le Blanc, without saying a word.

"This is the spacewoman. Her name is Uris. She is evidently a queen in her own world. She is responsible for returning Michael, or Kurege, as he calls himself, to earth."

"A queen in any world," Sid observed, "and a mighty sick young lady."

Uris was very stricken. Her breathing was becoming labored, and she was blue as Kentucky in springtime.

"Is that coloring normal?"

"No. She has always had a faint bluish tint since I've known her," Amy spoke, "but not like this."

"By the way," Jay remembered, "you had a phone call from Stark Raven."

"Did he leave a message?"

"He said that calls were breaking up going to him, but he would call you again. We told him what time your flight would arrive, and he said that he would give you time to get here and then call back."

"Did he say where he was?"

"Yes, he's still in Sumatra," Jay's answer chagrined them both. He looked at his watch. He should call any time.

As if in response to a magic summons the phone rang. Jay answered it. "Sid, it's for you."

"Sid Porter," he said taking the phone. "Yes, S. G., good to hear you," he paused. "Yes, I can hear you fine." He spoke a little louder into the receiver. "Can you hear me now? Fine. Yes. O.K. You remember that situation that we've been discussing about the XIT problem. Yes. That's it exactly. No, nothing new to report on that aspect, but you know these funny critters we were talking about? Yes. I got one. Yes. As a matter of fact, I sort of got two of them, but Stark, the reason that I made an emergency call to you is one of the critters is sick. No. something she inhaled. That's right. She. More, probably, something she didn't inhale. That's right. Can you help us?"

There was a long pause, and when Sid hung up, he was all smiles. "He will be coming himself, as fast as he can, which, with his resources, is usually fast. Now if the little lady can just hang in there."

Kurege was very agitated. He was drawing something again on a paper and showing it to Amy and then to Jay.

"What's he got there," Sid asked.

"Damned if I know. He's been drawing things and showing us for two days. I'm sure that he is trying to tell us what is wrong with Uris, but I'm damned if I can figure it out."

Kurege had drawn a matrix of seven boxes down the left side and eighteen across the top and gestured to the box that was the last one in the fifth row. He would reemphasize the edges and then circled the last one in that same fifth row.

They passed the rest of the afternoon and part of the night puzzling over his doodling and watching Uris, helplessly.

It was nearly midnight when they heard the knock that they had been expecting. Jay answered the door and ushered Stark and another man carrying a black bag with him. He was distinguished looking, with white hair, tussled. He had obviously been taken out of bed.

Nobody said anything but turned their attention straight to the stricken form. The doctor, as he apparently was, listened for her heart with his stethoscope. A perplexed look crossed his face.

"She is evidently in heart arrest. I can get almost no heartbeat," he began to look through his bag.

Kurege was becoming very agitated, pacing at the edges and waving his papers of the doodles he had been doing all day. "Who's this," Stark asked? He took the papers from the distraught man.

"This is a man who came to earth with the spacewoman. Her name is Uris. The man, Kurege, was evidently kidnapped from earth as an infant. This is his mother Amy Hodge, who came to my friend Jay," Sid filled him in.

Stark examined the papers that he had taken from Kurege. "He is my son Michael," Amy added. Stark looked at her. She was exactly what she appeared. He could tell nothing about the young man. He was to upset to be judged. The doctor found the bottle he was looking for and filled a syringe.

Kurege eyes got very big at this and when the doctor moved to inject Uris, Kurege grabbed his hand. "Here, just a minute there," the doctor protested "Stark, she needs a stimulant."

"Hold on a second, Doc," Stark stopped him. "I've got an idea." He continued to study the doodles. Kurege, still holding the doctor's hand, pointed excitedly at the papers.

"Have you got a chemistry textbook in the house," Stark asked.

"Yes, I think so," Jay responded. I believe I still have a text from a college first year inorganic course."

"Perfect. Would you get it please," Stark asked him? "Hold on a minute Doc. That injection might not be a good idea."

"Something is going to have to happen fast, if you want to save her." He sealed the point of the needle and lay the syringe back in a box in his bag.

"Here's the book," Jay came back blowing the dust of the binding and top edge of the pages, where it had settled, undisturbed for years. "I haven't seen it in a long time. I went right to it."

"Great, thank you."

Kurege got up from beside Uris and stood beside Stark. He was pointing at his papers. Stark opened the cover of the chemistry book and then turned to the back cover. "Here it is."

Kurege became very excited and began pointing frantically at the fifth-row right hand column of the cover, which Stark had turned sideways.

"What is it?"

"It's a periodic chart of the elements," Stark informed them. "Did you say you thought something was lacking in the atmosphere?"

"Yes," Amy spoke up. "Michael keeps gesturing to the air."

"Xenon," Stark said. "That's what she is lacking."

"Say, Stark," Doc looked confused. "What's going on here?"

"I'll explain it to you later Doc," Stark hustled the doctor out the door with a few words to the chauffeur in the limousine, that had brought him. He came back quickly. "We don't need a doctor. We need a welding supply," he said to the group.

"A welding supply?"

"That's right. And a big one, with all the noble gases, nothing else will do," Stark laughed. It was inconsistent with the grim faced, worried countenances that looked back at him.

"Xenon," he said again. "We need Xenon, and I know where there is some, just a few minutes away."

"No welding supply will be open at this time of night," Jay reflected. "Not any retail suppliers anyway," Stark agreed with him. "Wrap the girl up and hurry. Follow me, but I can only take four of us. Me, the girl," he looked at Kurege's fiercely determined face, "looks like he will have to go and one more."

"You're not going without me," Jay spoke up.

"It's OK," Sid put in to Stark. "Just keep me informed S. G. I'll be right here."

"We'll let you now as soon as we can, now let's move." He scooped up Uris and carried her out the door with Kurege and Jay Martin in tow. Uris eyes were open and focused on Stark as he carried her down the stairs. Kurege took her from Stark when they reached the sidewalk.

Stark had parked a helicopter in the field behind the condos. The ground was wet and it was a sloppy mess. They got Kurege in with Uris, and then Jay climbed in the copilot seat next to Stark. "Where are we going," he yelled as Stark warmed up the engine?

"I've got a little cryogenics plant for LOX and other stuff here in Houston. We liquefy a little L. P. on contract, but mostly, we just freeze air."

"You have some Xenon there in small quantities for some reason?"

"No. It's a small, very small percentage of earth's atmosphere, so we get a little of it. When we get the helium, we get everything."

"Oh," Jay held on to his stomach, as they jumped off the field. The tracks in the mud came lose all at once and they swooped into the dark night.

It was almost two thirty, when the maintenance man was startled awake by voices in the building. He looked at his watch and jumped up off the couch in the back of the monitoring room. The big compressors had just turned off, and it was quiet until they would kick in again. The compressors pumped in giant amounts of air and compressed it to thousands of pounds per square inch, and then the air was cooled, until its various gases condensed out. It was a smooth way to make money. One operator tended the whole plant. He watched the dials and responded to any warning signals. During the day, trucks with seven cylindrical, insulated, tanks came and hauled the product in liquid form to more labor-intensive bottling operations.

"Who's there?" He called out. He was also responsible as security, but who would want to steal liquefied air?

"S. G. Raven, son. What is your name?"

Tim Miles had never met Stark Galileo Raven, but he knew who he was, of course. The corporation that

Miles worked for S. G. Raven Enterprises, was private, he knew that. That the main man would come visiting at two-thirty AM was too suspicious. "Hold it right there. I'm calling the police. How did you get in here?"

"Now hold on, son," Stark used his best voice. "I have a key to this place. I'm Stark Raven, and in the next few moments, you are either going to get promoted or fired."

Tim stared back at him and wondered if maybe this was some kind of test.

"Now son, you must have seen pictures of me?"

"Do I get a hint as to which way to jump," Tim tried to hedge his bets, as he was beginning to realize that the situation cut both ways, if this were some type of trial by fire.

"I'll tell you exactly. If you hit that alarm, you are fired. On the other hand, if you recognize the man you work for, and do exactly as I say, including discretion, you are going to get a raise in salary and a great big bonus, at the end of the year."

"I recognize you, Mr. Raven, my name is Tim Miles," the guard conceded. "It's just that you startled me, and it is the middle of the night."

"I know, but we've got a situation here."

"How can I help?"

"That's the attitude. Lead me to the Noble Gas section."

"This way," Tim lead down an aisle of cryostats. 'Warning-No Smoking-LOX' was stamped on the sides of the cryostat tanks, others had big red letters saying, 'Liquid Oxygen.' Next, they passed tank after tank marked 'Nitrogen'.

"Here. This is the Noble Gas section," he eyeballed Kurege with Uris in his arms. His eyes got very big, and a perplexed look settled on his face. Jay brought up the rear.

They walked briskly past the tanks. Helium, Argon, several rows of Argon, were walked by, and then on the end, two marked 'Neon', and two marked 'Krypton', and one small cryostat marked 'Xenon', and color-coded blue as Uris was. It was at the end, near a fire door leading outside.

"Tim, how can we get some Xenon loose in the building," Stark asked?

"You can't," he answered. "The building is designed to prevent that from happening. It has to flow into the trucks."

Stark knew that already. He had been in on that piece of thinking. His eyes looked around hastily. He was a big believer in immediate answers. He was committed to a 'make do' philosophy, which maintained that the answer came before the question, and was usually close at hand. His eyes often scratched this way and that when grappling with a problem. They focused on the 'exit' sign. It was a fire exit. "Where is the fire hose," he demanded.

"There is a water hose coiled in a box on the back wall," Tim pointed behind the cryostat.

Stark ran to the box. He found what he was looking for, the fire ax. An alarm began when he jerked the door open. It would bring the fire department, en mass, if not shut off in thirty seconds. "Tim, run reset that alarm," he said to him. Tim ran back to the control and monitoring booth.

Stark sized up the cryostat and took a couple of tentative chops. "The damn foam insulation is going to stop me from getting a good whack at the tank."

The alarm shut off. Tim came out on the ramp and started moving down the catwalk stairs.

"Son, stay there," Stark yelled at him. "Couldn't get through that tank anyway," he said to himself.

"What can we do," Jay asked?

Stark looked up at him, from where he had keeled, and examined the piping. He looked back toward Tim. "Dump the Xenon into the fill line, like there is a truck being filled, but don't open the fill valve to the truck," Stark yelled at Tim. "Get back a little and pray," he said to the three huddled around him.

Tim waved OK and disappeared back inside the control room. In a second, the hissing rush of liquid under pressure was heard in the myriads of pipes running from the tanks.

Stark traced one from the little Xenon tank and followed it to a spot where he could get some force against it. He stretched the ax up and tested his swing path. He chopped away the insulation that was covering the pipe and then hit it really hard. The ax glanced menacingly off the special low temperature, high chromium stainless steel. The building echoed with the blow.

"Stand back," he warned, worried the head would break off and fly into them. He came forward with another whack, and the pipe reverberated.

Whang!

Whang! Whang! Whang, he stressed the metal over and over again! He hit the pipe repeatedly with increasing strength and abandon. He tried to concentrate on hitting the exact same spot. He hit the pipe ten or twelve times and wondered if he could break it. The steel was very thick. He redoubled his strength and hit the pipe with all the force he had.

Whang! The building sang with the blow. He could feel his strength would ebb. He gave it one more try, trying to think through the pipe. He swung the ax with everything in him.

Blewey! The pipe exploded, sending the ax straight up and narrowly missing his head. He sprang back, but not before the liquid had sprayed all over him. He was frosted from head to foot. The liquid Xenon escaped from the rupture with a mighty rush, spreading vapor up from the liquid that pooled on the floor to effervesce into vapor almost instantly. The building was filled with the vapor.

Stark came to Jay and Kurege. He motioned Kurege to move her closer. He couldn't talk without cracking the skin on his face. His eyebrows, lashes, hair, and mustache were frosted white, and part of his mustache had been frozen and blown off by the force of the rupture, giving him a comical look.

"Don't crack a joke," Stark said between clenched teeth, without moving his lips. "I'll crack up."

Chapter Twenty-Two Tres Negras

The three black basaltic rocks thrust up from the sea in a breathtaking, and majestic way. The black backgrounded the green that clung in sparse but vibrant patches to the inhospitable and craggy slopes. The feel of tropical water was in the air.

Jacob held the tiller wheel. Uris and Kurege lounged forward on the gently undulating teak wood decking. Stark came up the hatch with drinks for everyone. The big ketch was a forty-four foot motor sailor with about four hundred square feet of sail out with twenty-five thousand pounds of displacement. She moved easily through the light seas.

"Beautiful, it's turned out just beautiful. Drink?"

"Thank you."

He took two glasses forward to Uris and Kurege. He came back to where Jay steered the boat. "She's nicely making way," Stark observed to him.

"She be yar, cap'in," Jay complimented. "It's good to get out. We've been under to much pressure. Although, your people have been wonderful."

"Well, it's just so important that she learn to speak to us as quickly as possible." Stark looked at Uris. She seemed to be enjoying the sun. She reached over and took a sip from the glass and then breathed from a mask leading to a little blue tank. After a few breaths, she put it down again.

"I haven't seen her since that night in the air plant. I spent some time in the hospital in aloe vera treatment for burn from frost bite. How is she doing?"

"The indications are very good, S. G." He had taken to calling Stark by his initials, like everyone at the Tres Negras complex. "She seems to be in good health,

176

and both of them are learning very fast. She seems to understand almost everything that is said to her. She is reading at a ninth-grade level and has a voracious appetite for science fiction and technical magazines, but she asks for endless explanations. Her teachers are busy. The man on the other hand, has taken to reading Romance Novels. I think he is love struck. I believe they both must be, but don't think they are mates. They don't object to separate sleeping quarters."

"She still looks a little blue, to me."

"That seems to be her natural color. She thinks she is perfectly all right and gives the medical people hell. I don't know much about her yet, but one thing I can tell you is that she is used to getting her way."

They were rounding the last of the three black rocks. A reef and island lay beyond it in a naturally protected anchorage. The concrete and dome like construction made it look like an old hippy commune, but the domes were pressure domes for submergence under the sea. The same design and fabrication was used on top side buildings. A giant warehouse assembly building stood in the center with tracks leading down to the other end of the island harbor, where several old Ariane I, II, and III's were in various stages of launch campaigns. One Ariane IV stood at the door of the giant assembly building. As they moved, it moved imperceptibly forward on its tracks.

"I guess your operation is going to be obsolete here with the new United States launcher."

"I'm sure we will be," Stark shrugged. "We can probably buy a launch from them cheaper than we can do it ourselves, even with this old surplus equipment that we bought from the European Company, Ariane." He paused and turned a winch a couple of notches, drawing the ship closer to the wind. "Prepare to tack," he called in warning, as the boom came across, and they made a tack across the front of the reef. "We will still have time to use up what we've got before they start selling time. Right now, the military has it all sewed up, not to mention other powers that be. The only way to ensure that it can be done is to be ready to do it for yourself. Otherwise, the doors have a nasty habit of getting closed. So, we'll probably maintain this facility."

"Listen, I can't tell you how much I appreciate you taking me on board like this."

"I figure that it is your story."

"It belongs to Sid, also. Have you heard from him?"

"That's where I came from last. After I recuperated, we had a pow wow. I set up some security bugging for the Pantex plant. We're going to use that guard, Sam, and see if we can find out what is going on inside there."

"Pantex, the nuclear assembly plant?"

"Yeah, it seems there is another group of aliens that are doing something inside the plant. Sid is doing some sleuthing around. We've been looking into the background of Reginald Tellur."

"Tellur? He was at the Pathfinder launch. Boy did he look sour. Nuclear is his big item, and he wasn't seeing much that pleased him."

Uris got up and moved to the railing. She looked at the launch facilities and the out-of-date rockets on the pad. "What ith thith," she lisped? She couldn't seem to get the s sound down.

"Those are rocket ships," Stark answered her. He moved closer. This would be a good chance to get acquainted. She looked at him.

"Ith thith you," she spread her hands?

"Yes," he nodded.

"I remember you," she said plainly and looked in his eyes.

"I doubt it," he said.

"You sa..saved me," she said intently. "You carried me."

"Yes."

"They didn't speak for a minute and looked out at the launchers. He squeezed her hand and she looked curiously at him.

"What ith," she demanded gesturing toward the launchers?

"Rockets for putting satellites in space," he told her.

"s...Pathe?"

"Yes," he made a fist with one hand and circled it with his other. He pointed up to the sky. "Sky," he said, "Beyond sky. Space." He took his pipe lighter and lit it pointing at the rocket ships and making a whooshing noise. "Rocket," he repeated. "Space."

Her eyes got big in disbelief. "You go pathe with fire," she asked incredulously?

"Yes," he nodded.

She got very tickled and moved back to her chair. She continued to find this fact amusing for quite some time. She confided in Kurege, who was looking at her perplexedly, and he joined her in merriment. They positively guffawed over the very idea of it. They gestured to the rockets and made whooshing sounds, imitating Stark, until they had tears of laughter in their eyes.

Stark couldn't see it was that funny and went back to talking to Jay. "I don't see it is that funny," he observed.

"Well, to them, it must be. From what I can understand about the way they move around. That brings up another point. Evidently, from what I can find out, the military recovered her space vehicle. They came looking for her in Louisiana."

"Louithianna," Uris chimed in.

"Would you like to see our space launch facility," Stark gestured toward the rockets on the pad."

"Yeth, thank you," she beamed back at him.

"I wonder if the military knows that she survived the crash."

"Yes," Kurege said firmly. He had been listening.

Jay and Stark hove the boat to and made for the cut in the reef. It would bring them inside the harbor. They made for a wharf between the aluminum domes of the housing, factory shops, and the large assembly building. They disembarked, and he led them along the gangway to the shore.

"This is the assembly building with an old surplus Arianne IV rocket in final stages of assembly and transfer to the launch pad."

Uris examined the whole rocket with wide eyed wonder. She walked into the giant exhaust nozzles and all around the giant rocket. "Men ride thith," she quizzed him, when she returned from her inspection?

"No, only payloads of materials. Men ride a bigger one. We don't do that here. We hire a government to do that for us, usually, the United States government." This obviously pricked her interest.

"Let me show you some of the small laboratories, where we assemble things for space."

"Who do you do thith for," she inquired? Kurege was walking along with them listening intently. Jay had gone off looking at the rocket.

"Hey," he yelled. He had to run to catch up with the other three.

"We might do this for a pharmaceutical company, a university, government, private enterprise. We make custom made apparatus for testing and experimenting in space."

"You do work for government?"

"Yes."

"What government?"

"Many. Mostly, the United States."

"United States government, bad government," she said emphatically.

"Why do you say that," he inquired?

"They hurt my friendth."

"Where?"

"In Louisiana."

"Is that where you crashed?"

"Yeth."

"And the government hurt the people who helped you?"

"Yeth," she was mad, all over again, thinking about it. "I kill them."

"You what!"

"I kill them."

"You shouldn't have done that."

"They hurt friendth, and they have my 'Pearl'," she said the name of her spacecraft in her own tongue, Stark did not understand.

"Huh?"

"The spacecraft, we came in," Kurege informed him.

"So, you killed a government agent, because they have your spaceship?"

"You have influence with government," she asked him?

"Not enough to do you any good."

"You do job for government, United States," she pursued it.

"It's not a matter of money. If you've killed someone," he let it hang.

"They might have killed me," she gestured with her thumb at herself.

"Yes, but it's still a sticky wicket."

"What ith thicky wicket?"

"It's a matter of principle of law."

"I am Government of my world," she said definitely.

"Yeah. I'm sure, only I don't think we have any diplomatic ties with your people."

"What do here," she changed the subject? She was frustrated because without the Pearl and Andro, she was practically helpless, and defenseless. She had only her knife with its blade of many forms.

"We manufacture equipment to do processing of drugs and medical experiments in the vacuum of space. This one is an experiment in genetic engineering."

"What genetic engineering," she looked puzzled?

"Us," Stark indicated, for a lack of a better way, pointing to himself, and making a figure eight with his fingers turned sideways. "Double helix."

Her look changed from puzzled to appalled, as he made himself understood. It brought up the image of Metastophiles to her mind. "This Metatophiles clone world," she fumbled with the word, and then she said the word 'clone' in her native tongue, and this was lost on Stark.

"Mephistopheles, now there is a legendary sounding name," Stark said. "What kind of world is it?"

"I no wordth," she shrugged.

Stark was intrigued. It brought up all the images that Sid had been talking about with the connection to the Chicago Boys, the XIT, the Pantex complex. It was big commitments, going way back to the roots of the government, and deeply entrenched interests in the current administration.

"Genetic engineering bad," Uris pointed at the experiments.

"We will cure sickness," Stark told her. "You don't understand."

"She thinks genetics here on Earth are being changed. She said 'clone world'," Kurege tried to explain.

"More," she impatiently overlooked the fact that Stark was arguing with her.

"I'll show you our wire drawing factory."

She was very interested in all the space factory construction. Especially the cryogenics section, where experiments in magnetism at low temperatures were going on. They spent much of the day in this way. Stark gathered that the vehicle she had come in was a cryogenic type of super gravitational field generator beyond anything he had ever dreamed of, and, apparently, the military of the United States had their hands on it. He would have to put out some feelers about that. A strange inching inside his skull told him that it should be discreetly done.

He led them to lunch in part of the Underwater City that had been built on contract, with taxpayer funds, for training and modular design studies for cities in space, and on the moon and Mars. When the project finished, it had become S. G. Enterprises' base of space operations. The whole thing had grown piece by piece from that first contract. Stark had started in unusual modern construction and building systems. It had been a natural place to start from, and he worked into the NASA subcontractors list in the early seventies. He went way back with them. Funny, he hadn't heard a word about the crash in Louisiana. He would have thought he would have heard.

Uris loved the city under the sea and attempts at deep communication were halted while they all got to know each other with a shared experience. The city reminded her of her home that was now shattered and gone.

Jay and Stark let the two young people explore, on their own, the tanks and aquariums of the undersea city. They had a chance to talk.

"What do you think," Stark asked him?

"About the girl," Jay asked him? "In what way?"

"Do you think she is being honest with us?"

"Yes, I do. I believe her story one hundred percent, and I can't tell you why."

"I can," Stark mused. "Because it fits. It's preposterous, but it rings true."

"She knows a lot of things that she could share with us."

"The military is going to be turning the country upside down, you would think."

"What is she running from?"

"This thing or creature, Metasomething or other."

"Metastophiles," Jay said. "Now, could that be the group in Pantex, or is a third group involved?"

"That is exactly what I intend to find out," Stark said.

"Obviously, I'm going to have to go back to the States."

"I might as well go with you. Until she has a wider command of the language, there isn't much else she can tell us."

"To much moving back and forth is going to gain attention we don't want," Stark observed.

"I've thought of that," Jay mused. "The people who got the ride on the cryo sled to the sky dome for me are counting on me to write some stuff for them. I've been sending in stories regularly, and I told my agent that I had gone to Tres Negras to check the down side of what the super magnetic launcher will do to some of the private companies, who have invested capital in space exploration."

"I suppose that is the best approach, but it will only work a limited number of times," Stark frowned. The circle was unavoidably growing. Things would naturally be harder to control. "I think I better put you on the payroll."

"Writers are just ad men," Jay smiled. "We don't get into conflict-of-interest problems." He raised his glass. "What do you want promoted boss."

"Think the military will see it that way?"

"Sure, I'll make it look good," he winked at Stark. "Put the proper demeanor on the demo."

"How well connected are you with the military," Stark inquired. It occurred to him that Jacob might be well placed.

"Not well. I've got one or two contacts."

"You must know someone to be on the first civilian launch?"

"I know one high place Navy engineer, that I went to college with."

"Is he well placed?"

"What do you think? He's inside the Mountain."

"I'll tell you why I ask," Stark confided. "I am not hearing anything from any sources on the crash of an unidentified flying object, like they claim to have come in to earth. My sources are usually good. Sid is one of the best. He's into every civic organization in West Texas, and he's a veteran. That, and being networked with the retirement crowd, makes him one of the best-connected men in grass roots America. Everybody owes him. He is checking out a few things right now. He originally brought me into this about three months ago when he ran into a guard from the Pantex Nuclear Assembly Plant, that had a very strange story. That's why he knew to call me in, when the girl and boy showed up."

"What do you think of them as a pair?"

"Do I think they are a pair?"

"Yes."

"Probably, but they seem to be in the early stages with a few problems to overcome. That's another reason that I want to see them left alone. They are special people.

They have survived and that makes them special. The human race needs that more all the time."

"That's the way I read it. So far they are maintaining separate quarters."

"Before we get sidetracked, I wish you would go to the States and do what you must, but put out some discrete inquires to your friend and the military, then come back to Tres Negras and help me gain Uris' confidence and understanding. She must be willing to share with us, and I need to know what she meant by saying that this is a 'clone world.'"

"That did bring to mind strange images."

Uris and Kurege returned laughing and talking.

"You have wonderful world," she laughed. "Many fithh."

They all laughed heartily. The day had been a delight to them all.

"You look cute, in your little blue suit," Sid shook his hand.

"Do I look the part," Stark asked?

"The picture of a red neck, West Texas, good ol'boy," Sid laughed. "A policeman friend of Sam's is going to join us. Have you got the I.D.s?"

"No problem," Stark produced the plastic electromagnetic strip tape from his pocket. "One of my subsidiary companies produced the system for the government." It was getting on toward ten o'clock, as they waited in front of Sid's house.

Sam Keogh, the Pantex security guard, and Sheriff Jim Knowles drove up in Sam's car. Stark and Sid went out and got in the car with them. All four men were dressed in alike uniforms.

"Sid introduced Stark to Jim and Sam. Civilities were clipped, as they got right down to business.

"Got the magnetic I.D.s," Sam asked?

"I got," Sid confirmed.

"Good," he started up. "Now that will get us all in the front gate, but it won't get you three into the high security containment building that we're going into. I'll have to watch for an opportunity, and open this door," he reached in his pocket and handed then a slip of paper each. "I made copies of the map for each of you." He turned the car dome light on so they could study the map as they went.

"Is this the outer wall," Stark pointed to an exit door.

"Yes, that's the exit door that can be opened," Sam said. "No one is supposed to be in that part of the building, and I don't check in but once an hour. It should be easy."

"A quick in and out," Sid said hopefully.

"We're all crazy. I guess you know that," Jim said skeptically.

"No, we're not," Sid bellowed at him. There is starting to be a good body of corroborating information," Sid rebuffed him.

"Now take it easy, boys," Stark tried to calm them down.

"I guess I'm overreacting," Sid admitted. "But the strange connections I've been coming up with, concerning the Chicago Banks that funded the Pantex complex, show some strange ties. Now we got a new mystery," Sid complained. "These same corporations out of Switzerland and Chicago also tie into some strange pharmaceutical firms that are in the hormone business."

"That's big business," Stark agreed. "All those pregnant horses furnishing piss so women can get control of their bodies. Weird business."

"What is he talking about," Jim asked?

"The hormone business," Stark informed him. One of the biggest businesses going."

"Now," Sid continued, "we've come up with a weird connection. These same pharmaceutical companies keep showing up as the owners of holding companies that are into abortion clinics."

"You suspect a connection," Stark asked? "It seems like a strange business for them to be into."

"Not when you think about it," Sid corrected him.

"The extraction of chemicals is their business."

"Oh, gross," Jim winced. "Now, not only are little green men after our plutonium, but they're collecting fetuses. Ugh. What am I doing here?"

"Shut up, you guys. We're coming to the gate," Sam cautioned them.

"Jim it's worth looking around, don't you think?"

"I guess so. I'm here, ain't I. If we get caught, they're gonna shoot us."

"Probably."

"Give me those cards," Sam reached his hand over the seat. He followed a line of cars into the entrance leading to the main gate where the security stations were with their armed guard in sight. He spoke cordially to the security woman who took his card. They knew each other and exchanged pleasantries, while she passed the card's magnetic strip through the machine. She did her job by looking the men over and matching the pictures. They got the go ahead and were in the first level of security.

Sam pulled into the guard parking and found a slot. People were coming and going with a change in work shift.

"I'm going in now. You three make for over there and around the building to the spot on the map. Just act like you're talking and when you find a clear spot, just disappear into the shadows. It'll take me fifteen, maybe twenty minutes or longer. Just hide by the trash barrels at the loading dock, and I will open the door, just wait," he emphasized 'will'. Sam got out with a 'good luck' all around. The other three men got out behind him and slowly separated and moved off talking.

Getting to the loading dock door proved to be the easy part. It was fifty minutes before Sam opened it and called. "Jim," he said. "You guys there," in a whisper?

"Yeah," Jim led them in. "We were just about frozen," he complained. "Where the hell were you?"

They crouched down just inside the door and the building felt warm to them after being outside.

"Bad luck, a security meeting, nothing I could do," he hastily explained. "You men ready to move?"

"Sooner the better," Stark encouraged him to lead on.

"I've been up the pipe a couple of times since the original time," he explained as he led them to the duct entrance. "There is a filter grill inside about ten yards farther than the room I heard Tellur in. It has a filter grill in it so we can get in."

Sam squeezed into the intake duct and crawled, followed by Jim and Sid with Stark bringing up the rear. They crawled for several minutes and then stopped. They were stopped and cramped while Sam unscrewed the retaining screws from the tenement nuts that held the grill front and filter in place. Stark was tempted to speak, but no one said anything. Finally, they were able to crawl out. The flashlights revealed them to be in a small conference room.

"Where are we," Stark asked?

"According to the building specs that I've seen," Sam told them, "This is outside the sub-basement. There should be no building here."

"Sid, see where that door leads," Stark took command, as he was in the habit of doing.

Sid cracked the door and took a look. "It's a long hallway in both directions," he told them in subdued voice.

"I want to check the room next to this one, that I overheard the conversation in," Sam put in.

"That's as good a place to start as any," Stark agreed

"We'll need some scouting, Sid and I will take the hallway," Jim said.

Jim and Sid slipped out of the door and took opposite direction down the hallway. Light filtered in from both directions from an unrevealed source. They slipped along the wall back along a paralleled course to the duct work they had come in.

They found the room next door had a lock in the knob. Stark held the light close to the door while Sam, who was skilled with a lock pick, went to work. He worked several minutes without success. The noise of footfall stopped them.

They held their breath as Sid and Jim materialized out of the dimness from the direction of the room they had first come into.

"Both hallways lead to a larger chamber in a rectangular fashion," Sid told them both.

"The halls emerge onto a catwalk about thirty feet off the floor," Jim added. They were both out of breath.

"There are hooded figures in what looks to be some sort of shielding, perhaps radiation clothing, moving on the floor of the chamber. There is some sort of train that is parked at the entrance to a tunnel leading out the rear of the chamber."

"Let's all take a look," Stark suggested.

They crept back to the catwalk and positioned themselves where they could see the activity below without being seen. They watched the radiation shielded figures moving crates from the floor of the chamber into a waiting conveyance that looked like a mining train of small flat cars hooked together. The cars were almost full of crates and as they watched one of the hooded figures stopped another and gestured toward the lurking men. For a moment, they thought they had been seen, but after a small discussion the two figures broke away from the others and came leisurely toward them.

"Two of them are coming toward us," Stark motioned them to follow him. "We better go back to the entrance." They made their way quickly back to the room they had entered through. They were just slipping inside when the lights came up and they heard steps coming down the hall. They held their breath as the steps passed them by. The sound stopped, and they heard the door of the room next door being opened.

Jim pulled a thumper, rawhide covered lead, out of his pocket and patted it gently in his hand. Stark nodded approval and quietly opened the door. They crept to the door of the adjoining room. It was ajar and the two technicians were bending over something they were taking out of what appeared to be a freezer. Smokey frost was boiling up from it. They had their backs to Stark and Jim.

Jim slipped through the door and thumped the nearest one. A crack was heard like an eggshell splitting and the form went down. The other hooded figure turned to see what was happening and Stark slammed his fist into the cowling. The creature howled as the protective covering flew off revealing an antlike head, with shiny black orbs on either side. It grabbed Stark and flung him against the far wall like so much spaghetti. He must not have been done, he thought, as he figured that he had hit the wall hard enough to stick. Jim grabbed up a heavy glass rod and shattered it against the creature's skull, cracking it open with a sickening sound. Green oozed out.

"W-What the H-Hell," he stammered. He went to Stark to help him up. The other two men flew into the room.

"My God," Sid said. "What in Christ's name are they?"

"Strong," Stark said shaking his wrist to get some feeling back in it. "Very strong, is what they are."

He took Jim's hand and pulled himself up off the floor and checked himself over. He still seemed to be all working.

"Better watch the hallway," Sid motioned to Sam, who took a look at the creatures and made a disgusted noise as he left the room.

The other three gathered around the lifeless bodies and gawked in disbelief.

"I'll be the son of a female dog," Jim said, his mouth hanging open. Sid began to peruse the room. He went over to the freezer the two ectomorphs had been bending over. Using a towel, he picked up one of the vials and looked closely at it.

Stark, still rubbing his arm, came over to the body that Jim was looking at. Its skull was crushed. It was dead, the vital fluid leaking in spurts, the creatures' heart pumping erratically.

"What are they," Jim asked soto voice to himself as much as to Stark?

"I don't know. Some kind of ectomorphic creatures."

"What is that?"

"Look how the skeletal structure is on the outside of the body. The tissue underneath is muscle and soft tissue."

"They look like ants," Jim moaned. "They make my skin crawl."

"Stark," Sid called softly. "Look at this."

He held the vial of greenish fluid up to the light.

"What is it," Stark stood up and reached out.

"Careful," Sid cautioned, "it will burn you. It's in the cryogenic temperature range."

Stark carefully took the towel that Sid had wrapped it in and carefully exposed the vial to the light. It took on an ethereal glow.

"There are some papers here in a hieroglyphic form of writing that's no earth script I've ever seen."

"I think it's safe to assume that we have extraterrestrials running around here," Stark said facetiously.

"I've seen some big red ants in West Texas," Jim said still staring in disbelief at the creatures, "but these two take away the whole picnic."

"There is one thing I can recognize," he thrust the papers in front of Stark's face. "See anything familiar." Stark looked where Sid indicated.

"That looks like genetic coding."

"I just happen to know," Sid pointed, "see, TAAGAC, that's human genetic coding. This extra part I don't understand, but that part is the scientific notation for double helix human genetic typing."

"These two are going to be missed," Stark was beginning to get his wits back. He stuck his head in the hallway. He couldn't see anything. "We need to see if we can get out of here."

Sid closed the freezer lid to stop the icy fog from filling the room. "I'm going to take that creature's head. That should give us the evidence that we need."

"Unless the rest of the evidence disappears before we can get back."

"Assuming we can get out of here," Jim said.

"Scared," Stark asked?

"Shitless, aren't you?"

"I was 'till I hit the wall. Now I got too much adrenalin going."

Sid was decapitating the creature with the head that was most undamaged. Sam came back in.

"Ugh, god, what are you doing?" Sam was disgusted.

"He's getting us some proof," Stark told him. "What's going on out there?"

"Nothing. They finished loading the tram, and they seem to be waiting for these two to come back."

"That's it. They came up here last thing to get this stuff."

"What's that?"

"We don't know for sure."

"Well, what do you think it is," Sam scratched his head?

"You don't even want to know what our guess is."

"That bad?"

"That bad!"

"One thing for sure. Our low profile mission is scrap. They're sure as hell gonna know we've been here," Sam looked at the carnage spread out over the floor, and the spreading green ooze under the knife work Sid was busy doing.

"Sid, you need to get on out of the plant," Stark said. "They won't wait patiently forever out there."

"Aren't you coming," he looked puzzled.

"We need time," Stark looked out the door. "If they tie in with the human security, and they must somewhere, we'll never make it out of the gate before we are eliminated."

"What are you going to do?"

"I need someone to come with me. Sam has to come out with you Sid or you can't get out of here. Jim, can I count on you?"

"What you got in mind?"

"Maybe dying, but it's the only way to ensure that Sid and Sam get out of the plant."

"I was afraid you were going to say that."

"Are you with me?"

"After what I've seen here tonight, I'm with you," Jim affirmed strongly. "What have you got planned."

"Strip the radiation suits off these two and get into one," Stark checked the automatic pistol tucked in his belt. He started quickly into one of the suits, after cleaning it up the best he could.

Sid got the head wrapped in a towel they had found on a shelf and got the two dressed. They separated and wished each other 'good luck'.

Stark and Jim waited as long as they dared.

"We'll try to deliver this stuff and then back away," Stark said.

Their hearts were pounding as they approached the catwalk. One of the figures was almost to the bottom of the ladder and made a disgruntled sound and motioned them to hurry it up and come on. Jim was close behind. Stark could hear himself breathing. He tried to control himself. He held a box of vials out in front of him. Jim carried another one.

The rest of the creatures had loaded themselves in the front of the tram with the flat bed cars behind them, loaded with plutonium in thick lead shielding. There were no seats up front. Two seats were vacant at the back of the last car. When Stark and Jim tried to leave the vials and back away, the two guards in that car came to attention with their weapons at the ready. There was nothing that they could do but just sit down in the seats.

The tram rose slowly off the floor and accelerated into the tunnel. The acceleration was slow but went on for about three minutes until Stark estimated that they were doing about two hundred miles an hour through the dark tunnel. Lights along the way disappeared in a blur. He thought by way of his best guess, that they were headed North.

They traveled that way for a little over thirty minutes. Fortunately, the speed made talking impossible, and they weren't required anything by the two guards After what seemed a long time, the tram began to slow down. He didn't feel relieved. A wave of nausea swept over him, and he needed to urinate badly. The time had been long enough that the adrenaline had worn off, and a shock reaction was beginning to set in. He judged that Jim probably felt the same way. They turned and looked at each other.

They came into one end of a chamber carved out of solid rock. It was breathtaking, being a football field high and three long. It was well lit from sources high above and on the ground. The tram came to a stop. Their guards stood up and came to attention.

A column of creatures came marching up to the train without any radiation suits on although they had several different types of adornment. Stark suddenly got a giddy urge to laugh. He suppressed it knowing it would be his last laugh.

The guards with them on the rear tram car disembarked and joined the troop that had marched up. Stark and Jim stood up and stepped off the train. His legs were a little wobbly, but they supported him. Jim was in the same shape as he stepped onto the curb, he stumbled and bumped Stark, making him almost loose the box containing the vials. The ectomorph that seemed to be in control raised an appendage and started to strike Stark. He thought it was over, right there. The creature stopped just short of clobbering him and raved and ranted in incomprehensible sounds for several seconds, and then, motioned vehemently for them to join the parade.

They fell into the middle of the guard and the creatures closed ranks behind them, and then all around. They marched at a fast pace straight up the center of the complex. There were many, many ant-like creatures busy with tasks of loading, shipping, fueling, and doing maintenance on several types of space craft, and machinery that Stark could only guess at. They were marched up to about the center of the building and taken aboard the lowered ramp of a small spherical saucer about twenty meters across.

Most of the guard left them at the front of the ramp, parting suddenly to either side to let Stark and Jim through. When they hesitated the guards behind almost ran over them saying something harsh. They decided to keep moving into the ship. The two guards followed right behind them.

As they entered the ship to their left there seemed to be a control console and someone, not an ectomorph, but more humanoid looking, was making notes at a wall screen. He looked up at them as they entered but said nothing. Since there was a hallway to the right, Jim turned right and Stark followed his lead. The guards didn't object. They had gone a few steps around the curve of the ship until they were about halfway around it. They had passed several doors with markings on them.

"Look," Jim said very softly. Stark saw they were coming to a door with the same markings on it as the door on the room that the vials had come from. He opened it and walked in. Jim came in behind him. Lights came on as they walked into the room. The guards stayed outside, and they were alone.

"I've filled my boots with shit," Jim said.

"Really," Stark asked worried?

"No, but I'll bet they have an inch of sweat in them," Jim took his helmet off.

"There's a camera device in this room, you can bet," Stark said. "Better keep the helmet in place."

"Think they're watching us?"

"If they were, we'd be dead. I think we are couriers, and we better finish our job."

"The vials?"

"We need to get them in these freezers," he said, lifting the lid of one. His box just fit into a place made ready to receive it."

Jim placed his in one exactly like it on the other side of the tiny room.

"Now what?"

"I don't know. But we can't stay in here. I think with our job done we should try to leave."

"I'm one hundred percent thinking on that idea," Jim gladly acknowledged. Jim put his helmet back on.

"Ready," Stark asked?

"Ready," Jim opened the door. The guards were in place on either side of it. They stepped between them. The creatures said something functionary sounding and Stark mimicked it as best he could keeping it low and returning a type of salute. They beat a hasty retreat, trying to keep it somewhere between a march and a route, around the curve of the hallway, amid curious looks from the guards. Miraculously the guards stayed in place.

Jim and Stark creped to the hatchway. The guard was still in place. The technician was still working at the console. They had a better look at him now. He was short for a human. Elfish looking with bushy eyebrows, but he could be taken for human in a human environment. He did not look human in the glow from the console.

They crept back the way they had come, back up the hallway, testing doors as they went. They couldn't get the portals to open. The third one they tried prying on, suddenly opened to them and they hurried through into what was apparently the galley. On one side, a cabinet with a sliding door offered their only possibility of secreting themselves. They squeezed in. It made a tight fit. They both removed their hoods and listened intently.

"I think we're safe for the moment."

"We'll never get out of here," Jim croaked.

"Don't panic, we ain't dead yet," Stark persuaded himself as much as he did Jim. They began a careful review of their options. There weren't many, and as they went over them, they didn't like any of the possible plans they could come up with. Knowing that waiting was an option, also, there was little else they could do. Surely the others would leave Pantex at the end of Sam's shift. If they could only stay undetected, and the couriers they replaced and stuffed in the freezer would go on not found Sid and Sam might get away.

After a while they fell silent. The waiting became very long as Stark hadn't got to piss yet. He thought he would burst. It was then that he felt a slight vibration to the ship and heard a distinct snap, as if airtight hatches were closing.

In a few moments the unmistakable feel of acceleration pinned them to one side of the closet.

"Hell, we're airborne," Jim gulped.

"I think so," Stark agreed.

They were swayed first one way and another as the craft wove its way through the mountain range, in a low, slow, path. At a point far from ground radar installations, it picked up speed, and altitude. All sensation of motion ceased as the craft climbed quickly off the planet.

"I think we've stopped," Jim said.

"I don't think so," Stark disagreed. "I think we've gone on interior gravity as we picked up speed."

He guessed part of it. Soon, they tore into hyperspace, toward the first warp door on the long way around to Near Standard Xinor time, and a fourteen-year trip to another galaxy on the far side of the known Universe.

Chapter Twenty-Four DEFCOM 1

Getting out of the Pantex facility had gone smoothly for the two men. Sam had gone back to his rounds after letting Sid out the door. Sid had carried the head of the alien and hid at the loading dock until just before six o'clock when the shift changed. Then he mixed in with people, headed for the parking lot and arrived at the car about the same time as Sam, just as a pink sunrise was breaking in the Eastern sky.

"Any problems," Sid asked?

"Smooth as silk. How about you?"

"Let's go."

They headed out without more conversation, still anxious to get out of the complex. The guard just waved them through after entering their cards. All hell was going to break loose when they tallied.

"How long until they will find the discrepancy in the numbers," Sid asked Sam.

"It will probably first pop up in six hours at the end of this shift, then depending on how the supervisor handles it, he will go to a stage three alert at least. That's a search of the grounds. He could call stage two, which would shut down the city. Failing to resolve the incongruity of the in and out figures, they will have no choice but take it state and national within no more than twelve hours."

"Then these two rabbits better find a hole."

They were on the outskirts of Amarillo headed South, down highway two=eighty-seven toward Dallas, and on to Houston.

"Just keep on headed South."

"To Houston?"

"That's the way that I've got it figured," Sam nodded agreement. "Jay was going to Colorado Springs to

201

see his liaison and friend of his in the Navy, Bryan, but he should be back at his apartment in Houston by now."

They were coming to a convenience store on the edge of the city.

"Better gas up and grab a bite. Use your cell phone to call and check. But watch what you say, remember AI is listening. Make sure we aren't running to the wrong hole."

Jay was asleep when the phone rang. He came awake fast enough when he heard Sid's voice.

"You know who this is," Sid asked?

"Did you guys do it," Jay asked?

"In and out."

"Everything smooth?"

"Not exactly."

"Somebody hurt? Where is Stark?"

"I don't know. We got separated. I can't talk about it. I need to be on the road. Can we come stay with you?"

"Sure. Everything is clear here."

Sid hung up after telling him they were a good nine hours away.

Jay was feeling very anxious the rest of the day. He couldn't go back to sleep, and he started back on the cigarettes he had just managed to give up for three weeks. His anxiety progressed through the day until he thought he would pace a hole in the carpet. He progressed in nervousness until he was lighting one cigarette off the end of the last one feeling very guilty at his inability to control himself, when the door burst off its hinges.

"Put your hands up. Federal Agents," someone screamed at him.

He dropped the cigarette and placed his hands high in the air. He found himself immediately shoved face down into the floor on top of the lit cigarette. It was right by his nose, and he got accidentally pushed into it.

"Woa, Woa," he kept yelling at the collection of feet gathering around him like he was on a runaway horse. They pushed him even harder, pinning his hands behind, and pushing him into the cigarette, burning his face. They thought he was resisting, and pushed him all the harder into the rug, until the cigarette sizzled out on his face.

"AAAyhh," he screamed. They cuffed his arms and legs, like in a calf roping, and rolled him over. He was staring into the big bores of various forty-fives.

"Jacob Martin," someone said, "you have the right to remain silent, anything you say may be used against you. Do you understand," one of the men above him spoke like a litany. He nodded in shocked disbelief.

"What am I being charged with," he asked?

"Investigation and questioning in violation of the Sedition Act. Uncuff his legs and set him up. I think Mr. Martin is going to cooperate with us."

They took the cuffs off his legs and sat him in a chair. Some of the men began to search the apartment. They had already checked, with guns drawn, the rooms for other occupants.

One of the men talked on a walkie-talkie, and within moments more men entered the room. These men all had on suits.

"Yancey, you and Clark take the hall and watch the porch," the man said, who had read Jay his rights.

"OK Cap'in Harris," the men left the room closing the door. Harris came over to Jay and sat a chair down backwards in front of him. He sat down and folded his hands on the back of the chair in a non-nonchalant, non-threatening way.

"Martin, I need some answers to some questions. Now, you're going to be taken to the station and arraigned after we question you, but I need some answers now, and if you're smart, you'll co-operate."

"Sure, Captain Harris," Jay sure wanted to get along with these guys if he could. His brain was scratching, trying to figure what kind of trouble he was in. He didn't know any specifics of the Pantex operation. He assumed that they had come because of Uris and his recent conversations with Bryan. "Bryan could have just ask me to come in and talk with you guys."

"Bryan who," Harris asked? When Jay realized his mistake, he shut up. Harris took out a notebook and jotted in it.

"What are you looking for," Jay asked, not wanting to reveal more.

"Four men broke into the security of the United States Nuclear Weapons Assembly Plant, and we have reason to suspect that they may be headed here."

"I don't know a thing about that," Jay truthfully told him.

"Do you know S. G. Raven, Sidney Potter, Samuel Keogh, or Jim Knowles," Harris asked?

"I know the first two. I was with Mr. Raven last week on his island in the South Java Sea."

"What were you doing there?"

"Working on a technical article. That is how I make my living."

"When is the last time you saw any of these men," he asked?

"Last week," he said.

"Or, communicated with them?"

"Last week," he lied. He could kick himself for jumping to the wrong conclusion and possibly dragging Bryan into this.

A two-way radio crackled and a voice spoke. "Got company coming. Two men, one carrying a bag. Could be two of our boys, over."

Harris positioned everyone. They threw a gag on Jay with prepared tape and elastic. There was nothing he could do. Keogh and Potter walked right into it.

"Good evening, come on in," Harris answered the door. They were both caught off guard, and Harris' men in the hallway moved right in behind them and put cuffs on both.

"I'll take that," Harris took the bag. They detained the two men near the door and patted them down for weapons. Harris placed the bag on the center of the coffee table in front of the couch that Jay was sitting on. He had a good view.

"Bring that counter in here," Harris told one of the men. "Hey you two," he asked Sam and Sid, "have you got something hot here? Maybe some plutonium to sell to terrorist?"

"Why don't you take a look," Sam coaxed?

"Wise guy, huh," the Captain snorted. "If it's radioactive, you're sure stupid to be carrying it this way," he untied the bag. The man came back in the room with a small device in a black case. Harris turned it on and checked the outside of the bag Sid had been carrying.

"Not hot," he said relieved. "Now let's see what we got." He peeled back the plastic garbage sack Sid had bought at the convenience store, and then the towel. "Ugh, God, it's a severed head. Oh," he groaned disgusted. "Bring a light over here quick."

Even in the dim light Jay could see the head wasn't human. One of Harris men turned a bright flashlight on the head; the eyes came alive with an unearthly glow.

"Oh, God," Harris continued to groan. "They cut some....," he stopped short. "Hey, what the hell is this shit?"

He took the flashlight and shinned it on the severed head and rolled it over. He was stunned and his mouth worked for words as he looked up at the other men. He didn't have time to say anymore, as two of his own men opened up on the other four.

Harris caught a slug right between the eyes and fell over on the coffee table.

Jay tried to duck under the table, as the other three men, who were only injured in the first volley returned fire. Sid and Sam crouched down by the door as a war erupted in the twenty-by-twenty apartment. When the smoke cleared the police and federal agents had all shot one another. All that was left was mangled bodies in various stages of final shock and trauma. The war lasted less than ten seconds.

Jay tried to talk to the other two but the tape over his mouth made it impossible. He had to kneel down while Sid worked it off behind his back. They were working to find a handcuff key and just had a hand on one from Harris' pocket, when one of the men that had first opened fire regained enough consciousness to trip a packet he had in his pocket.

"Look out," Jay screamed and made for the door. He fumbled the knob behind his back, and they just fell through the portal when the apartment exploded in flames.

They were scorched by the blast and fell down the stairs. At the street a small war was going on, with everybody shooting at everybody else. They took a couple of close rounds and beat it back for the safety of the doorway of the apartment on the ground floor. It wouldn't be safe long, as the fire was rapidly spreading.

A car, plain brown with a small antenna, came whipping into the middle of the fray and slid to a stop. A door swung open and Bryan stuck his head out.

"Jay," he yelled, "come on." The three of them piled into the back seat and the car accelerated away.

"God, am I glad to see you," Jay beamed at him.

"What the hell is going on. We saw the trouble and the explosion just as we drove up and, in a minute, I saw you try to come out the front," he looked tired and worried. "I've been up all night."

"What are you doing here?"

"When I asked that question that you asked me to ask, I stirred up a hornet's nest. Looks like you're into a nest yourself."

"FBI, they said," Jay told him.

"Funniest operation I ever heard of. Looked more like a busted dope deal."

"They think I know something I don't," he said, as he fumbled and finally got Sid uncuffed, who took the key and worked Jay and Sam free. "Actually, these two know more about this than I. Sid, better meet my very best friend, Bryan. Bryan is the one I told you about in the Mountain. Bryan, this is Sid Porter, and I don't know his friend."

They were up the road putting distance between them and the fire.

"Jay, you know the situation that we discussed," Bryan asked. "This man with me is Dr. Ruben McAuley, and he is in charge of the investigation into the crash that you asked about."

"It's all right, Bryan, to talk. These people know about the space people."

"People," the Dr. asked? "Are there more than one?"

"Dr., you don't know the half of it," Jay told him.

"Neither do you, Jay," Sid informed him. Sam nodded the affirmative.

The guards were being very thorough this morning, as they searched the packages and checked identifications at the entrance to the Congressional Rotunda, but they hardly looked twice at the bushy eyebrows of the man who strode quickly and purposely by them. He passed through the security with hardly a nod. He entered the Congress and turned right up the stairs to the Senatorial offices.

Something about the intensity of his expression made people move aside. Two reporters fell into conversation in hushed tones as he passed. He turned into a doorway with the title "Senator Prickle" emblazoned on it in gold.

The secretary looked up with a smile as he came into the room, but the smile faded and she assumed a very businesslike air.

"Go right in, Sir, the Senator is expecting you," she said and then punching the intercom, she said, "Reginald Tellur is on his way in, Senator."

The bushy brows never acknowledged the secretary, but steadfastly looked ahead, betraying a familiarity with the office. He opened the inner door and stepped in.

Senator Prickle stepped around his desk and offered the man his hand. It was returned in a limp oriental fashion, with a look of disgust that was lost on the Senator, who was all obliging smiles.

"Good to see you this morning, Reginald," the Senator beamed. "I'm glad to make some time for you this morning, although, I'm afraid that I can't spare you much time. I'm meeting with the President at ten AM," he shrugged as if to say, 'nothing I can do about that'.

Tellur seated himself in the proffered chair and the Senator retreated to the sanctuary of his desk. 'It was always good to get some expensive hardwood between you and another powerful man', was Prickle's belief.

"This won't take much time, Senator," Tellur began. "I wanted to see you before you talked to the President and make sure you understood the implications of the situation."

"And what situation is that?"

"This penetration of the Pantex complex."

The Senator's face took on a look of surprise. "How do you know anything about that?"

"Senator, when it comes to Atomics, I am very well connected to fellow scientist and technicians. Little happens in that arena, that I am not very familiar with."

Tellur's accent sounded German, but suddenly the Senator thought it wasn't German at all. The strangest thought crossed his mind, as he studied the little gnome like man before him. He shook it off as totally absurd.

"Really, Dr. Tellur, I'm not at liberty to discuss this now. I know very little beyond the essential fact, that Pantex has been compromised. This is the very subject of the meeting with the President this morning."

"I realize this Senator, but still, I believe there are things that you should know."

"I'm always glad for your input into any situation Doctor," but he was frowning.

"Rumor has it, and I believe this one is accurate, that Stark Galileo Raven is the driving force behind the Pantex raid."

"Stark Raven," the Senator's frown deepened?

"Yes, and I believe that this man is insane."

"You don't have to tell me anything about S. G. Raven," the Senator shook his head, "I've had personal dealings with the man."

"Oh?" Now it was Tellur's turn to frown. "In what capacity was that, if I may ask?"

"It was in the opening days of Operation Sundrop," the Senator reflected. "In a funny way, he was responsible for the Sundrop idea."

"I am not surprised," the bushy brows knit deeper.

"He suggested that in order to keep Nuclear Terrorism from occurring with our nuclear waste, that it could be dropped into the Sun. I find it hard to believe that he has become involved in this Pantex business."

"Well, he is involved, my sources tell me."

"And what sources might that be?"

"Senator, they wouldn't be sources if I told you that. I have a few friends in The Company," Tellur side stepped the question. "The main thing to realize about this man is one: He is dangerously unpredictable, and two: If he has obtained fissionable material from Pantex, he has the capability of delivering it to any spot on the globe."

"Damn, that is right. I forgot about that. He has a space launch capability somewhere in Java, doesn't he?"

"That is correct. He has four old Ariane IV launchers and several of the smaller Ariane III launch vehicles at his compound in Tres Negras, three hundred miles South of Java."

"Damn, he as good as told me he was going to do this years ago."

"He did?"

"Yes. He rejected an offer to help us secure the surplus fissionable material. The morning, he suggested Sundrop, he told me then that nuclear waste would inevitably fall into the hands of private individuals. Little did I realize that he was talking about himself," the Senator shook his head in amazement.

"The man is insane," Tellur said again," and should not be underestimated. That is the message I wanted to bring to you this morning."

"I'm beginning to understand your concern, and I will pass this on to the President this morning."

"Thank you Senator." Tellur observed the civilities. When he left the Senator's office, his lips had a sinister curl to them.

The meeting with the President started right on time. Prickle was reassured that this was a top level meeting. Not only was there a full complement of cabinet officers, but the Joint Chiefs were present as well as the directors of the FBI, CIA, and Homeland Security chiefs and staff. Also, both party whips from both houses of

Congress of which Prickle was Senate whip. The Vice President was sitting to his right.

"Gentlemen," the President acknowledged, "let's get right to business. First, I want a situation report from the Bureau, and then we'll throw it open for discussion. Mr. Gavin, would you fill us all in?"

John Gavin, director of the Federal Bureau of Investigation, led off the discussion.

"Twenty-eight hours ago the Pantex complex in Amarillo Texas, which as you can see if you will follow the brief in the red folder, marked 'eyes only', was compromised. This was done with the help of a guard, Sam Keogh. Four men entered the Pantex complex at the ten o'clock guard change. At the six AM change, the next morning, a discrepancy with the in and out figures was noted by the computer, and an automatic yellow alert was triggered. It called for a search of the grounds. When this proved unsuccessful, the head of security fortunately did not wait to upgrade the alert. The FBI was brought into the situation at eight-thirty AM. We have prepared a list of possibles. A list is kept in preparation just in case, and the security contractor is, of course, a prime possibility. S. G. Raven Enterprises is the security system contractor of first resort. There were others. Totally, some three thousand men were put into the field in various places. A check of Raven's associates brought up some fifty people, twelve of which had been at his launch base at Tres Negras in the Java Sea. One of these men, Jacob Martin, a free-lance technical writer, had recently returned to Houston from Tres Negras, and six agents were dispatched to the Houston address.

Some three hours later, or roughly nine hours ago, the Houston Police informed the local FBI in Houston, that a gun battle had erupted at the apartment, and all six agents were dead," he paused for a moment and leafed through some papers. "The admittance guard who admitted them to the complex the night before has positively identified the four men as Raven, a close associate of Raven's, Sidney Porter, guard, Sam Keogh, and an Amarillo police officer Jim Knowles, Keogh and Porter were checked back through at the six o'clock change of guard. That is the situation as we know it," he finished and sat back in his chair.

"Thank you," the President said. "Any comments so far?" No one spoke. "I find it hard to believe that such a prominent industrialist would be involved. It doesn't make sense."

"Maybe it does, Mr. President," Senator Prickle interjected.

"How so?"

"Based on a conversation I had with Raven some years ago, when we wanted him to help us secure the plutonium waste. Looking back on it now, he practically told me he would do this, then."

"What gives you that impression?"

"He had a mystic sense of atomics. I don't know how to explain it, but he seemed certain that the government could not expect to maintain control of plutonium stockpiles. He said that Atomics belonged to private interest, and the government couldn't maintain security. He seemed gleeful, and now that I think about it, in the light of developments, I believe he was making a brag and threatening to do this then. The man is quite insane; I don't care how rich he is. Sometimes the two go hand in hand."

"What would be his purpose?"

"To have nuclear weapons. He is an ego maniac. He wouldn't necessarily have any other purpose, but it must be realized that he has the capabilities to take fissionable material and encapsulate it and rig a detonator. Also with his Ariane launch vehicles, he can deliver it to any point on the globe."

"This is true, Mr. President," the Air Force Chief added. "He has that capability. If he's gone insane.....," he didn't finish the thought.

"All right," the President spoke forcefully, "I want a satellite on top of his Tres Negras base, so we can see what is going on."

"Mr. President," the Air Force Chief spoke again, "we should upgrade our strategic status."

"To Defcom Three," the President spoke hesitantly?

"I don't think that is enough."

"Anything higher, and the Russians and Chinese are going to get really nervous."

"They'll have to be brought in," the general insisted. "We must assume that we have a 'Broken Arrow'," he emphasized the point with dramatic terminology, meaning a possible loose nuclear device.

"They'll come up on alert. How high should we take it."

"I think it will have to be Defcom 1, sir. Only then, will we be prepared to stop incoming missiles."

"It's going to make the Chinese and Russians very nervous."

"Not as nervous as they'll be if they get one laid on them," he paused to let it sink in. "He could prepare a launch of his Ariane launcher in six hours maybe less."

"That means it could happen from now on. Damn it! Find out how long it will take to get some good surveillance of Tres Negras. Defcom 1, it's got to be. If they start to prepare one of those launchers SAC has got to be ready to stop them. The Chinese are not going to like that. It will involve an overflight of their territory from a base in Japan, and keep it conventional, if it comes to that. The first resort is going to be a look see by the Navy, and then I want control of that rocket port, so get the Marines ready."

The meeting broke up. Gavin lingered a moment and signaled the President that he wanted a private word. He was ushered into the oval office.

"What is it John?"

"I didn't want to chase too many rabbits in there Mr. President, but something very odd has come to my attention from the Houston Police."

"Go on."

"They did routine ballistics on the agent's guns, so they could figure out who fired what bullet, and figure a sequence of events and the damnedest thing turned up. Those agents all shot each other."

"What?"

"All the bullets came from the agent's own guns, or those of the Houston police officers, that were with them."

"So, they were surprised, disarmed, and shot with their own guns."

"That's what I thought too, but the men at the scene said, 'no way'. From evidence at the scene, the agents got into a gun fight and shot each other!"

"This thing gets worse as it goes along. We have that damned Probe or whatever it is at White Sands. Nothing can approach it. I got a damn funny feeling. You suppose it is all tied in together, I mean, could it all be connected. You suppose it has anything to do with that thing that crashed in Louisiana?"

"That's quite a jump."

"I know. I want a deep background check on all those agents."

"Yes sir."

"Keep me informed."

Stark and Jim waited in the cramped little room, crammed into the cabinet. There was little or no light and less room. The smells of sweat and fear were on them and the shock of what was happening began to make them tired. They whispered to each other at one point and decided to wait it out as long as possible. Every minute they were undiscovered was another minute for Sid and Sam to make good their escape. Stark tightened his grip on his forty-five. The cold steel felt reassuring.

Suddenly, there was a noise outside the door, and it slide back. The light blinded Stark for a moment, but he could see one of the ectomorphic creatures silhouetted in the doorway. The creature gave a grunt of surprise and lurched backward. Stark raised his pistol and fired once, striking the creature in the chest and knocking it back against the far wall. It squealed loudly, like a pig at slaughter.

"Die Jacta est," Stark said over his shoulder. It didn't matter whether Jim understood Latin or not, the fat was in the fire. Having tangled with these creatures before, knowing how strong they were, now that they were discovered, Stark felt that he had no choices left.

He lurched through the door and started around the curving hallway toward the ship entrance and flight deck. Two beings were in the control room. Both looked startled as Stark peered around the edge. One was like the creature he had just shot, the other was the humanoid that he had seen on entering the ship.

He stepped into the open and shot the ectomorph neatly through the head. The creature dropped without a sound. He turned the gun on the humanoid but hesitated a moment. The thought crossed his mind that if this were the pilot, and he shot him, it was as good as suicide.

"Wait. Don't shoot. I can help," the man said, raising his arm in a gesture to halt, as if he read Stark's mind. Jim had come up behind Stark. The impeccable English startled them both, and Stark turned to look at Jim. The move saved his life, but cost Jim his. He saw a flash and felt a searing pain in his shoulder as a laser blast came from a weapon built into the humanoid's arm. Jim had a look of amazement on his face, as the blast caught him full in the chest and burned a hole right through him.

"You son of a bitch," Stark yelled as he fired.

The air near the alien glowed blue as the bullet molecularized into white hot smoke, and the smell of burned flesh was mixed with the smell of lead vapor.

"The alien laughed. "Is that all the weapon you have, earth man."

Stark emptied the gun at him to no avail, as the room filled with vaporized lead. The creature only laughed harder.

"Holy shit," Stark said to himself. The smoke obscured them for a moment and Stark ducted back into the companionway. His shoulder throbbed from the searing burn, but he still had the use of his arms.

He made his way quickly back down the circular hallway the way he had come. He heard the alien coming after him and his brain scratched. He turned into the cryogenics storage room, where they had left the vials of strange fluid. It seemed important, and his only thought was that maybe he could get control over it and bargain with it, but although he found a manual lock on the inside of the door and it gave him a few seconds, he couldn't get the storage compartment open and even if he could have, he had no insulation to hold it as he had removed the gloves and helmet of the insulated radiation suit, he had been wearing, in the room next door.

He felt trapped. There was a blast from the other side of the door, and the metal smoked from the heat. It wouldn't hold. His eyes scratched the room for anything. There seemed to be an access panel to the right of the freezer, between the freezer and the wall. Fortunately, he had his knife, and he began to work on the panel. It was his father's motto. 'Never Be Without a Knife in Your Pocket'. This rule had been drummed into his head from his youth, stemming from an incident in the Philippines in World War II, when his father, pinned down under fire on a railroad bridge, whittled his way free, when his foot slipped between the cross ties, and he had caught his leg. Stark thought he could identify with his father at this moment. He scratched the panel free and crawled into the access just as the lock was blasted loose and the alien burst into the room.

Stark crawled quickly out of the sight of the access, up into the inner working of the ship.

"Earth man, little rabbit," the alien taunted him. "I'm going to pull your head off. I'm going to tear you into little pieces.

Stark clawed and twisted his way farther up into the service chamber, feeling his way. It got bigger in a few feet and he could stand up. His eyes were beginning to become accustomed to the dark. He could see a little. He felt around desperately for something loose although he didn't know what good it would do with some type of force field that protected the alien humanoid.

He found an open pipe. It was some kind of dump for some fluid system. He followed it back ten or fifteen feet. Feeling his way along until he found what he was hoping for, a manual valve. The pipe was extremely cold although there was insulation on it. He wiggled his way up between the pipes, where he could get good purchase for his foot on the valve stem.

"Little rabbit, your burrow goes nowhere," the alien called to him.

"Come get me, shit head," he called back.

He could hear the being crawling into the bulkhead. When he heard his feet hit the floor from the splash of condensation near the outlet dump, he got ready.

"Where have you gone, little bunny," the alien called to him? "This is the end of the line," the creature laughed sadistically.

Stark listened carefully for the next two steps. "I'm right here," he called, coaxing the creature forward. Just one more step, he heard the footfall and kicked the valve open. The creature was caught in the stream of cryogenic fluid. His force field glowed and the room took on a weird blue glow. The glow began to fade, and a strangled, shivering, scream came from the alien. Stark poured it on until the area was so cold he thought he would freeze. Vapor surrounded him. He moved to the other side and kicked the valve closed. In a minute the super cold vapor began to settle on the floor. In another minute, he could make out the form of the alien, smoking, frozen. He walked cautiously forward. The creature was stiff as a statue. He gave it a kick, and it fell over and shattered into a thousand pieces.

"Oh, too bad," Stark said wryly, "did I crack you up?"

He crawled back to the companionway and emerged very cautiously, but a search of the ship revealed he was alone. He didn't know whether to laugh or cry. He stowed Jim's body as dignified as was possible, although he could find nothing to cover it with, and this bothered him. He didn't know what the hell difference it made. He figured he was as good as dead. He didn't know anything about this ship.

The forward viewer or what seemed to him, the forward viewer was on. The ship was moving so fast through space, the stars were straight lines. He was afraid to touch anything as he figured some of the controls were probably peizo-electro, or heat sensing. He began to search the console for any familiar symbol.

There were none. Everything was unfamiliar, but eventually he thought he had located a navigational console. On closer examination, he found an old alchemist symbol for earth located on one of the consoles, along with many other buttons with unfamiliar symbols on them.

The clincher came when he was able to uncover two condenser microphones in the panel of the console. He was fairly sure he had some kind of communication device. He worked the buttons until he got a light on the thing and then punched the one familiar button on the console. He couldn't tell if anything was happening, or not. He wondered if he were communicating with the alien's base on earth. He knew he wouldn't be communicating with any earth man.

After a while he got tired of that and just left the radio on. He explored the ship a second time and came back to the console. He had found food and water. At least he wouldn't starve to death for a while. The ship's viewing screen showed that they were still moving stupendously fast through space. He watched the stars for a while and slept.

Eventually, he kept coming back to the communications problem and finally had one idea. He unhooked the condenser microphones and used the two wires from one microphone to tap out Morris Code. He liked this idea, and he sat down and wrote a short report of his situation, and how he got into it, along with all that he knew about the alien's operations, but he only mentioned Uris and Kurege in a positive light, leaving out any account of the fight at the shrimp shed, and calling her Queen Uris. After he sent this message out, he signed it, and then he sent it out repeatedly, while he whistled the

Star-Spangled Banner. He laughed to himself thinking he might be driving the aliens nuts. If only someone might hear him. He could think of one possibility. He reasoned that they must use long gravitational waves like Cherenkov radiation or the Tachyon Monopole. If so, there were several deep mine experiments going on that might hear his Morris message.

He was in the fourth round of sending the message, when his attention was suddenly drawn to the viewing screen. It was getting very bright in the room. He watched astounded, as a large stellar body loomed suddenly and brightly directly in the path the ship was taking.

He went back to the wires of his makeshift Morris unit, and began to send very rapidly, but barely had time to send his name and goodbye.

The room filled with a searing light, as they bore through the outer star material of a Supernova remnant. Suddenly, the screen went very dark, but in spite of the artificial gravitation, the ship was picking up speed again, and Stark was pinned from the acceleration. He screamed and the ship screamed with him, as it dove into the collapsed star.

He should have been strapped in. He was thrown around unmercifully, or perhaps, mercifully as the light went out and he loved the cool darkness. It was so comforting and deep and dark. That was the best. It was dark. He was thirsty after black.

He didn't know how long he drifted in the blackness. He dreamed he was dead. He must be dead. He had been falling for a long time, and now, he hit bottom. He felt it.

Roughly, he was picked up by his arms. He squinted against the light. So, this is what the bottom is like, he thought, in his groggy state. When you hit bottom, and you wake up, you're dead, he thought.

"I must be dead," he heard someone whisper. He squinted to see who was dragging him. Big Ants.

"You guys don't look very angelic," he whispered hoarsely. He remembered falling into the sun or black hole, whatever. "This must be the other place."

He fainted again and this time, when he awoke, he had no doubt where he was. He couldn't feel his body. All he could feel was pain. Somewhere, far away, someone was screaming. It vaguely sounded like his voice.

This went on long enough to convince him of the reality of Hell, then suddenly it stopped. He could feel his body. He could feel the pores sweating, smell the fear.

"Damn good," he mumbled to himself. "Just like really being alive."

"Think," something stirred him. His mind reached out to question. The pain began again. When it released him again, again came the urge to think. He obeyed.

He thought of the recent events. The pain stayed away. If he questioned his surroundings, the pain returned.

When he hit events about Uris and Kurege, the pain came. If he did not think of them, the pain demanded that he think of them. He went over and over the events and conversations with them, and the pain would demand more. At last, when he knew his mind would snap forever, it all stopped.

He was left in the dark. It was cold. He was beyond the end of his energy. He retched many times until he had nothing to vomit. He shook and moaned and knew he was in Hell. Then it got colder, much colder. Cryogenics was his last thought.

Bryan Mallory and John Gavin both held a steaming cup of coffee. They were observing the waking men, through the two-way mirror.

"They're beginning to stir," Gavin observed.

"You know John, I'm beginning to believe their story."

Gavin looked cynical and took a sip of the hot coffee.

"Else, how do you explain that ship?"

"You explain it. I gave it to you three weeks ago."

"We didn't have any better luck than you did."

"It closed up after we got it out from the back of the salvage boat. It closed up tight when some guy snapped a picture of the inside. The flash evidently, set off some security measures that locked it up. We have one picture of the inside."

"I sent it down to a lab in Alamogordo, last week. They have a big X ray scanner. The skin is some ceramic, that we can't touch for hardness. Diamond bits just shatter. That proves something doesn't it?"

"Maybe. Maybe it proves Raven is more diabolical than we know."

"Come on, now. He has his limits. Are you saying he could have the technology to create some kind of hoax like this?"

"Perhaps."

"Bullshit."

"It has to be considered a possibility."

"Alright. Then, at the same time it must be a possibility that these men are telling the truth."

"Yes," Gavin finally, reluctantly agreed. "It's a possibility."

"Dr. Ruben McAulley has been made head of a new Department of Extraterrestrial Contact by the President. He flew to Washington last night after we had talked Porter and Martin into coming in, and he went to report to the President. He will be returning here to Quantico when he is finished at the White House. He will be in later this morning to be in on the debriefing of Martin and Porter. The President wants him to have all the information that we have to be given to Dr. McAulley on all these incidents, from the Probe in New Mexico, the ship recovered in Louisiana, to what we can learn from Martin and Porter."

"Have you been watching them all night?"

"Not all night. I had security call me if they woke up. They've been asleep since we arrived. Jacob Martin got up at one point and paced around for a couple of hours, but he didn't say anything."

"I've got to sit on a panel later today to decide on cover during the Tres Negras landing that is being stagged."

"Evidently, the girl is on Tres Negras."

"We want her alive."

"That may be hard to do. From the experience in Louisiana, she has some sort of molecular separator. Very nasty weapon."

"The President wants her alive."

"SAC has orders to 'take out that Ariane Base launch potential'. Now they are going to interpret that very literally should the Marine force on the ground have any trouble."

"From what we saw in Louisiana, any ground forces might have considerable problems."

"What about the fight between agents in Houston? You guy's take jurisdiction squabbles pretty hard."

"Gavin cracked a smile. "Not usually that much, for them to all shoot each other."

"What gives?"

"We're looking into it. It has roots in the old CIA. Before it was reorganized."

"You mean the attempted reorganization."

"Hey. Now you've found my soft spot. Get off my toes. The President needs information too."

"You see that he gets it."

"Yeah, that's always a problem," Gavin reflected. Sid Porter was looking in the mirror on the other side of the glass. "For instance, a crazy piece of information has filtered into me about Stark Raven. In addition to him being spotted in reportedly half the countries of the world, there is this guy running an experiment for the department of astro-physics at the University of Colorado, and he has this instrument set up to monitor something from space, some kind of radiation that travels faster than light, supposedly. Anyway, his experiment is deep down in this mine there in Colorado, and he claims that he got several repeated messages over this thing, signed Stark Galileo Raven in old style Morris code."

"Huh, what kind of experiment?"

"I don't know. Maybe he's just trying to get publicity, attention, and a government grant. That's the point. I'm inundated with information. What is meaningful?" He gave an exaggerated shrug.

"You got to use your gut to figure it out."

"How?"

"I don't know. You just do the best that you can," Gavin looked at the men in the next room. They looked haggard from their ordeal. They all did.

"I'm convinced that they are telling the truth or a well-rehearsed story."

"What the hell. Let's debrief them. I need more information before that SAC meeting. Maybe sharing notes might clear the air. If it could shed some light on the thing....," Bryan let the thought hang.

"All right," John said after a moment. "I think I'm ready to talk to them. You know Martin. Go in and talk to him again, and I'll get them some breakfast, and bring it in. Do they know they're under observation."

"They suspect it, but they maintain they've got nothing to hide."

Admiral Brenda Green looked down on the ships in the flotilla from the bridge of her flagship and pondered the orders for her assignment. It was an invasion landing in the Pacific, and she was in charge of the Pacific fleet. The briefing had been clear enough. She was to land a battalion of Marines on the Javanese island of Tres Negras, and secure the launch base of S. G. Raven Enterprise. She pondered the irony of life. She had gone to high school in Dallas Texas with Stark Raven. They had been friends. They had double dated, with her first husband, and her best friend. Now she was to launch an all-out attack on his Ariane base, from which he placed his communications satellites in orbit. The Java Sea rolled in swells around her. The island was just over the horizon, and her orders called for her to maintain position until satellites could be brought to bear on the area, and the information analyzed by experts. In the meantime, the amphibious landing craft were being readied on a nearby ship, and the Marine battalion that would make the assault were preparing themselves, laying out equipment on the quarter deck.

Admiral Green took a deep breath and let it out slowly. Events would naturally follow a pattern set down in print from this point on. She would simply set it all in motion with the command to begin the operation when she received the order to commence the assault.

Enrico Ramirez watched as Uris expertly maneuvered the hang glider into place. Kurege helped her hold the wings up into the wind as she walked forward to the edge of the cliff that caught the never-ending breeze that blew off the sparkling turquoise sea far below. He had never seen anyone learn quite as fast or become so completely addicted to the sport. She had been up here every day for the past week. Kurege had taken to it also, but Enrico could tell that he was just trying to stay near her and take an interest in the things that she was doing.

She launched herself off the cliff and dove for acceleration, then pulled back and turned into the breeze, letting it carry her up, and up, and up. She whooped from the thrill of the lift, and then shifted her body weight, and dove down in a steep turning dive toward the blue of the ocean stretched out in front of her. Kurege launched soon after and tried to follow her, but she far out accelerated him, and he was just reaching the shore by the time she made a long, low, fast run up the tide line, on the black, volcanic sand in the distance. She waited for Kurege to land near her, and then the two of them folded the hang gliders into a bundle and trudged toward the lift chairs that would bring them back to the top of the cliff for another launch. They had been doing this over, and over for many days, as Uris could not get enough of the thrill of free flight.

Enrico had worried at first, but she could not be stopped once she had seen some of the others launching and sailing from the top of the cliffs. He was worried about other things, also. He had not heard from Stark for many days now, and that was very unusual. Now, reports were coming in from fishing boats, and planes that were coming to the island, that a large flotilla of United States Naval vessels was gathering a few miles over the horizon. They seemed to be doing maneuvers involving landing craft, and they were unaccountably staying put in the same area. He could smell trouble coming, and repeated messages to Stark at all of his normal places had gone totally unanswered. People were starting to call him, looking for Mr. Raven. Business appointments were going neglected, and several very irate men, who were normally cool and collected, had become angry with him, when he could not explain the lack of attention to businesses that were on-going, and depended on S. G. Enterprises for support.

Ramirez was glad when after another flight off the cliff, Kurege and Uris decided to go back to the complex for lunch and then spent the rest of the day scuba diving on the reef inside the harbor. That evening they ate together in the underwater aquarium, which was near the rooms that they had selected for their sleeping quarters.

It was a full moon night, and the moonlight poured into Kurege's room from a skylight in the ceiling. He was awakened by a soft noise, and when he opened his eyes, Uris was standing over him in the moonlight.

"Hold me," she said to him, as she slipped into the bed beside him. She was shaking, and as he held her close to him, she made sighing noise, as she slowly settled into sleep. He watched her sleep for many hours, and along toward morning, he drifted into a deep dream that he had many times before, only this time, he knew that the woman who said 'follow me' was the one that he loved, the one that was by his side.

She was gone the next morning, and he found her sitting in the commissary, sipping coffee, and having a fruit plate of pineapples, grapes, and yogurt. It was a routine for her, although his taste ran more to a bacon, egg, and potatoes meal.

"Hello," she spoke to him in English, which they were both trying to use more and more.

"Did you sleep well," he asked?

"Yes, the best that I have slept in a long, long, time. I am feeling very alone."

"You are not alone," he told her, and reached out to touch her hand. She smiled back at him, and a strong bond was forming between them. He was determined not to rush her into the future. It would come soon enough, of its own accord.

"I want to go hang gliding again," she chirped.

"Again? You are going to become a bird and fly away."

"If only I could. This has been such a lovely place to be, but my dreams are haunted with the faces of my people. I know that they are worried about what has become of me." She gazed into the glass, at the underwater scene that formed one side of the commissary. "I can't see how I will ever be able to go to them. It all seems so impossible."

"It is not easy to see the future, but it will work out. After all, it is the business of the future to be unknown, and an adventure."

"Do you think that there is such a thing as fate?" She wrinkled her nose at the thought.

"I know it," he said firmly. "I have met you."

"And that is fate?" She looked doubtful.

"Without a doubt. I have seen you in my dreams for all of my life."

She didn't respond to this but turned away from him and his gaze. He was a commoner, and in the society that she was raised in, they would have no contact, none at all. The needs that drove her, and the events that had happened were confusing. She had been trained to be resistant to suggestion and was independent by nature.

Eventually, as the week passed, they spent all of their time together, and she came to him each night. With the time passing and their becoming used to each other's touch, feelings took a natural course, and they were falling in love.

It was a clear and calm day, very early in the morning with a soft breeze blowing from offshore. A steady sound came to them from the ocean, but not the drumming of the waves. It was a deep throated hum of motors, many motors, and as they stood on the cliff, and were fixing to launch for the first flight of the day, a line of dots appeared on the horizon. As they watched, the dots grew, until they could make out a whole line of boats, coming fast toward the shore. They watched in fascination, and in a few minutes Enrico and several other men from the complex below joined them.

"I was afraid that this was what it was about," Enrico confided to them. The others were talking excitedly among themselves, and there seemed to be a stiffening of fear in the body language of all the men and women gathered about them.

"What is happening," Kurege asked Enrico.

"The United States military has been gathering offshore for several days, and we have been sensing that they were going to land on the island."

"Why would they do this," Uris asked, already knowing that the answer had something to do with her.

"We are not sure, but Stark has not been heard from for two weeks, and no one can find him or Jay Martin, which is the man that he told me that he would be with. Something has happened which has triggered this landing, and I am sure it has to do with our launch capabilities. That is why I stopped the assembly and roll out of our next launch, as I was sure that it would be seen as provocative action."

"You cannot find Stark Raven," Uris asked?

"Not since he left the island three weeks ago. He is never out of contact this long. Something has gone wrong."

"Do you think that this is somehow about me," she asked?

"I'm afraid so," Enrico looked her square in the eyes, and told her the truth. She got a very determined look on her face and touched the knife which she always carried in the belt by her side.

By this time, the first of the landing craft had made it to the surf, and they watched as the doors came down, and the men began to wade ashore with their gear. Next, armored vehicles came out of the second wave of craft, and the first wave of the attack began to position itself in classic battle stances on the shore, just past the break line, and another wave of landing craft could be seen approaching the shore from the distance.

Kurege was watching Uris very closely and was not surprised to see her pull her knife from its scabbard.

"Uris," he called to caution her. She had a fierce and angry look on her face. He had no effect on her.

She drew the knife up and turned the handle to another position and pointing it at the sand in front of the troops, drew it slowly across, directly in front of the troop positions. A blue line, thin as a razors edge leaped out from the point, and the sand directly in front of the ensconced men boiled with the heat of the the disruptor ray. Vaporized quartz and volcanic dust filled the air, and a thin line of blackish green volcanic glass marked its passage, where the ray had hit the beach. It was a warning shot, but it had the opposite effect, as the men had their orders. One of the armored vehicles opened up with rockets that poured into the cliff face directly below them and exploded with shattering force. Everyone quickly moved back, including Kurege, but Uris stepped forward and touched the launcher with the tip of the ray emanating from the knife. The launcher glowed and then vaporized in a huge explosion.

The troops on the ground opened up with everything that they had, but they didn't have the range and most of the weapons fell short, some overflew the edge, and exploded behind them. People screamed and ran toward the complex. Uris slowly, and purposely, cut every landing craft and vehicle into pieces, and then began destroying any fire coming from the individuals that were left on the beach. The landing craft that were coming on stopped and paused in the operation, but one fired a rocket from one of the craft still at sea, and Uris began to cut them out of the water, until they had turned and disappeared over the horizon into the distance.

Kurege stepped to her side. "Uris, no," he pleaded. She looked fiercely at him. "What are you going to do? Kill the whole planet?"

"It's been done," she said emphatically.

"That is a powerful weapon, and it can kill, and kill. But eventually, you will run out of charge. You cannot defend against the rockets that will fall out of the sky. We cannot win this way."

She gave him a cross look, but she heard the logic of what he had said, and it startled and shook her, as she knew that he was telling her the truth.

Dr. Ruben McAulley was approaching the flotilla in a transport helicopter. He was high enough to see the action on the beach, and the landing craft fleeing from the disruptor ray.

"Shit," he said to no one. He yelled at the pilot, "Raise Admiral Green on the radio, I want to talk to her now." The pilot gave a startled look, and pointed at the headset.

"Dr.," he informed him, "I can hear you very well, don't yell and bust my eardrums, please." McAulley looked sheepish at the man. This was not all new to him. He was an ex-marine, but in cryptography in a forward position during Desert Storm, and he had seen plenty of action. But lately, he had been a college professor, until his appointment as Director of Extraterrestrial Contact, by the President. "I have Admiral Green on the horn," the pilot informed him. "She can hear you now."

"Admiral Green," he asked?

"Yes, I can hear you."

"This is Dr. Ruben McAulley, and I have special orders from the President of the United States with me in writing. You should not be attacking."

"My order's stated that I was to begin an attack and secure that island and launch base at Zero Eight Hundred this morning."

"I don't know how you have those orders Admiral Green, but I can assure you that the President has given me written orders to bring to you that will countermand any such order. It is paramount to the security of the Nation, that this woman be taken alive. You will cease operations until I can get there, and we can thrash this out."

"Well, for the time being operations have been stopped, as I have requested orders for a bombardment of the facility from over the horizon."

"Do not fire on that facility, repeat, do not fire." There was a long pause. "Admiral Green, I am approaching your flagship and will be landing shortly. Do nothing more, understood?"

"I will be awaiting your arrival, Dr. McAulley, now I have a mess to attend to, with many wounded, over and out."

"Give me all the speed you can get out of this thing and give me a priority line to the President. I am to keep him informed moment by moment."

The pilot shook his head that he understood and pushed the throttles to their stops. He turned to the radio operations officer and ordered a secured line to the White House.

"Mr. President, McAulley here. Can you hear me?" He spoke into the microphone when he heard the President say 'Hello'.

"Yes, I can hear you clearly," the President stated firmly. There was a slight pause between communications, as the speech was delayed by the satellite system and the encryption.

"Admiral Green has a situation, a bad situation. She began an attack at Zero Eight Hundred local time this morning."

"Son of a bitch," the President swore. "Can't anybody get these orders straight? I sent a countermand to belay that first order. It was sent hours ago and confirmed."

"I don't know where the snafu is, sir, but I have convinced her to break off the attack. She was in the process of requesting permission to bombard the facilities from over the horizon. I have convinced her to wait until she sees the written orders that I carry."

"Good. Good," came the response.

"Sir," McAulley continued, "what about the Strategic Air Command? If these orders to Admiral Green went awry, what about the orders to SAC?"

"I will make certain, McAulley, right now. I'll make a direct call and make sure that the attack has been scrubbed."

"All right sir, we are coming up on the fleet, now. I will keep you informed."

"Please do so." They broke connection. Being the President and Commander in Chief, did not always mean that there was control. The people in charge of executing the orders had to do so.

The helicopter was making its decent and maneuvering for position on the flight deck of the carrier that was Admiral Green's flagship. McAulley could see Admiral Green waiting below. She was obviously nervous, and she held her hands stiffly at her side, with the palms down, and the fingertips straight out from her sides. She was walking back and forth, and this characteristic nervousness, which she did her best to control, had earned her the nickname 'The Penguin'. By her side, McAulley recognized a Marine Lt. Colonel by the name of Logan Wilson, who McAulley recognized as a man he knew in

Desert Storm. Colonel Wilson had lost his right arm in the second war in Iraq and wore a prosthetic arm. He had been a Captain in Iraq, and they had given him a steel hand, like a pincher, when it had first happened. It had given him the nickname of 'Captain Hook'. McAulley shook his head. It was just a strange scene, and he could not help but think of the movie, "Dr. Strangelove", as the helicopter set down on the deck. He hoped the President was able to control SAC.

Kurege and Uris had stayed on the cliff above the havoc below. No more weapons were fired at them, and they left the survivors alone. A boat had approached from the distance, and it had a red cross painted on the side. They didn't understand this symbol, but they guessed at the purpose of the men inside. When they began to tend the wounded on the beach, and picked up survivors in the water, the two of them watched without comment or interference. It was about a half hour later that Enrico came up the cliff edge in a four-wheeler.

"Please come back to the complex," he called when he had pulled up close. He left the engine running. "They are calling from the ships over the horizon, and they want to talk with Uris," he stated excitedly. "Please come with me."

Uris looked at Kurege for direction, and he gently touched her arm, and they moved to the back of the four-wheeler and held on, as Enrico took them pell mell back down the hill, over the rough terrain, and back toward the facility.

When they arrived, there was a video conference room set up in a wing of the entrance building that had been built for business conferences.

"The military has promised not to form another surprise attack," Enrico told Kurege. Uris was hanging back, suspicious of the surroundings. She was feeling very vulnerable, and her body language was tense. With coaxing from Kurege, she entered the room. There was a tall black man with a brief case in front of them seated at the round conference table. "This is Alton Reed," Enrico introduced him to Kurege and Uris. Kurege shook his hand when it was offered, and Uris did the same after some hesitation. "He is our corporation lawyer, and I think that he may come in handy for the discussion that is sure to take place here."

After everyone was seated, and some water had been served, Enrico turned the meeting over to Alton. He laid a few papers in front of him from the briefcase.

"Madam," he addressed her, "the cessation of violence and hostilities is the first order of importance, as I see it." He looked straight at Uris. "Can you understand what I am saying?"

"Yes," she affirmed, but looked at Kurege for some guidance.

"I understand your language a little better than she, although my understanding is small."

"I can appreciate that, and I will guide you both. If you will follow my advice, I think we may be able to come to terms with the forces that are out there against us and avoid further bloodshed. I have been in contact with the Admiral who is controlling the operations, and it is a woman by the name of Admiral Green. I have met her many times, and she is a person of the utmost integrity, intelligence, and honor. We can trust her words implicitly. I mean completely. Kurege and Uris, did you understand what I said to you."

"Yes," Kurege answered for the both of them. "The leader of the forces is someone you know, and trust."

"That is correct," Alton confirmed. "I have also been in contact with the man who will liaison, speak for, our national leader. His name is Dr. Ruben McAulley, and he is in direct contact with the President and speaks for him in this matter." Alton paused and looked from face to face. Satisfied that he was understood, he proceeded. "We will now video conference with Admiral Green, and Dr. McAuley." He nodded to the technician who was standing by in a control area to open the connection on the telecommunications conferencing.

A room with three people at the table came into view. One was a woman in a military uniform, and a man with a prosthetic arm, in a different military uniform, and a man dressed in a suit of civilian clothes. Alton greeted them.

"Admiral Green, Colonel Wilson, Dr. McAulley, I am here with Queen Uris, and Ambassador Kurege, and our Chief of Operations, Enrico Ramirez. Mistakes are being made here, and hopefully, a tragic situation can be defused before more damage is done."

"Is that a threat?" Colonel Wilson blurted. He was motioned quiet by Admiral Green.

"Sir," Admiral Green began, "do you have a nuclear device in your possession on Tres Negras?"

"A nuclear device?" Alton Reed was stunned. This subject had not been broached in the initial contact a few minutes earlier, before Kurege and Uris had been brought down from the ridge line. He looked at Enrico for clarification.

"Certainly not," Enrico stated firmly.

"Are you, or have you been in possession of any plutonium, or other fissionable elements," Admiral Green continued the question?

"Absolutely not," Admiral Green. This line of questions is a total surprise to us. What is this all about? Why would you think that we would have nuclear material here on the island?"

"Mr. Ramirez," Ruben McAulley joined into the discussion, "have you had any contact with Stark Raven?"

"Dr. McAulley," we have had no contact with Mr. Raven since he left the island over three weeks ago. We are very worried about him. We have made repeated efforts to reach him where he said he would be but have not been able to do so."

"Where did he say that he was going?"

"He told me to reach him through a free-lance writer named Jacob Martin. Mr. Martin has not returned our phone calls, and we are quite concerned about Stark's wellbeing." There was a pause. "Can you tell us anything about what has happened?" Enrico looked questioningly at the figures on the other side of the teleconference.

"I may be able to shed some light on your question, but let's leave that for a few minutes. I am thinking that we can answer a lot of questions that we each have, if we can just sit down and talk this out." There was another long pause, while the men tried to anticipate what was happening with each side's thinking. Uris looked confusedly at Kurege, and he reached her hand and held it under the table. The level of conversation had gotten past what either of them could understand, but he trusted Enrico, and he knew that they had to trust what was happening. The alternative was unthinkable for everyone concerned and would certainly end with both he and Uris being killed.

"Dr. McAulley," Alton Reed began, "we can realize the fear that may be in your minds, thinking that we have nuclear capabilities, with our launch ability. But this is not a realistic concern. If that is what this action has been about, you are totally misguided." He let this soak for a moment and then continued. "What is it going to take to resolve this situation for you?"

"Mr. Reed," Admiral Green interjected, "you are going to have to surrender that weapon, whatever it is. That is going to be a first, and uncompromisable part of any negotiation." She let the demand sink in and then continued. "There have been many men killed today, and many more wounded."

Alton had considered this and had an answer. "Admiral Green, it is true that a warning shot was fired, but your troops fired the first volley of shots with the intention of killing. It was your provocative action of attacking the island without warning that led to this situation. It was your troops that fired the first shots with violet intent to do harm. Anything done from our side was totally in self-defense, and we have the right to defend ourselves from harm."

"That weapon must be surrendered, and any others like it," Admiral Green came back to her first and most salient point. "I cannot risk any face to face meeting until this threat is removed. Please do not make us use bombardment to end this situation."

"Now who is threatening who," Alton Reed interjected. We have not in any real sense of the word threatened the national security. I fail to see how you think that because you have met a force that you cannot simply overpower, that you are threating destruction of United States Citizens without benefit of a hearing or trial. This is barbaric, Admiral. You must see that."

Dr. McAulley leaned over to Admiral Green and tried to calm her. He whispered to her that she was exceeding her authority as only the President could order the strike that she had implied, but that he understood her frustration and anger at the loss of men. She blanched and then reddened, and when he asked to be allowed to speak, shook her head yes, and shrugged her shoulders, signifying that she was reaching her wits end with this stalemate.

"Mr. Ramirez, Mr. Reed," we have a Mexican standoff here. Wouldn't you agree."

"Possibly a poor choice of words, Dr. McAulley," Alton said, looking over at Enrico, "but it does summarize the situations, as we both have weapons, pointed at each other's heads. Ours, however, are 'unloaded' so to speak, as I know that you cannot be assured that we are without any atomics here."

"No, Mr. Reed, you mistake my meaning. We cannot use the threat of bombardment against you. You may not be aware of this yet, but Queen Uris, as you call her, is of supreme importance to national security. I know this and have convinced the President of this fact. We do not wish her any harm, and we need desperately to talk with her to determine what she knows."

"Then give her diplomatic immunity for any perceived crimes," Alton proposed, setting this paper in front of him, and this was the first thing that he had seized upon, when Enrico came to him after the first wave of attack, and the first call had come in. That was his purpose of introducing her as a Queen.

"We would have to have established diplomatic relations with her kingdom for that to be a legal possibility, and it would have to be before the fact of the crime." McAulley had been over this ground with the President, and the party whips of the Congressional delegation that had met to discuss this anticipated meeting, before he was sent. "That would take an act of Congress, and the sequence is all wrong, but there is another way."

"A Presidential Pardon," Alton anticipated him.

"That is correct," McAulley confirmed. "I am in direct communication with the President, and I can assure you that this can be achieved. She will be fully pardoned, if she will surrender."

"She has to turn over the weapon, first," Admiral Green interjected.

"I understand," Alton Reed confirmed. "I will want that agreement in writing by fax with the President's signature on it, in my hand." He was a lawyer, and he knew the importance of sequence, and the written word. He pointed at his hand.

"It can be done. Can you get the surrender?"

Alton turned to Kurege, and looking at Uris, told him. "I can get her fully pardoned and protected, but she has to surrender the knife."

Kurege turned to Uris, and explained in the mutual language that they spoke, the diplomatic language of Xinor, that she was to be pardoned by the highest official of the Government of the United States, but she must give him her knife. She looked long into his eyes. She thought about the day that her father had given it to her. She withdrew it slowly from its scabbard, and looking at it for a long moment, placed it in Kurege's hand. A tear rolled down her face, one lonely tear, and fell upon the table in front of them. He took the weapon and placed it on the table between himself and Alton Reed.

"We have an agreement," Reed said to McAulley. "I will expect that fax within the hour."

"You will have it," Ruben assured him.

"Colonel Wilson will be coming in a helicopter to receive the weapon," Admiral Green instructed. She turned to conference with Dr. McAulley for a moment. "Another helicopter will be sent upon the weapons return to me, for the four of you."

"Dr. McAulley," Alton put in, at this note of his detention, "the pardon will hold all, everyone, blameless, in this action."

"I'll make sure that it reads in that way," Ruben assured him.

"We will call with notification when we have the Pardon, and are ready for the surrender of the weapon, and the transport by helicopter to the ship." Alton gave the last word, and the conference adjourned, waiting on the paperwork to be done and communicated.

It was less than thirty minutes later that the fax machine in the conference room whirred and clicked into life, and spit out a sheaf of documents that Reed pulled from the machine. Enrico had ordered a potato soap and herbal tea be brought for the four of them to eat, to soothe the jangled nerves, while they waited.

Alton looked the pages over carefully, and when he was satisfied, he made a copy and placed it into his briefcase. The original fax was placed by Enrico into the company safe, that was secured in a panel inside the wall of the conference room.

"That all seems in order, and now I think we are ready for the next step. I'll place a call to the Admiral, and have the helicopters start on their way."

Within some twenty-five minutes, Colonel Wilson was ushered in by Enrico, who met his helicopter on the landing pad near the entrance. He was looking sour. He was walking stiffly and he remained standing when he was brought into the conference room.

Alton Reed presented him with the knife. He accepted it with his prosthetic arm. He was wearing the steel pincer version, and grabbed the knife with it, and brought it close to his face.

"That's it," he asked incredulously?

"That is it," Alton told him. Kurege and Uris stayed seated in a room to the rear of the conference room, and Enrico stood in the doorway between the two.

"This is all the weapon," he asked again, in disbelief? The particle beam weapon that annihilated my troops, this is the total weapon?" He had a look of complete astonishment on his face.

"That is the total weapon, and I wouldn't hold it too close to your face," Reed cautioned the man.

Colonel Wilson's look got even more sour, but he quickly held the weapon straight out, stiff arm, and turned on his heels and marched out to his helicopter, which was waiting with the blades turning slowly. Bending low, to get under the whirling blades, he climbed aboard, and the craft lifted into the blue sky, and quickly tilted, and headed for the horizon.

It wasn't long before that helicopter or another just like it was seen returning, and Alton, Enrico, Uris, and Kurege got aboard for the trip out to the flagship. Uris carried her blue bottle of Xenon with her, knowing that she might be gone long enough to need it. Uris and Kurege talked low to each other in their own language, but the other two were content to watch the ocean out the side windows, and to watch the approach that was made to the flattop that was the flagship of the Admiral. The decks were clear of personnel, as Admiral Green rightly detected that feelings were running very high amongst the men who had lost friends in the engagement. No announcement of the pardon had been made. Information was on a need-to-know basis, for the time being.

They landed as close to the Admiral's briefing room as they might come, and McAulley, and Admiral Green met them. Admiral Green led the way to the briefing room, while Ruben closed the door behind them, and secured it. Enrico walked behind Admiral Green, and Kurege, and Uris, walked in the middle with Alton Reed and McAulley bringing up the rear. When they were all inside the briefing room, Alton approached the Admiral and shook her hand in cordial fashion, as they had met on several occasions. He made formal introductions.

"Admiral Green," he began, this is Queen Uris, and Ambassador Kurege, I think you know Enrico Ramirez." The Admiral was puzzled as to how to act. When one is introduced to a Queen they might curtsy, and with a foreign Ambassador, offer a hand to be kissed, especially with a European, which was the only type of Royalty she had ever met, but she was unprepared for this, and after a moment, simply placed her hand at her sides with the palms down, and the fingers out, and gave a slight nervous nod.

"Why don't we all be seated," she requested, indicating the chairs, and taking a seat beneath a map of the world that was pulled down on the rear bulkhead. The others followed her lead. They eyeballed each other for a nervous minute, and she and Uris locked eyes. Neither flinched. After a few moments, the Admiral let a small smile creep onto her face. "So, this is the little bit of trouble that put my Marines on the run." Uris had little experience with a motherly chiding tone of voice, but she recognized the slight smile for an attempt at either being friendly, or a deception. She returned the slight smile without a verbal response. She was not sure what had been said. She understood the word 'run' and knew that it had something to do with the engagement but turned to Kurege to help form a response.

"We are sorry to be trouble," he said. "We do not mean trouble, but we crashed." That was the long and short of it.

"Let's start with the crash," Ruben opened, "with your permission, Admiral," he asked.

"Please," Dr. McAulley, "you are much more knowledgeable than I about this whole situation. I simply followed an order that apparently had been belayed, and that has led to the deaths of many of the men aboard my ships. This is greatly to be regretted, but the President has seen fit to Pardon this action. Now, if we can find a way to sort this out, please do so."

"Thank you, Admiral," Ruben adjusted his seat and placed some papers in front of him. "Uris," he asked her, "do you recognize any of these people," he passed three photos to her, which she studied for a moment, and then smiled.

"This Danielle, Henri, and Joe Le Blanc," she shook her head back and forth in the fashion that Joe used, in imitation of his way of moving when he talked and laughed. "They help us when we crash." She passed the pictures to Kurege who looked at them one at a time.

"Yes," he added. "They saved our lives."

244

"When did you last see them?" Ruben directed the question to Kurege this time, as he could see that Kurege understood and spoke English a little better than Uris did.

"We saw them last in the shrimp shed."

"What was happening when last you saw them?"

"We returned in the car, and found them tied with metal," he gestured at his wrist.

"Handcuffed?"

"Yes, handcuffed." Kurege continued. "There were five men there," he held up his hand with all five fingers open. "One man had Uris's father's record of the Draco explosion." He had to use their word for the name of the Neutron Star, and McAulley didn't follow this, but let him continue for the moment. "One man kick Joe Le Blanc, and Uris pulled knife. She killed the man holding the recorder." Here again he had to use their word for the data box. "The man who kicked Joe fired gun at her. She killed him. I made her run. Others were coming. She got sick." He indicated the blue bottle that Uris had carried with her. "Stark Raven saved her life."

At the mention of Stark, Uris asked, "Where Stark Raven?"

Dr. McAulley waved a hand. "One thing at a time, please." He paused to collect his thoughts. There had been something that he wanted to ask. "What is this box that she killed the first man over."

"Important," Kurege said, and stretched out his hands. "Very important. Her father gave life so that she could have."

"What does it do," he tried to find words?

Kurege thought for several moments. He spoke with Uris in their language, but she only thought that it was like a door. "It is doorknob," Kurege said at last.

"Doorknob?"

"Yes, doorknob," Kurege restated. "It opens door."

"What door," McAulley was completely at a loss to understand.

"Here," Kurege gestured all around. "This place, Terra. It opens the door to Earth."

Dr. Ruben McAulley suddenly felt like he was going to faint. The blood pressure shot up so suddenly with the realization of what was said that he could not move or speak for several seconds. Finally, he stammered, "You mean this galaxy," he guessed at the magnitude.

"Yes," Kurege confirmed, "Milky Way, and much, much more."

"More," Dr. McAulley repeated. He was in shock. "Are you telling me that this box was a computer program that contained instructions for how to get from her home world to here?"

"Yes."

Ruben sat back stunned and tried to get over the numbness that he was feeling. He was smart enough to know that he was only seeing a small part of the importance of what he had just been told.

"And this is strange thing," Kurege continued, "I have not told this to Uris, but in working with Danielle's computer, I found Xinor code on your Earth computers."

"Wha.., what," McAulley was having a hard time following.

"I do not understand, but there must be a connection to Earth from Xinor." Kurege shrugged his shoulders the way he had seen Henri Usay do to accent confusion. "Uris thinks that Pandamon has messed with genetic code here."

"What?" McAulley could say nothing else. Revelation after stunning revelation was tumbling out. He fished through some of the papers that he had with him. "Do either of you recognize this man?" He handed the paper to Kurege, who looked it over and shook his head 'no'.

"It looks a little like Commissioner Beel of Regis Xinor," he said, "But that cannot be." He passed it on to Uris. She took one look and became very agitated in an angry way. She talked very fast to Kurege in their language.

"She says," Kurege interpreted, "that this is Lord Sargon. He is one of the clones of Metastophiles. She knew him from her childhood, and he was once Commissioner of Xinor, before another clone of Metastophiles, named Beel, took his place. This is a very bad man."

"Admiral Green, please get me a secured line to the President immediately," McAulley turned to the Admiral. She got a puzzled look on her face but complied with him at once without any questions. She was gone but for a couple of minutes, and Kurege and Uris continued to talk. She was very excited. At one point she pounded the table with her fist. Admiral Green returned with a phone and flexible cord, that she plugged into a receptacle in the desk near her chair, and handed it to Dr. McAulley.

"Mr. President," he spoke into it. "Ruben here, and I have some very disturbing news. In the incident in Louisiana, there was a computer data file that was recovered, that did not show up in our possession. Yes sir, it was a file that gave navigation instructions on how to reach earth from where Queen Uris has come from. That is right sir. It is apparently very important to all concerned, and our suspicions about Dr. Tellur are correct. No sir, worse than that, much worse. Yes sir, immediately." He handed the phone back to Admiral Green. "We are wanted in Washington as fast as we can get there. We need to leave now." He rose from the table.

"Are we going with you," Kurege asked?

"Yes," he gestured toward the door. "The President wants to have everyone involved in a meeting as soon as possible. There are many things to be sorted out,

and they can't be done long distance, we all need to sit
down and figure out what is happening."

Chapter Twenty-Seven The Conference

Reginald Tellur held the data box in his hand. His heart was absolutely singing. Finally, they had what they had wanted for so long. He turned it over and over examining the connections. Uriah's data recorder would be the opening of untold millions of new worlds. He gloated with the absolute power of it. But the implications of how it came to be on Terra, that was bothering him, and he looked nervously at the telephone on his desk. As if by physic chance, it rang. He placed it on the speaker phone and answered it.

"Yes," he quipped into the receiver, as he walked to a wall safe, and placed the data recorder inside and shut the door and spun the lock.

"Reginald," came the voice over the speaker, "are you alone. I can hear the echo, and I know you always like to use the speaker phone."

"I am alone, and I have been waiting for your call. Is this situation resolved?" He had a pent-up furor in his question.

"Yes, and no," the voice on the other end stammered.

"What is that supposed to mean?"

"Well, the island has been taken, sort of."

"Explain that plainly," Tellur snapped.

"Well, the Marines had trouble, just like we thought. She opened up on them with that disruptor of her's, and gave them a rough time. She killed a lot of men and ran the next wave back over the horizon."

"Good, then the SAC attack was carried out." He smiled broadly and rubbed his hands together.

"No. That is not how it played out."

Tellur's countenance fell, and a crease appeared between his eyes, as a worried expression replaced the one of glee. "Then what did happen, exactly."

"She surrendered."

"What?"

"She surrendered. She turned the disruptor over to Admiral Green and gave up."

"But I warned you, she had to be destroyed!" Tellur's hand clenched into a fist and struck the table with a bang, right next to the speaker phone. "Surely you continued the Strategic Air Command mission."

"I tried."

"What do you mean, 'I tried'?" Tellur emphasized every word.

"The mission was recalled."

"You let that happen?" Tellur was becoming furious. He saw the situation spinning out of his control.

"It was that damned Ruben McAulley. He convinced the President to scrub the mission."

"We talked about that. But you said that you could delay the belay order."

"I did. The planes took off. They had even been refueled, as the Chinese denied permission for an overflight. They were shortly to reach their target, when the President took a direct command line and talked to the pilots, and the command staff on the ground. He turned them around. I'm not the President, you know," the voice said accusingly, in its own defense.

"But" Tellur stammered, "one of those planes was under our direct control. It could not have been turned around." He wiped his forehead with the back of his hand in disbelief.

"The President had a supersonic fighter scrambled from Taiwan, and he ordered the plane overtaken and instructed to land. When the pilot was unable to respond to the fighter's order, the fighter pilot flew upside down over the cockpit and screamed his orders to the bomber pilot. The plane was ordered destroyed by the President. After some more attempts to stop the plane, the fighter destroyed it."

"This is a mess, now." Tellur spoke sadly. "We have totally lost control of the situation. If this is Uris that has come to Earth, she knows far too much about what is going on."

"There is more. Apparently, Dr. Ruben McAulley directed the head of the FBI, John Gavin, to investigate a report that had come in from a deep mine experiment in Colorado. The professor who was running the experiment claimed to have a communication coming in on tachyon monopole in Morris code, from Stark Galileo Raven. It included a report on the raid on Pantex, and also told in some detail about the woman, calling her Queen Uris."

"Queen Uris," Tellur asked confusedly? He was at a complete loss to understand this latest revelation. He knew that Pantex had been penetrated but thought that had been contained in Houston. Or at least, the perpetrators were on the run, and that probably, Stark Raven had returned to Tres Negras. The SAC attack was supposed to take care of both problems. This was totally bad news. And with the surrender, there was no telling what the President was hearing about the operations on Terra.

"The woman is calling herself Queen Uris," the voice confirmed, "and, she has someone with her that is saying that he is Ambassador Kurege from Pandamon."

"Now what the hell is going on?" Tellur mused to himself, more than to the voice. "How can Pandamon have an Ambassador named Kurege?"

"I will know more after the meeting that is scheduled to occur between the President's cabinet, party whips, and the two space people. Dr. McAulley will also be there."

"This is just great," Tellur mused sarcastically.

"What do you want me to do," the voice asked.

"Blow up that meeting, with yourself included."
There was a long pause. Nothing was said for several
seconds.

"I'm afraid you are talking to the wrong person, if
that is really what you want done. But, if you are going to
try to arrange that, I would rather not be at the meeting."

"Perhaps that would be best."

"What does that mean?"

"It means that you can forget about ever being
President," Teller disconnected the call. He sat wearily
into his chair, and after a moment, placed his hands over
his eyes, and slumped. He could see that this was going to
get away from him. After a few moments, he decisively
dialed the phone on his desk.

"Global Charter Airline," a woman's voice crisply
answered.

"This is Dr. Reginald Tellur," he spoke to her
through the speaker.

"Yes sir," she knew him from many occasions, and
he was big money to them. He was their very best
customer, and her voice dripped with sweetness and good
humor. "How may we help you today, Dr. Tellur?"

"I need my corporate jet made ready."

"Yes sir," she spoke positively and clearly, "and
where will you be traveling, and when, sir?"

"I will need it made ready immediately," he
ordered. "The destination will be the private complex at
Amarillo."

The meeting was scheduled for One PM, and
everyone was in place. Security came in and swept the
room one more time for anything that they might find,
from eavesdropping bugs to bombs. The cabinet was

seated first, followed by the members of congress, and each was checked with hand-held security detectors, and bomb sniffing dogs and chemical devices. John Gavin was taking no chances, and whoever might be offended could just register all the protest they might wish. He knew he had a leak, at the highest level, and he was taking no chances with this meeting. The President came in last, the Vice President was conspicuously absent, and his chair was empty and left in place. He suddenly had chest pains, and was rushed to the hospital for a checkup. Uris and Kurege were ushered in by Director Gavin, after everyone else was in place. They were placed at the end of the long conference table, opposite the President. A microphone was positioned in front of them. Kurege took Uris hand after they were seated and held it under the table.

"Well now," the President began, "we all seem to be present, and I assume that everyone has had their lunch. Is there anything that anyone wants, other than water, which is here, and glasses for each one. Please note that this is a closed meeting, and no notes are to be taken, at this time." He looked from face to face to make sure that everyone was comfortable.

"We are as secure as possible," John Gavin assured the President and the room, and then seated himself against the back wall, behind the President, where he could watch the room and all the men in it.

"Thank you John," the President said. "Please bring in Mr. Martin, and Mr. Porter, and Mr. Ramirez," he ordered. "Also, seat Mr. Alton Reed," the President instructed. "He is the counsel for Queen Uris," he explained to the other men, "and he has insisted, as a point of law, that he be present, while the Queen is questioned. The other men being questioned have also engaged him as counsel, so everyone here is being represented, and all have been duly sworn, although he has pointed out, that the swearing process can mean nothing to Queen Uris, or the Ambassador Kurege, as they are not of this planet, and we do not know their religious beliefs." The President paused to see if anyone had a comment to this. Several people moved uneasily in their seats, but no one seemed to want to address this issue, at the moment. "We will simply have to believe them on the evidence. I think that we can see that their input is invaluable to us, in determination of the course that we must decide to take, in light of several disturbing events. Some of these things, many of you know about already, some will be brand new, as they have, supposedly, been known by this office, only. Let me say, right up front, that any leaks coming from this meeting will be prosecuted as treason, under the Wartime Powers Act, as given to the Commander-in-Chief by the constitution. There is a Presidential Finding, Top Secret, to the effect that we are at war with an unknown power. This finding will now be distributed to you, the papers to be taken up, before you leave this room." He paused while John Gavin distributed a paper to each man around the table. "Gentlemen, let this sink in. Any breach of confidence, and I will try to have the perpetrator shot." He looked around the room. An uneasy wave passed throughout the meeting, but no one spoke.

Gavin opened the door, and the four men were brought in and seated in four chairs, that had been saved in the very center of the conference table on the President's right hand side. Enrico Ramirez and Alton Reed were brought from one holding area, and Jay Martin and Sidney Porter from another. Enrico was seated next to Jay Martin, with Porter closest to the President and Alton Reed at the farther seat. Jay looked twice at Enrico; there was something familiar about him. He leaned over and whispered to Enrico, "Do I know you?"

"You could have met my twin brother, Derek, at Space Station Apollo, when it was activated," he suggested.

"That's it," Jay snapped his fingers.

"Something that we all should hear," the President asked?

"No sir, sorry sir," Jay turned red. "I just discovered that I have met his brother."

"And where was that," the President continued?

"I was the civilian reporter on the initiation of the Tecumseh, Apollo mating, and Colonel Ramirez was the NASA officer in charge of the station. Sorry to interrupt sir."

"Interesting," the President observed. "It is sometimes a very small world. But it has lately gotten very much larger." He paused and looked at the papers in front of him. "To start," he continued, "I think we should have a report from Sidney Porter. Mr. Porter, please tell this assembly how you came to be involved, and how you came to be here this afternoon."

Porter sat forward and placed his hands on the table in front of him, folding the fingers together, organizing his thoughts. "For me, this began with a chance meeting one night in Amarillo, when Sheriff Jim Knowles was feeding coffee to a Pantex security guard named Sam Keogh. Sam had been doing some snooping in a part of the facility that shouldn't have existed, according to the plans, and he was puzzled. The night that I overheard his conversation with Sheriff Knowles, Sam was in quite an overexcited state, as he claimed to have heard the voice of Reginald Tellur inside the Pantex facility talking about moving plutonium out of the facility, and perhaps terminating the operations taking place there. Sam was scared out of his mind, and one of those strange meteoric occurrences that happen in the Lubbock, Amarillo area, had just occurred moments before. This was very interesting to me, as it fit a suspicion that I had for years, involving research that I had done on the facility. Several things about the operation did not stand up to analysis, and strange events attached

255

themselves to the Pantex plant, and the area in general, going back as far as recorded history. The overall feel of the story that Keogh told rang true to me, and I called Stark Raven, a longtime friend and discussed it with him. He flew into a small airport just West of the city, near Helium Rd. and I picked him up there, and we talked with Sam Keogh and Jim Knowles about the incident some, a short time after the incident, and could decide nothing, but talked Sam into returning to work at Pantex, and keeping quiet, and keeping his eyes open." Sid poured himself a glass of water and drank part of it. "Pardon me gentlemen, but telling this story makes me dry as West Texas in August, or dry as it used to be, anyway." He drank a little more. The men around the table were wrapped in interest. "Anyway, a short time, a matter of a few days later, I received a call from a passing acquaintance in the news business, Jay Martin, who had a fantastic story. He claimed to have a man at his apartment that had been kidnapped from Earth as a child, and taken to someplace," he didn't know how to say it, "somewhere far away, another civilization, for some unknown purpose. The man Michael Hodge had been the subject of some articles that Jay wrote, some eighteen years before, on missing children. His mother, Amy Hodge, called him when Michael showed up at her home in Kansas, and had a woman with him, that was deathly sick. Perhaps it would be best, if Jay Martin told this part of the story."

"Yes," the President agreed, "please Mr. Martin, continue with what you know of the events."

Martin cleared his throat, and composed his thoughts for a moment, and continued. "Amy Hodge, her son, who we now know as Kurege, and Uris, arrived at my apartment in Houston, about two days after my initial conversation with her. I had dismissed it from my mind, as I was writing an article about the flight that I was selected to make to the Apollo Station, but when she arrived, and I saw Uris, I placed a call to Sid Porter, because I knew that he was acquainted with Stark Raven, and I had a hunch that Mr. Raven might be able to help her. Sid came down to Houston, after contacting Mr. Raven. Stark came to Houston about twenty-four hours later. He was the one that determined and understood that she was in trouble because Earth's atmosphere was slightly under in content of the gas Xenon, which she evolved in, and was necessary to her system to survive. Stark has a gas plant in Houston, where he extracts common and noble gases from the atmosphere, and he flew myself, Kurege, Uris, and himself to the plant, where he was able to save her life." He stopped to take a drink of water before continuing. "After his recovery from frost burns that he received in the Houston rescue, he met us, where he had sent us, at his base on Tres Negras in the Java Sea. After some discussion, and a lot of thought, he determined that he wanted a look inside the Pantex facility."

"Why didn't you come to the authorities," the President asked?

"We simply did not know who could be trusted inside government, or even which bureau might even start to believe such a fantastic series of events."

The President nodded. "Please continue, Mr. Martin."

"Stark was the security contractor for the Pantex facility, and he was sure that with Sam Keogh's help, the plant could successfully be penetrated around the security, and that he could take a look around and leave. That was the plan. It didn't work out that way. The men involved got in way over their heads." He stopped and looked around the table, as he couldn't figure how to tell the next part, as the proof had been burned up in the Houston fire at his apartment.

"Please continue," the President coaxed.

"If you please sir, I think I will turn the floor back to Sid Porter for this part of the story. He was actually there, as I was not, but had returned to Houston."

"Thanks a lot," Porter said wryly. He composed himself and began trying to explain. "We were able to gain access to the Pantex facility, that is myself, Stark Raven, Jim Knowles, and Sam Keogh. We went into the unknown part of the building through an air conditioning vent that was discovered by Sam Keogh, who opened a loading bay dock door for us, and led us in through the vent. After some preliminary reconnaissance, we discovered that figures in radiation shielding were loading a tram or train-like conveyance, and Sam and Stark had tried without success to open a lock to a room that was the room that Sam had been sure was where he heard the voice of Reginald Tellur." At this point, majority party whip, Senator Samuel Prickle, squirmed in his chair. The President noticed.

"Senator," he asked, "was there something that you wanted to add," the President asked him, point blank.

"Ahemm," he cleared his throat. "Not at this time, I'm listening very closely."

"I would, if I were you, Senator, as the White House is very aware of your close dealings with Dr. Tellur over the years. There is, by the way, a federal warrant out for the arrest of Dr. Tellur, as of yesterday, but he seems to have left town for," and the President paused for effect, "Amarillo." There was a general stir. Prickle was not the only man in the room that had dealt extensively with Tellur in the recent past. "Please continue," the President instructed Porter.

"Stark wanted to take a look at what Jim and I had found, so we all slipped back onto the catwalk above the activity below, and watched as, what appeared to be, radioactive material was loaded onto the tram. At a certain point, a figure gestured in our direction, and we thought

258

we had been discovered. As we retreated to the room that we had emerged from the vent in, two sets of footsteps came down the hall and the lights came up. We thought we were going to be found, but they went next door, and unlocked that room, went inside. Sheriff Knowles had a thumper, you know, rawhide covered lead, and he showed it to Stark, who OKed its use, and the two of them crept into the adjoining room, while me and Sam stayed put. We heard a terrible scuffle, and when we ran into the room, well, all I can tell you is two of these big ant-like creatures were laid out on the floor, with a sort of greenish fluid running out of their heads. Sam went to keep watch in the hallway, and," he paused. "Where is Sam, anyway," he asked?

"Sam Keogh was judged by a psychiatrist as in no shape to go over these events, and it was thought best to keep him resting," the President explained.

"Oh," said Sid, "I am not a bit surprised. This is not fun to remember."

"Please continue, Mr. Porter. We can appreciate the trauma of these incidents, but it is very important, the testimony that you are giving here today."

"All right," Sid continued, "that is about all that I know. Except, after the fight, I got to looking around, and I found this weird green fluid, that almost glowed, in the freezer. We figured that this was something important that the two creatures, shelled aliens, were after. I got these vials out of the freezer and recognized human genetic coding on the label. Stark took them, and he and Jim Knowles dressed in radiation suits and went down among the aliens, to try to give us enough time to get out of Pantex." He paused in his story. Uris was becoming agitated, and she and Kurege were talking low. "That's about all I know, except what happened in Houston, where we headed when we got clear of the plant. But you know all that, cause we went over it a hundred times, except that

I cut one of the heads off the alien ant creature, but that was lost in the fire that started in the Houston apartment, when those police, or whoever they were started shooting each other up. But you guys know more about that, than I do." He stopped there, as Uris and Kurege were talking furiously.

"Is there something that you can tell us, Kurege," the President asked.

Kurege held his hand up to Uris, and she slapped it. He gave her a peeved look. "Just that she is confused and mad, because where we come from, these creatures that have been described are politically on the other side. The fact that they are here helping Lord Sargon, does not make any sense to her, or me, and she is very upset about what she is able to understand, or not understand, as it is."

"Hmm," the President mused. "It seems that politics makes interesting bed fellows in places other than Earth." He thought for a moment, and then asked, "Can you tell us who this Lord Sargon is? Who is the man that we know as Reginald Tellur?"

"I do not know him sir. I have never seen him, but Uris is very mad at finding him here and confused about it. He was once Commissioner of Xinor, the highest position in the Empire. He is appointed by the ruling counsel, and I do know his replacement, Beel. They are in fact the same. They are both clones of Metastophiles."

"Who, pray tell, is that, if you can explain? I have been trying to understand this for days."

"Metastophiles is Lord of the Pandamon Empire. He is a law unto himself, and has controlled the ruling counsel of Xinor for more than three hundred of your earth years. He is opposed on Xinor by a minority coalition. On Pandamon, he is worshiped as a god. In the Xinor Empire, religion is illegal, even punishable by death, but they have no power to enforce this on Pandamon. With the elimination of the position of Emperor as a political

260

power, centuries ago, the clones, and Metasophiles himself, are considered Barons. This is the highest Royal position that the Xinor Empire recognizes by birthright. But it is thought that he intends to destroy the minority coalition and make himself God Emperor."

"How can this be," the President was truly puzzled.

"I have never seen him," Kurege began. "He lives in down time, moving at the speed of light, except when he comes to take his life extension shots. That is the fluid that was taken by Stark Raven. That much I can tell you. Beel, the Commissioner of Xinor is the clone that currently rules the Xinor Empire, and that is about all I know of these beings." He turned to Uris, and they talked for a few moments.

"Sargon," she said, "is my father's sister's son, but no relation to me, even that he carries the family house in his name, Ur. He is Tellur. But he is no relation. He is clone. My father's sister was forced to bear him by Metastophiles. My grandfather made mistake. The House of Ur is at war with Pandamon, at war with Metastophiles. We tried Peace." She stopped. She was at a loss for words. No one spoke for many moments.

"Well, it seems that Earth is not the only place in a mess of trouble. We all would like to try peace. We all would like for it to work."

"Metastophiles puts his genetics into many worlds and steals the babies to make his life fluid to keep alive," she added. This was understood by the men around the table, and a disgruntled murmur grew up, until the President asked for quiet.

"This just gets worse and worse," he reflected. "I think we should try to turn back to the chronological order of the events as they unfolded. At this time, I am going to have John Gavin read a transcript into the record that we believe came from Stark Raven." He gestured to John. "John, skip the first part, and the part about Uris and

261

Kurege, as we have them here to tell us what they know. It runs almost exactly as we have heard already, and pick up where the others have left off."

"Yes sir," Gavin stood, and thumbing through a stapled sheaf of papers, found the spot, and began to read. "Jim and I covered ourselves with the radiation suits, and made our way, carrying the fluid down to the waiting train. We were seated at the very back, and with what appeared to be a load of plutonium bombs, were taken about one hundred miles in a due North course, as best I could tell. It could be less, as I could not tell the speed we were traveling. We arrived at a huge chamber, and were loaded onto a saucer type ship, some fifty feet in diameter. Managed to secret ourselves into an area, and after a short time, the craft accelerated. We were discovered, and a fight ensued. Jim was killed. I managed to overcome the pilot, and I am hoping that this message reaches someone." Here Gavin stopped. "This message was repeated almost verbatim several times. Three to be exact. In the middle of the fourth repeat, it suddenly reads, "Black light all around, making everything brighter than the sun. Goodbye, Stark Galileo Raven." That is it. Gavin sat down.

The President addressed Kurege. "Kurege can you tell us what this last sentence means?"

"He was entering the core of a Warp Star in hyperspace, and his shielding was not properly in place," Kurege speculated.

"Could he have survived," the President showed concern?

"It is possible," Kurege told him. "The ship would have survived, as it would be on an automatic guidance system. As for Stark Raven, it is hard to know."

"Well, let us hope so. He is a hero of the nation, and of the Earth." The President paused for a moment to collect his thoughts. "John, do you have anything to add," the President turned to his Director.

"No sir. I think that we have covered the salient points that we wanted to make known. There is new information to be understood that has come out of this meeting. But that about covers it."

"All right," he sighed, "obviously we have to make a plan to stop this activity that is headed by Tellur, and to clean out this mess at the nation's Nuclear Assembly Plant. A plan is being formulated, and men on the appropriate committees will be informed when we have completed planning and are ready to act, and that will be soon, so please stay in Washington, gentlemen, and hold yourselves ready for any emergency meetings that may need to be held. Any questions?" He looked around the room at the stunned faces. No one spoke. "All right," he said. "John, if you would bring the Chaplin in, I think we will be dismissed with a prayer."

Chapter Twenty-Eight A Small Surprise

Uris woke early. She was not feeling well, and she slipped out of the covers, and was careful not to wake Kurege. She went to the bathroom and silently closed the door. Her stomach was in a flutter, and her head was swimming. She retched a little and then got violently sick. She washed her mouth, and shook her head a little, and went back to bed to lay down, but when she closed her eyes, the room went all around. She fought not to get sick again. She had been drunk before on sweet fruit wines, but never sick like this. She wondered what could be wrong with her. She bit her lower lip to try and make it go away.

Kurege woke and turned to her with a smile.

"Good morning, Queen of my heart," he said to her in English.

She jumped out of bed and ran for the bathroom and dry heaved. He followed her with a very worried look on his face. He held her head, and then wet a rag with cold water, and washed her face while she sat shaking on the floor in front of the toilet. She was pale, and her face had lost its characteristic blue hue. He was very concerned and led her back to the bed when she could get up. He dressed in front of the apartment window. There was a magnificent view of the nation's capital, as they had been placed in a very nice hotel near the center of the city. There was an FBI agent assigned to keep watch, and the man looked up when Kurege stepped out into the hall. He didn't know the man's name, as there were several who were taking shifts, and he had not become acquainted with each one, as they had only been in this apartment for two days.

"Could I speak with John Gavin?" He asked the man seated in the hallway, and the worried look on his face registered with the agent.

"I'll see if I can get him on the phone for you," the man responded. "It is still very early, and he may not answer, but I'm sure that he will call back immediately, if he is out of touch, as his instructions to me are to reach him with any request." He punched the cell phone that he was carrying, and while it was dialing, looked up a Kurege with concern. "Is there some emergency?"

"I'm not sure," Kurege told him. "Uris is sick, very sick."

This made the man get an even more worried expression on his face. "John," he spoke into the phone, "I'm glad you answered. The girl is sick. No, I haven't seen her, but the man said that she is very sick. Yes sir, I'll do that. Thank you. See you there. He immediately speed dialed another number, and giving the name of the hotel and the room number, his name and FBI badge number, had an ambulance on the way to them in a matter of moments." He closed the cell phone cover and turned to Kurege. "John has instructed me to call an ambulance, which I have just done. She is going to be transported by paramedics to the nearest hospital, or, if judged by them to be able to make the journey, to Walter Reed Hospital." He rose from his seat and turned to face Kurege. "Please get anything that she may need for a hospital stay, and get ready to go immediately. The ambulance will be here in a few moments." The sentence was punctuated with the scream of an ambulance coming toward them from somewhere near.

"I'm going with her," Kurege said firmly.

"Of course, the agent assured him. That's a given." He turned as if to go down the elevator, and meet the ambulance, thought better of it, and went part way toward the elevator, and stopped.

265

Kurege felt terrified and was sure Uris would feel the same way. Their lives just seemed to be spinning more and more out of their control. He went back into the room to tell her. She was not happy at the plan, but he began to gather things that he thought she might need, and last, placed the blue bottle of Xenon on top of the case he had packed. There was a rap at the door a few minutes later, and the agent and three other men, big men, entered the room.

One immediately put a blood pressure cuff on her arm and began to take her blood pressure. Another asked questions about what type of distress she had been in, and when they learned that she had been sick in the toilet, made a quick look at each other. Kurege saw one roll his eyes at the ceiling and wondered what that meant.

"OK," the one in charge said. "We are going to transport her to Walter Reed," and he spoke into a walkie talkie attached to his shoulder, and a voice spoke back. One of the men left the room. The one that had taken her blood pressure put a thermometer near hear ear and took her temperature. He then started writing things on a palm pilot that he was carrying attached to his belt.

In a few minutes the man that had left the room returned, and he was helping another man bring a gurney, which they unfolded, and then waited for Uris to load herself on the mat, which took her and Kurege a second to understand. This seemed to confuse the two men, and one of them asked Kurege, facetiously, "What part of the galaxy are you from, anyway?"

"Oh, we're not from this galaxy," Kurege answered him straight. This got a really puzzled look on the faces of the paramedics, and the FBI man burst out laughing, and then stifled it behind his hand. The paramedics thought they were being carried on some sort of joke they didn't understand and clammed up and rolled Uris to the elevator and carried her down and into the waiting ambulance with

Kurege trailing behind. No one spoke again until they were loaded and the ambulance screamed off through the traffic. Kurege began to talk to Uris in their language, and the paramedic in the back with them got a quizzical look, which progressed into a fully wrinkled forehead, and then he just sat and listened with his mouth hanging open. It was like no language that he had ever heard, and in Washington, he had heard them all.

At Walter Reed Hospital, they were taken to the emergency entrance, and Uris was wheeled into the doors that slid open as the paramedics approached. Kurege watched helplessly, and he was unsure and upset when a nurse stopped him and told him to 'wait here' as he watched Uris distraught face wheeled in through some swinging doors, that said, "Doctors and Patients Only" in red letters. He was greatly relieved when, a few seconds later, John Gavin came in, and gave him a friendly wave, and came over to where he was standing, helplessly holding on to her blue colored Xenon tank and mask.

"Kurege," John greeted him, shaking his hand. "Have you been here long."

"No," he told him, looking toward the door that Uris had disappeared through, "we just arrived. They took Uris through that door."

"Don't worry," John reassured him, "they will find the problem and get her well. She probably has just contracted a virus of some type that she had no immunity for. We have been worried that that would go both ways, as you two have been loose on the planet with microorganisms that were possibly unknown to this planet or the other way around. It's amazing that one of you has not come down with a disease that you had no immunity to before now."

"What will they do to her?"

"Oh, normal things. They will check her blood and take samples of fluids. Those will tell them pretty quickly what is wrong with her." John tried to reassure him.

"But she can't talk very well."

"They won't need her to. She can talk good enough to answer the basic questions about where she is hurting. Maybe she will just have to point at the problem. If they need some help, they will come and ask you to explain. I have been in touch with the doctor that will see her already by phone."

"You have," Kurege asked?

"Of course, I have." John touched his arm, and gave it a squeeze. "You know that you and she are important, and we are making every effort to keep you both safe and sound."

Kurege was somewhat reassured and his posture relaxed a little. John motioned him over to a chair in a waiting area around the corner.

"You wait here and I'm going to get some paperwork from the admissions desk and fill it out. There is endless paperwork in being admitted to a hospital, and I'll be right back, and then we can try to fill it out together." He went around the door and disappeared, leaving Kurege looking at a television screen going on and on with endless commercials. He was back in a few moments.

Gavin started in on the paperwork, which was hard to do, as he had no address, last name, social numbers, phone numbers, or medical history that he could record. He just used his own information for much of it. In a minute, he came to the medical history section, and asked Kurege if she had any previous problems that he knew of.

Kurege thought for a moment and then told him what he knew. "She is very used to always getting her way, and she can be violent at times, especially when she does not." He said that last part with definite emphasis.

John burst out laughing and gave up trying to fill out the form for the moment. He was still tickled, when a few moments later, Dr. Ruben McAulley came around the door with a very worried expression on his face.

"How is she. "What is wrong with her," he spoke staccato. "I'm sorry," he said, "John," he shook Gavin's hand. "Kurege," he greeted the young man and sat down next to him with Gavin on the other side. "Oh, me, this was just not in the plan. I had hoped to take her to Alamogordo in the next day or two." He shook his head. "What seems to be the problem?"

"I think she's just got a bug," Dr. McAulley, "hopefully nothing to debilitating." He spread his hands in a gesture of helplessness. "What is this about Alamogordo?"

"Well, in talking with the President today, I suggested that we should try to see if she would tell us about the ship, and I thought that taking her to it would be the best way to get that done." He looked at Kurege. "Do you think that she would be willing to help us to understand the spacecraft?"

"That is possible," Kurege stated flatly.

"Kurege," John ventured, "You have not known her for very long, have you?"

"No, only a short while." He wanted to add that he had known her in his dreams all of his life but stopped himself.

"Something is confusing me," Gavin continued. "At the conference, she said that 'Ur was at war with Pandamon', but I think I remember that Alton Reed said that you are an Ambassador of Pandamon."

"I came to Saphos, the Ur home world, as an Ambassador, there were diplomatic relations at that time with Saphos and it was a possible rotational position for an Ambassador being initiated into the Navigational Guild."

"I see," said Gavin, but he really didn't. "So, how did you get to be an Ambassador at your age? You seem young for a position like that."

"I'm not," Kurege confessed. "It was a made-up story and part of the way that I escaped from Pandamon. I was about to be imprisoned as breeding stock for the Royal House."

"Really? But I thought you were kidnapped from earth," he chuckled. "That's how I come to be your guardian, as your fingerprints match those of the kidnapped child Michael Hodge."

"I am, that is true."

"So, how are you breeding stock for, how did you say it, the Royal House, of what, Pandamon?"

"That's right. That is one of the reasons that Uris is sure that this is one of the clone worlds that are being genetically altered. Because I was chosen."

"I don't think I understand. What specifically were your genetic traits that were sought."

"I'm a Betazoid," he used the Xinor word for it.

"Huh," Gavin looked perplexed?

"It has to do with the dreams that I have. I dream of the future. I'm a physic."

"Is that right," Gavin looked skeptical. "So, there is a physic gene?"

"Yes," Kurege told him matter of fact.

"Well, I'll be a monkey's uncle," Gavin said.

"You will," Kurege asked him back, taking the saying literally? The two men gaped at each other, and neither spoke or explained.

"So," Ruben asked, "you have dreams of the future?"

"Not that much," Kurege added. "I have had many dreams of Uris, all my life. Long before we met." He thought for a moment. "I do not think that this is that uncommon for species that dream," he added.

"Easy for you to say, buddy," McAulley shrugged. "It has never happened to me, not that I can remember."

"I think it is a matter of remembering the dream," Kurege told them. "But how or why it happens is a puzzle to me." He wanted to tell them what he thought, and he tried to put it into words. "We know that space and time are relative occurrences. They are variables along the same path. So, in a way it should be expected."

"Definitely not following you there, friend," John put in.

"Well," Ruben added, "the phenomenon of déjà vu is well known. But psychologist believe it to be a slip in the brain that associates something already seen and confuses it with another occurrence."

"That is an explanation, perhaps," Kurege agreed, "But I remember more, and also, events can happen as they are dreamed, or they can be changed in the moment of happening into a different happening. I know this."

The other two men looked wonderingly at him, and then at each other. "You got us, there, buddy," Gavin humored him. He gave a pause but then had another question. "What do you mean by 'time and space are relative'? Like Einstein?" He had answered his own question with another question.

"Like whom?" Kurege was curious.

"The man that discovered relativity here on Earth," Ruben answered. "But nobody understands what the hell he was talking about, except that light is bent by large gravitational fields, yet it has no mass. Make sense of that if you can," he said to no one in particular.

"What did you mean by the words 'Down Time' that you said this Meta-creature lives in," Gavin asked?

"This is a very complicated question that no one fully understands, having to do with oneness," Kurege tried to tell him. "Space, time, speed, and place are all interrelated through a relationship that is unknowable. It is

271

as if the entire Universe is existent at all places in an infinite time yet changing. Each moment is for always. But even this is too simple, as it can be interacted with. We know this and use it to travel in Xinor Standard Time."

The two men exchanged glances. "You lost us again with that one Kurege," Gavin had to admit.

"Don't feel alone," Kurege told them. "No one fully understands this. It just is."

"If you say so," Dr. McAulley added with a shrug.

"I have studied Navigational Theory, but I have not been shown many of the secrets of the Guild." Kurege admitted to them. "I am not a Navigator, but Uris is."

"She is?" They both said it at once.

"But of course she is. She is a Queen of Ur, and a full member of the Navigational Guild. She is one of the brightest mathematical geniuses of the entire Guild. She is renowned for her skills. It was her work that led to the accord to send the probes. She averted a galactic war. I was there when she persuaded the Guild that the ceramic plutonium pellets coming from Earth were garbage, not weapons in an attack."

"God, I wish I knew what you were talking about," Gavin said. "I can see that it is important to us, but I'll be damned if I can understand what you're saying, half the time." He shook his head. "What's this about a probe?" He snapped on that and looked at McAulley. "Could he be talking about that problem that we had land at White Sands," he asked Ruben?

"Are you saying that some plutonium, that we dropped into the sun to burn it up, found its way to your world and probes were sent to seek us out," Ruben asked.

"Some of your plutonium garbage from your power plants, that you must have dropped into your sun, ended up scattered all up and down time. One hit a Pandamon diplomatic shuttle and almost caused a galactic war. It was Uris that used her mathematical skills to calculate where it had come from, and probes were built and sent to confirm that conclusion."

John Gavin had a puzzled look on his face. Ruben McAulley rose immediately from his chair and saying that he had to talk to the President, stepped out into the hall, away from the television noise, and opened his cell phone.

It was at that moment that a nurse came into the waiting room. "Mr. Gavin," she said to John. "The woman, Uris, I believe her name is, the one you signed in, has been moved to private room 209 on the patient's floor. She is calling for someone named Kurege, and she is very insistent. The Doctor is waiting for some test results. He will be along to see her in a little while."

"Is she going to be all right," Gavin asked?

"Probably," the nurse gave him a wink, "in about nine months." She turned to Kurege and placed her hands on her hips. "Is this the husband," she asked?

"Yes," Gavin told her.

"Good job, big boy," she threw over her shoulder as she turned and crisply walked from the waiting room back toward the nurse's station at reception.

Kurege gave her a curious look. She twitched her hips at him, as she walked back to the nurse's station. "Why did you say that I was the husband," he asked John?

"It seemed best, under the circumstances. They won't let you into her room, if you are not a relative, and husband is what I filled in on the form, so that you could get into her room to see her."

"Oh," Kurege agreed.

"And" John paused, "you are the father, I am assuming?"

"Father of what," Kurege was truly in the dark.

"Of the child she is carrying," John told him. "Haven't you figured this out yet?"

"Child?"

273

"Yes," John's eyes twinkled. "You know what sex leads to, don't you."

Kurege visibly reddened. He swallowed hard. "She's not going to like this," he reflected. "She's going to kill me," he reflected.

"A real black widow, huh."

"She is going to kill me," Kurege reaffirmed.

They moved off down the hall toward the elevators, passing Ruben on the way. He was talking on the cell phone. "One moment, sir," he held his hand over the phone and looked up at Gavin. "Is she going to be all right," he asked.

"In about nine months," Gavin told him.

"Ah Oh!"

"We'll be up on the patient's floor in room 209," he said, and they moved off down the hall. Kurege heard McAulley exclaim on the phone.

"She's pregnant!"

He shut his eyes tight and tried to imagine how she was going to take this news. Now, his stomach was feeling a little sick. He followed John to the elevator, and they waited for it to arrive. John kept glancing at him, with a wry smile. He felt numb.

After they cleared the nurse's station on the second floor, and got instructions toward her room, they made their way along the corridor, and John let Kurege enter first with a flourish like a courtier of old. Kurege took a deep breath and cracked the door and peeped in. Uris looked small and forlorn with her knees drawn up, and her arms wrapped around them so that her head was resting on top of her knees. She looked up at the movement of the door, and Kurege stepped into the room. She visibly brightened when she saw him, but it was somewhat of a smile.

"Hello, Queen of my heart," he chirped in English. He went over and rubbed her back and sat on the bed behind her. John entered and took a chair. "Are you feeling well?" he asked in their language.

"I feel fine, now," she told him and shrugged. "Except these vampires keep coming in a stabbing me for more blood every few minutes. I want to get out of here," she pleaded. "What do they need so much blood for, anyway?"

"I don't know," Kurege told her in English. "They said the Doctor would be up to talk with you shortly." He looked over at John. "She said that they keep taking blood from her."

Gavin shrugged. "That's the hospital for you. Bleed you dry. I think they sell it," he tried at a lame joke. No one laughed. Uris stretched out and lay back on the pillows and raised her bed to a sitting position. She seemed pleased with herself, that she had figured out how to control this little piece of her life, and wiggled her eyebrows at Kurege when he had gotten up from behind her to let her lay back. He stood beside her and stroked her shoulder. The door opened and Ruben McAulley stuck his head inside in a tentative inspection and seeing that nothing was exploding came in with a sheepish smile. Uris looked from one to the other. They all had the same idiotic smiles on their faces.

"What," she demanded.

"What, what?" Kurege asked back with as much innocence as he could muster.

"You all have the same idiotic grins on your faces," she said to him in their language, with suspicion mixed with annoyance.

He stopped smiling, and so did the other men.

She looked from one to the other.

McAulley started a conversation with Gavin, more to cover his nervousness, than to convey information. "I told the President what we had learned about the Probe," he began. "Uris," he addressed her, "Kurege has told us of devices that were sent to investigate Earth. Devices sent to find where the plutonium waste came from. Some of our nuclear power plant waste got in your space?" He stopped to see if she understood. Kurege repeated to her, in their language, what Ruben was trying to ask her.

"Yes," she confirmed in English. "Your garbage is scattered all up and down time and space. It is stupid," she said with emphasis.

"Probes were sent out?"

"Yes," she told them, "Many were dropped into Draco, but we had no tachyon communication with the other side, so if any made it to Earth, they would have just sat."

"One did," McAulley confirmed. "It sits in the middle of a military reserve where our first atomic explosion took place."

"That is what it is designed to do," she nodded that she understood. "It would maintain, until some communication was established, and then send its location."

"Well, it has destroyed anything that approached it. We can't get near the thing, and it just sits there."

"Good," she said, "It is working properly." She recognized the exasperated look on his face. "I can deactivate it," she added.

"You can," he asked?

"Yes."

"How?"

"I am a member of the Navigational Guild, and I have a code to deactivate the Probe."

"Can you give us that code?"

"No," she said matter of fact, with just a hint of arrogance. "Only Guild member, and I will need my knife and my Pearl," she used its name in her language.

"What does she need," McAulley asked Kurege.

276

"Her knife," he explained and the spacecraft in working order." Neither explained about Andro. "Her knife is a genetically coded key to open the ship." He paused to let them understand. "They will only respond to her. The knife is the key to the ship, among many other things that it can do."

"Hmm," McAulley pursed his lips. "That may be tricky, as the Navy and the Marines have that, and they won't give it up. It killed too many of their men, and even the President may have a devil of a time getting it loose from them."

"Without it, even Uris cannot open the ship."

"If we could get it back, and she could open it," Ruben speculated, "what is wrong with the spacecraft? I mean, why did you crash?"

"The anti-gravity coils must be surrounded by a very rare substance. It is rare anywhere in the galaxies of time and space, perhaps the rarest and most prized of substances."

"And what is that," Ruben asked?

"It is a form of one of the first elements in what you call the periodic chart."

"Helium?"

"Yes," Kurege confirmed, "but a rare form of it that has very strange properties. It is a superconducting fluid, for one thing, and it will flow against gravity."

"You are talking about helium III," McAulley confirmed.

"Yes," Kurege agreed, "that is what you call it."

"What are you two talking about," John Gavin looked totally puzzled?"

"Helium III," Ruben told him. "It is the only known superconducting fluid, other than plasma. It also displays a very strange property called negative viscosity. It can't be contained but will flow up and out of any container."

"That's a strange one," Gavin scratched his head.

"Is there any on this planet," Kurege asked?

"There is one source on Earth," Dr. McAulley confirmed.

"Where is that," Gavin asked?

"Wouldn't you know it," Ruben told them. "The oil wells in the Amarillo field, just West and North of the city, produce hydrogen in small amounts, and helium in even smaller amounts, and the wells along Helium Road, are the only wells in the world that produce small amounts of the isotope of helium, helium III." The two men looked at Uris while Kurege tried to explain what he had understood about what he had heard from Dr. McAulley. "How much helium III does it take to make the spacecraft operational?"

Kurege asked Uris and she measured a square area with her hands of about a foot and a half square.

"Whew," McAulley whistled. "That is a lot of that stuff. Getting our hands on that much from the production people is going to be a problem. Mostly, we just see very small amounts for experimental purposes, and that's always like pulling teeth."

"Maybe someone has been holding out," Gavin suggested. "I believe a FBI inspection would be warranted."

"That is a possibility," Ruben agreed.

It was at that moment that Dr. Curtis made an entrance into the room.

"Well young lady," you've got lots of company. He chirped at Uris. "Which one of you is the father," he asked looking from one man to the other. Kurege lifted his hand a small amount.

"What do you mean, father," Uris asked?

"Young lady," the Doctor peered over his glasses at her, "you only had morning sickness. You are pregnant. Didn't you know that?" He was amused at her surprise.

"Not possible," she answered in shocked concern.

"Oh, my dear, it is not only possible, but I assure you it is so," the Doctor told her point blank.

She buried her face in her hands and burst into tears. The Doctor got a very confused look and turned to look at each of the men.

"There, there," he chided. "It's not a death sentence, after all. It is good news, and you can go home. You are as healthy as a horse."

"My mother died in childbirth," she stammered at him between the howls of tears welling up.

Dr. Curtis was totally taken aback. "Well, my dear, we are not going to let that happen to you." He made a note on his charting and left it for the others to calm her down. He motioned for John Gavin to follow him into the hall. Ruben McAulley tagged along, leaving Kurege to comfort Uris as best he could.

Dr. Curtis took his glasses off, after he had finished writing on the chart and tucked the chart under his arm. He turned to face the other two men with a very perplexed look on his face. Ruben McAulley spoke first, wanting to ask the doctor what was on his mind before the man could hurry away.

"Dr.," he questioned, "can she travel. I mean across country?"

"Flying in low pressure would not be good for her at this time, but I see no reason she couldn't take a car trip, or train."

"Even across the country," Ruben asked?

"I don't see why not," the doctor confirmed. "At least for the next several months, there is no trouble with her traveling anywhere she would like, as long as she is in full pressure, and not exposed to radiation in the upper atmosphere."

"Good. Good," Ruben could see that he could take her to Alamogordo.

"John," Dr. Curtis remarked, "I don't know who you've got here, but her blood work is very strange."

"Don't worry, Doc," that's to be expected, Gavin reassured him.

"Maybe so," the doctor continued, "but you know here at Walter Reed, we have the best equipment in the business. We have state of the art DNA machines, and while I had her blood, I ran it through the system, and try to explain this one to me," he fixed Gavin with a hard stare. "She is related to every person on this planet." He defied John to grasp that fact. "If she is not 'the mother of all that is living' the original Eve, she is pretty damn close to it. Can you explain that one to me?"

Gavin did a double take on the doctor and on Ruben. "You got me there, Doc," and shrugged.

"Well neither can we, or even make a guess. It's got to be the strangest case that I have seen or ever will see." He took another look at the chart to verify that he had everything, and since both men were scratching their heads, he shrugged his shoulders and turned and walked away down the hall.

When they reentered the room, Kurege was rigging the Xenon mask and blue bottle for Uris to take a few breaths. She had stopped crying, but she looked far from happy.

No one said anything for several moments, and the men all shuffled their feet nervously. Ruben McAulley, determined to make some progress on the item that was on his mind, finally spoke up.

"Did the spacecraft crash because it ran out of helium III," he asked Kurege.

"Yes," he answered.

"Then it uses it up," McAulley asked?

"It slowly gets converted, and has to be drawn away from the coils," Kurege told him.

Uris had managed to hear that they were talking about the Pearl, and this brought back the memory of her time with the only woman who had been like a mother to her.

"Where is Danielle Usay," she asked taking the mask away from her face. "I want to see Danielle Usay."

John Gavin went dead still. "I thought you knew," he said. "The Usays and Joe Le Blanc were killed. They were shot execution style and found in the shrimp processing plant."

Uris took this in with total horror, and then she slumped and turned and buried her head in the pillows on the bed and burst into tears all over again. This time she was inconsolable, and she cried until she cried out and then just whimpered and heaved. All three of the men were crying with her. John and Ruben finally left the room, and left Kurege to manage alone. It was the worst day of her life.

Uris looked at the Pearl setting on a stand in the middle of the warehouse. There was both scanning and X-ray equipment arrayed around the ship. Ruben McAulley and Kurege were talking with John Gavin and several other men at the office to one side of the complex.

"The ship is basically atomic powered as far as the electrical systems are concerned, so that part of it will function, and as Uris has told you, she will need her knife back to be able to send the code to open the door. The knife will respond only to her. It is genetically coded for her and will not work for any other person or being." He had already been over this part of the operations of the Pearl. He gazed over at Uris, who had approached the craft and was running her hand over the smooth surface.

Brian Mallory had been the Navy man selected to be present when the spacecraft was opened. "Logan Wilson will be arriving in a few minutes," he said, looking at his watch. "He will be bringing the weapon, the key, or knife, with him from where it has been stored."

"Have you met Lt. Colonel Wilson before," Ruben McAulley asked Mallory?

"I know that he is straight up military, and a no-nonsense officer," Brian stated. He had his hand on a cart that carried a thermos-looking cryostat about the size of a very large ice chest. Smokey fumes were wafting from the top of the container. Insulated lines were coiled and lay around the top. "Do you know him," Brian asked Dr. McAulley?

"I knew him a long time ago," he reflected. "We served together at the very end of Desert Storm. He was always a great Marine. I was very sorry to hear of his injury in Iraq, but it didn't end his career. Your friend Jay

Martin wanted to be here today," Ruben commented, continuing to touch base with mutual acquaintances. "He just wasn't selected. This part of the operation is not getting any press, and people involved are being kept to a minimum. The President is very concerned about news leaks. Surprise is pretty much all we have going for us, and with the inspection and confiscation of this cache of helium III, they probably know that we are coming soon."

"How soon," Mallory asked?

"That somewhat depends upon today, but the Marines that will form the shock troops are in place, at least for the front door raid on the Pantex complex. Normal operations are still going on there, but many of the workers have been replaced with Marines that will make that part of the attack. We just don't know how or where the back door is yet. We have men in position over a very wide area, but we still don't know exactly where that exit door is, or how we are going to get inside from that end. The plan is a coordinated attack at the plant and at the exit where the spacecraft go in and out, but we still have to find that exit."

McAulley moved over to a group of maps that were rolled and sitting on the top of a table. He unrolled one of the maps and began to study the details. "This is where we are concentrating the search," he said to Mallory, pointing at several different spots. "From the Morris message that we decoded from Stark Raven, it should be somewhere along this line. Starting from the Pantex facility, we have allowed for an increasing margin of error as the line gets farther from the plant."

A black SUV with a US seal, pulled up inside the hanger. The group of men moved toward the vehicle. The back side door opened, and Logan Wilson stepped out and adjusted his Marine dress uniform hat on his head, looked around the hanger complex, and then reached inside and took out a box, which he tucked under his good left arm. He walked erectly toward the group.

"Good afternoon, gentlemen," Logan greeted them. He shook hands with Ruben McAulley, and then with Brian Mallory. He didn't shake Kurege's hand, and the other men hung back, as they were technicians. John Gavin stood back with the technicians.

"We were just looking over some area maps here at the table and trying to get some perspective on the possible back door. We know that we will be looking for a valley that would protect any flying craft from detection at the entrance. That only makes sense, as this sight has gone undetected by radar for all these years," Ruben showed him, trying to bring Wilson up to speed. "There are numerous anomalies that have occurred on radar through the years, and these have been plotted, as you can see by these yellow triangles here on the map, but there are an awful lot of them, and they don't point at any specific spot, as they are just not concentrated in any one location."

Colonel Wilson set the box he was holding down on one side of the map, spread it wide with his good hand, and then held it there with the prosthetic hand while he reviewed the markings. Uris joined the group, and Wilson gave her a disgruntled look, but allowed her a spot at the table."

She had only looked at the map for a few moments, when she asked for a smaller grid. Ruben choose from among the other maps, and unrolled one on top of the larger area map. She ran her finger along the line of action that had run due North from the Pantex facility and stopped at a marking. "What is this," she asked?

McAulley looked closer. "That is private land, old historic ranch land of the old XIT," he told her.

"This is mark of Xinor," she stated firmly. "They name with their mark and starting letter of the planet. This means Xinor Terra. This is where to look." She held her finger in the middle of a long valley running North and South. All three men bent over the table for a close look. Kurege moved to the other side, and studied the map upside down.

"I'll be damned," McAulley exclaimed, "it has been right in front of us the whole time. It even sounds like 'exit', so how much clearer can it get. He looked closely at the map. Wildcreek Canyon was written in small letters along what was probably a dry stream bed, that would flow during wet weather. I'll have scouting parties moved into the area immediately."

"Uris has told me of an idea that she has been thinking of," Kurege told the men. "You must not come near this cavern door with anything metal, or anyone with metal on, not even metal in their teeth."

"Why is that" Colonel Wilson asked?

"There will be extremely good detection devices set up in the area, and they will be set to detect any metal, even small amounts."

"Looks like we are going to lose the element of surprise," Brian Mallory reflected. "How are we going to get any troops close enough to make an attack?"

"Uris has told me of an idea, and it might work," Kurege continued. "The detectors are set to ignore animal life. Small and large animals, bugs, reptiles, and the like, would be always setting the sensors off, so they are set to ignore such signals. It is assumed that no attack can be made without weapons with some metal in them." He paused to see if he had been understood.

"That is helpful," Ruben said, "we might be able to make use of that information."

"Also," Kurege added, "they will ignore large flying birds. There are many planets where such large flying creatures are common. Our experience with hang gliding has given her this idea. She thinks an attack can be made with hang gliders made of animal bone, glue, and feathers. No one in the advanced force can have any metal, not in their teeth, or on their bodies. They will have to be armed with knives made out of bone. This advanced group will have a chance of penetrating the security of the spaceport. Any other way, and the attackers will simply be disintegrated by disruptor before they can get inside to secure the door."

The men looked from one to another. "Bone knives against ray guns," Colonel Wilson shook his head in mystification. "It sounds like a long shot."

"We cannot see any other way to go about it," Kurege assured them all. "This is the one flaw in their security that can be used against them."

"I will convey this to the President for his consideration, and I will suggest that this exact area be examined by men carrying no metal, nor any radio equipment. They will have to slip in and out by foot to carry out the recognizance." He rolled the maps back into rolls and laid them in order on the tabletop. "And now, I think it is time that we see if this spacecraft can be opened and perhaps put back in working order." He looked at Logan Wilson and handed him a sealed envelope. "This is an Executive Order, from the President of the United States, ordering the return of the weapon-knife to the possession of Queen Uris. Please do so now, Lt. Colonel Wilson."

Wilson received the envelope and opened and read it in detail. He folded the Executive Order back into the envelope and handed the box to Brian Mallory, the Navy engineer that was there to receive it from the Marines. Mallory opened the box and carefully removed the knife, looked it over, examining the intricate engraving on the handle and blade, and handed it, by its handle, pointing it down, to Ruben McAulley, who handed it to Uris.

Uris walked back to near the Pearl, and adjusted the handle, readjusted it, and sheathed the knife in its scabbard, but kept her hand around the grip.

She said a sound that sounded to the men standing around like, "Gilleemmmm." Immediately, a small slit opened in the seamless side of the Pearl. Kurege heard her say, "My Pearl," in her own language. The seam got slightly larger. The men had gathered around her and to either side. Suddenly, a puff of dust shot out of the slit with some considerable force, which startled the men, and several raised an arm to shield their face. Next, about a cup full of salt sprayed out and fell to the floor, then about two cups of salt. These gathered in a little pile, about halfway between the people and the ship. Nothing happened for another several seconds, and then three very dried fish suddenly shot out the hole and landed right at the feet of Lt. Colonel Logan Wilson. His eyes got big and round at this, but he held his ground. Uris laughed out loud with glee. "Andro," she chirped. The slit opened into a full-size door, and slowly something peeped around the side of the slit. After a good look at what was happening, Andro came gliding smoothly out of the door and stood hovering in front of the astounded group.

"Princess," his mechanical voice hailed Uris, with obvious joy, and he glided forward toward her, very fast. Guns came out of holsters.

"Andro, Protect!" She commanded him. A blue bubble of light shot out all around him, and instantly enveloped Uris.

"What the hell is that?" Two or three men said at the same time, and the rest of them were thinking it.

"That is her military robot, and it would be good to put your weapons away, and make no sudden movements," Kurege told the group.

"You didn't tell us about this," Ruben McAulley protested.

"He wasn't working the last time I saw him. But he can self-repair. He must have repaired himself, and I guess, cleaned up the ship."

The men began to slowly relax, with no apparent threat from Andro, they holstered their weapons one at a time.

"Uris," Kurege tried to soothe her, "there is no danger, you can deactivate Andro's defenses."

"They pulled weapons," she said, "they might have shot him."

"They did not know that he was coming out, or what he was," Kurege reasoned with her. "They were frightened, and they reacted," he persuaded. "It is all right now."

She spoke the command to turn off his defenses, and the light of the force field around her disappeared. She was so glad to see him up and running that she went to him and put her arms around him and gave him a hug.

"My lady," he said with some surprise apparent in his mechanical voice, "you are with child."

She lost much of her color and physically started at his comment. "You are to tell no one," she commanded him.

"Who would I tell?" He questioned her. "We are stranded on an unknown planet halfway across the Universe from Saphos."

"She disengaged from the robot and walked toward the ship."

"Kurege," Andro said monotone.

"Keep it under your lid," she admonished him again, and he fell silent, but his mechanical gaze moved to Kurege, and examined him very closely.

She disappeared inside the ship, and the group of men moved with her and one by one came in the door. Andro, who had seen enough of the inside of the ship of late, stayed put, and looked all around the hanger complex.

He moved slowly about observing items, and when his attention was drawn to the cryostat of helium III, he moved toward it, and a sensor came out from him, and he sampled the gas that was wafting in wisps from its top.

The engineers, Brian Mallory, and Ruben McAulley moved in behind her, and began to examine the inside of the ship with complete fascination. Logan Wilson, and John Gavin hung at the door and looked in but did not go deeply into the ship. Uris moved toward a locker and opened it. She extracted a nozzle and, holding it up to Dr. McAulley, showed it to him.

"This can be fitted to fill the ship with helium III. It is put here," she showed them. Brian Mallory took the nozzle from her and looked it over. He could see that he could easily adapt his hose to the fitting, and he took the nozzle and left the ship. He ordered some of the technicians to bring the cryostat closer, and talking it over with one of the men, sent him for a special hose clamp that would not fracture from the temperature of the liquid helium III. He then supervised the moving of the cryostat inside the Pearl, and in a few minutes the man he had sent after the insulated hose clamp had returned with the clamp and a set of Alan wrenches. Working with the wrenches and the hose that he had prepared for the procedure, he soon had the nozzle attached and inserted it into the fill valve that Uris had shown him.

"Wait," Uris told him. She went to the controls and set some of the touch pads to the proper settings. "Now it can be filled," she told him.

"Here goes," he said, and turned the valve on the cryostat, which pressurized the top of the tank with its own exhaust gases, and the liquid began to flow from the cryostat into the ship. "What kind of mileage do you get from this," he asked Kurege.

"A complete filling is good for millions of parsecs," he told Brian." He and Ruben both whistled softly in pure amazement.

"That is pretty good mileage on a fill up," McAulley observed.

"I would say so," Mallory agreed, "since a parsec is the distance that light travels in a year. That is amazing."

"The universe is a very large place," Kurege told them, "And on Pandamon, this amount of helium III is priceless. It's value is almost beyond count. This much helium III would buy an entire planet in some places. It is that rare, and cannot be synthesized." He gestured a helpless shrug. "There are no building blocks smaller that it can be built from. It is composed of the origin material."

Earth, as a source, is a very rich planet."

When the fueling had been completed and the hose removed, Uris told Kurege that she wished to test the coils, and he informed the group that she would have to shut the door to let the field complete. Mallory and McAulley stayed on the ship with Kurege and Uris and the other men moved back and away from the ship. She called Andro inside, and he glided smoothly in the door. She told Kurege to warn the men outside to move back and away from the hanger door. He warned them not to be near the ship, as the field would react against them, and to stand clear of the path to the door. When they were positioned, she shut the door, and taking the controls, began to generate the gravity field, and then the anti-gravity field, so that they were on an interior gravity when they accelerated.

The men outside watched in amazement as the Pearl lifted off the stand and slowly moved toward the hanger door. Once at the door, the spacecraft gained speed, and moving into the open increased speed and altitude at an astounding rate. Within seconds, the craft had disappeared into the sky, to be punctuated with a sonic boom that resounded through the area and shook the building.

The people inside the craft had no sense of movement except a very slight sensation of acceleration, but not nearly the amount in which they were truly gaining speed. Uris opened a screen to the outside, and the two men and Kurege got a view of the terrain that they were traversing outside the craft. She flew East over Cloudcroft, generally following the highway, and then circled up the Eastern side of Alamo Peak, the tallest peak in the area, and came around its Southern flank, about a mile above the mountain top, steering clear of jet traffic that was traversing in the area.

"I am getting a fix on the Probe in a desert just forward of our path," she told them. "Do you want me to disable the Probe?"

"Can you do that from this distance?" McAulley was amazed.

"Yes," she told him. "In fact, if I don't disable it shortly and keep the same path, it is going to react to my ship."

Andro interrupted, "Princess, we are being scanned by a Xinor Probe droid," he told her. "Do not approach closer as it will react, if we do not identify ourselves." She brought the ship to a stop in midair and they hovered there.

"If I do identify myself, there is no telling who is listening to its possible transmissions," she told the men. And then without waiting for them to make a decision, she told Andro. "Send a Navigational Guild directive command for the Probe to shut down all activity," she directed Andro.

"It is done, Uris," he told her almost instantly.

"These Probes," she told the two men, as Kurege already knew, are built to respond to a Navigational Guild directive command to turn off, as it was unknown when they were sent out when they might transgress into some space already settled by a Guild member world. In this way, mapping of areas that were secret could be avoided, and the Probes could search unsettled space for the source of the plutonium polluter."

"The plutonium polluter," Mallory questioned?

"Earth," Kurege confirmed for him.

"Oh," he responded.

"There was a mapping vote," Kurege tried to explain. "Among the independent worlds, navigational secrets are the most valuable of secrets. Where a Guild House is located, and even when, are closely guarded secrets." The two men gave him a blank look. "Where, and when, are relative to angle and speed on the entry of a Warp Star, and these parameters are the way in which the independent Houses keep themselves from being attacked. If it is unknown where in time and space the home world exists, then it is not easily attacked, so the Empire is only mapped in Xinor Standard time. Other parameters are closely held secrets by the Houses that are outside of the Empire. Mapping of time and space is a hotly debated issue where we are from."

"Oh, I see," Mallory affirmed, but he had only a very small glimmer of the magnitude of the debate that raged during Guild meetings on Xinor.

"Have you disarmed the Probe," Ruben McAulley asked?

"It is done," Uris confirmed.

"It can be approached," he asked.

"It is a dead pile of metal," Uris told him.

"Can we take it apart," McAulley asked?

"There are parts of it that would be best left alone," Kurege cautioned, "but for the most part, yes."

"Wonderful," Ruben exclaimed, "the President is going to be very pleased."

"The Pearl is in good working order," Uris told Kurege, "we shall return to the hanger where it was stored."

The men heard it coming from the sonic shock wave that ran in front of the spacecraft, when she brought it in at supersonic speed, and then slowed it, and brought it slowly floating back into the building. It stopped short of the platform, and three landing pod legs rotated out from the hull to hold it level and upright on the building floor. The humming sound stopped and the door reappeared, and the three men emerged, followed by Uris.

Dr. McAulley opened his cell phone and contacted the President to tell him of the Probe's termination. Uris moved back to the map table and unrolled the maps one at a time and began to study them. The other two men followed her, and Lt. Colonel Logan Wilson joined the others around the table. She studied the maps for some time, and then made a decision.

"After the initiation of the attack," she told Kurege in their language, "once the door has been secured, I will bring the Pearl, and Andro into what is bound to be a desperate fight, as they are not going to just give up and go away. They have too much invested here in time and energy. Such a source of helium III is not going to be surrendered without a fight. That is not even counting the life extension drug, and whatever combination of other genetics that have been introduced by Metastophiles. And then, there are the plutonium bombs to be considered, as Metastophiles, and Sargon, and the rest of this conspiracy, are obviously planning an attack at some point in time and space on the other Houses. This has been in preparation for a long, long time. They are not going to just give it up."

"Uris," Kurege told her, "you cannot go anywhere near this fight." They glared at each other, and the other men around them did not know what was going on, but they could tell that they were arguing. Several more exchanges were made, and they were getting toe to toe in what was starting to look like a very nasty domestic argument to the others. Ruben McAulley finally noticed and told the President that he would have to call him back, and hung up the phone. He approached the furiously arguing couple, and hoped to figure out what the trouble was, and make peace, but the gestures were getting way out of bounds. He was well aware, from past experience, of the danger of stepping into the middle of a domestic argument. It looked like Uris was about to pull the knife on him. "But you are pregnant with child," Kurege told her. "I will not allow you to do this."

"You will not allow me," she screamed at him. "You will not allow me!"

"You cannot endanger yourself and the child," he screamed at her in English, hoping to enlist the aid of the men around him, by letting them understand what they were arguing about.

"There is no way that this fight can be won without Andro and the Pearl, and that means me," she enunciated in very clear English. "Otherwise, Boom!" She threw her hands in the air. "Earth goes Boom!"

Collin Rains, the Marine Lieutenant leading the attack, carefully streaked his face with the greenish black camouflage make up that was used in covert night attacks. He looked around him at the men that had volunteered. He knew some of them, others from the Army Rangers, and Navy Seals, were unknown, but one common thread linked them, other than that they were all from service elite core units. They were all excellent at the sport of hang gliding, and where their teeth were not perfect, and fillings had been, the teeth had been recently pulled. There were twelve men in the initial assault unit. They had only had two days to train together, but the team had melded into a tight group. They were dedicated individuals to begin with, each with a high sense of purpose, and a love for the flag that they served. Coming to understand the nature of the mission had been somewhat harder. Aliens from another world were not the enemy that they had envisioned themselves as fighting. Leaving behind the weapons that they had trained themselves to use, was a tough idea to get used to having.

Dustin Holliday was going to form the point. He and Collin were both Marines, and he moved closer to Rains among the rocks. They were positioned about two miles from what had been identified as the entrance to what was assumed to be a large underground cavern. It had taken more than a week to locate the mouth of the cave. Ground surveillance had been used, and several possibilities had been watched, until three nights earlier, a spacecraft had been observed emerging from this one. It had slowly moved up the valley, hidden from distant radar installations, and had gained velocity and emerged into the open atmosphere near a high mountain peak some twelve miles distant, at a time when there was a gap in satellite observation. The squad had been moved into place the next evening and had rested and stayed still among the rocks of a hill some eighteen hundred feet above the valley floor to the Northeast. They would be able to catch a prevailing Southwest flow of night breeze to carry them to the cavern entrance.

"Dusty," Rains acknowledged him quietly. "Any movement being reported," he asked. Jaron Wakeman was observing through night goggles from a position hidden along the path that Holliday had just come down.

"Nothing but bats coming out about dusk," Dusty reported to him.

"Anything on the horn," he asked.

"Eric says that he has a standby. They are saying that the FBI group has started into the plant. The four wheelers have been brought up to be unloaded and positioned, and as soon as the complex has been secured, they are going to blow a way in for them. Once they have controlled the opposition from that end, they will start toward our position, and we are to begin the attack from this end." Eric Alcántara was just visible in the star light hunched over the radio receiver, listening intently. Dusty gave Rains a toothy grin. He was famous for his broad smile, but Collin could see the missing right front tooth. Dusty had injured the tooth in a football scrimmage in his high school years, and it had been saved with indodonture, but as the procedure had replaced the nerve with a metal plug, the tooth had been removed a week earlier for this mission. The smile twitched a little with the nervousness that he was feeling. With the group entering the Pantex facility on the move, it would not be long before the order to commence would be given, and almost everything about the attack was unknown.

Several miles to the Southeast, Uris was in position with the Pearl. She was listening to the same radio wavelength to which Eric Alcántara was listening. She would be moving into the area when the fighting had commenced, and hopefully the cavern entrance had been gained and secured. It was believed that there must be a door between the outside and the cavern, and this needed to be blocked open when she brought the Pearl, and Andro to bear on the resistance that would surely come from inside.

Kurege had gone with Ruben McAulley, John Gavin, and the rest of the Inspection team that would gain and secure the Pantex plant itself. It was thought that once the alien part of the plant was opened and any collaborators were identified and subdued or eliminated, there might be alien prisoners that were captured, and if that happened, Kurege would be of value in being able to question them in a common language. He had been reluctant to separate from Uris, but she and he were still arguing over her part in the fight, and John Gavin, seeing the sense of having Andro in action, and realizing that only Uris could command him, had suggested that Kurege would be invaluable with his group. He had reluctantly been persuaded.

Ruben McAulley, John Gavin, and Kurege had received passes and an appointment had been made with an administration official inside involving procedure to oversee that undocumented aliens were not working inside the plant. The irony of this ploy was not lost on Gavin, who had been the one to think it up. The administration had a big push on to make sure that paperwork on all employees was in order, and that workers everywhere in the US workforce were properly documented. This was going to be, simply, a procedural discussion to make sure the Pantex plant had the latest rules and was keeping their paperwork up to date.

Gavin was driving and pulled smoothly up to the guard post, with the armed guards, and the admissions clerk that was on duty. The woman that was in charge of admissions took their picture ID information from each one and looked them over to make sure the ID matched the face of each person in the car and turned to her appointment list. The guards took a perfunctory look at the passengers in the car, and continued to stand at attention, with weapons at the ready. She finished looking at the list on her clipboard and turned to the telephone that was hanging on the wall of the booth, and checked with the appropriate party involved. Satisfied, she returned their ID cards to the men, and motioned them through, opening the gate.

They parked and went into the front lobby where they were asked to sign in by the secretary at the front desk. They asked for Julian Burkman, and she made a call and gave them name tags to be worn while they were in the building, as Burkman had confirmed that they would be going to his office in Human Resources. She looked them up and down, and said not an unnecessary word, taking them for some salesmen, probably of forms or reams of paper. She was a typical, tight lipped, Dragon Lady on guard for solicitors trying to crash the front door and bring their products inside. It was her personal mission in life to stop this type of time-consuming annoyance at the front desk.

Burkman soon appeared in the lobby through a secure door that led to the interior of the front building complex. He was balding and short, a mid-management man doing a staggering job of keeping track of the paperwork of hundreds of employees, and making certain that the files were all in order. After perfunctory information exchanges and introductions, assuring him that they were looking to confirm routine procedural practices, he escorted them inside the plant and took them into the heart of the Human Resource section where the hiring and firing and record keeping was done. Security also had an office in this section, in case someone gave trouble if they were found in a violation, and summarily discharged, and escorted from the building.

"What can I show you gentlemen, today," Burkman asked? He plopped himself in a swivel chair behind his desk and clasping his hands behind his head in a nonchalant manner. "We have filed all the necessary paperwork on each employee with Homeland Security, and I really am at a loss to understand what it is that can call for a new procedural inspection. Can I get you gentlemen anything to drink, water, whatever?" He was being as friendly as an eel. There was only one chair in the office. "Have a seat," he said to John Gavin. He didn't offer to let the underlings sit, as he thought Ruben McAulley and Kurege were subservient.

Gavin came right to the point. "We're going to inspect the entire facility for any aliens which may be undocumented and working in some of the areas that are sensitive.

"You mean in the nuclear assembly area," Burkman got a very puzzled and concerned look on his face?

"Yes," John told him in one word.

Burkman shook his head. "I'm afraid that is quite impossible. I would have no access or authority to escort you through to those areas, or any area, other than this office. That was the only arrangements that were made."

"You will need to get your supervisor in here in that case to grant access," Gavin told him smoothly.

Burkman gave him a long look and glanced at the other two men for any clues as to what was happening. Ruben and Kurege both smiled and shrugged in a good-natured way, as they had practiced when this scenario was formed. He reached for his phone, hesitated for a moment, and then punched a line. "Brent," he spoke, "this is Julian Burkman in Human Resources, and I'm going to need your help in here in my office. No, nothing like that. I've got a federal inspection team in here, and I can't comply with what they are saying they want to do. I'm going to need you to explain things to them. Thanks." Burkman hung up the phone, and with a sly grin in place, turned back to Gavin. "I'm going to have Mr. Brent Simon of the plant security join us," he said.

"Good," Gavin crossed his legs, and sat back easy in his chair. Kurege and McAulley moved to put their backs against the wall on the side of the room opposite the door. It was only a few moments before two rather large men entered the office.

Brent Simon was scowling, and the frown got bigger when he saw John Gavin. "John," he said, "what the hell are you doing here?" He looked at Burkman. "Julian, what's going on here?" Without waiting for an answer, he turned back to Gavin." "I thought this was a routine paperwork request."

"Not exactly Brent," Gavin told him. They knew each other from college, and training. Gavin had gone to the FBI, and Simon had joined the CIA, and moved into national security with the NSA. He had joined in nuclear security for the DOE and was the top of the security chain at Pantex. Gavin let him think about it.

"What exactly are you doing," Simon restated the question.

"I'm going to search this facility for aliens, Brent." The double entendre was not lost on Simon, and he visibly started.

"We have no undocumented workers in this plant, and you have no authority to search this facility."

"Brent," Gavin leveled at him, "I'm not playing a game of Simon Says here. I've got an executive order that is a Presidential Directive, signed by the President. I also have a search warrant signed by the Chief Justice of the Supreme Court." Will that give me authority enough," Gavin said in a level tone. He handed Simon the papers.

Simon looked them over for a few moments and then looked back with a disarming grin on his face. "I'll need to check this out," he seemed to muse, pursing his lips, like he was reflecting deeply. "You will need to make another appointment with me, as I am tied up all day," he said with great sincerity and good humor.

"Well," John agreed smoothly, I guess we're stymied today. He turned to Ruben and Kurege and rose from his chair, facing the door. "Hey Rube, I guess we're finished here for today. Can I buy you guys some lunch somewhere in town?" This was the code sentence, as he was wired to a transmitter that was being listened to by Colonel Logan Wilson and a large attack force gathered just out of sight of the security cameras that dotted the landscape around the complex. Ruben, and Gavin both pulled nine-millimeter automatic pistols from arm holsters, and leveled them at the two men by the door. "Brent," he said levelly, "you and the other gentleman step inside a little farther and close the door behind you. Brent," Gavin told him, "You know that I will not hesitate to shoot you both, and these pistols are silenced, so don't do anything heroic. That's right," he encouraged, as the two men complied. "I knew you would see reason, in the long run." "Colonel Logan," he spoke out loud, "we have the security head in custody, come on in."

"You're crazy," Simon tossed at him.

"Brent," Gavin told him straight. "I have an arrest warrant for Reginald Tellur, and we have good reason to believe that he is in or near this facility. I know that you are in association with Tellur, and what is going on here, and you are under arrest. Both of you men hold very still while I pull your guns, and Burkman, don't open that drawer, and move away from that button under your desk."

Ruben McAulley carefully did the duty of disarming the two men, and then they sat them on the floor, hands on their heads.

"You have no idea what you are into here," Simon snapped at Gavin. "You're going to get half this planet blown sky high. One shot in the wrong place and a thousand nuclear bombs are going to go off."

"Maybe so," Gavin told him. "But this is as far as it goes, and yes, I do know exactly what I'm into here. Your inventory says that you're only supposed to have six-hundred-thirty bombs on hand at present. Where are the other three-hundred-seventy stored, I might ask. Now keep it shut."

Outside in the guard shack, the two guards received their orders from Colonel Wilson, and they turned and disarmed the DOE guard and moved her away from the alarm on the wall by the phone. Trucks full of men were rolling up the access road and they opened the gate and let them in. At the same time, men positioned all over the facility secured the areas around themselves, and within moments, key areas of the Pantex plant were under the control of the Marines commanded by Colonel Wilson, and agents that were handpicked by John Gavin. This part had gone flawlessly, and troops flooded into the foyer, to the total shock of the Dragon Lady on the desk. Gavin handcuffed his three, and let the troops in the security doors, and brought them up to the areas where resistance might be mounted and surprised the remaining security staff. Gavin was on the second floor near the security heads office when Colonel Logan Wilson found him.

"Looks good, Colonel," he reported to Wilson, we've got most major areas under control and haven't fired a shot yet.

"Good work," Wilson congratulated him. "I'll bring up the ATVs and the electric trucks. Sam Keogh is being brought in now."

"Let's find that secret section," Gavin started for the first floor. Wilson was following closely with a squad of his men. Employees were being segregated and then taken to the entrance area and loaded onto trucks, to be taken to a holding center some miles away in Amarillo, and questioned there for information that some of them might have.

"Sargent Carson," Wilson barked at one of them.

"Yes sir," Carson responded, "right here sir." Carson came up on a run.

"Go to the command center vehicle and bring the maps of the Pantex complex, and when Keogh arrives, bring him to me here. I will be in this first area."

"Right away sir," Carson hurried toward the front door.

Colonel Wilson and Dr. McAulley walked the perimeter of the front area, while John Gavin checked with his men that were prepositioned throughout the facility. The front section was part-engineering cubicals, and some precision machining back toward the rear, separated by a center wall. Every employee had been contained and moved toward the front, and by the time the two men, with Wilson's squad following, had reconnoitered the edges of the two areas, Carson had returned with the maps, and Sam Keogh in tow.

"Sam," Ruben addressed him, as Colonel Wilson unrolled the maps, "show us where you penetrated the hidden section."

Sam looked quickly over the map. He traced to one that showed the layout of the boiler rooms, where the air conditioning and the huge gas furnaces that heated and cooled the complex were placed. "This is where I originally went into the hidden section. As you can see, this wall is the termination of this part of the main energy plant that provides the complex with its own power supply, and the boilers for the heating." He pointed at the Western edge of the front building. "We have to go out that way to building six, and then down to the basement. That is also the building that has a loading dock that was used when I brought Raven, Porter, and Knowles inside."

"Carson," Colonel Wilson ordered. "Take this map and bring the ATV and the electric trucks around to building six loading dock. We will secure the inside and then open the door. We will try to penetrate the subbasement from that area."

"Right away, sir," Carson took off at a dead run.

"Lead on, Sam," Ruben motioned to him to lead the way. Sam led then through the Western exit and across the complex to building six, where they entered cautiously, finding two of John Gavin's men in control of the facility. They moved to the loading dock area and opened the loading bay doors. Carson was already driving up with a convoy of car haulers loaded with ATVs and electric trucks. Wilson stayed near the dock and supervised the start of the unloading. Sam and Gavin and McAulley went to the area where Sam had originally gained access to the rooms secreted on the other side.

"Blow it," Gavin told Colonel Wilson. He had some explosives that were prepared for this brought up. There was also a small dozer that was the first item unloaded off the car haulers. It had a strong cage built around the driver. It was a modified dirt mover, like one used in construction. They quickly set charges and retreated to the loading bay for the explosion. The dirt mover tore through the rubble and made short work of gaining access to the rooms on the other side. They sent three squads of men in around the dirt mover, and in about three minutes they heard a muffled explosion from inside. One of the squad leaders came back to Colonel Wilson to report.

"We found a catwalk down a hallway and a large room. Some of those creatures were loading an electric tram looking engine about to head into a tunnel, with crates that are all around it, scattered on the floor," he told Wilson. "I had a rocket propelled grenade put in the engine, and the critters went into a confused huddle."

"No resistance," Wilson asked?

"Not so far, sir. They just grouped into a huddle and stood there, sort of confused. I don't think they have any armament, sir."

"Can we get these vehicles down to the floor and into that tunnel," Wilson questioned him.

"Not this way, sir," he shook his head. "It is too far from the rooms up here to the floor."

"Take a couple of squads and find the way into that room. There has to be a link with the main complex, or those crates could not have been brought down. And secure those prisoners but just hold them where they are. We have someone coming that may be able to talk their lingo."

"Yes sir," the squad leader saluted, and was off to carry out his orders.

"Kurege," Colonel Wilson addressed him, "let's go see if these critters can be persuaded to talk."

The four men, with an armed escort leading the way in front made their way through the rubble and out onto the catwalk. Climbing down, they walked near the group of huddled aliens.

"Who is your leader here," Kurege addressed them in Xinor standard language. One of the creatures stepped forward.

"You know our language," he asked?

"I have been on Pandamon," Kurege told him. I can speak either dialect. Tell me quickly, he told the creature,"Where does this tunnel lead.?

"It will lead to the ships."

"Are you loading to leave," he asked?

"We are not told. We were simply to load the carrier and bring it to the ships." The creature looked questioningly at Kurege. "You are with Lord Sargon," he asked?

"Is Sargon at the ships," Kurege ignored the question.

"Yes," he told Kurege.

"How many are with him," he continued to question?

"There are six of Pandamon, and thirty workers from Pran and the outer rim of Regis."

"How many ships?"

"Two are present, and being loaded, one other is expected soon."

"You will all stay still, and you will not be hurt. I will question you more later." Kurege turned away from him. "John," he addressed Gavin. Tellur is still on Earth. He is in the chamber at the end of this tunnel, and he has two ships being loaded. They are expecting another ship to arrive soon. That would indicate that Tellur has already sent the information on the Draco Supernova back to Xinor, and they are using it to bring ships back and forth through Draco. That is not good. They could come in force at any time now from the Imperium."

The squad leader came running up to Colonel Wilson. He had to catch his breath for a moment before he could talk. "Sir, we have found a way to bring the vehicles into this area."

"Good Wilson told him. Get it crackin'. I want to get started up that tunnel, immediately."

Uris heard the radio crackle, and then a code given. "This is Bright Star," the voice said. "Commence with Hey Rube. Be aware that another ship is expected. Repeat, another spacecraft is expected to enter your area." She knew that this would commence the attack on the cavern. The implications of the spacecraft arriving would mean that some prisoners had been taken, and that Kurege had managed to get information from them. The news was not good, as a spacecraft arriving would imply that Sargon had sent craft through Draco, and it was now being used. That would mean that any number of ships might be arriving to reinforce the alien group, or it could be coming from some other group already on Earth. Either way it was bad news, and with the time that had passed, it was very likely that Sargon had sent the information from the data recorder back to Regis Xinor, and also to Pandamon.

Eric Alcántara took the head set from his ears and motioned to Dusty Holliday and Collin Rains that he had an order to commence the attack. Alcántara set the headset down and moved toward Rains until he could be heard while he talked softly. "Collin," he spoke in a quiet voice, "they are saying that there may be a spacecraft arriving tonight. You are going to have to watch over your shoulder at something coming from behind you. Apollo station is on the move and will be able to cover this side of the planet within the hour. Satellites have been brought in to get high resolution video images of this area, and I will be able to see you in infrared until you go into the cavern. When you have secured the area, and have the door open, if there is a door, then you will have to send someone on the advanced team back out to the entrance where we will pick up his body heat. That will be the signal for the spacecraft and robot to enter the fight. I will also be relaying this to command so that the force coming from Pantex will be aware that the forward area is being engaged."

"I know how this goes, Eric," Rains huffed at him. "We've been over this plan two dozen times in the briefings."

"Well, I just wanted to go over it one more." Alcántara gripped his hand. "Best of luck, Collin, I wish I were going in with you."

"I wish you were too, but someone has to relay the info to command. We're depending on you."

"Wakeman will be watching every move. He and I won't goof on you, Collin."

"Well, here we go," Rains raised his arm to a cocked position and pumped it up and down. The men watching in the rocks began to position themselves for the hang glider flight into the dark Texas Panhandle night."

The hang gliders had been manufactured of a composite of bone ground and glued and formed into the proper shapes. The cloth covering had been replaced with feathers glued to a framework made of sinew. They carried wicked looking knives tucked into a leather waistband. They were curved, about fourteen inches long, made from the jawbone of horses, and sharpened razor sharp. They would work very well for decapitation of an enemy. They also carried a long leg bone club. Every stitch of clothing was leather. They had to pass as animals, if they were to fool the sensors that were sure to be at the entrance to the cavern. Two of the men, Jacob Goldman, and Justin Marshall, who were both Navy Seals, would be the last to launch, and they held the hang glider in place as each man ran from a rocky precipice and launched himself into the night. Dustin Holliday was the first to go, as the point man.

"Good luck, Dusty," Rains gave him a pat on the shoulder, both as a go signal and a personal encouragement. "I'll be right behind you," Rains assured him.

"See you in Hell," Holliday threw at him, as he started his run for the edge. Rains watched him disappear into the dark night. He stepped onto the little plateau that led to the edge, and Goldman and Marshall positioned the sail of the hang glider for him and he started his run for the edge. There was a moon in the sky in the third quarter, and he could just see a glimmer of reflection from Dusty in the distance, making his way down into the valley toward the cave entrance. He caught a full sail of air and let it lift him and then dove down to pick up speed. The night air was exhilarating, and the adrenalin began to pump hard in his veins.

Two more Marines, Eric Rojas, and Juan Salinas were next to launch. They were followed by the contingent of Army Rangers, Christian Jaralos, and Charlie Long, the only black man on the squad, both made quick launches one after the other. Brandon Heinlein adjusted, and readjusted his knife and club, until Brad

Blackwell coaxed him. "Come on Brandon, it's going to be over by the time you get there."

"Just tend your own shit, Blackwell," Heinlein told him surly, as he started for the edge. He slipped and almost fell but stumbled forward and made the launch. Blackwell shook his head and got in position.

"Good luck," Justin Marshall told him.

"Break a leg," Jac Goldman tossed at him carelessly as he released the sail when Blackwell started forward. Goldman held the sail from behind for Marshall and watched him launch. Goldman was the most experienced with far more hours on hang gliders than the others, and he declined an offer by Wakeman to help, telling him to just keep his eyes on the men. Wakeman and Alcántara watched with envy as the last man made his leap into the dimly lit night. They understood that their missions were important, but they were going to miss the excitement and the glory that the others would find. These were all men who loved to live on the edge, pushing the danger, and feeding on the adrenalin rush that it brought.

Dustin Holliday had made his landing by the time that Goldman had made his leap into the unknown. Wakeman saw Holliday make a smooth landing on a little knoll in front of the cave entrance, which was situated low in the wall of the far side of the valley. He watched as Dusty disentangled himself from the harness, and as Collin Rains made a fairly good landing near him, stumbling in the run at the last and sliding on his face in the rocks. The big Marine took it without a sound more than a soft grunt. He rolled out of the tangled harness and wiped some blood on his sleeve. He tasted a little blood on his lips, where he had a small cut.

"Collin," Dusty whispered as he came toward him.

"I'm all right," Rains softly called back. They shed the hang gliders and began an approach to the cave entrance. Probing slowly inside. They had progressed only a few feet, when they both stopped and crouched.

"Shit," Dusty said. "It's black as the inside of a witch's cauldron in here. Collin, I can't see my hand in front of my face."

"Me either," Rains told him. They waited for the others to join them. They could hear movement outside. In a few minutes, Salinas and Rojas had joined up with them. The Ranger team would come next.

They heard a lot of noise, and in a minute, heard Jaralos tell Long that he was damned hard to see in the dark.

"My advantage," Long shot back quietly. They were starting for the mouth of the cave. Brad Blackwell was about halfway across the valley, and he could just make out Brandon Heinlein in front and under him in the distance, when a large object, moving very fast, pasted between them. As it passed over Heinlein, Blackwell heard him call out loud, a sort of choked scream, and saw him plummet straight down, as if a huge hand had caught him, and slammed him into the ground. As he passed over him, he could see his form twisted, and his neck and head broken where he had slammed into rocks that had been directly below him.

As the saucer passed across the entrance to the cavern, it went close over Jaralos, and he hit the ground hard with a grunt. Charlie Long was not directly under its path but felt the side force of the anti-gravity units, and the searing heat from the hull, that was still almost white hot from the spacecraft's passage through the atmosphere. Collin Rains and Dustin Holliday were off to one side of the cave entrance on the right. They were not exposed to the force, but felt the hot blast, and could see a glow from the hull as the ship slowed and entered the cavern, disappearing into the depths of the cave, as it made a curving path where the cave turned as it went deeper. Jaralos and Long stumbled up to join them.

"This is crazy impossible," Long observed. Jaralos was dazed, and Long had helped him up, and buddy carried him to join the others.

"Are you all right," Rains asked him.

"I got the breath knocked out of me, like a fist the size of a car hit me," Jaralos gasped.

They heard someone else land, and then shortly two more. In a few minutes Blackwell, Marshall, and Goldman joined them.

"What about Heinlein," Rains questioned?

"He bought it," Blackwell told him. "That damned saucer flew right between us. I could almost reach out and touch it. It flew right over Heinlein, and when it did, it slammed him into the ground, hard. He was broken up bad." Somewhere deep in the cave, and far forward, light came on.

"This is a chance," Rains told them. "No more talking, and move, move now, and move fast." He led out on a run and took a position farther inside. Dusty passed him by and the other men followed quickly. He and Dusty leap frogged into the depths of the cavern as fast as they could go, and as they reached the curve and rounded it, the light got brighter up ahead.

Wakeman had seen the ship approach and watched helplessly as the craft overtook the hang gliding men, and saw Heinlein slammed into the ground. He had Alcántara report the situation to command, and Uris heard the radio message. She had seen the craft approaching with her own sensors, and now she made a decision to move in, although that was not the plan. She was to wait for a go ahead from the central command center, but she sensed an opportunity, as she was sure they would have to open the outer door to admit the arriving spacecraft. That would be her chance to put Andro into operation. She came over the

311

mountain range and moved close to the terrain, and hugged the valley floor at tree top level, even at times in and out of the forest. She drove the Pearl across the valley at a frightening speed. Wakeman did not see her approach until she came into view at the cave entrance and instantly disappeared into the mouth of the cave. It happened so fast that he only had an impression of what he had seen. He rubbed his eyes, and looked again, but could see nothing more.

"Tell command,"He instructed Alcántara that I think I saw the spacewoman take her ship into the cave mouth.

"They want to know what you mean by 'I think I saw,'" Alcantera told him in response.

"Tell them it happened so damn fast that I am not sure what it was, but something went into the cave, and it had to be her from the size of it."

Alcantera relayed the message. "They are saying to keep them informed of every movement that you think you see."

"Tell them that Heinlein bought it, and to bring an air ambulance, but it's not going to do any good, from what I saw."

Reginald Tellur watched the ship come slowly through the door leading to the outside. It settled in a landing area and was immediately drenched with liquid argon gas to cool the hull. The vapor rose in boiling waves from the ship's hull, and giant exhaust fans came on and shoved the vapors into the outer area toward the entrance to the cave. The door opened in the side of the ship, and a humanoid somewhat thick bodied and short with bushy hair and brows, much like Tellur emerged.

"Lord Sargon," he saluted, "I have word from Lord Metastophiles." He approached the podium from which Tellur was observing the operations around him. He was near the ramp leading to a superb silver saucer directly behind him. He watched the new arrival come toward him without returning the salute.

"Tell me his biding," Tellur requested as the Pandamon captain came within easy hearing.

"His pleasure at the opening of the Draco Warp Star. He has emerged from Down Time and will be awaiting your return on Pandamon.

"Yes, continue," Tellur ordered. "What is his biding on the termination of Earth."

"He wants it intact. The genetics are far too successfully implemented to be destroyed. He wishes that we join him on Pandamon. Then Terra will be subdued in another fashion, or it will be taken by force, if necessary. Those are his instructions."

"Make ready for departure." Sargon's ship's captain, a Pandamon, similar in body type to Sargon, turned and waved to a ship being filled with helium III on the other side of the cavern. There was a general increase in activity. "Make your ship ready for an immediate return," Sargon ordered the captain who had just arrived.

"I must have a replenishment of cryofluid," he objected. "There is not enough to get me halfway to the Draco Warp Star let alone through it."

"You should have had plenty to make the round trip," Sargon said accusingly

"The Neutron Star is yet unstable," the captain objected. "I was lucky to withstand passage," he gestured helplessly. "There are serious anomalies in the core, and the added stress during passage through converted more to regular helium and had to be drawn away from the coils. I will have to be refueled before the ship is suitable for the return trip."

"You will have to wait until the other ship is readied, as both these ships have a full freezer of protofetal fluid, and as many plutonium bombs as they can carry."

It was at that moment that a disruptor flash was seen just beyond the inner door. Dusty Holliday had just leaped ahead of Collin Rains position and had approached the open inner door. He had been caught in an automatic disruptor blast and incinerated in front of the horrified eight men remaining of the squad. They crouched down unsure which way to go. Rains had seen where the blast came from, and looking closely he spotted the infrared sensor on one side, near the disruptor, and the receiver that reflected the signal back. Dusty had walked right into the beam, and that was it for him. Rains signaled the men to break into four groups of two, as it was thought that in any hand-to-hand combat, it would take two humans to overpower one of the aliens. They had surmised that from the descriptions that Porter and Martin have given of what they knew of the fight that Stark Raven and Jim Knowles had with the two they had encountered.

All four groups made for the edges of the cave walls on either side, where they could get their backs to the wall. Rains took himself and his three men to the right and Charlie Long took command of Blackwell, Rojas, and Goldman. They had just positioned and dropped down behind some boulders on either side, when an alien exomorph came out to the disruptor that had discharged with a weapon at the ready. Another two approached just behind the first.

Collin motioned for Salinas, and Marshall to crouch down. Chris Jaralos was already glued to the ground as low as he could go. They were out of sight of the alien who lowered some night vision, and infrared sensing goggles and scanned the other side of the cave. Charlie chose that moment to take a peek over the boulder he was behind. The alien turned and fired, and the rocks around Charlie began to burst from the heat and then melt. Charlie scrambled for cover, but not fast enough as the blast caught him in the back and blew a hole right through him. The other three men were able to get safely out of the way, unseen, and the alien ceased fire, and turned fully toward where Charlie had fallen. The two with him turned and stepped a couple of steps that way. That was enough for Rains who stepped to the top of a boulder and drew his bone knife. He leaped onto the back of the alien who had fired, and took his head off with a deft movement, catching him around the throat, and slicing deep in a left to right pull. Salinas, Marshall, and Jaralos came right behind him, and managed to knock a hole in the next one's head with clubs, after Salinas had knocked the weapon out of his hand. The other alien stepped back and caught Jaralos coming on him with a blast that burned through his chest. Marshall caught the weapon and tried to hold on, and was spun off to one side, but delayed the creature long enough so that Salinas got a knife deep in his back. A long high, wailing, scream like a pig at slaughter came blood curdling from the creature as he twitched and tried to get at Salinas, who backed away. Rains and Salinas attacked the wounded creature from two sides, and when Rains made a feint that it went for, Salinas clobbered him and ended the struggle.

The other three men arrived at the scene of the struggle, and watched together, as the aliens' troops raised their weapons. Rains grabbed one of the fallen alien weapons, and after a couple of attempts to fire it, succeeded at figuring out the triggering, and cut loose with a burst at the horde of alien troops moving toward the five men.

"Spread out," he yelled, and threw the weapon he was holding at Salinas, and dove for the second weapon that was on the ground a few feet in front of him. It saved his life, as a blast tore the air just over his head where he had been standing. Goldman was in back of him, and didn't move fast enough. The blast caught him from the neck up and tore his head off in an inferno of explosion.

Rojas, Blackwell, and Marshall backed away behind a rock, and Rojas was able to get the third weapon, and was aiming and trying to fire it, when all hell broke loose, as ten or more weapons discharged in their direction at the same time. The five men could only find the biggest rock around and try to keep behind it and hope that it would not melt.

It was at that moment that the Pearl sailed serenely into the edge of the inner cave, and the firing stopped. Tellur stepped off the podium and began walking quickly up the ramp into his starship. The door port on the Pearl began to open.

"Andro," Uris gave him his commands, "protect and destroy."

"Uris," Andro's mechanical voice rose in pitch, "there was a time track in Draco that I have not had a chance to tell you about. It was early, before any of the Probe tracks, and I believe that it must have been an escape pod from Uriah's ship."

"Andro," she was stunned, "why have you only now told me this?"

"You are sending me into battle. There is a Pandamon starship out there. I can see it through the portal. I may not come away intact."

"Andro," she warned him, "that ship is probably carrying many plutonium bombs. Your destroy order cannot include that ship or any of the ships. Be careful not to detonate any of these bombs that may be stored and have been loaded on these ships. We would all be destroyed."

"I understand my lady," he moved toward the portal.

"You must protect the Pearl, and myself, and yourself. That will be the extent of what we can do here."

"Understood." He moved beyond the ship. He began to generate a force field to protect himself and the ship and Uris moved to the portal and jumped to a large boulder near the Pearl that was above the cavern floor. Andro covered her with a glowing blue force field. She drew out her knife but was fearful to turn the disruptor ray in any direction, not knowing the location of any bombs that might be on the floor. A hum of electric motors was heard approaching from the tunnel at the back, and several of the electric trucks emerged. Kurege was in one of the first ones into the cavern and he saw Uris immediately.

"Uris!" He screamed at her.

Andro went to work on the twenty odd armed exomorphs who had opened up on him in sheer terror with disruptors. Their hand-held weapons were of no effect upon him. He made very short work of the resistance, hitting them with laser, electrical charges, and disruptor weapons that were at his command from his own frame and the Pearl itself. The captain of the spacecraft that had shortly before arrived, made for the ramp of the starship that Sargon had boarded, but he was too late, and the two other star ships rose up and moved slowly toward the door with Sargon leading.

Uris turned on Sargon's ship with her knife, concentrating the beam from the knife directly in its center. She knew it would be fruitless, as the forcefield around the spacecraft took on an iridescence that became more intense as Andro also concentrated his weapons on that craft as well. The contest grew in intensity, and at the critical point an intense electrical charge shot out from the departing craft, and enveloped Uris, Andro, and the Pearl. Andro began to overload, but so did the starship. A huge explosion ensued, and the forcefield that Andro was generating collapsed. The rock that Uris had been standing on burst from the pressures all around it, and Uris was thrown to one side, and fell to the ground. Kurege was terrified and came running across the blazing cavern floor to get to her.

The starship with Tellur reached the cavern entrance and accelerated on its way. It was watched by Wakeman and Alcántara from the hill opposite the valley as it came toward them gathering velocity, the other ship was right behind it. Both spacecraft passed by as they went supersonic, and the concussion of the pressure waves knocked them both to the ground. In moments, the two craft were high above the earth on their way to the Draco Warp Star. Aboard Lord Sargon's starship the captain was looking worried at his instruments. He made some adjustments, but he began to fall behind the acceleration of the companion ship.

"Lord Sargon," he reported, "the fight with the robot has damaged our coil. We cannot maintain the anti-gravity field without a repair."

"Can you fix it here in space if we continue."

"I can repair the coil. We have everything that we need, but it will take time. We will be coasting. I can not attain hyperspace until the repair is completed."

"Very well," Sargon took it at his ease. "Tell the other ship to continue. We will catch them before they can reach the Regis System."

The captain contacted the other starship and did as he was told. He then went below deck to instruct on the repairs of the field coils.

Derek Ramirez was sitting in the firing chair of the Apollo plasma cannon. He was adjusting telemetry to get the aiming just right on target.

"Yes sir," he said into his headset. The plan to overload their coil that Uris devised seems to have worked on one of the ships. The other has moved out of range. Yes sir, we have a full charge on the plasma cannon."

"You have permission to fire at will, Colonel Ramirez," the President calmly gave the order.

Sargon could see it coming as it was coming from the Earth's horizon some eight thousand miles across the curve of the Earth, just above the ionosphere. It took just slightly longer than forty-three one thousandths of a second to reach him. It was long enough to register that something was coming, but he didn't have time to know what it was. The plasma ball struck the unshielded hull of his ship and tore into it like a hot knife into butter. The inside of the ship instantly exploded as the plasma ball disassociated, and the immense quantity of electrons contained in its field dissipated into every particle of matter on board. The temperature shot to near the surface of the sun, and some three hundred megatons of plutonium bombs being carried on board, exploded. The aurora created in the Earth's atmosphere was more intense than ever seen before by hundreds of times in magnitude, and the people of the Earth stood in the night of New York to Hawaii, and in the daylight of Tokyo to London, and marveled and feared that the end of time itself had come.

Space station Apollo fired rockets to bring it back around the curve of earth to protect itself from the shock wave coming at it, and the debris from the exploding ship. Derek Ramirez got a very rough but very satisfying roller coaster ride.

"Mission accomplished, Mr. President," he transmitted to Earth when the radiation interference from the explosion was dissipated.

Uris awoke in a hospital bed with the television going on and on about the strange Aurora Borealis that had been seen around the world. There were pictures and more pictures of the unparalleled occurrence from every major city on the planet. It was being played as a fierce group of prominences that had shot out from the sun, interfering with Earth's magnetically charged field.

She saw Dr. Curtis, with his back to her, and Dr. Ruben McAulley, sitting to the right. John Gavin was in a chair on her left, and Colonel Logan Wilson was holding a big bunch of flowers, which he was trying to find a spot to place among bunches placed in the window, and on the shelf below the television. She felt someone squeeze her hand and she looked to see Kurege sitting by the bed holding her hand in his.

"Well," he said to her, "you are finally back among the living. We were getting worried about you."

She gave a weak smile and tried to sit up. Her head was splitting. Dr. Curtis heard Kurege speak to her and came over to the bed and took her other hand and, holding the pressure point in her wrist, pulled out a stopwatch and began to take her pulse.

"Just lay back and take it easy, young lady," he told her. "You've had a rough go of it."

She remembered the explosion, and she came to herself. "Dr. Curtis," she asked, "what about my baby?"

"You are just fine," he assured her, "and so is your baby." He shook his head at her. "The very idea of you putting yourself and child in such danger." He frowned very deeply at her.

The other men all gathered around her. They pressed in with grinning and anxious faces. She could see their concern, and it touched her heart.

"You men give her some air," Dr. Curtis elbowed them back.

"The President is coming to speak with you," John Gavin told her.

She looked at them and smiled and squeezed Kurege's hand. "I have about all the men I need, right here," she told them.

"I've got a present for you," Kurege told her, "Pulling a box to the side of the bed from the floor." She looked at him with a questioning look. He opened the box and pulled out the pair of gru skin boots that he had been making for her. She got a look of wonder in her eyes and took them from him. She stroked the skin. She thought of her father.

"How did you get them so soft," she asked, misty eyed.

"How do you think," he said, "I chewed them." She reached up and hugged his neck and buried her head in his shoulder and started crying. He looked up at the men around them and wiggled his eyebrows. "You know how women are about shoes," he explained.

Continued in Mergatroid
by Raymond Walter Seibert